IN THE MOON
OF RED PONIES

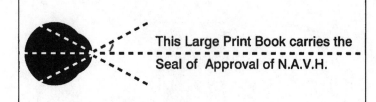

This Large Print Book carries the
Seal of Approval of N.A.V.H.

IN THE MOON
OF RED PONIES

JAMES LEE BURKE

LARGE
PRINT
PRESS

Waterville, Maine

Published in 2005 by arrangement with Simon & Schuster, Inc.

The text of this Large Print edition is unabridged.
Other aspects of the book may vary from the original edition.

Set in 16 pt. Plantin.

Printed in the United States on permanent paper.

The Library of Congress has cataloged the Thorndike Press® edition as follows:

Burke, James Lee, 1936–
    In the moon of red ponies : a novel / James Lee Burke.
      p. cm.
    ISBN 1-58724-778-X (lg. print : hc : alk. paper)
    ISBN 1-59413-067-1 (lg. print : sc : alk. paper)
    1. Holland, Billy Bob (Fictitious character) — Fiction.
2. Vietnamese Conflict, 1961–1975 — Veterans — Fiction.
3. Attorney and client — Fiction.   4. Indian activists — Fiction.   5. Trials (Murder) — Fiction.   6. Montana — Fiction.   7. Large type books.   I. Title.
PS3552.U723I53 2004b
  813'.54—dc22   2004053569

In memory of
Thomas Edmund Kroutter, Jr.

ACKNOWLEDGMENTS

Once again I would like to thank my wife, Pearl, and our children, Jim, Jr., Andree, Pamala, and Alafair, for all the help and support they have given me over the years. I would also like to thank Father Jim Hogan and Father Ed Monroe for their friendship along the way, and I'd like to mention my ongoing debt of gratitude to all the librarians and booksellers who have promoted my work without ever asking for any type of thanks.

Lastly, I owe a tip of a battered hat to my old Montana compadre Paul Zarzyski for the Larry Mahan quote.

God be blessed for all dappled things.

CHAPTER 1

My law office was located on the old courthouse square of Missoula, Montana, not far from the two or three blocks of low-end bars and hotels that front the railyards, where occasionally Johnny American Horse ended up on a Sunday morning, sleeping in a doorway, shivering in the cold.

The city police liked Johnny and always treated him with a gentleness and sense of fraternity that is not easily earned from cops. He had been awarded the Distinguished Service Cross for bravery in Operation Desert Storm, and some cops said Johnny's claims that he suffered Gulf War syndrome were probably true and that he was less drunk than sick from a wartime chemical inhalation.

More accurately, Johnny was a strange man who didn't fit easily into categories. He lived on the Flathead Reservation in the Jocko Valley, although his name came from the Lakota Sioux, and his relatives told me he was a descendant of Crazy Horse, the shaman and chief strategist for Red Cloud, who actually defeated the United States Army and shut down the Bozeman Trail in Red Cloud's War of 1868. I don't know whether or not Johnny experienced mystical visions as his ancestor supposedly did, but I had no doubt he heard voices, since he often smiled during the middle of a conversation and asked people to repeat themselves, explaining nonchalantly that other people were talking too loudly, although no one else was in the room.

But on balance he was a decent and honorable man and a hard worker, who took pride in tree-planting the side of a bare hill or digging postholes from sunrise to dark, in the way ranch hands did years ago, when love of the work itself was sometimes more important than the money it paid. He was handsome, full of fun, his hands shiny with callus, his face usually cut with a grin, his coned-up straw hat slanted on his brow. His higher ambitions were quixotic and of a kind that are doomed to destruction, but he was never dissuaded by the world's rejection or the fate it would eventually impose on him.

I just wished Johnny hadn't been so brave or so trusting in the rest of us.

Montana's history of rough justice is legendary. During the 1860s the Montana Vigilantes lynched twenty-two members of Henry Plummer's gang, riding through ten-foot snowdrifts to bounce them off cottonwood trees and barn ladders all over the state. Plummer's men died game, often toasting the mob with freshly popped bottles of champagne and shouting out salutes to Jefferson Davis before cashing in. Plummer, a county sheriff, was the only exception. He begged his executioners to saw off his arms and legs and cut out his tongue rather than take his life. The vigilantes listened quietly to his appeal, then hanged him from the crossbeam at the entrance to his ranch, the soles of his boots swinging back and forth three inches from the ground.

But that was then. Today the Montana legal system is little different from any other state's, and the appeals apparatus in criminal convictions sometimes produces situations with which no one can adequately deal.

The most dangerous, depraved, twisted, and unpredictable human being I ever knew was a rodeo clown by the name of Wyatt Dixon. With my help, he had been sentenced to sixty years in Deer Lodge Pen for murdering a biker in the Aryan Brotherhood. On an early spring morning, one year after Wyatt had begun his sentence in Deer Lodge Pen, I walked from the house down to the road and removed the daily newspaper from the tin cylinder in which it was rolled. I flipped the paper open and began to read the headlines as I walked back up the incline to the house, distracted momentarily by a black bear running out of the sunshine into the spruce trees that grew on the hill immediately behind the house.

When I glanced back at the paper, I saw Wyatt's name and a wire service story that made me swallow.

I sat down at the breakfast table in our kitchen and kept the newspaper folded back upon itself so the story dealing with Wyatt was not visible. Through the side window I could see steam rising from the metal roof on our barn and, farther on, a small herd of elk coming down an arroyo, their hooves pocking the snow that had frozen on the grass during the night.

"Why the face?" Temple, my wife, asked.

"For spring it's still pretty cold out," I replied.

She straightened the tulips in a glass vase on the windowsill and lifted a strand of hair off the glasses she had started wearing. She had thick chestnut hair and the light was shining on it through the window. "Did you say something about Johnny American Horse earlier?" she asked.

"He got himself stuck in the can again. I thought I'd go down to morning court," I replied.

"He needs a lawyer to get out of the drunk tank?"

"This time he had a revolver on him. It was under his coat, so he got booked for carrying a concealed weapon."

"Johnny?" she said.

I folded the newspaper and stuck it in my

12

coat pocket. "Meet me for lunch?" I said from the doorway.

"Can you tell me why you're acting so weird? Why are you taking the newspaper with you?"

"No reason."

"Right."

The phone rang on the counter. I got to it before she did. "Hello?" I said, my mouth dry.

"Well, God bless your little heart, I'd recognize that voice anywhere. Howdy doodie, Mr. Holland? I wasn't sure you was still around, but soon as I come into town, I looked in the phone directory and there was your name in the middle of the page, big as a horse turd floating in a milk shake. Bet you don't know who this is?"

"You're making a mistake, partner."

"Sir, that injures my feelings. I have called you in good faith and as a fellow American, 'cause this is the land of the free and the home of the brave. I don't hold no grudges. I have even used your name as a reference in the many letters I have wrote to our country's leaders. In fact, I have wrote President Bush himself to offer my services. Has he contacted you yet?"

"I'm going to hang up now. Don't call here again," I said, trying to avoid Temple's stare.

"Now listen here, sir, I'm inviting you and your wife to a blowout, all-you-can-eat buffet dinner at the Golden Corral Restaurant. Do not hang up that phone, no-siree-bobtail —"

I returned the receiver to the cradle. Temple's eyes were riveted on mine.

"Who was that?" she said.

"Wyatt Dixon. He's out," I replied.

She began to straighten the tulips in the window again but instead knocked over the vase, shattering it in the sink, the tulip petals red as blood among the shards of glass.

As I left the house for work the sun was bright on the hillsides of the valley in which we lived, and to the south I could see the timber climbing up into the snowpack on the crests of the Bitterroots. I turned onto the two-lane into the little town of Lolo, then headed up the road to my office in Missoula. My reluctance to tell Temple that Wyatt Dixon was out of prison had nothing to do with the reasons people normally conceal bad news from their loved ones. Rather, it had everything to do with Temple's own propensity for immediate and violent retaliation against anyone who threatened her person or that of her friends or family.

Back in Texas, before she became a private investigator for small-town lawyers such as my-self, she had been a patrolwoman in Dallas, a deputy sheriff in Fort Bend County near Houston, and a corrections officer in Louisiana. She had also been buried alive by Wyatt Dixon.

I parked in my rental space not far from the Oxford Bar, whose doors have stayed open since 1891, and walked down the street toward my office close by the courthouse. The maple trees on the courthouse lawn were in new leaf now, riffling in the breeze, the shadows shifting like lacework on the grass. At the corner, across from a pawnshop and bar, I saw a man watching me, his arm hooked on top of a parking meter.

He was lantern-jawed, his red hair like cornsilk, his eyes as pale and empty as a desert sky, his teeth big and square, his hard buttocks no wider than the palms of a woman's hands. He wore skintight Wrangler jeans, boots that were cracked from age, a beautiful Stetson with an eagle feather in the band, and a heavy, long-sleeved cotton shirt printed from collar to shirttail with a collage from the American flag. When he grinned, his skin stretched back from his teeth, his lips a strange, purplish color in the shade.

"How 'bout I take you down to the Oxford and buy you a breakfast of eggs and corned beef? Guaranteed to put a chunk of drill pipe in your britches," he said.

"You get the hell away from me," I said.

He twisted a finger in his ear and looked down the street at two college-age kids, a girl and boy, jogging through the intersection, both of them sweaty and hot, their faces bright. His eyes came back on mine. "I ain't got no grief with you, counselor. Left that back at the joint. Know why?" he said, his eyes widening.

"Not interested," I said.

"They dusted off the electroshock machine, wired me up, and made blue sparks jump off my Johnson. I was definitely in the spirit when they pulled them electrodes off my head, yes sir."

"Electroshock isn't used anymore."

"They said in my case they was making an exception, although they didn't give me no explanation on that. Put me naked in an isolation cell and hosed me down with ice-cold water, too," he said, fitting his hand on his scrotum, watching the college girl jog by a few feet away. "I'm putting together a company to provide the best rough stock on the Northwestern circuit. Horses you couldn't hold in with a barbed wire hackamore. Need you as my legal point man."

"Are you out of your mind?"

He seemed genuinely puzzled, his jaw hooked forward like a camel's. "I'll pay you top dollar, cash money, Brother Holland," he said.

"*Brother?*"

"I joined a church when I was inside. You are not looking at the same Wyatt Dixon who traveled the Lost Highway and went to the Wild Side of Life where the scarlet waters flow. You have probably noticed them are

16

lyrics written by the greatest songwriters of our time. I hope you can feel the depth of sincerity in each of them poetic words."

"I want you to work real hard on this concept, Wyatt. You come anywhere around me or my wife or son, if you send any of your neo-Nazi friends after us, if I see that barnyard, white-trash face anywhere near —"

I stopped. Each of my statements seemed to connect with and energize a neuron inside his head, causing his face to jerk, his mouth to flex, his legs to cave, his feet to splay, as though he were being struck with invisible blasts of air. He stared at me, his eyes dilated with awe.

"I did not believe it possible, but once again your word skills has done blowed away this simple rodeo cowboy," he said. "I know now I have chose the right man to recommend me to President Bush. God bless you, sir."

I went inside the office. Through the window I could see him stretched out under a tree on the courthouse lawn, the side of his face propped on his hand, watching the passersby, none of whom had any idea that a man wearing a shirt stamped with the colors and design of the Stars and Stripes was thinking thoughts about them that would cause the weak of spirit to weep.

I called Temple at home, but no one answered. I called the agency where she worked as a private investigator with a man and another woman. "He was waiting for me outside the office," I said.

"He's going to reoffend. Just wait him out," she said.

"Temple?"

"Yes?" she said.

"If he comes around the house and I'm not there, shoot him," I said.

"I'll shoot him whether you're there or not," she replied.

The morning court judge was Clark Lebeau, known for his egalitarian attitudes, short tolerance for stupidity, and unusual sentences for people who thought they would simply pay a fine and be on their way. Businessmen found themselves working on the sanitation truck; animal abusers cleaned the litter boxes at the shelter; and drunk drivers mowed grass and weeded graves at the cemetery. Rumor had it he kept both a gun and a bottle of gin under the bench.

"What the hell were you doing with a pistol?" he asked from the bench.

"I guess I was gonna pawn it," Johnny American Horse replied.

"You guess?" the judge said.

"I was pretty drunk, your honor."

"The officers said it was under your coat. That means while you were passed out you managed to commit a felony. Where's your goddamn brains, son?"

"Left them in the Oxford, your honor," Johnny said.

I winced inside.

"You took a gun to a saloon?" the judge said.

"Your honor," I began.

"Shut up, Mr. Holland," the judge said. "You carried a gun into the Oxford?"

"I don't remember," Johnny said.

The judge rubbed his mouth. He was old and sometimes irritable but not an unfair man. "I'm letting you go on your own recognizance. Come back in here on a firearms charge, I'm going dig up the jail and drop it on your head. Am I making myself clear?"

"Yes, sir," Johnny said.

We walked outside into the brilliance of the morning, sunshine on the hills above the town, birds flying through trees on the courthouse lawn, the noise of traffic, a world of normalcy as dissimilar from life inside a jail as the quick are from the dead.

That is, except for the presence of Wyatt Dixon, who was now sitting up in the shade, sailing playing cards into his inverted hat. His pale eyes looked up at us, a matchstick rolling in his teeth.

"Know that dude?" I asked Johnny.

"You betcha I do," Johnny said. "He was shacked up with a girl on the res. Her ex and a couple of his Deer Lodge buds decided to remodel Wyatt's cranial structure. One of

19

them walks with a permanent limp now. The other two decided to start new careers in Idaho."

Johnny reached down, picked up a small pinecone, and threw it at Wyatt's head. "Hey, boy, I thought you were in the pen," he said.

"Hell, no," Wyatt said, his eyes looking at nothing, his matchstick flexing at an upward angle.

We walked to the corner, then crossed the street to my office. I didn't speak until we were a long way from Wyatt Dixon.

"Why not just put your necktie in the garbage grinder?" I said.

"Telling a man you're afraid of him is the same as telling him he's not as good as you. That's when you have trouble. Fellow as smart as you ought to know that, Billy Bob," Johnny said. He hit me on the shoulder.

"Why were you carrying a gun?" I said.

He didn't answer. Inside the office, I asked him again.

"A couple of guys are here to fry my Spam," he said.

"Which guys?" I asked.

"Don't know. Saw them in a dream. But they're here," he said.

"That'll make a fine defense. Maybe we can get a couple of counselors from detox to testify for us."

He told me he'd work off my fees at my small spread outside Lolo, then went to search for his pickup truck so he could drive back to his house on the reservation in the Jocko Valley.

It's probably fair to say that welfare dependency, alcoholism, glue sniffing, infant mortality, the highest suicide rate among any of our ethnic groups, recidivism, xenophobia, and a general aversion to capitalistic monetary concepts are but a few of the problems American Indians have. The list goes on. Unfortunately, their troubles are of a kind most white people don't want to dwell on, primarily, I suspect, because Indians were a happy people before their encounter with the white race.

The irony is, except for a few political opportunists, Indians seldom if ever make a claim on victimhood. Individually they're reticent about their hardships, do their time in county bags and mainline joints without complaint, and systematically go about dismantling their lives and inflicting pain on themselves in ways a medieval flagellant couldn't dream up.

Johnny American Horse didn't belong in the twenty-first century, I told myself. He lived on the threadworn edges of an aboriginal culture, inside a pantheistic vision of the world that was as dead as his ancestor Crazy Horse. I told myself I would help him with his legal troubles, be a good friend to him,

21

and stay out of the rest of it. That was all decency required, wasn't it?

Temple joined me for lunch by a big window in a workingmen's café near the old train station on North Higgins. Across the street were secondhand stores and bars that sold more fortified wine than whiskey. Brown hills that were just beginning to turn green rose steeply above the railyards, and high up on the crests I could see white-tailed deer grazing against the blueness of the sky. The café was crowded, the cooks sweating back in the kitchen, frying big wire baskets of chicken in hot grease.

"Johnny was carrying a gun because of somebody he saw in a dream?" Temple said.

"That's what he says."

She bit a piece off a soda cracker and stared out the window at a freight passing through the yards, her mouth small and red, her chestnut hair freshly washed and blow-dried and full of lights. "I think Johnny's looking for a cross. If he can't find one, he'll construct it," she said.

I started to speak, then saw her eyes go empty and look past me at a group of men entering the door. Three of them were probably wranglers, ordinary blue-collar men, brown-skinned, their stomachs hard as boards under their big belt buckles, their hats sweat-ringed around the crowns. But the fourth man had teeth like tombstones and a vacuity in the boldness of his stare that made people look away.

"That bastard is actually on the street," Temple said.

I set down the iced tea I was drinking and wiped my mouth. "Let's go," I said.

"No," she replied.

Wyatt Dixon and his friends sat down at a table by the door. Outside, a trailer loaded with horses was parked in a yellow zone. It didn't take long for Wyatt's vacuous gaze to sweep the restaurant, then settle on us.

The cast or composition of his eyes was unlike any I had ever seen in a human being. They had almost no color and showed no emotion; the pupils were black pinpoints, even in bright light. They studied both people and animals with an invasiveness that was like peeling living tissue off bone.

He sat with one booted foot extended into the aisle, causing the waitresses to step around it, his eyes focused curiously on Temple's face.

The waitress brought a chicken basket for Temple, fried pork chops and mashed potatoes and string beans for me. I looked back once more at Wyatt, then picked up a steak knife and started to cut my food. Temple scraped back her chair and walked to the pay phone by the front door, no more than five feet from Wyatt Dixon's table. She punched in three numbers on the key pad.

"This is Temple Carrol Holland, down by the depot on North Higgins," she said into the receiver. "A psychopathic bucket of shit by the name of Wyatt Dixon and some of his friends have illegally parked a horse trailer by the restaurant. Please send a cruiser down here so we don't have to breathe horse sweat while we eat. Thank you."

The level of sound in the restaurant dropped precipitously as she hung up the phone and walked back to our table. Wyatt's jaw was hooked forward, exposing his teeth, a smile denting the corner of his mouth, like a thumbnail's incision in tan clay. He told one of the wranglers to go outside and move the truck, then came to our table.

"Howdy doodie, Miss Temple?" he said, standing above us. " 'Member me? Bet you still think I was one of them men dug a hole and stuck you in it."

"Go back to your table, Wyatt," I said.

"Let him talk," Temple said.

"Truth is, I don't know what I done before I got filled up on chemical cocktails and had my brains electrified at Warm Springs. But in this time of national trial, there is no excuse for one American doing mean things to another. Here's two tickets to an ass-buster down in Stevensville. There you will find this humble rodeo clown entertaining the throngs of people that follows our greatest national sport."

24

I brushed the tickets off the tablecloth onto the floor. "You're about to have the worst day in your life," I said.

He looked down at the tickets, then back at me in mock disbelief. A waitress stepped around him, a loaded tray balanced on her shoulder. He admired her rump a moment, then squatted down, eye-level with me. He was clean-shaved, his skin without tattoos or scars. I could smell horses and an odor like hay and buttermilk in his clothes. He looked at the steak knife that rested in my right hand. "I had a lot of bad nights up at the Zoo. A lot of time to study on things, Brother Holland. Glad I found Jesus. 'Cause I wouldn't want to act on the kind of thoughts that was tangled up in my head," he said.

Through the window I saw a city police cruiser pull to the curb.

"Your cab is here," Temple said.

Wyatt glanced over his shoulder, then scratched his cheek. "I will not pretend I can contend with the smarts and humor of Miss Temple. Instead, I salute both y'all as fellow Texans and patriots defending the U.S. of A. against the ragheads that is attacking our great country," he said. "I'll be out to your ranch directly with a haunch of sirloin to slap on the barbecue. Y'all live up that gulch right outside Lolo?"

He grinned idiotically, his teeth shiny with his saliva.

Later, after he and his friends had eaten and gone, Temple and I sat in the quietness of the now almost deserted restaurant, the glass in the window vibrating with wind. I felt both inept and angry at myself for reasons I couldn't define. I kept reviewing in my mind what I should have done to Wyatt Dixon, like a schoolboy who has been shoved down in the playground and done nothing about it.

"Forget it," Temple said.

"He spit on us."

"Don't get the ego mixed up in this, Billy Bob."

"I'll see you at home," I said.

"Where are you going?"

I paid the check and went out the door without answering.

The District Attorney was a Northern California transplant by the name of Fay Harback. She was a petite woman with a small, attractive face and white skin, and hair that was mahogany-colored and thick on the back of her neck. She'd graduated at the top of Stanford Law and, like many of her fellow Californians in the aftermath of the Rodney King riots, had moved into the northern Rockies.

But her husband, an organic truck farmer, had bad luck in lots of ways. His ideals drove him and his wife into bankruptcy, and after he died in a hunting accident, she became an assistant district attorney, then ran for the D.A.'s job and won, largely because she had helped shut down an industrial waste disposal group that had tried to construct a PCB incinerator on the river, one that would have probably poisoned the entire valley.

I liked Fay and I liked her toughness in particular, even though she was sometimes ambitious, but I could never guess which way her wind vane was about to blow.

"Let's see if I understand. I sent Wyatt Dixon up the road, but I'm responsible for the fact he's on the street?" she said.

"I didn't say that," I replied.

"Look —" she began. She pinched her temples and got up from her chair and stood at the window. I heard her take a breath. "I screwed it up."

"How?"

"Failure to disclose exculpatory evidence. A jailhouse gum ball claimed Dixon was shooting pool with him when the biker was killed. His only problem was he drooled when he was off his medication."

"Why didn't you give his statement to the defense?"

"An A.D.A. we later fired said he'd taken care of it. I forgot all about it. It was worthless information, anyway. But I got sandbagged on appeal," she said.

"Get Dixon for the burial of my wife."

"We can't prove he did it."

"You've got his fall partner's testimony."

"Terry Witherspoon's? He died from AIDS in the prison infirmary last week." She looked at the frustration in my face. Her expression softened. "You were a Texas Ranger?"

"Yes."

"Have days you miss it?" she asked.

"No."

"Montana isn't the O.K. Corral anymore. If I were you, I wouldn't listen to the wrong voices inside my head."

"Box up the psychobabble and ship it back to Marin County, Fay," I said.

"I grew up in Weed. So run your redneck shuck on somebody else, Billy Bob."

Lesson? Don't mess with short women who have law degrees from Stanford.

That night the sky was black and bursting with stars above the valley where we lived, then clouds quaking with thunder moved across the moon and snow began to fall on the mountaintops, sticking on the ponderosa and fir trees that grew high up on the slopes. In my sleep I dreamed of small-arms fire in the dark, the running of booted feet, the smell of wet mesquite, scrub oak, burned gunpowder, and ponded water that had gone stagnant. In the dream I raised my revolver and fired at a man silhouetted against the sky, saw his arms reach out horizontally, then clutch the wound that burst like a rose from the top buttonhole on his shirt.

Fay Harback had asked if I missed my career as a Texas Ranger. The truth was I had never left it. It returned to me at least every third night, in the form of my best friend's accidental death down in Old Mexico.

L. Q. Navarro had long ago forgiven me, as the priests at my church had. But absolution by both the living and the dead did not reach into my nocturnal hours. I woke at 3 a.m. and sat alone in the coldness of the living room, looking out at the moonlight that had broken through the clouds and at the caked snow steaming on the backs of my horses in the pasture.

Just before dawn I fell asleep in the chair and did not wake until I heard Temple making breakfast in the kitchen.

CHAPTER 2

Johnny American Horse's dreams did not involve past events from his own life, guilt, erotic need, or even people or places he knew. His dreams were filled with birds and wild animals on alluvial moonscape, rivers and pink mesas he had never seen, herds of mustangs racing across a darkening plain forked by lightning. Sometimes the people in his dreams carried obsolete flintlocks, drove bison over cliffs, and sat by meat fires among cottonwoods whose leaves flickered like thousands of green butterflies.

He told a bartender in Lonepine and one in Big Arm he'd dreamed where the grave of Crazy Horse was located, although no historian had ever been able to find it. He built a sweat lodge in the Swan Mountains and fasted and prayed on the banks of a creek that had been melted snow only the day before, and inserted himself at dawn, hot and naked, between boulders that roared with white water out of fir and spruce trees.

When he performed the Sun Dance ceremony over at the Northern Cheyenne Reservation and tore the hooked pieces of antler loose from his pectoral muscles, he saw a burning white globe spin out of the sky and burst inside his head, blinding him to all images of the earth except those given to him by an ancient deity who had no English name.

But none of these things brought Johnny American Horse peace of mind. Instead, he joined radical Native American groups and fought with oil, pipeline, and timber companies, and sometimes became a shrill and obsessive voice to which no one listened. Some nights he slept in the woods or the reservation jail. Some nights he wasn't sure where he slept.

But one week ago the content of his dreams had changed. He had fallen asleep in a chair on his front porch overlooking the Jocko River. The wind was cool blowing up the valley, smelling of pines and woodsmoke, and Johnny slept with his hat pulled down on his eyes and a sheep-lined coat spread across his chest. In his dream he heard a car engine roar to life, then saw a Firebird speeding at dawn out of an industrial city on the shore of a great lake, two men seated in the front, the exhaust thundering on the asphalt.

The man in the passenger seat had gold, peroxided hair, cut military-style, his arms tattooed with roses and green parrots that had yellow beaks. His chest was flat-plated, his face like tallow that had been warmed next to a flame and wiped clean of either joy or remorse, then allowed to cool, retaining no trace of any humanity it might have possessed.

The driver was middle-aged and wore horn-rimmed, thick glasses and had tiny red and blue veins in his jowls. He was dressed in a tweed coat, brown pants, a tie and white shirt, and shined shoes. Except for the intensity and concentration with which he drove the Firebird, he could have been a department store floorwalker or an accountant.

For three nights Johnny saw the two men on their journey westward, their vehicle low-slung, hammering hard across the Great Plains, through mesa country and badlands that were the color of chalk. They ate in truck stops, with neither pleasure nor distaste, ordering whatever was the special for the day, usually snuffing out their cigarettes in their unfinished food. At the Super 8 and the Econo Lodge they slept in beds that crackled with static electricity and smelled of other people's copulation.

They drank brandy and soda in roadside bars, staring without interest at sports television, picked up two whores in Belfield, North Dakota, blew out a tire in Billings, hit an icy stretch on the Grand Divide, and whacked a swatch out of the guardrail west of Butte. To the men in the dream, one activity was no different in meaning or significance from another.

Then one morning Johnny American Horse woke in the coldness of the sunrise, his mind empty of images, the fir trees and ponderosa on the hillside above the Jocko wet and shining, the whole world as bright and clear as a spoon ringing against the rim of a crystal glass, and he knew he would not dream of the two men again. There was no need to. The horn-rimmed man and the man whose face had melted next to a flame were here, someplace around Missoula, waiting, but he did not know where.

The day after Johnny was released from jail on the weapons charge, he was turning over the thatch in his vegetable garden, the sun warm on his shoulders, when the scene around him seemed to dissolve and break apart, replaced by a collage of neon-lit smoke, green felt, a brass rail, and a man in a tweed jacket hunched over a bowl of chili by a window lighted from the outside. He heard pool balls clattering inside a triangular plastic rack and saw a man with roses and green parrots tattooed on his arms sight along a pool cue and smack an eight ball into a side pocket.

Johnny got into his pickup truck and drove into Missoula and on down West Broadway toward the business district. In the distance he could see the huge brown slopes of the mountains that enclosed the eastern end of the city, the trees a deep green in the saddles. On his right the Clark Fork of the Columbia River paralleled the street he drove on, its banks fringed with willow trees. The current was a greenish-coppery color from the first snowmelt, the water braiding between the chains of rocks that protruded from the surface. To the south were the beginnings of the Sapphire Mountains and the Bitterroot Valley, the fresh snow on the peaks a blinding white in the sunlight.

But here, on each side of the street, was a different world, one of $19.95 motels, a self-service filling station that advertised itself as AMERICAN OWNED, and bars where women fought with knives and the clientele came to the door at 7 a.m.

He parked down by the river and entered the back of a bar that smelled of coffee, flat beer, and cigarette smoke that had soaked into the walls and vinyl booths. A swamper was swinging a wet mop on the floor, the bartender loading a cooler with long-necked bottles of beer. A man with peroxided hair, wearing a yellow muscle shirt and stonewashed jeans and polished military boots, split a nine-ball rack with such force the cue ball jumped the rail and rolled across the floor.

Johnny picked up the ball and set it back on the felt.

"Thanks," the pool shooter said, his eyes flat.

"No problem," Johnny said.

He sat at the bar, ordered a soft drink, and peeled a hard-boiled egg. The pool shooter ran the balls in a string down to the nine ball, chalking his cue before each shot, his eyes never leaving his game. Then he replaced his cue in the wall rack and started to leave the bar.

"Where's your friend?" Johnny asked.

"Which friend?" the man asked.

"The guy you drove out with."

"You lost me."

"No matter what you guys are getting paid, if I was you, I'd give the money back."

"Yeah, I guess that's good to know. But I got no idea what you're talking about," the man said.

"Maybe I got you confused with somebody else."

"Yeah, maybe you do," the man said.

Johnny watched the man with roses and parrots tattooed on his arms go out the door and cross the street, then walk down an alley, where a car was parked. The man walked gracefully, light-footed, like a prizefighter, his back a triangle of sinew and muscle. Just before he reached the car, a Firebird, he turned and looked back at the bar.

When Johnny got back home, he strung tin cans on wires around his house and removed a box from under his bed containing a bowie knife that had been forged from a car spring, and a trade hatchet, with an oak handle and a half-moon hook on the head, given to him by his grandfather. He went into his toolshed and ground the hatchet on an emery wheel, then sharpened both it and the bowie knife on a whetstone and returned to the house.

The day was growing warmer, and through the window he could see flies hatching out of the reeds on the riverbanks, drifting onto the riffle, where rainbow trout popped them as soon as they touched the surface. He fell asleep in a chair on the porch and thought he heard dry thunder on the far side of the mountains that ringed his land.

Every defense attorney has clients who enter his life on a seemingly temporary basis, then become the human equivalent of chewing gum on the bottom of a shoe. Celebrity defense attorneys who appear regularly on CNN talk shows may lead glamorous lives, but the average practitioner of criminal law has a clientele with whom he does not want to be seen in public. These include grifters of every stripe, jackrollers, pimps, paperhangers, drug dealers, Murphy artists, cross-dressing prostitutes, court-assigned women who kill their children, and lifetime recidivists who are convinced they are criminal geniuses and try to outwit the system by lying to their attorneys.

Private investigators deal daily with the same bunch, although occasionally there's one who doesn't fit into the box. Temple called me that afternoon. "It's Amber Finley again," she said. "She's in on a drunk and disorderly. She also hit a cop. Actually, she threw her underwear in his face."

"Why is she calling you?"

"She's burned herself with every attorney in town. At least with the good ones," she replied.

"She wants me to represent her?"

"She's not a bad gal, Billy Bob."

"Answer is no."

"You pretty busy now?"

"She can call her father. I don't want to get involved."

"She says she knows why Johnny American Horse was carrying a pistol."

"How does she know anything about Johnny?"

"They've been seeing each other. At least that's what she says."

"Her old man must love that."

"You want me to tell her to get lost?"

A few minutes later I walked over to the sheriff's department and a deputy escorted me to a holding cell, where Amber Finley sat on a metal bench, her legs crossed, looking at the wall. She was around twenty-five and wore beat-up cowboy boots, jeans hitched tightly around her hips, a Harley T-shirt, and long earrings with blue stones in them. Her hair was blond and cut short, her eyes an intense blue. Even though she was hung over, her face still possessed the lovely features and complexion that Hollywood had idealized and turned into a national icon in the Technicolor films of the forties and fifties. But Amber Finley's mind-set was far removed from that earlier, more innocent time.

She was a biker girl one night, a cowgirl the next. She drank in busthead bars and was probably the wet dream of the men and college boys who hung in them. But the clothes she wore and the life she led were a self-abasing deception. She spoke French and German, had an IQ of 160, a degree in English literature from the University of Virginia, and was the daughter of United States Senator Romulus Finley.

"How do you commit battery with undergarments?" I said.

"It's easy when a cop kicks open your motel room while you're dressing," she replied.

"What were you doing in a dump like that, anyway?"

"To tell you the truth, I don't remember."

I paused a moment. "Your old man won't spring you?" I said.

She seemed to think about it. "If I asked him, yeah, he probably would. Yeah, he might," she said. She looked at me, as though confused by her own words and the sad implication in them. She got up and walked to the bars. I could smell the cigarette smoke in her hair and the mixed drinks that had gone sour on her stomach. "Get me out of here, Billy Bob. I'm *really* hung over this time."

★ ★ ★

An hour later we walked out of the jail. "Why was Johnny American Horse carrying a gun around?" I asked.

"It's those oil companies he's trying to stop from drilling on sacred lands. He thinks they put a hit on him."

"A hit? From an oil company? Maybe some of their CEOs are moral imbeciles, but oil companies don't have people killed," I said.

"Right, that's why we're taking over Third World countries — we don't care about their oil. See you later, B.B. I'm going to sleep for three days."

B.B.?

As the sun dropped behind the ridge of mountains on the west side of the Jocko Valley, Johnny American Horse walked the perimeter of his four-acre lot, examined the wire and tin cans he had strung earlier in the day, then continued on up the slope into the trees bordering the back of his property. The sun became a hot red spark between two mountains, and a purple shade fell across the valley floor just as the moon rose over the hills in the south. He sat for a long time among the trees, his arms folded across his knees, studying his land, the dirt road that traversed it, the dark green shine on the river winding out of the cottonwoods.

The men who had driven across the plains to find him were urban people, he thought.

They would come for him at night because they were cowards and they killed for hire. They would drive their Firebird as close to his house as possible because they did not like to walk, nor did they feel confident when they were separated from the machines that gave them both power and anonymity.

But their greatest mistake would be their assumption that their prey thought as they did.

He returned to the house and turned off all the lights except the one in the bathroom, leaving the door ajar so that it shone on his bed. He stuffed a rolled sleeping bag under the blanket on the bed and pulled the blanket up onto the pillows. In the kitchen he filled a thermos with black coffee, threaded the sheath of his serrated bowie knife on his belt, and put on his sheep-lined coat and a shapeless cowboy hat.

Make entry as hard as possible for them, he told himself.

He locked all the windows and both the front and back doors, then walked back up the slope with his thermos in his coat pocket and his grandfather's trade hatchet swinging from his right hand.

He sat on the ground inside the cover of the trees, his back against a boulder. He could smell elk and deer droppings in the pine needles and the tannic odor of horses in the gloaming of the day. The surrounding hills were black now, but the sky was still full of light from the sun's afterglow. He unscrewed the top from his thermos and drank, then screwed the cap back on. He heard the sound of an automobile coming down the dirt road, rocks pinging inside the fenders.

The car was low-slung, the body weather-scoured almost paintless, the engine far more powerful than the age of the car would indicate. It passed his house in a rooster tail of dust and disappeared around a bend, beyond a grove of cottonwoods. Less than two minutes later it came back up the road, gradually slowing, pulling into the cottonwoods. The driver cut the headlights and in the darkness Johnny heard at least one car door squeak open on an ungreased hinge.

He stood up in the pines and strained his eyes at the road. The air was cold now, smelling of the river and damp stone and timothy grass that was sodden with dew in the fields. When the wind gusted across the valley floor the leaves swirled like water in the cottonwoods, and suddenly Johnny could see two men, standing as stationary as statues, amidst thousands of fluttering green leaves.

The men crossed the road and headed toward his house, stooped in simian fashion, as though somehow their abbreviated posture would make them less visible. One of them stopped and raised his hand in a clenched fist, as a foot soldier would in order to signal a halt. Then the two of them stepped carefully over the trip wire that Johnny had strung with tin cans, each containing a handful of gravel.

The two figures moved around the side of the house, peering in each window. One of them went to the shed and put his hand on the hood of Johnny's pickup truck, as though to determine if the metal was still warm. He rejoined his companion, and the two of them stepped gingerly onto the back porch and went to work on the door lock.

Johnny followed a deer trail that wound laterally through the pines in the opposite direction from his house, then walked down the slope on the far side of his barn, so he could remain out of view and beyond the angle of vision of the two men picking the lock on his door.

As he came out of the horse lot, he let his heavy coat drop to the ground, moving quickly into the lee of his house. He worked his way toward the back corner, no more than ten feet from the men, who were still on the porch. He held his bowie knife in his left hand, the trade ax in the other, breathing slowly through his mouth, his back flat against the clapboards. Out in the darkness he heard horses nickering, their hooves thudding on packed earth.

The two men had been unsuccessful with

the lock. One of them stood back and smashed the door out of the jamb with his foot, shattering glass on the floor. Both men burst into the house, crashing into the bedroom, only to discover that Johnny was not there.

"I told you he was onto us. You wouldn't listen." It was the voice of the man Johnny had seen shooting pool that morning, a man who wore roses and parrots on his arms to tell him who he was because someone had stolen all expression from his face.

"Turn off the light," the other man said.

"We got to finish it, Eddy."

"No." One of the men clicked off the light in the bathroom. "Another day. We find his cooze, then we whack him."

"The guy's an Indian. He's out there."

"Tell me about it."

Johnny heard them move into the front room and unlock the door. A moment later a board squeaked on the porch and the two men walked into the yard, into the moonlight, each of them turning in a 360-degree circle as they did. Johnny picked up a rock and pitched it over the peak of the house to the far side. Both men jerked around, staring into the shadows at the source of the sound.

The man named Eddy, who wore thick, horn-rimmed glasses, held a cut-down double-barrel shotgun in both hands, the shoulder stock wood-rasped into a pistol grip.

The man with tattoos carried nothing in his hands but was reaching behind him now to extract the blue-black heavy shape of a semi-automatic stuck down inside the back of his belt.

Johnny closed his eyes briefly, heard the words *hokay hey* inside his mind, and hit the two men running, just as they were turning toward the sound of his work boots coming hard across the grass.

The man with horn-rimmed glasses seemed the more surprised of the two men, his eyes distorting like a goldfish's behind the thickness of his lenses. But nonetheless he was able to raise his cut-down shotgun for what should have been a deafening explosion of flame and lead shot into Johnny's chest. Instead, his angle of fire was obstructed by his friend, the man incapable of expression, whose weapon had caught in his belt.

Johnny whipped the trade hatchet into the neck of the man named Eddy and slashed his knife across the face of the man who did not know how to smile or to be sad. Later, he would not recall with any exactitude the struggle that followed, but he knew the blows he visited upon the intruders from an industrial city on the shores of a great lake were more than enough to ensure they would not present themselves to him again, at least not outside the bright edges of his sleep.

CHAPTER 3

The man named Eddy was on the surgeon's table four hours. His full name, according to his driver's license and a GI dog tag tucked down in his wallet, was Edward T. Bumper of New Baltimore, Michigan, a lakeside community on the shores of Lake Erie. The next day an information check through the National Crime Information Center would indicate that Eddy Bumper had no criminal record whatsoever, not even a traffic citation. In fact, other than the eleven years he had spent in the lower ranks of the United States Army, he seemed to have been hardly more than a cipher in the Detroit area, where apparently he had spent most of his life.

During the ambulance ride to the hospital, he offered no explanation for his presence at the house of Johnny American Horse, nor did he make any entreaty to his attendants, in spite of his obvious pain, or express interest in contacting friends, family, or minister. His only request of any kind was to the surgeon: If possible, he wanted a local rather than general anesthetic.

At 2:43 a.m. Edward T. Bumper opened his eyes wide on the operating table, stared up into the brilliant glare of lights overhead, and said, "I need to get to the airport."

Then he died.

His fall partner in the home invasion was another matter. Raised in a state-run orphanage, released from juvenile court at age seventeen to the United States Marine Corps, Michael Charles Ruggles served eight years in the Third World, received a general discharge, and began to get into trouble again, as though his time in the Corps was simply a respite from his true career.

But the charges filed against him were those consistent with a run-of-the-mill miscreant rather than a professional killer: solicitation of a prostitute, jackrolling an elderly person, possession of marijuana, failure to pay child support, drunk driving, solicitation and battery of a prostitute, and passing counterfeit currency at a racetrack. In each instance the charges were dismissed without explanation.

But I knew none of these things until the following day, when Johnny American Horse called my office from the jail.

"Have you been charged?" I asked.

"No. They're just talking to me," he replied.

"Cops don't just talk. As of this moment you answer no questions unless I'm present."

"Amber's with me," he said.

"Did you hear me?"

At the courthouse a deputy escorted me to

46

an interview room, where two plainclothes cops were sitting with Johnny at a wood table on which there was a can of Coca-Cola and a Styrofoam cup, a video camera mounted high on the wall. Johnny could not have looked worse. He had washed his skin clean, but blood splatter had dried in his hair and horsetails of it were all over his clothes.

"This ends now, gentlemen," I said.

One of the detectives was a towering, bull-shouldered man named Darrel McComb, whose clothes always seemed to exude a scent of testosterone. "We were talking about baseball. Think those Cubbies are cursed?" He grinned.

I sent Amber and Johnny across the street to my office and went downstairs to see the district attorney. "Put Darrel McComb back in his kennel," I said.

"Treated unfairly, are we?" she said, looking up from some papers on her desk.

"McComb questioned Johnny without Mirandizing him. He also ignored Johnny's request for a lawyer."

"Your client is not under arrest. So get lost on the Miranda. Also quit pretending Johnny's an innocent man."

"These guys tried to kill him, in his own house. What's the matter with you?"

"He lay in wait for them with a tomahawk and a knife. Why didn't he dial 911, like other people?"

"The Second Amendment says something about telephones?"

"Don't drag that right-wing crap into my office."

"I don't want Darrel McComb anywhere near my client."

"What's wrong with McComb?"

"For some reason the words 'racist' and 'thug' come to mind."

"Get out of here, Billy Bob."

Twenty minutes later, after Amber Finley had driven Johnny back to the res, I glanced out the window and saw her father cross the intersection and enter my building, his face effusive, his hand raised in greeting to street people who probably had no idea who he was. Romulus Finley's political detractors characterized him as an ignorant peckerwood, a Missouri livestock auctioneer who fell off a hog truck and stumbled into the role of United States senator. But I believed Romulus was far more intelligent than they gave him credit for.

He sat down in front of my desk, pulling a wastebasket between his feet, and began coring out the bowl of his briar pipe with a gold penknife. The indirect lighting reflected off the pinkness of his scalp.

"My daughter has already retained you?" he said, his eyes lifting into mine.

"Yes, sir, she has."

"I wish she'd called me. It's hard to keep

them down on the reservation sometimes."

"Sir?" I said.

"Can't keep them down on the farm is what I mean. Or at least I can't keep my daughter there. Damn if that gal isn't a pistol."

His language and use of allusion, as always, were almost impossible to follow. "What can I do for you?" I said.

"I just want to pay her fees and take her off your hands."

"If she wants to discharge me as her attorney, that's up to her," I replied.

He cleaned the blade of his penknife on a crumpled piece of paper and put the knife away. He smiled. He was a stout, sandy-haired, sanguine-faced man, with manners that struck me as genuine. He clucked his tongue. "My daughter is a source of endless worry to me, Mr. Holland. Will you let me know if there's anything I can do?" he said.

"I will."

"Thank you," he said, rising to shake hands. His grip was meaty and powerful, his eyes direct. "Did she leave with that Indian boy?"

"Excuse me?"

"Take exception to my vocabulary if you want. But that fellow American Horse is trouble. Not because he's an Indian. His kind tear things down, not build them up. You know I'm right, too."

"I don't know that," I said, nonsensically.

"Each to his own. Thanks for your time," he said. "Tell that daughter of mine she's fixing to drive her old man to the cemetery or the crazy house."

By that afternoon no charges had been filed in the invasion of Johnny American Horse's home, not against him, nor against the surviving member of the assassination team that had obviously been sent there to kill him.

Long ago, even before I fell in love with her, I had come to think of Temple Carrol as one of the best people I had ever met, certainly the most fun, perhaps the most beautiful, too. Her social attitudes were blue-collar, in the best sense, her personal loyalty unrelenting. She loved animals and hated those who would abuse them, thought all politicians worthless, and carried a nine millimeter in her purse. Bad guys messed with her once.

That evening she showed her P.I. badge to the deputy sheriff standing guard in front of Michael Charles Ruggles's hospital room.

"You can't come in," he said.

"Really?" she said, flipping open her cell phone. "Let's call the sheriff so you can tell him you're countermanding his permission. He's at the county commissioners' meeting now."

The nurse had left the blinds open inside

the room so the man in bed could see the blue light in the evening sky and the rooftops of the town and the chimney swifts that swooped and darted above the trees. His head was propped up on the pillow, one cheek heavily bandaged; an IV was clipped to an index finger. When Temple entered the room, he tried to push himself higher up in the bed in order to look at her more directly. His face winced peculiarly at the effort, as though the tissue were dead and had been touched alive by electrical shock.

"Looks like you're doing pretty good for a guy who has forty stitches in his cheek and two stab wounds in the chest," she said.

"Who the hell are you?" he said.

"Gal who doesn't want to see it put on the wrong guy. You don't have to talk to me if you don't want to."

"Answer the question, bitch."

Temple held a capped ballpoint and a yellow legal pad in her hands, the cover folded back as though she were about to start taking notes. She sat down in a chair by the bed, placed the ballpoint in her shirt pocket, and closed the legal pad. She looked idly into space a moment.

"Let me line it out for you," she said. "You tried to whack out a Native American political leader. You tried to do it in the middle of a United States government reservation, which shows how smart you are. You also managed

51

to do these things in the geographical center of all political correctness, Missoula, Montana.

"So what does that mean? you hurriedly ask yourself. It means either the FBI is going to prove it's an equal opportunity law enforcement agency by jamming a mile-long freight train up your ass, or you'll do state time in Deer Lodge, where the bucks will take turns shoving something else up your ass."

"That's an entertaining rap you do. I like it," he said.

"You're going down for an attempted contract hit, Michael. That's probably worth twenty years here. You want to take that kind of bounce to protect some rich guy?"

"Michael's my first name. I use my middle name. Everybody calls me Charlie. Charlie Ruggles."

"You're looking at double-digit time, Charlie. Your bud gave you up in the O.R. They didn't tell you?"

He looked at the light in the sky, then turned his head toward the nightstand, where a glass of ice water sat with a straw in it. "I can't reach over to pick it up," he said.

Temple lifted the glass to his mouth and held it there while he drew through the straw. She could feel his breath on the back of her wrist, his eyes examining her face.

"Thanks," he said. "You got nice tits. Are they implants or the real thing?"

★ ★ ★

That night the moon was full above the valley and there were deep shadows inside the fir trees on the hill behind our house. Temple had been quiet all evening, and as we prepared to go to bed she put on her nightgown with her back to me.

"You still thinking about Ruggles?" I said.

"No, not Ruggles."

She sat on the side of the bed, looking out the window. I placed my hand between her shoulder blades. I could feel her heart beating. "What's the trouble?" I asked.

"Johnny American Horse is a professional martyr. He's going to hurt us," she said.

"I don't read him that way."

"That's why he comes to you and not somebody else."

"He's our friend," I replied.

She peeled back the covers and lay down, the curvature of her spine imprinted against her nightgown.

"Temple?" I said.

"Ruggles is a Detroit button man. So was the other guy. Johnny has to know who sent them."

I couldn't argue with her. Maybe in some ways Johnny was enigmatic by choice. People who claim mystical powers don't spend a lot of time feigning normalcy at Kiwanis meetings. But I still believed Johnny was basically honest about who he was.

"I'll talk to him tomorrow," I said.

"It won't do any good," she replied.

Moments later she was asleep. I lay in the darkness with my eyes open a long time. We had a wonderful home in Montana, one hundred and twenty acres spread up both sides of a dirt road that traversed timber, meadowland, and knobbed hills. It was an enclave where distant wars and images of oil smoke on desert horizons seemed to have no application.

Why put it at risk for Johnny American Horse?

I heard a vehicle on the road, I supposed one of the few neighbors living up the valley from us. But a moment later I heard the same vehicle again, then a third time, as though the driver were lost.

I put on my slippers and went into the living room. Through the window I could see a paint-skinned pickup truck with slat sides stopped on the road and a man in a snow-white Stetson, a long-sleeved canary-yellow shirt, and tight jeans leaning on our railed fence, studying the front of our house.

I went back into the bedroom, slipped on my khakis and boots, then stopped in the hallway to put on my hat and leather jacket. In the living room I removed a .30–30 Winchester from the gun rack. Every firearm in our house was kept loaded, although no round was ever in the chamber. I heard Temple behind me. "What's wrong?" she said.

"It's Wyatt Dixon," I replied.

I stepped out on the gallery and levered a round into the Winchester's chamber. Wyatt positioned his hat on the back of his head, the way Will Rogers often did, so that his face was bathed in moonlight. I steadied the rifle against a post and aimed just to the left of his shoulder and pulled the trigger.

The bullet struck rock on the opposite hillside and whined away in the shadows with a sound like a tightly wrapped guitar string snapping free from the tuning peg.

Wyatt looked behind him curiously, then scratched a match on a fencepost and cupped the flame to a cigar stub clenched between his teeth. He flicked the dead match into our yard.

I ejected the spent casing and sighted again. This time I blew a spray of wood splinters out of the fence rail. I saw Wyatt touch his cheek, then look at his hand and wipe it on his jeans.

My third shot blew dirt out of the road six inches from his foot. I started to eject the spent casing, but Temple grabbed the barrel and pushed it down toward the gallery railing.

"Either put the gun away or give it to me," she said.

"Why?"

"He knows you won't kill him. He knows I will," she replied.

I put my arm around her shoulder. She was wearing only her nightgown and her back was shaking with cold. "To hell with Wyatt Dixon," I said.

We went back inside and closed the door. Through the window I saw him get inside his truck and puff his cigar alight. Then he started the engine and drove away.

"Billy Bob?" Temple said.

"What?"

"You're unbelievable. You shoot at somebody, then say to hell with him," she said.

"What's unusual about that?"

She laughed. "Come back to bed. You know any cures for insomnia?" she said.

The next morning was Friday. Fay Harback was in my office just after 8 a.m. "Where do you get off sending your wife into a suspect's hospital room?" she said.

"It's a free country," I replied.

"This isn't rural Bumfuck. You don't get to make up your own rules."

"Have you charged Ruggles yet?" I said.

"None of your business."

"I'm getting a bad feeling on this one."

"About *what?*" she said.

"The other half of the assassination team, what's his name, Bumper, had no record at all. Ruggles has at least a half-dozen arrests, including passing counterfeit, but the charges were always dismissed."

Her eyes shifted off mine, an unformed thought buried inside them.

"Any Feds been to see you?" I asked.

"Feds? No. You're too imaginative."

"My client isn't going to get set up."

I saw the color rise in her throat. "That takes real nerve," she said.

"File charges against Ruggles and we won't be having this kind of conversation," I said.

"The investigation is still in progress."

"Seems open and shut to me. Who's running it?"

"Darrel McComb."

"You're not serious?"

"If you have a problem with that, talk to the sheriff."

"No, we'll just give your general attitude a 'D' for 'disingenuous.' Shame on you, Fay."

She slammed the door on the way out.

I headed up to the Jocko Valley. Western Montana is terraced country, each mountain plateau and valley stacked a little higher than the ones below it. To get to the Flathead Reservation, you climb a long grade outside Missoula, between steep-sloped, thickly wooded mountains, then enter the wide green sweep of the Jocko Valley. To the left are a string of bars and an open-air arena with a cement dance floor where Merle Haggard sometimes performs. Across the breadth of the valley are the homes of fairly prosperous feed growers as well as the prefabricated tract houses built for Flathead Indians by the government. The tract houses look like a sad imitation of a middle-income suburb. Some of the yards are dotted with log outbuildings, rusted car bodies, parts of washing machines, and old refrigerators. Often a police car is parked in one of them.

But through it all winds the Jocko River — tea-colored in the early spring, later boiling with snowmelt, in the summer undulating like satin over beaver-cut cottonwoods and heavy pink and gray boulders. Johnny American Horse wanted to save it, along with the wooded hills and the grasslands that had never been kicked over with a plow. He also argued for the reintroduction of bison on the plains, allowing them to crash through fences and trample two centuries of agrarian economics into finely ground cereal. Some people on the res listened to him. Most did not.

I parked in his yard and sat down on the front steps with him. A sealed gallon jar of sun tea rested by his foot. A calico cat rolled in the new clover. Part of the mountains behind his house was still in shadow, and when the wind blew down the slope I could smell the odor of pine needles and damp humus and lichen and stone back in the trees.

"A couple of things are bothering me, Johnny," I said.

"Like what?" he said, watching the cat trap a grasshopper with its paws.

"Why'd you have to use a knife and hatchet on those guys?"

"The only gun I own is the one the cops took away from me."

"Why'd you lay in wait for them? Why didn't you get some help?"

"This is the res. People take care of themselves here. Ask any federal agent what he thinks about Indians. An Indian homicide is just another dead Indian."

"I think maybe you know who sent Bumper and Ruggles after you."

He seemed to study a thought that was hidden behind his eyes. "Ever hear of wet work?" he asked.

"Maybe," I replied.

"You were a Texas Ranger and an assistant U.S. attorney, Billy Bob."

"You're saying the G sicced these guys on you?"

"What's the G? It's just the guys who are currently running things. I trained with people just like Bumper and Ruggles. Some of the old-timers had been in the Phoenix Program."

The screen door opened behind us. "You telling Billy Bob about your dream?" Amber Finley asked. Her eyes were the bluest, most radiant I'd ever seen, her complexion glowing.

"What dream?" I said.

Johnny got up from the steps and walked across the yard toward the barn, his face averted. Amber watched him, a hand perched on one hip. "Isn't he something else?" she said.

"What dream?" I said.

"He just told me, 'All those dudes are going down. There's nothing to worry about.' I wish I could have dreams like that. Mine suck," she said.

CHAPTER 4

My son was Lucas Smothers. Illegitimate, raised by a tormented, uneducated foster father, Lucas was living testimony to the fact that goodness, love, decency, and musical talent could survive in an individual who had every reason to hate the world. He had my eyes and reddish-blond hair and six-foot height, but oddly I thought of him as my son rather than of myself as his father. When I had a moral question to resolve, I asked myself what Lucas would do in the same situation.

He was in his second year at the University of Montana and lived in an old, maple-lined neighborhood west of the campus. His small apartment looked like a recording studio more than the residence of a college student. Microphones, stereo systems, amplifiers for his electric guitars, stacks of CDs and old vinyl records, as well as his instruments — a banjo, mandolin, fiddle, stand-up bass, twelve-string mariachi guitar, and his acoustical HD-28 Martin — covered every available piece of space in the living room.

He answered the door barefoot, wearing no shirt, his stomach flat inside his Wranglers.

Over his shoulder I saw a young woman go out the back door and clang loudly down the fire escape. "Who was that?" I asked.

"A friend who stayed over. She's late for class," he said.

"It's two o'clock in the afternoon."

"That's what I said. She's late," he replied.

I nodded, as though his response made perfect sense. "Wyatt Dixon is out of prison," I said.

"I read about it in the newspaper," he said. He started picking up clothes from the floor, some of which included a woman's undergarments.

"I ran him off our place last night. But he'll be back. Watch yourself," I said.

"He's not interested in me."

"People like Dixon hate goodness. They try to injure it whenever they can, Lucas."

"I ain't afraid. I know you sure as hell ain't. So what's the big deal?" He pressed a button on his stereo and the amplified voices of Bonnie Raitt and John Lee Hooker almost blew me out of the room.

But I couldn't get Wyatt Dixon off my mind that afternoon, or Johnny American Horse's cavalier attitude about sharing information with me. I worked until late, my resentment growing. At 5:30 p.m. the courthouse square was purple with shadow, the trees pulsing with birds. I called Johnny at his house.

"You told Amber, 'All those dudes are going down.' How about some clarification on that?" I said.

"All power lies in the world of dreams. I have a dream about red ponies. It means I don't have to worry about these guys who are after me," he said.

"Then why were you carrying a gun?"

"Don't represent me."

"What?"

"You heard me."

I felt my old nemesis, anger, flare inside me like a lighted match. *Don't say anything,* I heard a voice say.

"You got it, bud," I said, and hung up the phone.

I wish it had all ended right there. But it didn't.

That evening, Temple and I had supper at a Mexican restaurant in town. The streets were full of college kids, people riding bikes over the long bridge that spanned the Clark Fork, tourists visiting the art galleries that had replaced the bars and workingmen's cafés on Front Street. A tall man in a hat and a western-cut suit walked past the restaurant window. His face was lean, his skin brown, his lavender shirt stitched with flowers. He could have been a cattleman out of the 1940s. But Seth Masterson was no cattleman.

"What are you staring at?" Temple said.

"That guy at the corner. He was a special agent in Phoenix."

"You sure? He seemed to look right through you."

"I'll be right back," I said.

I caught up with Masterson before he could cross the intersection. "Why, hey there, Billy Bob," he said, as though my face had been hard to recognize in the failing light. "What are you doing in Missoula?"

"Chasing ambulances. You know how it is," I replied. "How about you?"

"A little vacation," he replied, his eyes twinkling.

"Right," I said.

"You ought to come back and work for the G."

"Got any openings?" I said.

"You know me. I stay out of administration. Hey, I don't want to keep you. Call me if you're in Arizona."

"Sure," I said.

He crossed the intersection, then went into the Fact and Fiction bookstore. My food was cold when I got back to the table.

"What's the deal on your friend?" Temple said.

"Remember the story about the FBI agent who wrote a memo warning the head office terrorists were taking flight instruction in Phoenix? The memo that got ignored?"

"That's the guy?"

"He was at Ruby Ridge and Waco, too. Seth gets around."

"You want your food reheated?"

"Why not?" I said. But even after the waitress warmed up my plate, I couldn't eat. I wasn't sure why Seth was in Missoula, but there were two things I was certain of: Seth Masterson didn't take prisoners and I didn't want him as an adversary.

Saturday morning I received a call at home from a man who was probably the most effective but lowest-rent attorney in Missoula. If a human being could exude oil through his pores, it was Brendan Merwood. His politics were for sale, his advocacy almost always on the side of power and greed. What he was now telling me seemed to offend reason.

"You represent Michael Charles Ruggles and he wants to see me?" I said.

"He likes to be called Charlie."

"Why would 'Charlie' have any interest in me?"

"Put it this way — he's not your ordinary guy."

"My wife got that impression when he called her a bitch and expressed his thoughts about her anatomy."

"I'm just passing on the message. Do with it as you wish, my friend," he said, and hung up.

I drove to St. Patrick's Hospital in

Missoula and rode the elevator up to Charlie Ruggles's floor. A sheriff's deputy stopped me at his door. "You're supposed to be on an approved visitors list, Billy Bob," he said.

"Better check with the man inside," I said, and grinned.

The deputy went into the room and came back out. "Go on in," he said.

Instead, I stayed outside momentarily and pulled the door closed so Charlie Ruggles could not hear our conversation. "Was Seth by here?" I asked.

"Who?" the deputy said.

"Seth Masterson. Tall guy, western clothes, nice-looking?"

"Oh yeah, you mean that Fed. He was here yesterday afternoon. What about him?"

"Nothing. We used to work together."

I went inside the room and shut the door behind me. Charlie Ruggles watched me out of a face that seemed as dead and empty of emotion as pink rubber.

"You made remarks about my wife's breasts and called her a bitch. But since you're in an impaired condition, I'm not going to wrap that bedpan around your head. That said, would you like to tell me something?"

"I want one hundred grand. You'll get everything your client needs. Tell the Indian what I said."

I stood at the window and looked out at the treetops and the old brick apartment houses along the streets. "Why would anyone want to pay you a hundred grand?" I said, my back turned to Charlie Ruggles.

"Considering what's on the table, that ain't much to ask," he replied.

The personality and mind-set of men and women like Charlie Ruggles never changed, I thought. They believe their own experience and knowledge of events are of indispensable value and importance to others. The fact that their own lives are marked by failure of every kind, that their rodent's-eye view of the world is repellent to any normal person, is totally lost upon them. "Hey, did you hear me?" he asked.

"I don't have one hundred grand. Neither does my client. If we did, we wouldn't give it to you," I replied.

"Your client knows the people he can get it from. They'll pay him just to go away."

"I don't want to offend you, Ruggles, but are you retarded?"

His facial expression remained dead, but his eyes were imbued with a mindless, liquid malevolence that I had seen only in condemned sociopaths who no longer had anything to lose. "Step over here and I'll whisper a secret in your ear. Come on, don't be afraid. You're safe with me. I just want to tell you about a couple of liberal lawyers who got in my face."

He rubbed his tattoos with the balls of his

fingers and waited for me to speak. I walked close to his bed.

"What do you think hell's going to be like?" I asked.

"What?"

"Nothing."

"Say what you said again."

"I'll give you something else to think about instead. You and your bud were armed with a semiautomatic and a cut-down double barrel, but an Indian with a knife and tomahawk cleaned your clock and didn't get a scratch on him. If I were you, I'd stick to beating up old people and hookers."

I could feel his eyes burrowing into my neck as I left the room.

On the way to my car I passed the sheriff's detective, Darrel McComb. I had used the words "racist" and "thug" when talking about McComb to the district attorney, Fay Harback. Like most slurs, the words were simplistic and inadequate and probably revealed more about me than they did about McComb, namely, my inability to think clearly about men of his background.

The truth was he didn't have a background. He came from the hinterland somewhere, perhaps Nebraska or Kansas, a green-gold place of wheat and cornfields and North European churches we do not associate with the Darrel McCombs of the world. He was

68

big, with farm-boy hands, his head crew-cut, his face full of bone. He had been a crop duster, an M.P. in the Army, and later had worked as an investigator for CID.

But there were rumors about Darrel: He'd been part of the dirty war in Argentina and connected up with intelligence operations in Nicaragua and El Salvador; he'd run cocaine for the Contras into the ghettos of the West Coast; he was an honest-to-God war hero and Air America pilot who had been shot down twice in Laos. And, lastly, he was just a dumb misogynistic flatfoot with delusions of grandeur.

As a sheriff's detective, he operated on the fine edges of restraint, never quite crossing lines but always leaving others with the impression of where he stood on race, university peace activists, and handling criminals.

Ask Darrel McComb a question about trout fishing while he was sitting in the barber's chair, he'd talk the calendar off the wall. Ask him where he lived twenty years ago, Darrel McComb would only smile.

"I hear your man is on the street," he said.

"Which man is that, Darrel?"

"Wyatt Dixon," he said, feeding a stick of gum into his mouth, his eyes focused down the sidewalk.

"Fact is, he was out at my house. I shot at him a couple of times. Did he check in with you on that?"

McComb's eyes came back on mine. "Your aim must not be too good. I just saw him eating at Stockman's."

"Nice seeing you, Darrel. You try to jump Johnny American Horse over the hurdles again, I'll be seeing a lot more of you."

I heard him laugh to himself as I walked away.

Temple and I and my son, Lucas, had moved to western Montana from Texas only two years before. But moving to Montana marked more than a geographic change in a person's life. The mountains and rivers of the northern Rockies are the last of an unspoiled America. To live inside a stretch of country that still bears similarities to the way the earth looked before the Industrial Age humbles a person in a fashion that is hard to convey to outsiders. The summer light rises high into the sky and stays there until after 10 p.m.; the stones in a river quake with sound in the darkness, giving the lie to the notion that matter does not possess a soul; the sunset on the mountains becomes like electrified blood, so intense in its burning on the earth's rim even an unbeliever is tempted to think of it as a metaphysical testimony to the passion of Christ.

But I did not need the grandeur of the Northwest to make me dwell upon spiritual presences. The friend I'd slain, L. Q. Navarro, was never far from my sight, regardless of where I happened to be. Sometimes he stood behind me while I groomed our horses in the barn, or perhaps he walked past a window in the starlight, still wearing the ash-gray Stetson, pin-striped suit, and boots and spurs he had died in.

L.Q. had an opinion on everything. Usually I didn't listen to him. Most of the time I wished I had.

Don't stick a burr in that McComb fellow's shoe, he said to me that night as I was loading a wheelbarrow in the barn and hauling it out to our compost pile.

He started it, I replied.

That's what we'd always tell ourselves before we scrambled somebody's eggs.

I don't need this, L.Q.

You should have parked one between Wyatt Dixon's eyes and put a throw-down on him. No serial numbers, no prints but his own.

Would you give it a rest? I said.

He climbed up on the stall and sat on the top slat. He had a black mustache and his hair grew in black locks on the back of his neck; his shirt glowed as brightly as snow in moonlight. *This American Horse business is starting to develop a federal odor,* he said.

You were always a closet states'-righter, L.Q. You just never accepted it. Now shut up.

When I looked up, the stall was empty. From up the slope I could hear an owl screeching in the trees.

I dumped the wheelbarrow on the compost pile just as the phone rang in the house. The message machine didn't click on and the phone was still ringing when I entered the kitchen. For some reason I thought it might be L.Q. It wasn't.

"What do you want, Johnny?" I asked.

He was clearly drunk. In the background I could hear country music and loud voices. "Come have a drink with me and Amber," he said.

"Don't make me get you out of jail," I replied.

I heard someone pull the phone from his hand. "Drag your butt down here, you wet blanket," Amber's voice said.

"Thanks for the call," I said, and hung up.

Later, in the early hours of Sunday morning, a diminutive man, one for whom joy was an emotion he experienced only in stealing it from others, lay in the semidarkness of his hospital room, the maples outside alive with wind, the mountains to the east rounded softly like a woman's breasts, the clouds veined with lightning.

The Demerol flowing out of the IV into his finger was the best dope he'd ever had. It made him neither high nor low but instead created a neutral space inside him that was like warm water in a stone pool or the fleeting sense of tranquillity he experienced after sexual intercourse. He paid little attention to the deputy who looked in on him occasionally or the nurses who came and went or a solitary figure in greens who gazed benignly at him out of the shadows, then reached down to puff up his pillow.

In fact, the Demerol made Charlie Ruggles feel so good about his situation he was sure the right people would once again show up in his life, as they always did, and set matters straight. It had started to rain, a warm, beautiful, steady rain that pattered on the tops of the maple trees. He could not remember a night that had been as perfect in its combination of colors and sensations. When he turned his head toward the figure in greens, the coolness of the pillow being placed across his face made him think of a woman's kiss, perhaps from years ago, although in truth he did not recall any woman whose touch had been this cool and gentle.

Then a terrible weight crushed down on him, sealing his eyes, pressing his skin back from his teeth, as though he were trying to smile for the first time in his life.

CHAPTER 5

Darrel McComb and another detective served the search warrant at Johnny's house on Monday morning. What happened as a result became a matter of perspective. Amber Finley told one story, Darrel McComb and his partner another. I tended to believe Amber.

"What do you expect to find in his closet?" she said to McComb.

"A set of greens, the kind hospital personnel wear?" McComb said.

"You're an idiot," she said.

While Johnny sat on the porch, McComb tore the closet apart, throwing all Johnny's hangered shirts and trousers out on the floor. Then he reached down and picked up a pair of tennis shoes and placed them in an evidence bag. He was resting on one knee now, his stomach hanging over his belt, his broad shoulders about to split his suit coat. He squinted up at Amber's silhouette framed against the window, the tautness of her shirt against her breasts. His eyes drifted to the bed, where the sheets and covers had slid off the mattress onto the floor.

"It's true Indians do it dog-style?" he said.

"Ask your wife," she replied.

McComb threw the bagged shoes to his partner and laughed. "Keep your eye on American Horse," he said.

McComb ripped a sheet loose from the bed, then dumped the contents of Johnny's chest of drawers on the mattress, poking through socks and underwear. "I'm not married," he said.

"I'm shocked," she replied.

"If he's dirty, you're probably going down with him. Your old man will be hard put to bail you out of this one."

"Why is it I think you're full of shit?" she asked.

He surveyed the room and pulled his collar off his neck, as though it chafed him. "I'd like to help you with any troubles that might come out of this," he said.

He was positioned between her and the door, massive, the bulk of his shoulders like small sacks of cement. She could hear him breathing through his nose, smell his hair oil and the body heat and odor of testosterone in his clothes. He took a business card from his shirt pocket and lifted her hand and slipped the card between her fingers. She could feel the sharp edges of his calluses against her palm. "You get jammed up, just call me," he said. "I grew up in a midwestern farm town, just like your old man did. We're the same kind of people."

He tried to keep his eyes respectful, his

expression neutral. But she saw his tongue touch his bottom lip, the slackness in his jaw, the flush in his throat, the way his stare dipped momentarily.

She crumpled the card, letting it drop into a trash basket as she brushed past him into the front of the house. Behind her, she heard him make a sound like he had bitten a word in half.

"What did you say?" she asked, turning toward him.

"Maybe one day you'll learn who the good guys are."

"I can't wait. In the meantime, kiss my ass," she said.

Outside, the air was clear and bright, the mountains a deep blue-green against the sky. Johnny American Horse was still sitting on the edge of his porch, his legs crossed, his coned straw hat slanted forward. "You really think I snuffed that guy at the hospital?" he said to McComb.

"I think you'll do anything you can god-damn get away with," McComb said. He picked up the evidence bag containing Johnny's tennis shoes from the hood of his cruiser. He shook the bag and grinned. "Size ten and a half. I think we might have a match."

Johnny stared into space, his hands pressed between his thighs, his face in shadow. He pushed himself off the porch and approached

McComb, his hands pushed flatly into his back pockets. "I want a property receipt for the shit you took out of my house," he said.

"It's on your table," McComb said.

"I didn't sign it."

"You don't need to, asshole."

"I think I do," Johnny said, his face averted.

McComb stepped closer to him, covering Johnny with his shadow. The men were now so close together they looked almost romantically intimate. "You don't deserve to live in this country," McComb said.

"Could be. You gonna write out another receipt?" Johnny scratched an insect bite on his forearm.

Maybe his boot brushed against McComb's shoe, or his coned hat touched McComb's face. Or maybe McComb, staring at Amber over Johnny's shoulder, simply could not deal any longer with his own rage and sense of sexual rejection. He swung his fist into the middle of Johnny's face, then pulled his blackjack from his back pocket and whipped it down on Johnny's head, neck, and shoulders, slashing with all his strength, as though attacking a slab of meat on a butcher block.

That afternoon I went into Fay Harback's office without knocking. "I just left St. Pat's. Go down there and look at what your trained goon did to Johnny American Horse," I said.

"I know all about it," she replied.

"No, you don't. McComb used a blackjack on him, for God's sake. Without provocation."

"That's what you say. Both detectives tell a different story."

"McComb came on to Amber Finley. She told him to take a walk, so he tore Johnny up. *That's* what happened."

"American Horse is a violent man. Quit pretending he's not."

"You ran on a platform of personal integrity. You're a big disappointment, Fay."

"At least I'm not an ex-prosecutor who became a hump for any criminal with a checkbook."

She was standing now, her nostrils white-rimmed, her throat streaked with color.

"*Adios,*" I said.

"I didn't mean that," she said at my back.

I walked across the grass, through the shade trees on the courthouse lawn, toward my office at the intersection, my blood singing in my ears. Parked by the curb was a dented, paint-skinned pickup truck with slat sides bolted onto the sides of the bed. Wyatt Dixon lay on the hood, wearing aviator shades, his shoulders propped against the windshield, his fingers knitted behind his head. The muscles in his upper arms were as big and hard-looking as cantaloupes. He wore dark Wranglers brand new from the box and an elastic-ribbed, form-fitting T-shirt stamped with the words *SEX, DRUGS, FLATT 'N' SCRUGGS*. He pulled a matchstick from his mouth. "I hear that Indian boy got his ass kicked," he said.

"Get a job," I said.

"Want to stick it to Darrel McComb? Got some information might hep you do that, counselor."

"I doubt it."

He sat up on the hood, hooking his arms around his knees. "Before I seen the light and changed my ways, I was in the Aryan Brotherhood. The only trouble with the A.B. is it's infiltrated. Know how come that is, Brother Holland?"

Don't let him set the hook, I told myself. But there was no doubt about Wyatt Dixon's knowledge of criminality and his insight into evil. He was a genuine sociopath, totally without conscience or remorse; but unlike his psychological compatriots, Wyatt enjoyed sharing the secrets of the inner sanctum.

"Spit it out," I said.

"Sometimes the G likes to employ folks that ain't on the computer."

"Such as yourself."

"Not me, counselor. I wouldn't get near them government motherfuckers with a manure fork. I'm just saying Brother McComb was not un-known to the fallen angels of backstreet bars. Also had a way of spreading money around when some work needed doin'."

"When you can clean the collard greens out of your mouth, we might have ourselves a conversation."

He unhooked his aviator sunglasses from his ears and rubbed a place next to his nose with his thumbnail. Perhaps because of the sky overhead, his eyes had taken on a degree of color, a grayish-blue, with pupils like burnt matchheads. He picked up a battered work hat, one with dents in its domed crown, and fitted it on his head. "About ten years ago Darrel McComb offered me five thousand dollars to do a job on a man — the tools could be of my choosing. Believe that?" he said.

"No."

"Don't blame you. If you seen what I seen of the world, you wouldn't be no different from me. Study on that the next time you and Miss Temple are at the church house," he said.

"There's a parking ticket under your wind-shield wiper."

"I declare, this life is sure fraught with trouble, ain't it?" he said. He wadded up the ticket and tossed it on the sidewalk.

You didn't get the last word with Wyatt Dixon.

I was tired of feeling like the odd man out, somehow allowed to know only the edges of a situation that even a morally insane person like Dixon seemed privy to. I called the Phoenix office of the FBI and told an agent there who I was. He did not seem impressed. I asked if he would call Seth Masterson in Missoula and tell him I'd appreciate his contacting me immediately.

"I'm not real sure where he is. But I'll see if I can get a message to him," the agent said.

"That's really good of you. Keep up the fine work," I said.

Fifteen minutes later Seth called my office. "Trying to light up my colleague's pinball machine down in Arizona?" he said.

"Why do federal agents always sound arrogant over the phone?" I said.

"Search me."

Seth was notorious for his laconic speech and his reticence about his job. In fact, a joke about him in the Phoenix office went as follows: There were three words in Seth's vocabulary — "Yep," "Nope," and, when he was in a talkative mood, "Maybe." But Seth also had a weakness.

"Want to meet a rainbow trout I know up Rock Creek?" I asked.

"That's a possibility," he replied.

An hour later he met me outside my office, dressed in khakis, a fly vest, and a bill cap with a green visor on it. We drove east up the Clark Fork in my Tacoma, through Hellgate Canyon, past the confluence with the Blackfoot River and into alluvial floodplain dotted with cottonwoods and bordered by thickly wooded mountains whose slopes were already dropping into shadow.

We turned off the four-lane at the juncture of Rock Creek and the Clark Fork and entered a long, steep-sided valley where the afternoon light had turned gold on the hilltops and the meadows were full of grazing deer and the creek was steaming in the cooling of the day.

Seth rode with the glass down, the wind in his face, as we passed beaver dams, flooded cottonwoods, and dalles where the creek coursed over boulders that were larger than my truck. I almost felt guilty at the pastoral deceit I had perpetrated on him.

"Gonna ask me a question or two?" he said, looking straight ahead, his eyes twinkling.

"You working the home invasion at Johnny American Horse's place?"

"Yep."

"But his spread isn't on res land. He's an independent ranch owner."

"Doesn't matter. The perps were crossing and recrossing a federal reservation during the commission of a felony," he replied.

"So the Phoenix office is now investigating reservation crimes in the Northwest?" I said.

He grinned at me. "Think a wooly worm might bring those big ones up?" he asked.

Trout season had not opened yet, so we released the half-dozen rainbows and the one bull trout we caught, and walked back up through fir trees toward the truck. The sun had dipped down through a crack in the mountains, and the water and the rocks in the creek were bathed with a red glow. Upstream, a moose clattered across the stream and chugged huffing uphill into woods that were now black with shadow.

I unlocked the shell on the bed of my Tacoma and put my fly rod, vest, and waders inside. Seth was quiet for a long time, his eyes obviously troubled by an unresolved conflict inside himself. "I've been thinking about taking early retirement," he said.

"Doesn't sound like you," I said.

"I don't always like the cases I catch anymore. Get my drift?"

"I'm kind of slow sometimes," I said.

"You've stepped into a pile of pig flop, Billy Bob. I'd get a lot of gone between me and Johnny American Horse."

"Hate to hear you talk like that."

"Not half as bad as I do," he replied.

In the cab he pulled his hat down and pretended to sleep the rest of the way back to town.

That night I visited Johnny at St. Pat's Hospital. He had taken stitches in one eyebrow, behind his ear, and on the jawbone. "Quit looking at me like that. I get out in the morning," he said.

"You're being charged with attempted assault on a law officer. Why'd you have to get in McComb's face?" I said.

"Dude leaves a big footprint. This is still the United States. I fought for this damn country," he said.

"When wars are over, nobody cares about the people who actually fought them."

"Doesn't matter. McComb tore up my home. He tried to hit on Amber. He didn't do it because he's a cop, either. He did it because he's a white redneck and he knew he could get away with it," he said.

"I've got to know why Ruggles and Eddy Bumper came after you, Johnny."

He raised his hands and dropped them on the sheet. "My coalition has sued a couple of oil companies to stop them from drilling test wells on the east slope of the Divide. In the meantime we're trying to kick a pipeline off the res. I kind of went out on my own on this anthrax stuff, too."

"Say that last part again?"

"A private grudge I brought back from the first Gulf war, I guess. Sometimes I see things in my head, in broad daylight, that make me wish I wasn't on the planet," he said.

I didn't want to hear it.

It was late and I was tired when I got back home. Temple had already gone to bed. I fixed a ham-and-egg sandwich and poured a glass of buttermilk and ate at the kitchen table. The moon was up and through the side window I could see elk and deer in the pasture and hear our horses nickering in the darkness on the far side of the barn.

I grew up on a small ranch in the hill country of south-central Texas. My mother was a librarian by profession and my father a tack and hot-pass welder on pipelines all over Texas and Oklahoma. Both of them dearly loved our ranch, in spite of the meager income it provided them. They also loved the Victorian purple brick home in which I grew up. They loved the horses, dogs, goats, cats, sheep, beehives, fish in the ponds (called tanks in Texas), and even poultry in the chicken run on our land. My father named our ranch "Heartwood," and he burned the name into a thick red-oak plank with the intention of hanging it from the front gate.

But the man who had landed at Normandy, and who had walked all the way across Europe to the Elbe River, was killed in a natural gas blowout at Matagorda Bay and never got to hang his sign. So I hung it for him down in Texas, and now I had hung it above our gate in Montana, up a valley that was the most beautiful stretch of land I had ever seen.

I brushed my teeth and lay down next to Temple. I felt her weight turn on the mattress and her hand touch my back. "Your muscles are stiff as iron. What's wrong?" she said.

"Heartwood is the best place I've ever been. It's not one spread, either. It's the place where I grew up and it's the place we've built together, here, in Montana," I said.

She raised herself on her elbow so she could look into my face. "What happened tonight?" she said.

"Seth Masterson tried to warn me off Johnny's case."

"Who the hell does he think he is?"

"You don't know Seth. He broke all his own rules. Johnny American Horse is in the meat grinder. You were right. Johnny might pull us down with him."

She pressed her face next to mine. "Listen to me, Billy Bob. You tell the FBI to screw themselves. Nobody threatens us," she said.

I turned and looked into her eyes. They were milky green, the color of the Guadalupe River in summer, sometimes with shadows in them, the way the river was when it flowed under a tree. "You're special," I said.

She pulled her nightgown over her knees and sat on top of me, then leaned down and kissed me on the mouth. I cupped her breasts, then heard her say "Wait." She worked her gown over her head and I put her nipples in my mouth and ran my hands over her baby fat and felt my own hardness touch her stomach.

I rolled on top of her, then she reached down and held me with her hand and placed me inside her, her knees widening, her face turned to one side, her eyes closing, then, slowly, her mouth puckering as though she were warming the air before she breathed it. Her skin was moist and pink in the glow of the moon through the window, then she began to come and I felt as though the two of us were dropping down inside a well that swirled with starlight at the bottom.

She held me tighter, then even tighter than that, and made a sound in my ear that was like the cry of the loon, and I was sure in that moment no evil would ever touch our lives.

CHAPTER 6

On Tuesday morning, when Johnny was about to be transported from the hospital to face the trumped-up attempted assault charges filed against him by Darrel McComb, he was formally placed under arrest for the murder of Charlie Ruggles and taken in handcuffs to a cell at the county jail. I caught Fay Harback at the coffee stand by the back entrance of the courthouse. "No," she said, raising her hand prohibitively. "I don't want to see you."

"This is bogus, Fay. You're being a dupe," I said.

"How would you like to have this coffee thrown in your face?"

"My client is the victim, not the perpetrator. You're helping a collection of assholes gang up on an innocent man."

"Did I ever tell you, you make my blood boil? I want to hit you with a large, hard object," she said. People were starting to stare now. "Come outside."

We went through the big glass doors onto the lawn. It was cold in the shade of the building and the grass was stiff with frost. "Which collection of assholes are you talking about?" she asked.

"I'm not sure."

"That's beautiful. You just slander people in public without knowing why?"

"The Feds are involved in this stuff. An agent tried to warn me off last night."

"Let me make it simple for you. American Horse's tennis shoes matched a perfectly stenciled impression on the floor right next to Charlie Ruggles's bed." She raised a finger when I started to speak. "Hear me out. Your client not only left behind a signature with his foot, he dropped a Jiffy Lube receipt on the floor. It has his name on it and his fingerprints. We found a pair of greens in a service elevator. They smelled of booze."

"How could Johnny have gotten past the guard at the door? All the deputies know him," I said

For just a second, no more than a blink, I saw the confidence weaken in her eyes. "The deputy went to help an elderly man use the bathroom. It's not his fault," she replied.

"Who said it was?"

"Johnny was in a bar down the street from the hospital. He's a mercurial, unpredictable man. He killed Ruggles. There's no conspiracy here," she said.

"Hell there's not."

She looked into space, as though my words contained a degree of credibility which, for reasons of her own, she would not acknowledge. "I do my job. I don't always like it. Don't ever try to embarrass me in front of people like that again," she said.

That afternoon, I visited Johnny at the lockup. We sat at a wood table in a small room that contained a narrow, vertical slit for a window, through which I could see the old buildings and brick streets down by the train yards. Johnny wore a bright orange jumpsuit with the word JAIL lettered in black across the back.

"How do you explain the Jiffy Lube receipt and the prints of your tennis shoes in Ruggles's room?" I said.

"Somebody must have taken the shoes out of the house and put them back later. The receipt for the oil change was in my pickup."

His eyes wandered around the room. I touched him on the wrist to make him look at me. "You get pretty swacked Saturday night?" I said.

"No."

"No blackouts?"

"Amber was with me all night. We were at the Ox, Charley B's, and Stockman's. I went down to Red's for a few minutes to meet a guy who wants to buy my truck. But he wasn't there."

"You went to Red's by yourself?"

"Like I said."

"Has a Fed named Masterson been in here?"

"No. Who is he?"

"Johnny, nobody wants to believe in conspiracies anymore. People want to trust the government. They don't want to believe that corporations run their lives, either. But everything you do and say sends them another message. You hearing me on this?"

"Not really," he said.

They're going to burn you at the stake, I thought. I banged on the door for the turnkey to let me out.

"You still my attorney?" Johnny said.

"Nobody else will hire me," I replied, and winked at him.

Darrel McComb belonged to an athletic club downtown, one frequented primarily by middle-class businesspeople during their lunch hour or just before they drove home from work. But Darrel did not go to the club for the tanning services it offered or for the state-of-the-art exercise machines most members used while they read magazines or watched a television program of their selection, the audio filtering through the foam-rubber headsets clamped on their ears. Darrel was there to clank serious iron, benching three hundred pounds, curling forty-pound dumbbells in each hand, the veins in his muscles rippling like nests of purple string.

He also liked to smack the heavy bag,

getting high on his own heated smell, diverting an imaginary opponent with a left jab, then ripping a vicious right hook into the place where his opponent's rib cage would be, under the heart, driving his fist so deep into the leather the bag rattled on its chain.

But on that particular Tuesday evening Darrel was disturbed for reasons he couldn't adequately explain. As he sat in the steam room by himself, he experienced a sense of depression about his life and about who he was that few people would understand.

Not unless they had grown up abandoned by their parents in a town that was hardly more than a dusty crossroads inside several million acres of Nebraska wheat. Not unless at age fifteen they had blown an orphanage where the kids scrubbed floors with rags tied on their knees. Not unless they had piloted Flying Boxcars through AK-47 ground fire with a guy named Rocky Harrigan.

Rocky was a legend. He had dog-fought the Japanese in the skies over the Pacific, made airdrops to the Tibetan Resistance, and lit up the Pathet Lao with fifty-gallon drums of gasoline mixed with Tide laundry detergent. Then, in the mid-eighties, Rocky had hooked up with a CIA front in Fort Lauderdale, telephoned his young friend Darrel McComb, who was spraying crops and dodging power lines in Kansas, and invited him to join the fun down in Central America.

But planes crashed, names spilled into headlines, and the era of Ronald Reagan came to an end. Darrel McComb always believed he had shared a special moment in history, one whose complexities and dangers few people were aware of. The Iron Curtain had collapsed, hadn't it? American companies were opening textile mills and creating jobs in Stone Age villages where Indians still lived in grass huts, weren't they? None of that would have happened if it hadn't been for men like Rocky and himself, would it?

Let the peace marchers and the bunny huggers light candles and sing their hymns, he thought. They would never be players. This was a great country. Guys like Rocky gave up their lives so the jackoff crowd could revel in their own ignorance. In Cuba they'd be diced pork inside somebody's taco.

But the splenetic nature of his thoughts brought him little peace. What was really on his mind? he asked himself, sitting on the tile stoop in the steam room, his skin threaded with sweat. For an answer he only had to glance down at the erection under his towel.

Amber Finley.

He thought about her all the time, in ways he had never thought about a woman. In fact, women had never been an issue in his life. He went to bed with them occasionally and had even been married for a few months. An Army psychiatrist had once told him he was probably homoerotic, a categorization that oddly enough didn't offend him. But the sight of Amber Finley filled his head with images and sounds that beset him like a crown of thorns, leaving him sleepless at night and throbbing in the morning.

What was it that attracted or bothered him most about her? The blueness and luminosity of her eyes? Her heart-shaped face? Or the throaty quality of her laugh and the irreverence in her speech? Perhaps the perfect quality of her skin, her education and intelligence and the fact she spent it like coin in lowlife bars with people like Johnny American Horse?

No, it was all of it. Amber Finley could walk down a street and make his innards drain like water.

He shouldn't have lost it with that Indian kid. American Horse was going down anyway; he might even ride the needle for the gig on Ruggles. Why did Darrel have to make a martyr of him and probably earn himself a civil rights beef in the bargain? He'd flushed himself good with Amber, and acquired a dirty jacket on top of it.

He showered, dressed, and ate supper by himself in a workingmen's café on Front Street. The evening was warm, the color of the sky as soft as lilacs, the flooded willows on the riverbanks clattering with birds. There were many places he could go — a movie, a concert in the park, a minor league baseball game, a bar where cops drank and he sometimes joined them with a soda and sliced lime. But Darrel had no doubt where he would end up as soon as the sun began to sink, and that thought more than any other filled him with an abiding shame.

Amber lived with her widower father, the senator, up Rattlesnake Creek, in a two-story home built on a slope above a sepia-tinted stream. Darrel parked his car and walked through a woods that looked down on the back of the house, the hot tub on the deck, and the lawn where Amber's yoga class met on Tuesday evenings. His binoculars were Russian Army issue, the magnification amazing. He could see the down on her cheeks, the shine on the tops of her breasts, the way she breathed through her mouth, as though the air were cold and she were warming it before it entered her lungs. No woman had the right to be that desirable.

Was this what people called midlife crisis?

A black Mercury pulled to the front of the house, and two men and a woman got out and were greeted at the door by the senator. The woman looked familiar, but Darrel could not be sure where he had seen her. Then he heard a noise behind him.

A man in a cowboy hat and jeans was sitting on a big, flat, lichen-stained rock, shaving a stick with the six-inch blade of an opened bone-handled knife. Even though there was a chill in the air, the man's corduroy shirt-sleeves were rolled, exposing biceps that were as big as grapefruit.

"Late for bird-watching, ain't it?" the man said, without looking up.

Think, Darrel told himself. He opened his badge holder. "I don't know who the hell you are, but you're interfering in a police surveillance. That means haul your ass out of here, pal," he said.

The man closed the knife in his palm and stuck it in his back pocket. He picked a piece of wet matter off his lip and looked at it. "You don't 'member me?" he asked.

"No."

The man removed his hat and the afterglow of the sun fell through the trees on the paleness of his brow and the moral vacuity in his eyes, the chiseled, lifeless features of his face. " 'Member me now?" he asked.

"Maybe," Darrel said.

"I want in on it," the man said.

"On *what?*"

"Chance to serve the red, white, and blue, sir. You want serious work done, I'm your huckleberry."

"Is that right? Well, I think you're crazy. I think your name is Wyatt Dixon and you're about to get yourself put back in a cage."

Wyatt fitted his hat back on and pushed himself up from the rock, advancing toward

Darrel so quickly Darrel's hand went inside his coat. Then he realized Wyatt Dixon was not even looking at him but instead was un-zipping his jeans.

"Drunk a horse tank of lemonade this afternoon. Ah, that's better," he said, urinating in a bright arc down the side of the hill.

Wyatt's voice was loud and had obviously carried down into the Finleys' yard. Amber went into the house and came back out the sliding glass door with her father, both of them now staring up the hill. *Don't lose control. Handle this right,* Darrel told himself. *Never surrender the situation to perps.*

He turned on Wyatt Dixon. "You're in a shitload of trouble, boy. Wait right here till I get back," he said.

Darrel went hurriedly down the incline, stepped across a series of rocks that spanned the stream at the bottom, and entered Amber Finley's backyard, while she and her father and their guests stared at him in dismay. His shield was open in his hand.

"I'm Detective Darrel McComb, Senator. I was following an ex-convict by the name of Wyatt Dixon. He seems to have taken an interest in your house," he said.

"Why would he be interested in us?" Romulus Finley asked.

"He was in Deer Lodge for a homicide. But unfortunately he's out," Darrel said.

"You didn't answer my question."

"This man beat Johnny American Horse with a blackjack," Amber said.

"I see," Romulus said.

"I've intruded on you, but I thought you should know, I mean about this fellow up in the trees," Darrel said. He folded his badge holder and put it away, glad to have something to occupy his hands.

"I appreciate your concern. But we're not real worried about this," Romulus said.

The two men and the woman who had arrived in the Mercury were on the patio now, watching Darrel as though he were part of a skit. Where had he seen the woman? Somewhere down in the Bitterroot Valley? She wore a suit and was auburn-haired and attractive in a masculine way. Her eyes seemed to look directly into his.

"I guess I'll go. I'm sorry to have disturbed you," Darrel said.

"It's no problem," Romulus said.

Darrel recrossed the stream and climbed the incline back into the woods, wondering if his story had been plausible at all or if he had looked as ridiculous as he felt.

But at least Wyatt Dixon was gone. From the shadows Darrel looked back down into the yard of Amber Finley. The auburn-haired woman dressed in the suit was standing on the deck, steam rising from the hot tub behind her. He thought she was gazing up at the treeline where he stood, perhaps wondering where she had met or seen him. Then he realized she was watching a child launch a kite into the sunset, and his presence in the Finleys' backyard had been of no more consequence to those gathered there than his absence.

A white-tailed doe bolted out of the trees and thumped across the sod and down a gully. The woods felt dark and cold, the air heavy with gas, more like autumn than spring. Darrel struck the trunk of a larch with the heel of his hand, hard, shaking needles out of the branches, cursing the quiet desperation of his life.

Amber called me at the office early the next morning and told me of Darrel McComb's bizarre behavior at her house. "He was lying. He's a voyeur," she said.

"He told you he was following a man named Dixon?"

"Right. Who's this guy Dixon, anyway?"

"A guy who left his pancakes on the stove too long." I glanced out the window.

"What's he want with us?" she asked.

"I'll let you know. He's looking through my window right now."

After I hung up, I opened my door and went into the reception area just as Wyatt came through the front door. He wore a purple-striped western shirt with scarlet garters on the sleeves. The bottoms of his jeans were streaked with water, as though he had walked through wet weeds. He grinned stupidly at the receptionist, his gaze raking her face and breasts.

"What were you doing at the Finley place?" I said.

"Taking a drain," he said, his eyes still fastened on the receptionist. He started to speak to her.

"Hildy, go down to Kinko's and pick up our Xerox work, will you?" I said.

"Gladly," she said, picking up her purse.

I walked inside my office and closed the door after Wyatt was inside.

"Nice little heifer you got out there," he said.

"You have thirty seconds."

"Got the goods on Darrel McComb. Seems like he's been doing some window-peeking up the Rattlesnake. My official statement on the matter might do a whole lot to hep that Indian boy. I might also have some information about that senator always got his nose in the air."

"What do you want for this?"

"You got to sign on as my lawyer."

"Why me?"

"I need investors in my rough stock company. Folks don't necessarily trust their money to a man who's been jailing since he was fifteen."

"Forget it."

"We're more alike than you think, Brother Holland."

"You're wrong," I said.

"Tell me the feel of a gun in your hand don't excite you, just like the touch of a woman."

"We're done here."

"Violence lives in the man. It don't find him of its own accord. My daddy taught me that. Every time he held my head down in a rain barrel to improve my inner concentration."

"Get out."

"Walked the rim of your pasture this morning. I'd irrigate if I was you. A grass fire coming up that canyon would turn the whole place into an ash heap."

But my morning involvement with Wyatt was not over yet. Two hours later Seth Masterson came into the office, sat down in front of my desk, and removed a Xeroxed sheet from a sheaf of documents inside a folder. "Read this," he said.

The letter had probably been typed on an old mechanical typewriter; the letters were ink-filled and blunted on the edges. The date was only one week ago, the return address General Delivery, Missoula, Montana. It read:

Dear President George W. Bush,

I am a fellow Texan and long supporter of the personal goals you have set for yourself and our great country. I particularly like the way you have stood up to the towel heads who has attacked New York City and the Pentagon. With this letter I am offering my expertise in taking care of these sonsofbitches so they will not be around any longer to get in your hair. Let me know when you want me to come to Washington to discuss the matter.

My character references are William Robert Holland, a lawyer friend in Missoula, and Rev. Elton T. Sneed of the Antioch Pentecostal Church in Arlee, Montana.

Your fellow patriot,
Wyatt Dixon

"Is this guy for real?" Seth said. His legs wouldn't fit between his chair and my desk and he kept shoving the chair back to give himself more space.

"You must have pulled everything available on him. What do you think?"

"He's a nutcase. The question is whether he should be picked up."

"Wyatt does things that give the impression he's crazy. At the same time he seems to stay a step ahead of everyone else, at least he does with me. Is he dangerous? When he needs to be."

"You seem pretty objective about a guy who kidnapped and buried your wife."

I paused a moment. "Two years ago I tried to kill him. I got behind him and shot at him four times with a forty-five revolver and missed."

Seth looked at me for a beat, then lowered his eyes. "Got a little head cold and can't hear too well this morning. Keep me posted on this guy, will you?" he said.

"You bet. He was just in here."

"This is quite a town," he said.

"Why you bird-dogging Johnny American Horse, Seth?"

"I've got to get something for this dadburn cold. My head feels like somebody poured cement in it," he replied.

Some people have no trouble with jail. In fact, they use jails like hotels, checking in and out of them when the weather is severe or if they're down on their luck or they need to get their drug tolerance reduced so they can re-addict less expensively. But Johnny didn't do well inside the slams.

Fay Harback called me on Thursday. "Been over to see American Horse?" she asked.

"Not since Tuesday," I replied.

"Go do it. I don't need any soap operas in my life."

"What's going on?"

"I'm not unaware of Johnny's war record. Maybe I've always liked him. I don't choose the individuals I prosecute."

"Yeah, you do."

"I'll say good-bye now. But you have a serious problem, Billy Bob."

"What might that be?"

"An absence of charity," she replied before hanging up.

I put on my hat and coat and walked over to the jail in a sunshower. The trees and sidewalks were steaming in the rain and the grass on the courthouse lawn was a bright green. Upstairs a deputy walked me down to an isolation cell, where Johnny sat on the cement floor in his boxer undershorts. His knees were pulled up in front of him, his vertebrae and ribs etched against his skin.

"It's his business if he don't want to eat. But he stuffed his jumpsuit in a commode. We probably mopped up fifty gallons of water," the deputy said.

"It's pretty cold in here. How about a blanket?" I said.

"I'll bring it up with his melba toast," the deputy said, and walked off.

"Why provoke them, Johnny?" I said.

"I wouldn't wear the jumpsuit. But it was another guy who plugged up the toilet with it."

"Why not just tell that to somebody?"

"Because they know I'm going down for the big bounce and they couldn't care less what I say."

He combed his hair back with his fingers. His hair was black and had brown streaks in it and in places was white on the ends. He looked up at me and grinned. "Dreamed about red ponies last night. Thousands of them, covering the plains, all the way to the horizon," he said.

"You're going to be arraigned in the morning. You have to wear jailhouse issue," I said.

He shrugged his shoulders. "They're going to ask for the needle?" he said.

"Maybe."

"Ain't no maybe to it, partner," he said. His eyes seemed to glaze over with his inner thoughts.

At 9 a.m. Friday, Johnny stood in handcuffs before the bench and was charged with capital murder. His bond was set at two hundred thousand dollars. That afternoon I called Temple at her P.I. office.

"Johnny doesn't have the bondsman's fee and his place has two mortgages on it," I said.

"And?" she said.

"I'd like to put up a property bond."

"You're going to risk Heartwood on Johnny American Horse?"

"They're taking the guy apart with a chain saw, Temple."

The line was so quiet I thought the connection had been broken. "Temple?" I said.

"Do it," she said.

"You're not upset?"

"If you weren't the man you are, I wouldn't have married you."

How do you beat that?

CHAPTER 7

Saturday morning I went fishing by myself on the Bitterroot River. It was a grand day, cool and full of sunshine and blue skies. The rain had turned the slopes on the mountains a velvet green and fresh snow blazed on the peaks, and the river had risen along the banks into cottonwoods that were just coming into leaf. I was on a sandspit that jutted into a long riffle eddying around a beaver dam when I saw a man in hip waders working his way across the channel toward me.

He had the cherry-cheeked face of the professional optimist, his upper half like an upended hogshead, his hand lifted in greeting, although I had no idea who he was or why he was wading into the riffle and ruining any chance of my catching a trout there.

"Your wife told me where you was at, Mr. Holland. Name is Reverend Elton T. Sneed. I think we got us a mutual friend," he said, laboring out of the water onto the sandspit.

Where had I heard or seen the name?

In the letter written to the President of the United States by Wyatt Dixon.

"I hope you're not talking about who I think you are," I said.

"Wyatt's a member of my congregation, but I'm troubled about him. The boy needs direction."

"The man you call 'boy' is the residue people clean out of colostomy bags. Except that's offensive to colostomy bags," I replied.

Suddenly his eyes became like BBs and the corners of his mouth hooked back as though wires were attached to his skin, turning his smile into a grimace. He studied the trees on the far bank, searching for a response. "I guess my job is saving souls, not judging folks," he said.

"The FBI came to see you?"

"Yep. But since that visit, Wyatt has told me about somebody he seen with Senator Finley. I get the feeling it's some kind of past association Wyatt don't need to pick up again. Thought you might be able to hep me out."

"My advice is you get a lot of space between you and Wyatt Dixon, Reverend."

"Man seems all right when he takes his chemical cocktails. Thought I was doing the right thing coming here."

When I didn't reply he looked wanly down the stream, his vocabulary and frame of reference used up. "I mess up your fishing?" he said.

"No, it's fine," I said.

He nodded. "Been catching some?"

"Let's wade on up past the beaver dam and give it a try," I said.

When I handed him my fly rod his face once more broke into an ear-to-ear smile.

Monday morning I started the paperwork to put up our property as bond for Johnny's release. Then I looked up Amber Finley's number in the directory and called her at home. "Is your dad there?" I said.

"He flew back to Washington," she said.

"Too bad. Look, those guests you had at your house Tuesday evening? Is there any reason Darrel McComb would be interested in them?"

"Darrel is interested in watching women through their bedroom windows."

"Would this guy Wyatt Dixon be interested in your father's friends?"

"How would I know?" she replied.

"Could you give me their names?"

"Greta Lundstrum and a couple of campaign contributors. I don't remember their names. What's this about?"

"It's probably nothing. Who's Greta Lundstrum?"

"The Beast of Buchenwald. Go ask her. She runs a security service in the Bitterroot Valley. Are you getting Johnny out of jail or not?"

What's the lesson? Don't call boozers before noon.

★ ★ ★

That afternoon, Temple walked into the office of a company named Blue Mountain Security and Alarm Service down in Stevensville, twenty-five miles south of Missoula. The office was located inside a refurbished two-story brick building that had once been a feed and tack store. An ancient bell tinkled above the door when she closed it. Through the window she could see the huge blue shapes of the Bitterroot Mountains against the sky.

"Ms. Greta Lundstrum, please," she said to a man working at the reception desk.

"She's in a meeting right now. Can you tell me what this is in reference to?" he said.

Through a glass partition in back, Temple could see a thick-bodied woman in a gray business suit, talking from behind her desk to a man who stood in her cubicle doorway. "It involves a criminal investigation. Would you ask her to come out here?" Temple said.

The man at the reception desk looked over his shoulder. "Oh, I see she's out of the meeting. Just a moment, please," he said.

"Right," Temple said.

The receptionist went to the cubicle in back, and the woman in the gray suit gave Temple a look, then nodded to the receptionist. But she didn't get up from her chair. Instead, she seemed to make a point of looking at some documents on her desktop.

Temple walked back toward the cubicle.

"Just a minute, ma'am," the receptionist said.

Temple brushed past him and entered the cubicle without knocking. "You're Greta Lundstrum?" she asked.

"Yes, what do —"

"I'm a private investigator. You know a sheriff's detective by the name of Darrel McComb?" Temple said, opening her badge and ID holder.

"No, I don't think so. Who did you say you work for?"

"Billy Bob Holland. You were at Senator Romulus Finley's home Tuesday evening?"

"How did you know that?"

"You were being surveilled by a sheriff's detective. Who were the two men with you?"

"That's none of your concern, madam. What do you mean 'surveilled'?"

Greta Lundstrum had thick hair, wide-set green eyes, and a broad face. Temple removed a small notebook from her shirt pocket and wrote in it. "Nice place you have here. You know a man named Wyatt Dixon?"

"I never heard of him. Answer my question, please."

"A sheriff's detective and an ex-convict by the name of Wyatt Dixon were watching you while you stood in Romulus Finley's back-yard. You never heard of Wyatt Dixon?"

"I told you."

Temple made another entry in her note-book. "That's strange. He used to live at that white supremacist compound not far from here. He went to prison for murder. There was a great deal of publicity about the case and also about the white supremacist compound. But you never heard of him?"

"If I can assist you in some meaningful way, I will. But you're being both rude and intrusive. I think our conversation here is concluded."

"Ms. Lundstrum, Wyatt Dixon buries people alive. I know because I was one of his victims. You want to be cute, that's fine. But if I were you, I'd give some thought to who my real friends are."

Greta Lundstrum looked momentarily into space, then picked up the telephone receiver and punched in three numbers on the key pad. "This is Blue Mountain Security. We have a trespasser here," she said.

The next morning, Temple used a friend at San Antonio P.D. to run Greta Lundstrum through the NCIC computer. Then she went to work on the Internet.

"Lundstrum was a security consultant in Maryland and Virginia. Divorced twice, no children, no police record of any kind. Her second husband ran a martial arts school. Greta came out to Montana seven years ago and settled in the Bitterroots," Temple said.

"A dead end?" I said.

"I think she lied about not knowing Wyatt Dixon. The question is why."

"Sometimes people don't want to tell strangers they know bad guys. As soon as they make that admission, they're asked what the bad guy is like, or how it is they came to have a relationship with him."

"When they lie, it's to cover their butts," she replied.

Lucas's band played three nights a week at a busthead nightclub just off the Flathead Indian Reservation. That afternoon he arrived early at the club to set up the band's equipment. While he wound new strings on his acoustical Martin, tuning them simultaneously with a plectrum, *ping-ping-ping,* at the back of the club, a young Indian woman and her boyfriend stood at the bar, knocking back shots with beer chasers. Both of the Indians were drunk, kissing each other wetly on the face, hardly aware of their surroundings.

Outside, the sun was hot and white, the glare through the open front door so bright Lucas could not make out the face of the cowboy who entered the club and sat at the end of the bar and ordered not just coffee but the whole pot. His posture on the stool was rounded, his boots hooked in the rungs, his face shadowed by his hat. He smoked a thin cigar and dipped the unlit end into his coffee before he puffed on it.

A middle-aged Indian man, with a stomach that hung over his belt like a sack of bird-seed, came through the front door, hesitating a moment to let his eyes adjust to the dark interior. He wore a peaked, battered hat, and the sunlight from outside shone through the holes in the felt. He could have been either the Indian girl's father or her husband, or an uncle or an older brother. Or perhaps he was none of these. But he slapped the girl full in the face, so hard her eyes crossed.

It took her a moment to recognize who had struck her. Then she said in a subdued, wan voice, "Oh, hi, Joe, you want a drink?"

The middle-aged man ripped off his hat and whipped her head and face with it. The boy with the Indian girl did nothing, watching her humiliation in the mirror behind the bar as though it had nothing to do with his life.

The cowboy at the end of the bar unhooked his boots from the stool, went to the front door, and threw his cigar outside. Then walked toward the middle-aged man. The cowboy wore a heavy white long-sleeved shirt and a silver buckle that reflected light like a heliograph.

"Whoa there, bud," the cowboy said, grabbing the Indian man's wrist. "You done hit your last woman for today. Least while I'm around."

"Stay out of —" the Indian man began.

The cowboy grabbed the man's arm and shook him with such power the man's teeth rattled. "I'll walk you to your truck. Don't be hurting that young woman again, either. I hear about it, I'll be back and you'll be walking on sticks," he said.

He took the Indian man outside and watched him climb into the driver's seat of an old pickup. "Hold on a minute," he said. The cowboy went back inside the club and returned with the man's hat, then dropped it inside the truck window. "That means you ain't got no reason to come back."

He reentered the club, picked up his coffeepot and cup, and walked to the back, where Lucas still sat at a table by the bandstand, his Martin across his thighs.

"Know who I am?" the cowboy said.

"I do now. I ain't got anything to say to you either," Lucas replied.

"I come out of the pen a different man."

"Tell it to somebody else, Wyatt."

"Me and you got a lot in common. I was a woods colt, too. My daddy knowed it and that's why he made every day of my young life what you might call a learning experience."

"Got nothing to say to you."

"Want a beer or a soda pop?"

"No."

"Maybe I'll see you at the rodeo, then."

Lucas continued to tune his Martin and

didn't answer. Wyatt Dixon was framed against the light like a scorched tin cutout.

"Johnny American Horse has got your old man jumping through hoops," Wyatt said.

Don't bite, Lucas told himself, his heart tripping. "How?" he asked.

"American Horse ain't no shrinking violet. He's a stone killer. Ask them two men he cut up with an ax and a knife. You get an Indian mad, run his pride down, make fun of his woman, he'll either come at your throat or turn into a pitiful drunk like that 'un I just kicked out of here."

Lucas looked into space, this time determined not to speak again.

"Here's what it is," Wyatt said. "American Horse's sixteen-year-old nephew got executed by a white man. The word is executed. Boy was breaking into the white man's truck and the white man come up behind him and put a bullet in his brain from three feet. That white man was turned loose with just an ankle bracelet on him. American Horse ain't no mystic holy man. On the sauce he's a mean machine out to put zippers all over white people. Take care of yourself, kid."

Wyatt set his coffeepot and cup on the bar and walked out the front door, his boots loud on the plank floor.

"Dixon just didn't seem like the same fellow," Lucas said that night at the house.

"Believe it, bud, he's the same fellow," I replied.

We were eating dinner at the kitchen table; the moon was yellow on the side of the hill behind the house and up high snow was drifting on the fir trees.

"People change. That's what your church teaches, don't it?" Lucas said, his eyes playful now.

"The Bible doesn't have a chapter on the likes of Wyatt Dixon," I said.

Later, the three of us washed and put away the dishes, then Lucas went out on the front gallery and watched the deer grazing in the meadow. He looked pale and handsome in the moonglow, his body lean and angular, his jeans high on his hips, his flannel shirt rolled above his elbows.

Before he was born, his mother had run away from her husband, a hapless and violent man, and had moved in with me when I was a patrolman with the Houston Police Department, living in the Heights. After Lucas was born, his mother was electrocuted trying to fix a well pump her husband had previously repaired with adhesive tape from the medicine cabinet.

Lucas's early life should have embittered him against the world. Instead, he became a loving and brave and decent kid, with an enormous musical talent. As I watched him leaning against a post on the gallery, his hat cocked on his head, serene inside his youthful thoughts, I wished I'd killed Wyatt Dixon years ago, when I had the chance.

The next morning, Wednesday, I saw Darrel McComb coming hard from the courthouse, crossing between cars to get to my office. I saw him glance behind him, almost getting hit by a truck in the bargain, then I heard him talking loudly in the reception area.

I went up front to meet him. "What's the problem?" I said.

His face looked heated, the skin under his nose nicked by his razor.

"Sorry, Billy Bob," Hildy said.

"It's all right. Come on in, Darrel," I said.

He followed me into my office and closed the door.

"Leave it open," I said.

"Screw you."

"What?"

"You sent your wife down to Stevensville to question this woman Greta Lundstrum. Your wife told her I was following Lundstrum around. Lundstrum just called the sheriff and gave him hell over the phone."

"You deny you were in the woods above Romulus Finley's house while Lundstrum was there?"

"I was following Wyatt Dixon. I filed a report on that," he said.

"I bet you did."

"What's that supposed to mean?"

There were circles under his eyes and a raw odor in his clothes. His coat was open, and I could see the small leather clip-on holster he wore on his belt. I walked past him and opened the door. "I can respect your problems, Darrel. But you beat up Johnny American Horse with a sap and we both know why you did it," I said. "I think it's time for you to leave."

His scalp glistened inside his crew cut. "I've seen Lundstrum before. I don't know where," he said, his brow knitting.

Then I realized he was somewhere out on the frayed edges of his life. "I've got appointments all morning. How about we have a talk after lunch?" I said.

"That's out. I shouldn't have come here. Tell your wife, no matter what you people think, I got a good record as a police officer and I don't need a P.I. dragging my name in the dirt," he said.

Who "you people" referred to was anybody's guess.

But Darrel McComb's quest for personal vindication was not over. That afternoon he went to the home of Amber Finley. She was working in the garden, barefoot, wearing only a halter and shorts. There were sun freckles on her back, and when she sat up from her work to talk to him, her stomach creased above her exposed navel, causing him to fix his eyes intently on her face so as not to reveal the weakness he felt in his loins.

"I just wanted to clear up why I was watching your house. This lady Ms. Lundstrum has gotten hold of a crazy idea and I thought maybe you had some false notions, too," he said.

"I know exactly why you were watching us," she replied.

He looked away in desperation, then knelt down so he could talk to her at eye level.

"You're making me uncomfortable," she said.

"Listen, the evidence against Johnny bothers me. The tennis shoes that matched the prints at the crime scene were under a bunch of other shoes and boots. But if Johnny had just worn them, why would they be under other shoes, unless someone wanted to disguise the fact they were placed there to be discovered? The Jiffy Lube receipt on the floor of the hospital room doesn't flush, either. The killer was wearing hospital greens. So where was he carrying the receipt — in his underwear?"

"The prosecution will say he had jeans on under his greens. Why are you doing this?" she said.

"I want to let all that bad blood go. I'm sorry for what I did to Johnny."

"So tell it to Johnny and Billy Bob."

He got up and tried to brush the grass stain off the knee of his slacks. "If I acted disrespectfully to you, I apologize. I don't mean to be a bad guy, but sometimes —" He didn't finish.

No, you're just a geek, she thought, then felt oddly uncharitable as she watched him try to tuck his shirt in with his thumb and disguise his pot stomach.

The next morning I drove up to Johnny American Horse's small spread on the res. Amber's Dakota was parked in the yard and she was sweeping a cloud of dust off the front porch. Johnny had just finished shoeing a sorrel mare inside the barn, a leather apron that was almost yellow with wear tied around his waist. He slapped the mare on the rump and watched her trot into the pasture, where she joined a sorrel stud. I leaned on the railed fence Johnny had made from shaved lodgepole.

"Ever see a pair with that much red in them?" he said.

"Not really," I said.

"Gonna breed a whole herd of them."

I looked at him to see if he was serious. "Sounds like a lifetime job," I said.

He grinned and took off his apron and hung it over the fence. "You eat breakfast yet?" he said.

"A sixteen-year-old boy from the res was

killed a while back by a white man whose truck he broke into," I said, ignoring his invitation.

Johnny nodded, his eyes on the two sorrels in the pasture.

"That kid was your nephew?" I said.

"What about it?" he asked.

"The court released the guy who did it. It's reason for a family member to bear a lot of anger toward the system. It's the kind of stuff the prosecution is going to use against us. Why didn't you mention you were the boy's uncle?"

"I remember when a white rancher ran over an Indian kid hitchhiking outside Missoula and got a twenty-dollar traffic fine. The kid died. The only cost to that rancher was his twenty bucks. That's the way it is."

He opened the gate to the lot and came outside, then looped the gate secure. He propped his arms across the top rail on the fence. The wind was up, balmy and smelling of distant rain, denting the alfalfa and timothy in the fields, puffing pine needles out of the trees on the slopes. The two sorrels were running in tandem across the pasture, their necks extended, their muscles rippling. In the distance I could hear thunder echoing in the hills.

"You think all this is worth fighting for?" he said.

"Damn straight it is," I replied.

"I think one day the bison will run free again," he said.

I kept my eyes straight ahead and didn't reply.

"Let's go see Amber and drink some coffee," he said.

The next morning, Fay Harback said she wanted to see me in her office.

"I'm a little busy. Why don't you come over here?" I said.

"Let me define the situation a bit more clearly. How would you like to have American Horse's bail revoked?" she replied.

The previous night there had been a break-in at an agricultural research lab outside Stevensville. The intruders were not amateurs or vandals. They had used bolt cutters on the gate chain, cut the telephone line on which the alarm system was dependent, and called the alarm service to report the downed wire, using the owner's password.

Once inside, they had rifled all the hard-copy document files, downloaded computers, rounded up all the floppy disks they could find, and drilled the floor safe under a canvas tarp they spread over themselves to conceal the glow of their flashlights and the noise of the drill.

A man returning from a bar in town around 3 a.m. reported that he saw four men and a woman exit the back of the building and cross a field to a grove of cottonwoods, then drive away in a van. As he rounded the bend, his headlights swept across the group and he was sure of what he saw: the woman was white but the men were dark-skinned and wore pigtails on their shoulders.

"So you're saying four Indians and a white woman broke into a research lab? What's that have to do with Johnny?" I said.

"American Horse is involved in this. If not directly, he knows who did it."

"You're calling Johnny an ecoterrorist?"

"Your friend Seth Masterson has already been here. This whole business smells of American Horse's ongoing war with the federal government. I don't like being the last person on the telephone tree. I don't like being used, either."

"I don't know anything about the break-in, Fay. I doubt if Johnny does, either."

"Where was your client last night?" She looked at me expectantly, and I realized she secretly hoped I could provide an alibi for him, perhaps for his sake, perhaps so she would not have to feel deceived.

But I didn't answer her question. In reality, I was already wondering how the intruders had pulled it off. I was also wondering if some of Johnny's friends, who had been in the pen, weren't indeed a likely group of suspects. "How did these guys have the password? It sounds like an inside job to me. Maybe it's industrial spying," I said.

"Most security services pay minimum wage

to their employees. So their employees come and go and often have little loyalty to their employer. You have no idea who the woman might be?"

"No, I don't," I replied.

She walked in a circle, her frustration obvious. "I hate a lie. I hate it worse than anything in the world," she said.

I fixed my gaze on the trees rustling on the courthouse lawn and a long line of bicyclers moving through the traffic.

"What's the story on this guy Masterson?" she said.

"He's like a lot of people who work for the G. He's a good man who has to take orders from a bunch of political shitheads," I replied.

She tried to look serious but couldn't hide a smile. "You see Amber Finley?" she asked.

"Sometimes."

"Tell her what it's like to cell with a bull dyke up at the women's pen."

Darrel McComb had never belonged to a church, but he did believe in spiritual entities. In his mind there was a Valhalla where slain heroes lived in a giant meadhouse and feasted on roasted boar and watched over the few who fought to protect the many. One of those slain heroes was Rocky Harrigan, Darrel's mentor in a half-dozen clandestine operations, killed when his cargo plane crashed into a mountain during an airdrop to anti-Russian forces in Afghanistan.

Rocky's handsome face grinned at Darrel from a framed photograph on top of Darrel's dresser, Rocky wearing shades, a fatigue cap, and a skinned-up leather jacket, his arm cocked on the open window of an old DC-6.

Why'd Rocky have to go and get himself killed? Darrel thought. And for what? Dropping ordnance and C-rats to Muslim fanatics who one day would fly planes into the Twin Towers and the Pentagon. What a travesty. Who wrote the damn history books, anyway? Names like Rocky's never got in there. Instead, the whole nation lionized fraternity pissants who had never heard a shot fired in anger in their lives.

Darrel couldn't shake the funk and depression that had plagued him ever since he had beaten the Indian with the blackjack. His career and his life were unraveling. His rage against Johnny American Horse was just the symptom, not the cause. But what *was* the cause?

He didn't know.

He'd always been straight up as a cop, true to his own ethos, but now he'd lied and filed a fraudulent report to cover up the fact he was a voyeur, after being caught in the act by Wyatt Dixon, who at some point would undoubtedly try to blackmail him. All because he literally ached with desire whenever he set eyes on Amber Finley.

He went out on the balcony of the apartment where he lived above the Clark Fork River. Three stories below were sharp rocks and a slope that dropped precipitously into the water. All he needed to do was step on a chair, fit one foot on the handrail, and launch himself into space. For just a moment he saw his body being lifted off the rocks onto a gurney by firemen and paramedics, all of them solemn-faced at the passing of one of their own.

Who was he kidding? He didn't have two friends in the whole town, nor did he want any, at least not here, in Ho Chi Minh City West.

Don't get mad, get even, he thought.

Why not start with this Greta Lundstrum broad? Who did she think she was, dimeing him with the sheriff, accusing him of bird-dogging her at Romulus Finley's house, bringing down a shitload of departmental grief on his head? He pictured her in his mind's eye again. He was sure he'd seen her before. But where?

Good God, he thought. It was on a surveil-lance two years ago. He and another plain-clothes had followed Wyatt Dixon to a motel in Alberton, down the Clark Fork, and when Dixon had tapped on a door, a thick-bodied woman had let him in the room. An hour later, Dixon had driven away. Darrel had run the woman's car tag but had decided she was

126

simply a casual girlfriend of Dixon's and of no consequence in the investigation of white supremacists in western Montana.

What an irony, Darrel thought. A connection between Dixon and the Lundstrum woman had suddenly validated his lie and justified his own presence at the Finley house. He looked at the framed photograph of his dead friend on the dresser and felt that somehow Rocky was watching over him, maybe even winking his eye and lifting a tankard of mead from Valhalla in salute.

At the department Monday morning Darrel opened a fresh legal pad, wrote the date and time at the top of the page, then clicked Greta Lundstrum's name into the departmental computer and hit the search key.

What he saw on the screen made him tap the heel of his hand against his forehead. The burgled agricultural research lab down in the Bitterroots had used an alarm system operated by Blue Mountain Security, owned by one Greta Lundstrum.

It was too much for coincidence, Darrel thought. The B&E report from Ravalli County had been put on his desk because of a possible tie-in between ecoterrorists, Indians, and Darrel's arrest of Johnny American Horse. Now Lundstrum's name had surfaced in the same investigation. He called Blue Mountain Security and asked to speak to her.

"This is she. Who's calling, please?" the

voice on the other end of the line said.

"Detective Darrel McComb, with the Missoula County Sheriff's Department. I'd appreciate your coming into the office for an interview," he replied.

"You would appreciate *what?*"

"We've been investigating a group of Native American environmental activists for some time." He positioned the B&E report by the phone so he could see it more clearly. "We think they may be involved with the burglary of the Global Research facility. Your company handles security for them, doesn't it?"

"McComb? You're the detective who followed me to Senator Finley's house?"

"That's incorrect, ma'am. My concern there was about an ex-convict by the name of Wyatt Dixon, who was watching the Finleys' home. I believe you have a past relationship with Dixon, don't you?"

He could almost hear her heart beating through the phone receiver. "Ma'am?" he said.

Then she surprised him. "Unfortunately, I did know him. About two years back. A brief and mistaken relationship, if you get my meaning. Now, what the hell is this about?" she said.

"I'd rather talk to you in person. I'll drive down there," he replied.

"Suit yourself," she said, and hung up.

Now, there's a woman who wrote her own

rule book, he thought. The kind, as Rocky used to say, who would read your mind, slap your face, then ask you to stay over for breakfast.

It took him only a half hour to drive to her security service. In the background the Bitterroot Mountains rose high into the heavens, the dark green of the timber marbled with new snow. He liked being down in the valley, away from university and liberal influences, among people who were of a mind similar to his own. It was going to be a fine day in all respects, he told himself.

Greta Lundstrum came out of her cubicle as soon as she saw him through the glass partition, her wide-set eyes fixed on his. "So what do you need from me, Detective?" she asked.

The boldness of her stare was at first disconcerting. Long ago, in his dealings as a police officer, Darrel had concluded that aggressive female business executives fell into one category only: their authority and their successful imposition of it were entirely dependent upon their ability to destroy any male challenge to it.

"The people who broke into Global Research called in the password after they cut the telephone line," he said. "Do you —"

"I've pulled the files on all our ex-employees," she interrupted. "Two of them are people I fired for coming to work with alcohol on their breath. One of them is an Indian. He still lives in Missoula. The other man moved out of state."

"The password didn't necessarily have to come from an ex-employee," Darrel said.

"If you mean one of our current employees might have given it out, yes, that could have happened. But it didn't."

"How do you know?"

"Because they've been with me for years and they have no motivation for betraying me or the client. Come into my office and sit down," she said.

His eyes slipped down her back, her hips, and rump as he followed her into her cubicle. "You know a woman named Temple Holland?" she said. She sat forward in her swivel chair, her elbows on the desk, her back stiff.

"She's a P.I., the wife of a local attorney," Darrel replied.

"Why did you tell her you were following me?"

"I didn't."

"Then why did she tell me that?"

"My guess is, she and her husband want to cause trouble. He's the lawyer for an Indian named Johnny American Horse," Darrel said. He looked at the hardness in her green eyes and the set in her jaw. He decided to test her affinities. "I arrested American Horse for attempted assault on a law officer. During that arrest I hit him several times with a blackjack.

Mr. and Mrs. Holland aren't fans of mine."

Her expression showed no reaction. "You think this man American Horse is involved with the break-in?" she asked.

"Hard to say. He's cut out of different cloth," Darrel replied.

"In what way?"

"He was awarded the Distinguished Service Cross during Desert Storm. Maybe he just hangs around the wrong kind of people."

"Funny attitude for a sheriff's detective."

"Give the devil his due," Darrel said. "Give me the name of the guy you fired, the one still living in Missoula."

She wrote the name and the address down on a piece of paper and handed it to him. Her auburn hair was thick and had a deep part in it, her scalp gray and clean-looking. "Sorry I was a bit rude over the phone," she said.

"It was a misunderstanding," he said.

She straightened her shoulders, and her breasts seemed larger than he'd noticed earlier. He looked at his watch. "There's a Mexican joint up on the highway. You ever eat there?" he said.

That evening, Darrel McComb sat down at his home computer and on the hard drive recorded all the important events and the names of people connected with the investigation of Johnny American Horse. This case went far beyond the boundaries of Missoula

County or the Feds wouldn't have come down on it like flies on pig flop, he told himself. The issues were much larger than the usual reservation problems over water rights, grazing fees, and control of the bison range. And the backgrounds of the two dead hit men out of Detroit were altogether too familiar to Darrel.

But who was actually turning the dials? From his own experience in clandestine operations, Darrel knew that the grunts on the ground kept it simple, trusted the larger cause they served, and didn't question the moral authority of their leaders. But the old cause was the war against communism. What was this one about? Whatever it was, Darrel McComb knew he was going to be a player again.

CHAPTER 8

I wanted to believe Johnny American Horse had nothing to do with the break-in at the research lab. I had put up the equity in our home and one hundred twenty acres of land for his bond so he could be released from jail, and I expected thereafter he would have only one goal in mind — to be found not guilty of Charlie Ruggles's murder. Johnny was an honorable man and would not hang a friend out to dry, I told myself.

But Johnny was also an idealist, and it's the idealists who, given the chance, will incinerate half the earth to save the other half. Tuesday morning I found him at work, cleaning and burning brush under an abandoned railroad trestle that spanned a gorge on Evaro Hill, ten miles outside Missoula.

It was shady and cool inside the gorge, but Johnny was sweating in the heat of the fire, his forearms and yellow gloves smeared with soot.

"Say all that again," he said.

"It's a simple question. Did you bust into that research lab or not?" I said.

"No, I did not."

"You know who did?"

"I'll tell people anything they want to know about me. But that's as far as it goes." He piled a rotted ponderosa on the flames and stepped back when it burst alight. Down below were the home and a warehouse owned by a famous antique and vintage arms dealer. A Gatling gun stood in the front yard and a World War II tank and armored personnel carrier in a side lot. The wind shifted and Johnny walked out of the smoke and sat on a rock. "I had a bad dream about a fire last night."

I really didn't want to hear more about Johnny's dreams or visions or whatever they were. But I suspect, as the Bible says, that Johnny was one of those who was made different in the womb and he saw no fence between this world and the one that lay behind it. "I saw an animal running in a woods. The woods were burning. The trunks of the trees were like a big cage and the animal couldn't get out," he said.

I sat down next to him and placed my hand on his shoulder. His muscles were as hard as rocks under his shirt. "Listen to me, bud. There's enough misery in this world without a guy using his dreams to create more of it," I said.

"You don't get it. Somehow I'm responsible for the fate of that animal."

"I think you ought to contact the V.A. and talk to someone," I said.

He looked into my face and I saw the injury in his eyes. "I better get back to work. See you around," he said, turning his back to me.

I walked back down the slope, past the armored vehicles on the property of the dealer in vintage and antique arms. Their steel tracks were spiked with weeds, their turrets and machine-gun slits a haven for birds and deer mice. But rusted and ugly as they were, their true history unknown, these relics would remain objects of fascination for all those who would never be required to journey into foreign deserts or live inside the nocturnal experiences of a man like Johnny American Horse.

Lester Antelope graduated from high school on the res, tried the Army, and even worked a short time for a security service before he decided he didn't like uniforms or being bossed around by other people. In fact, Lester took pride in doing grunt work that required nothing of him except his labor and physical presence. He carried hod, stacked sacks of cement as though they were filled with mulch, gathered fieldstones by hand and turned them into rock fences that were artworks.

He wore braids, a traditional Indian flat-brimmed, high-domed hat, and had a face like a dented pie plate. One night he took on four millworkers outside the Oxford Bar and, with his back against the building so they couldn't get behind him, put them away one by one as though he were swatting baseballs inside a batting cage.

Lester Antelope worked hard, spoke seldom, ate his meals in workingmen's cafés, and kept few close friends. Until he met Johnny American Horse in the drunk tank of the county jail. Lester listened to Johnny talk of a range dotted from horizon to horizon with bison and red ponies, and for the first time in his life felt he was part of a world much larger than himself, one that was not only attainable but perhaps worth dying for.

Lester knew instinctively that Johnny's courage was unlike other men's. Johnny was brave in the way an animal is brave when it fights for its life or protection of its young — without problems of pride or self-pity or desire to vindicate or avenge oneself. Johnny's soul had the iridescence of the archer's bow the Everywhere Spirit hung in the sky after a thunderstorm. Johnny's indomitable courage and resilience gave not only voice but hope to those who had none.

Lester Antelope lived downtown by the tracks in a rooming house with a bath at the end of the hall. Tuesday evening, after work, he found the business card of a detective named Darrel McComb stuck in his doorjamb. He threw the card in the trash sack under his kitchen sink, bathed and changed into fresh clothes, then strolled down to Stockman's Bar to eat supper and shoot pool.

It was early and except for the bartender the pool table area was deserted. Lester was shooting a solitary game of rotation when a man entered the back door, silhouetted against the soft evening light and the river down below. The man was thin and dark-haired, and wore a cheap suit and a white shirt that had gone gray with washing and was frayed on the collar and cuffs. Lester could hear the man dropping a series of coins into the pay phone, then speaking with his back to Lester, as though he wanted to conceal the urgent nature of his conversation.

"Can you wire a money order? The car battery is dead. Even if I get a jump start I hate to take Ellie and the baby over the pass like that," the man said.

There was silence while the man listened, his free hand clenching and unclenching at his side.

"We just need to get to Spokane. I'll get paid in two weeks and everything will be fine," the man said. "I wouldn't ask you if it wasn't a dire situation . . . No, operator, I don't have more change. Did you hear me? No, please don't cut me off."

Then the man was staring wanly at the receiver, which had gone dead in his hand. He replaced it in the cradle and pinched his temples between his thumb and forefinger. Lester glanced out the back door of the saloon. A battered car with a Washington State plate was parked down by the river, a blond woman in the passenger seat, an infant wrapped in a blanket on her shoulder. "You want to borrow a buck or two?" Lester said.

"Oh, no, thanks. But I could sure use a battery jump. I got cables in my trunk," the dark-haired man said.

Ten minutes later the battered car with the Washington tag was seen roaring up the entrance ramp to the interstate highway. A tramp living in a hobo jungle on the mountainside close by the ramp walked hurriedly to a filling station and made a 911 call. He swore he had seen a baby thrown from the car's passenger window.

The bartender at Stockman's brought a fried pork chop sandwich, a plate of hash browns, and a cup of coffee to the table where Lester ate his meals. But Lester never returned from the parking lot, and the food grew cold and finally the bartender took it away and tipped it into the garbage can.

At 8:14 a.m. Wednesday, Darrel McComb called my office from a cell phone. "Ever know an Indian named Lester Antelope?" he said.

"Yeah, he does fence work for Johnny

138

American Horse sometimes," I replied.

"Describe him."

"What for?"

"I need somebody to do an ID. I'm looking at a guy I *think* is Antelope but I can't be sure."

"I'm not understanding you."

"He's dead. You know Sleeman Creek Road?"

"Lester's dead? Up Sleeman Creek? That's close to my house."

"Good. You know the way," he said.

I drove ten miles south of Missoula through Lolo, then west on Highway 12 toward Idaho. I turned up the dirt road that led past my home, then entered a long, deserted valley where the hills were round on the tops and steep-sided, with ponderosa growing hard by the rock outcroppings. A collection of police cruisers and emergency vehicles were parked on a slope at the bottom of an arroyo. The coroner had just arrived.

Midway up the arroyo, in deep shadow, was a tin shed built on a cement pad, the door hanging half open. Darrel McComb walked down to meet me. He wore a rumpled suit with a blue shirt and dark tie. His face had no expression.

"Last night a bum called in a 911 on an infant thrown from an automobile. The 'infant' turned out to be a plastic doll," he said.

139

"We have a feeling Antelope got lured out of Stockman's Bar by some people posing as a hard-up family trying to get to Spokane."

"Why would anyone want to kidnap Lester?"

"He used to work for Blue Mountain Security. I have a feeling he was one of the Indians who broke into the Global Research lab. This morning a hiker got caught in a shower and took shelter in the shed. Take a look inside, then talk to me."

"Why me?" I said.

He wrote in a small spiral notebook and didn't answer.

"I asked you a question," I said.

"You got a vested interest in this case, Holland. Maybe we're on the same side," he replied.

I walked up the slope and looked inside the shed, which was bolted down on a concrete pad and had probably once been a storage place for logging equipment. The coroner was squatted down by the body of a large Indian man who lay on his side, his face pointed toward me. A uniformed deputy had placed a lit flashlight on the floor. One of the Indian's pigtails had been cut from his head. I looked at the walls, floor, and ceiling, then backed out of the shed and blew out my breath.

"Is it Lester Antelope?" Darrel said.

Before I could speak I had to clear my

mouth and spit. "Yeah, it's Lester Antelope. He didn't have any identification on him?" I said.

"Picked clean. Ever see anybody take a beating that bad when you were a cop?"

"No."

He looked back over his shoulder, as though he did not want anyone else to hear our conversation. "How do you read it?" he asked.

"Someone cuffed him to a U-bolt and used the two-by-four that's on the floor. Then Lester broke the chain on the cuffs and went after them. That's when he got shot in the forehead. I think some of the blood on the walls might belong to his kidnappers."

"Think Antelope creeped the research lab down in the Bitterroots?"

"How would I know?"

"He's buds with your client, Johnny American Horse, Native America's answer to Jesus Christ."

"I knew Lester. He was a good man. This happened right up the road from my house. I'm not in a light mood about it," I said.

"Maybe these guys are sending you a message. You think of that?"

"Be more specific," I said.

"You and I both worked for the G. All this Indian stuff is cosmetic. There's a much bigger issue at work here. I just don't know what it is. You still pissed because I got

141

rough with American Horse?"

"I don't like cops who blackjack unarmed people."

"Maybe I don't, either," he said.

Darrel stuck his notebook in his shirt pocket, the wind flapping his coat, his revolver and holster exposed. Then he scratched his cheek and seemed puzzled. For a moment I thought he could actually be a likable man, except for his abiding insecurity and desire to control others. He was standing slightly higher on the slope than I was, I suspect not by accident. "They didn't get what they wanted, did they?" he said.

"I think Lester spit in their faces, then signed off with his hands on their throats. You want anything else, Darrel?" I said.

"Nope," he said.

I turned to go. The valley down below was green and blanketed with sunlight now, and just around the bend in the road was my house, where Temple and I would have supper together that night, safe from all the intrusions of the world.

"Antelope had information these guys wanted real bad. That means they're going to have another run at it. You think about that," Darrel said.

I walked back up the slope until I was a few inches from him. "Run that by me again?"

"I was being straight up with you, Holland.

No second meaning intended. I don't want any beef with you," he said.

Late that afternoon it turned cold and snowed unexpectedly. Through the back window I could see the ravine and trees behind the house turning gray, the white-tailed deer heading through the undergrowth for cover. Temple had spent the day in Red Lodge, deposing witnesses in a civil suit, and had heard nothing of Lester Antelope's death. I fixed her a cup of tea, then told her of the events that had occurred that morning. She stared out the window at the snow drifting in the trees.

"They drove him up our road to do it?" she said.

I nodded.

"Coincidence?"

"Maybe. Except the doll was thrown from the car up on I-Ninety. The abductors were headed in the opposite direction from us."

"Maybe Lester was put in another vehicle."

"Maybe. Johnny American Horse told me he'd had a dream about an animal trapped in a burning woods. He said he felt responsible for the animal's fate."

"I don't care about Johnny anymore. I care about what he's doing to us."

"Guys like him and Lester are on their own. They don't have many friends, Temple."

"Forgive me. I guess I shouldn't worry

about the prospect of losing our home," she said.

"It's not that bad," I said.

She walked to the sink and stood with her back to me, looking up the ravine at the trees misting over and disappearing inside the weather. I went to the pantry to get some food for supper, and I heard her use the name of God bitterly under her breath.

In the morning the sky was bright and clear, and the snow that had fallen during the night was melting in the trees on the hillsides. I walked down to the front gate to retrieve the newspaper from the metal cylinder next to the mailbox. As an afterthought I flipped open the mailbox in case I had forgotten to pick up the mail the previous day. Inside was a blood-spotted black pigtail braided from human hair.

Later that day I got hold of Seth Masterson. "I need some help," I said.

"Sure, what is it?" he said.

I told him about Lester Antelope's death up the valley from me and my discovery of his severed pigtail in my mailbox. "Yeah, I already got the paperwork on it," he said.

"So?"

"There's no federal jurisdiction here," he replied.

"It's a kidnapping."

"Not per se."

"We don't have local resources to deal with what's going on here, Seth."

"You want my advice? Disengage from Johnny American Horse. Or buy yourself a high-end security system or a lot more guns."

"How about losing the Okie-from-Muskogee routine?"

"We're living in a different era, partner. Before it's over, the body count will be higher than anyone could have ever imagined. I'm talking about right here at home. None of us will be unaffected. That's just one guy's opinion."

In the silence that followed I could hear the receiver humming in my ear like wind in a cave.

That evening the sunset was orange on the hills and trees above our house, and before dusk I began opening the irrigation trenches that ran from the hillsides down through our pasture. We had no twelve-month creeks on our land, but the snowmelt and runoff in the spring gave us good grass, and during the end of summer we got by with temporary irrigation from a three-hundred-foot well. We kept six horses — a sorrel, a buckskin, two Appaloosas, a Morgan, and an Arabian I bought from a circus. From the far end of the pasture, as shadows grew across the valley, I could see the red metal roof of our barn and the one-and-a-half-story house we had built, with a wraparound veranda and cupolated corners that gave a wide-angle view of the valley and the snow-covered peaks of the Bitterroots in the south.

The air smelled cold and heavy as the water coursed through the irrigation trenches in the shade. Then the wind shifted and blew from the opposite hills, out of the sunlight, and I heard our horses nicker behind me and the sorrel, for no apparent reason, begin galloping through a stand of aspens toward the barn.

I stared up at the lighted hillside in the east and saw a flash on metal or glass among the trees. Then I saw it again. I went to my truck and got my binoculars from the glove box and swept the lenses across the hillcrest. A man in a sportsman's cap and down vest was crouched next to a ponderosa trunk, looking straight at me. Two other men, both dressed in jeans and caps, stood behind him. All three men turned their faces in the opposite direction, then worked their way up the slope through the Douglas fir and disappeared on the other side.

I could feel my heart beating when I lowered the binoculars from my face.

I said nothing about the men on the hill to Temple. That night she fell asleep with her back turned toward me, her hip molded under the thin blanket. The darkness was alive with sound — deer or elk thumping down the trails on the hillside, an owl screeching, a bear knocking over the garbage can in the barn, a hoof clacking like a punctuation mark on the top rail of the fence as an animal vaulted over it. I placed my hand lightly on Temple's back and could feel the swelling of her lungs through my palm. A moment later she got up and walked to the bathroom, then returned to bed, covered her head with a pillow, and went back to sleep.

I woke before first light and drank coffee by myself in the coldness of the kitchen. As the stars began to fade in the sky, I saw a skinned-up truck with slat sides parked on the road and a hatted man in a thick canvas coat leading our buckskin gelding back through a break in the fence. I put on a coat and walked down to the road.

"Why are you here, Wyatt?" I said.

He slipped the lariat off the buckskin's neck and popped him on the rump to encourage him though the collapsed fence rails. He hoisted the top rail into place and began hammering the torn nails into the post with a rock. "You got a mixture of crested wheatgrass and alfalfa in that pasture. Good dryland combo, but when elk come off a winter range a fence like this don't even slow them down," he said.

"Let that be. Tell me what you want and leave," I said.

He tapped the nails snug and removed a thermos from inside the truck. He unscrewed the top with his thumb while he stared at me with a crazy light in his face. "Got me a Sharps buffalo rifle with a fifty-caliber barrel. At three hundred yards I can core a hole big as a tangerine through a cottonwood tree. I know all about the Indian got killed up the road yonder. Know about the pigtail they left in your postbox, too. You need backup, Brother Holland. I'm the huckleberry can do it, too. You know I am."

He lifted his thermos to his mouth and drank.

"My God, what is that? It smells like a septic tank," I said.

"More like lemon-flavored paint thinner. It's my chemical cocktail. Medicaid will pay for it, but so far I ain't had to take no money from the government. There was men watching you from up on that ridge last night."

"How'd you know that?"

"I got connections."

"I don't think you do. I think you were probably spying on us, and just like me you spotted those guys up on the hill."

"Suit yourself. That Indian went out full throttle and fuck-it, didn't he? Know why? Indians ain't afraid of dying. That's 'cause they think this world is already part of the next. But white people ain't got that kind of comfort. How'd you like them motherfuckers who did Lester Antelope to go to work on Miss Temple or that boy of yours?"

He upended his thermos and drank it empty, his Adam's apple working smoothly, an orange rivulet running from his mouth, his lidless eyes waiting for my response.

Later, I called our new sheriff, a stolid and unimaginative man who was more bureaucrat than law officer. I asked him what he had on the murder of Lester Antelope.

"It's under investigation," he said.

"I know that. I was at the crime scene. One of his pigtails was in my mailbox," I said.

"I'm aware of all those details, Mr. Holland. You don't need to raise your voice," he said.

"Look, some men were watching me through binoculars yesterday. I think these guys are sending me and my wife a message."

"I'm not quite sure what you're talking about. If you want, you can come in and make a report. We'll look into it. Sending you a message? About what?"

I walked across the street to Fay Harback's office. I told her of my conversation with the sheriff. I also told her of Wyatt Dixon's early morning visit to my house.

"What's Dixon up to?" she said.

"I don't have any idea."

"We think we may have found the car that

was used to abduct Lester Antelope. Or at least it fits the description given by the homeless man who saw the doll thrown from the window. It was burned in a canyon up Fish Creek. The tags were gone, but the vehicle ID matches up with a car that was stolen in Superior a couple of weeks ago. The sheriff didn't tell you any of this?"

"He didn't get around to it."

"So you think the guys who murdered Antelope might come after you or Johnny American Horse now? Because you or Johnny might have access to the material that was stolen out of the Global Research lab?"

"They *think* I may have access."

"No truth to that?"

"No."

"Johnny doesn't know anything about it, either?"

"He wasn't involved." I tried to hold my eyes on hers.

"I feel sorry for you," she said.

"Why?" My face started to tingle, as though someone had popped me contemptuously on the cheek.

"You're going to take his bounce," she replied.

At lunchtime Lucas came into the office, his jeans hitched up above his hips, the legs tucked into his boots. "You eat yet?" he said.

"Can't do it. Got to work."

He looked disappointed for a moment, then he smiled. "I got invited to play at the bluegrass festival in Hamilton," he said.

"That's good, bud."

"Y'all coming?"

"Couldn't run us off with a shotgun."

He stared idly out the window at the trees on the courthouse lawn. "Weird thing happened this morning. Somebody stuck a crunched-up license plate in my mail slot," he said.

"What kind of plate?" I said.

"Washington State. It was twisted into a cone and jammed into the slot. Why would somebody do that?"

"Where is it?"

"In my trash can. What's going on?"

"Let's go," I said.

We drove over to his apartment and I removed the tag from his garbage can with a pencil and dropped it in a plastic shopping bag. I called Fay Harback on my cell phone and read the tag numbers to her. I heard her shuffling papers around on her desk.

"Bring it in. We'll see if there're any latents on it. It came off the burned vehicle we found up Fish Creek . . . Hello?" she said.

"Where's Wyatt Dixon live?" I said.

CHAPTER 9

Wyatt lived up on the Blackfoot River, on a grassy bench north of a sawmill and an unused railroad trestle. Several years back an ice jam had crashed through the cottonwoods, sweeping away the owner's truck, automobile, and machine shop, depositing great chunks of frozen flotsam inside the downstairs area of the main house. Wyatt rented the house for a song. He strung canvas over the holes in the first story and moved into an upstairs bedroom that allowed him a view of the only two ways the property could be accessed — either by a steel swing bridge suspended over the river or by a single-track log road that wound over the hill behind the house.

The sky was still filled with light when I parked on the riverbank and headed toward the swing bridge. The wind blowing down the canyon smelled of damp stone, pine needles, and wood smoke, and a fisherman was down below in the current, flipping a dry fly out on the riffle, taking up the slack in his line with his left hand. The swing bridge pinged and bounced with my weight as I crossed it, then the sun dropped behind the mountain, filling the gorge with shadow, and

I swore I saw a figure in the willows at the far end of the bridge.

Ain't nobody home, Billy Bob. Better be glad, too, L. Q. Navarro said.

Mind your own business, I replied.

You're trying to use Dixon as a cure for your problem. That's like shopping in hell for an air-conditioning unit.

What do you suggest?

Inside his black coat he wore a white shirt with pale gray stripes in it. A red ribbon folded in the shape of a shepherd's hook was pinned to the place where I had shot and killed him. *The problem is you haven't figured out what he's really up to. This boy ain't your reg'lar psychopath,* he said.

I sure could use you now, L.Q. I hate myself for what I did down there on the border.

But he was gone. I turned around and walked back across the bridge, my boots clanking on the steel grid. The fisherman down below, who had witnessed my conversation with someone no one else saw, was looking at me strangely. I waved at him, but he didn't respond.

I sat in my truck, trying to think. As L.Q. had indicated, I had never figured out Dixon. He was born twenty miles from the birthplace of Audie Murphy, on a dust-blown, locust-infested farm where his parents apparently raised children as they would livestock. Then the family moved to another rental farm, in an even more godforsaken place, not far from the birthplace of Clyde Barrow. Somehow it seemed more than coincidence that Wyatt's early life was geographically linked to names that were so antithetically juxtaposed in connotation.

At age fifteen, Wyatt ran away from home and enlisted in the United States Army. At bayonet practice a drill instructor who had a particular dislike for Wyatt made the mistake of choosing him for a demonstration with a pugil stick. Wyatt broke the drill instructor's jaw with the pugil stick. The Army found the drill instructor at fault but later realized it had underestimated Wyatt's potential when he waylaid a black mess sergeant in a San Antonio alley, cut off his stripes, and stuffed them down his throat.

He picked chickens in a Texas slaughter-house, hauled illegal Mexican beef, and did time in a Coahuila prison, where the guards made him kneel on stones with his wrists chained to a log stretched across his shoulders. He wandered the American West in stolen cars and pickups, sleeping under the stars, working cockfight pits, breaking mustangs in Nevada, gypo logging in the Cascades, running a bale or two of weed up from Baja when he ran short of cash. His body looked as though it were made from whipcord. The muscles in his forearms swelled into balloons; his grip was like steel cable. Then at age nineteen

Wyatt discovered the world of a full-time, honest-to-God rodeo man.

As a bull rider, he would tie himself down with a suicide wrap and either ride to the buzzer or take his chances on being dragged, stomped, hooked, or flung into the boards. As a steer wrestler, he would fly from the saddle, grab the steer's horns, and slam it to the ground with such force he and the steer would seem to disappear inside a brown aura of dust and desiccated manure. From Big D to Calgary, the crowds loved Wyatt Dixon.

Barroom women sucked his fingers, and mainline ex-cons, neo-Nazis, and outlaw bikers walked around him. His skin was stitched with scar tissue but clean of tattoos, the skeletal structure of his face like a Roman soldier's. He spent large sums on fine boots and embroidered western shirts, drank tequila with a beer back, and belonged to Aryan supremacist groups out of convenience rather than need. He ate his pain, let his enemies break their fists on his face, and grinned like a jack-o'-lantern at the condemnation of the world.

It was Dixon's courage that made no sense. Sociopaths are invariably cowards, and their cruelty exists in direct proportion to their own fear and self-pity. If they show any calm when they're executed by the state, it's because they've forced their executioner to do what they could not do themselves.

Wyatt Dixon didn't fit the category.

As I started the truck, I remembered the two rodeo passes he had tried to give me and Temple at the café in Missoula, tickets I had brushed off the table onto the floor. Then I remembered seeing an ad in the morning paper. The rodeo, in Stevensville, began that weekend.

When I arrived the fairgrounds were teeming with people, neon-scrolled carnival rides revolved against a turquoise light in the sky, and crowds of rodeo fans were packing into the grandstands while Bob Wills's original version of "San Antonio Rose" blared from loudspeakers. I bought a candied apple and sat up high in the stands, where I had a wonderful view of the bucking chutes and the arena. But I saw no sign of Wyatt. He usually worked as a clown, dressed in a cherry-red, bulbous nose, face paint, baggy pants, firehouse suspenders, and fright wig, staring the bull down, pawing the ground with his cleats, arching his back away from the horned charge with only an inch or two to spare, sometimes mooning the bull as it turned for another pass.

I watched the bulldogging and calf-roping competition, the ladies' barrel race, and a comedy routine involving a monkey named Whiplash who, dressed in cowboy garb, charged about the arena strapped to a dog sprinting after sheep.

Then it was time for the bareback riders.

Almost all the riders came from Montana and Wyoming. Most were young and wore red or purple or green chaps, outrageous shirts, and hats with huge crowns and sloping brims; none of them had a teaspoon of fat on his body, and all of them seemed to glide across the ground rather than walk. When they came out of the chute, the only thing between them and a ride into the sky was a suitcase handle stitched to the slender piece of leather rigging on the horse's withers. Larry Mahan once said bareback riding was easy, that it was just like loading a suitcase with bricks, hefting it up by the handle, then stepping out of a ten-story window.

Then I saw Wyatt Dixon mount the side of a bucking chute, rosin the palms of his gloves, and slide down inside the boards onto the rigging of a horse named Drunkard's Dream. At first it seemed Wyatt was having trouble getting set, dipping his hand repeatedly into the rigging and tugging back on the suitcase handle. The horse began rearing its head, banging Wyatt's legs into the boards, trying to clear space to get off a solid kick.

For no reason that made any sense a rough stock handler poked a battery-powered hotshot through the boards and jolted the horse's forequarters with it. The horse went berserk. But Wyatt hollered, "Outside!" anyway, and he and Drunkard's Dream exploded into the arena.

First bounce out of the chute, he roweled the horse's neck, his legs extended in front of him, his back almost touching the horse's rump. Drunkard's Dream corkscrewed, sunfished, and came totally off the ground, but Wyatt's lock on the suitcase handle was so tight his small, muscular buttocks seemed stitched to the animal's hide.

"Wyatt Dixon, thirty-nine years young! Look at that cowboy ride, ladies and gentlemen!" the announcer yelled with genuine excitement and admiration.

But in a blink it went south. Wyatt seemed to slip and lose balance on the horse's back, as though the arena were tilting. Drunkard's Dream raked him against the boards, and Wyatt and his rigging went over the side, under the horse's hooves.

The crowd was on its feet, horrified. They could see Wyatt through the horse's legs, curled in a ball, his forearms raised defensively. They could even hear the uneven sound the horse's hooves made as they trod over both the sod and Wyatt's body.

The clowns and a pickup rider were the first people to get to Wyatt. When they tried to lift him onto a stretcher, he pushed them away and rose to his feet, falling back against the boards for support. His face was dazed, filmed with dust, blood leaking from a cut in his scalp. He reached over, almost falling down again, picked up his hat, and slapped it clean against his leg.

Regardless of his injury, Wyatt had ridden to the buzzer, and the judges gave him the highest score so far in the bareback competition. But Wyatt seemed to be completely indifferent to either the crowd's applause or the points just given to him for his ride. He left the arena at the far end, where the rough stock were kept, then circled back under the stands.

I walked to the concourse, where I could see the unlighted area behind the concession stands and under the seats. The man who had used the hotshot on Wyatt's horse was eating a chili dog out of a paper plate, his face bent close to his food. He was a tall man with a pot stomach, narrow shoulders, and flaccid arms. He was a rough stock handler, not a rider, a man who would always be a candle moth and never a player. When he looked up from his food, his face turned gray.

"The cinch busted. It didn't have nothing to do with the hotshot, Wyatt," I heard him say.

Wyatt's back was turned to me, so I could not see his face or hear his words. But when he spoke, the handler nodded his head up and down, then shook it from side to side. His chili dog slid off his plate onto the ground. People were starting to gather now. An older man stepped forward and patted

Wyatt on the shoulder, then I saw Wyatt look away at the people passing by the concession stands, as though he were leaving one reality and entering another. In profile his face and exposed eye possessed the same flat, bloodless and brutal luminosity as a passing shark's.

Then he simply walked away, his mouth down-hooked, his shoulders sloped forward, a rivulet of blood glued to the side of his eye and down his cheek, like paint on an Indian warrior.

I was sure he had not seen me. I drove back to his house by the Blackfoot River and left the following note in his mailbox:

You think a jailhouse jerk-off like you is going to sell information about us to a defense attorney? That cut cinch was just a warning. Take it to heart, sperm breath.

He called the house Saturday morning. "I just received a communication that's a test for my thinking powers, Brother Holland," he said.

"You need to take my number out of your Rolodex," I said.

"Got the shit kicked out of me under a horse last night. This morning I find this note in my mailbox, accusing me of trying to sell information about certain parties to a defense lawyer. You been telling people I done that?"

160

"I sure did. To anybody who'd listen."

"I am very disappointed to learn that. I thought we was operating on a basis of lawyer-client confidentiality."

"I want you to hear this, Dixon —"

"Brother Holland, I know you wasn't raised up on a pig farm. It's impolite to call folks by their last names. You done sicced some bad people on me, sir. That means you owe me."

I hung up, but I knew he'd taken the hook. He called back fifteen seconds later. "I think somebody put acid on my cinch so it looked like it busted from dry rot. Last night I was fixing to rip the arms off the wrong man. Glad I have calmed down and got my Christian attitudes back on the front burner," he said.

"Leave me out of your life."

"No-siree-bobtail, we're in this together. Remember, I have already given your name as my reference with President Bush. That means both you and me are in the service of the red, white, and blue. I 'spect I'm gonna be making some home calls on a few folks. But whatever I do, I'll keep you updated as my counselor. Have you been to Brother Sneed's church up at Arlee? I think you would find it an uplifting experience."

"Have a great weekend, Wyatt," I said, and eased the receiver into the phone cradle.

The kitchen was full of sunlight, the hills a soft green from the spring melt. Temple stood in the doorway, staring at me in disbelief.

"You're trying to manipulate a lunatic like Wyatt Dixon?" she said.

"Got any other solutions?" I replied.

She started to speak, to fling a rejoinder at me. Then she gave it up and shook her head. I put my arms around her and pulled her close against me, my face buried in her hair, and could take no pleasure in either her verbal defeat or my having just stepped into the moral basement that constituted the world of Wyatt Dixon.

It was the weekend and Darrel McComb was off the clock, but he could not get Amber Finley off his mind, nor the whole business involving the Indians and what he had come to believe was some form of intelligence operation. What had Rocky Harrigan always told him about being a player? Kick ass, take names, and don't look back. But kick ass.

Saturday afternoon he showered, shined his shoes, put on a Hawaiian shirt, what Rocky used to call a "goon" shirt, and knocked on the Finleys' door. When she opened it she looked absolutely stunning, in a purple dress printed with green flowers, with big red beads around her throat and straw sandals on her feet. In the rush of cool air out into the sunlight he could smell her perfume and the odor of her shampoo. It was obvious she had been on her way out. "This is an official visit," he said.

"Then I'd be more comfortable if somebody was accompanying you," she replied.

"We don't have a lot of budget for weekend overtime," he said, half smiling.

She stepped aside to let him in. "Get it over with, whatever it is," she said.

The living room was furnished with green velvet drapes and massive, dark furniture, but the morose effect was attenuated by the flow of light through the French doors that opened onto the backyard and creek. As his eyes adjusted, he realized the glass tabletops, the pale marble in the mantelpiece, and the big mirror above it gave contrasts to the room that were a mark of taste and planning inconceivable in the homes of most people he knew. He waited for her to ask him to sit down. But she didn't. He removed a notebook from his shirt pocket and sat on the couch, anyway, folding back pages and clicking his ballpoint to give the impression he was all business and at the same time controlling the situation, not letting her use social protocol to achieve the upper hand.

"You knew Lester Antelope?" he said.

"He worked for Johnny sometimes. I knew him around. Why?"

"He was murdered."

"I know that. Why don't you find the people who did it?"

She was standing by the mantel, one forearm propped on the corner. Darrel smiled at her. "Believe it or not, that's the purpose of my visit. I think Antelope was mixed up with the burglary of that research lab down in Stevensville. I suspect it had something to do with ecoterrorism. But we're pretty sure four Indians did the job." He paused a moment to give emphasis to the rest of his statement. "A white woman was with them. Maybe somebody who just got caught up in things."

She didn't blink. Her eyes stayed riveted on his, the most radiant blue eyes he had ever seen. "You said, '*We're* pretty sure.' The Missoula Sheriff's Department is investigating crimes in Ravalli County?"

He'd slipped and she'd caught it. "I'm getting a crick in my neck looking up at you. Could you sit down?" he said.

"There's no 'we,' is there?" she said.

He tried to look bored. "It's a cooperative effort. In this instance, a burglary and a homicide are linked together in two jurisdictions. Who do you think that woman was?"

"Snow White, with four of the dwarfs. Get a life, Darrel."

He grinned at her humor and wrote in his notebook. He was on top of it now — generous, confident enough to be indulgent. When they cracked wise, they had unknowingly admitted they were amateurs and probably guilty as well. In the old days, mainline hard cases took the beating. Today, the pros asked for an attorney and became deaf-mutes.

"About five years ago, I knew a gal from your background who went inside. Educated, smart, nice-looking, used to ski in Aspen and hang out in Malibu. Her daddy was a state senator, a big rancher, a wheeler and a dealer, with juice all the way to D.C. But the girl fell in love with a junkie who maxed out all her credit cards and made her drive the car whenever he turned over a liquor or convenience store.

"One night the junkie had a fierce jones going and decided to hold up a store in a strip mall. He killed three people, including a twelve-year-old kid. Our girlfriend got raped by a male guard her first week inside and the next week by a couple of dykes. She never came out. She hung herself. Think I'm kidding? I'll give you her name. You can check it out."

He had driven the barb in deep. Amber's eyes were shimmering, her throat spotted with color. He felt paternal and wanted to stand up and touch her cheek and hair, to reassure her things were not out of control yet, that he would be there as her friend. His thoughts, although not deliberately erotic, caused a thickening in his throat.

But he saw the flicker of weakness and humiliation leave her eyes and her jawbone flex, her posture straighten as she removed her hand from the mantelpiece.

"Do anything you goddamn feel like, but in the meantime take yourself, your horny attitudes, and your hair tonic or cologne or whatever that stink is out of my house. If you come back again without a warrant, my attorney will pull the nails out of your shoes."

He rose from the couch, clicked his ballpoint pen, and stuck it in his pocket. His face burned, then his embarrassment turned to anger and he had to bite down on his lip so he would not say the words he was thinking. He walked to the door and opened it, the sunlight blinding his eyes. When he looked back at her, her arms were folded on her breasts, one knuckle poised on her lips while she watched him. She had not only bested him again but insulted him physically. A bilious fluid rose in his throat.

His desire for vindication, even revenge, should have made him willing to pull out all the stops. But as he looked at the composure in her face, the paleness on the tops of her breasts, her cocked hip, her refusal to be bested by him, only one thought coursed through his mind: *What an incredible woman.*

Why couldn't she accept his feelings for what they were?

Darrel and Greta Lundstrum had made a date that evening. Before he left his apartment on the river, he made an entry in the computer file he was now keeping on the case of Johnny American Horse and the individuals who threaded their way in and out of it. The entry read:

Greta Lundstrum — smart, confrontational, I suspect territorial as hell, maybe a sexual adventurer. Would she get in the sack with a guy like Wyatt Dixon just for fun? Or is she a player? Why was she at the house of a U.S. senator? An easterner out here among the cowboys just for kicks? No way.

As he drove down to Stevensville to pick her up, he tried to convince himself that his motivations were professional in nature. But his unrequited obsession over Amber Finley was taking its toll. Night and day he felt a vague sense of sexual need that left him not only uncomfortable but irritable and discontent, almost hostile, as though he were less in the eyes of others, an inept, clumsy man who smelled of locker rooms and had to wear his military history like an invisible uniform to know who he was.

Greta Lundstrum lived in a white bungalow with blue shutters, a solitary spruce tree planted on each side of the small porch. In the late afternoon light the yard, the spruce trees, and the house looked like a demonstration home removed from a 1940s subdivision development. She opened the door and came outside without inviting him in, dressed in a black skirt and a white blouse, a gold chain around her throat. A shiny black purse hung on her arm.

"Am I late?" he asked, looking at his watch.

"I made reservations at the Depot for six-thirty," she replied, walking ahead of him.

"I didn't know we were going to the Depot," he said.

"You don't like eating there?"

"No, it's fine," he said.

"Good. That's where I usually eat when I'm in Missoula," she said. She opened the car door for herself and got inside, her purse on her lap, waiting for him to start the engine.

The restaurant's main dining area and the bar across the foyer were crowded. Outside, on the terrace, a jazz combo played under a striped canopy, the sun a soft orange ball above the hills behind the railroad tracks.

"I'm glad you got reservations," Darrel said.

"You have to. On Saturday night university types take over everything," she said.

"It's that kind of town, all right," he said.

She ordered wine and he a glass of seltzer with a slice of lime.

"You don't drink?" she said.

"Not too often. But I can if I want to," he replied.

"When do you want to?" she said, and smiled when she said it.

"When I feel like it. I just never had the taste for it."

"Give me the sirloin, well done, sour cream and chives on the baked potato. No butter," she told the waiter.

"Yeah, same for me," Darrel said.

During dinner he realized she spoke to no one at the other tables, although her eyes seemed to take note, without personal interest, of everyone in the room. She had firm arms, square shoulders, a small cleft in her chin, and medium-size hands with clipped, pink nails. She ate with a good appetite and midway through the meal ordered another glass of wine. "Sure you won't join me?" she said.

"Why not?" he said, nodding to the waiter.

Later, she had Bavarian cake for dessert, and when the waiter brought coffee, she looked sated, happy, her face a bit flushed. She didn't order anything else to drink and he knew she wasn't a real boozer. "I always like the food here," she said.

"I've been looking into that guy Dixon's background. You know, the rodeo guy?" he said casually.

She picked up her spoon from her coffee saucer and looked at it and put it back down. "I think I already told you I strayed into a dalliance with Wyatt. It was my fault, not his. But I'm not really interested in hearing any more about him," she said.

"The Feds say he writes letters to the President. He's a definite head case."

He looked out the window, waiting for her reaction. "Is this why you asked me out?" she said.

"I shouldn't have brought this guy up. Cops have a hard time getting off the clock. That's why they hang out together. Lot of times in late night bars. I'm glad you wanted to go to dinner tonight."

She let her eyes rove around the dining room, her thoughts veiled. "Ever been married?" she asked.

"For a little while. I was in the Army, moving around from place to place."

"You seem like a frank man. What do you think of me?"

"You're a classy lady. I got a feeling we're a lot alike," Darrel said.

"Who knows?" she said.

"Want to take a walk down by the river? There's a concert in the park tonight. Actually, my apartment is across the river from the park. Sometimes I listen to the music on my balcony," he said.

"You saying you want to go to the concert or to your apartment?"

"Whatever," he replied.

She rested her chin on her fist and looked directly into his face again. "You go to Vegas or Reno very much?" she said.

"Yeah, how'd you know?"

"Because I go there, too. Know why?" she said.

" 'Cause you never know what's going to happen next. Twenty-four hours a day, you can have any kind of adventure you want," he replied.

She kept her eyes on his and kissed the air with her lips.

A few minutes later, he and Greta were sitting on a grass embankment by the river and listening to a band pound out "The Eight-Thirty Blues." The park was crowded with college kids, young couples with children, Frisbee throwers, skateboarders, hobos who slept in the willows along the riverbank, and punked-out street people who dealt drugs in the shadows by the public restrooms and looked as if they had been shot out of a cannon.

But Darrel had little interest in street dealers or the strips of maroon cloud on the mountains in the west or the yellow light that filled the sky or the breeze that blew off the water and smelled of fern and wet stone. Instead, his entire attentions were now focused on two people dancing on the clipped lawn in front of the bandstand — Amber Finley and Johnny American Horse.

Amber wore a knee-length black spaghetti-strap dress and Mexican cowboy boots, and danced with her fists held in the air, swinging her hips from side to side, kicking one booted foot when she made a turn, totally indifferent to the impression she made on anyone else. By contrast, Johnny American Horse looked like a post, his face shaded by a light-colored Stetson, his skin dark, his black jeans and tight-fitting silver shirt stretched to splitting on the leanness of his body.

Greta's eyes followed Darrel's line of vision.

"A penny for your thoughts," she said.

"The country's turning into a toilet," he replied.

"It's not that bad, is it?"

He picked a blade of grass off his shoe and flicked it into the breeze. "I guess not," he said.

"You want to go?" she asked.

"I'll go get us a couple of snow cones, then we'll see," he said.

He worked his way through the crowd to the concession stands that had been set up under a huge canvas awning. The band had stopped playing and he could see Amber and Johnny by the bandstand, talking to the musicians, Johnny's arm draped across her shoulder. Darrel felt his jaw tighten, the fingernails of his right hand rake across the heel of his palm.

Then Amber left the lawn area and walked

directly toward him, the black fringe on her dress swishing on her knees, the yellow light in the sky reflecting on her shoulders.

"Your snow cones, sir," the kid at the concession stand said.

"What?" Darrel replied.

"Your snow cones? You want them?"

Darrel took one in each hand and found himself standing in Amber's path, awkward, stupid-looking, like a giant clod just arrived from Nebraska, grains of colored ice sliding down his hands and wrists. Why was she bearing down on him? What had he done wrong this time? "Hi, Amber," he said.

She turned, her blue eyes searching for the voice that had called her name. Then he realized she had been completely unaware of his presence in the crowd.

"What are *you* doing here?" she said.

"Checking out the music," he said, trying to smile.

"*What* is your problem? Are you following me again?"

"No."

"You peek through my windows, you come to my house uninvited, you beat up my boy-friend with a blackjack, and now you trail your BO into the concert I'm attending. Do you see a pattern here?"

People were turning to stare now. His face was burning, his armpits sweating inside his coat. He tried to find words to speak but couldn't. He shoved his way through the crowd back toward the grass embankment where Greta waited for him. Behind him he thought he heard people laughing.

Greta pulled the snow cones out of his hands. "You look terrible. Sit down. What happened over there?" she said.

"Senator Finley's daughter holds a grudge. It's no big deal," he said.

"Who cares? She's a brat who should have had her butt pounded a long time ago," Greta said. She got up from the grass and threw the snow cones in a trash barrel. "Come on, big fellow. Show me where you live."

She walked a few steps toward the parking lot, then turned and waited for him to follow.

They drove across the bridge and turned into a shady side street that bordered the river. But he couldn't concentrate. He had started out the evening convinced he was investigating both ecoterrorists and a rogue intelligence operation. Now he'd been made a public fool and he was in the company of a woman whose complexities and motivations he couldn't begin to guess at. He felt like a man being pushed into a fistfight after his arms had been torn off.

His apartment was located in a century-old refurbished brick building with a grand view of the river and the city. He walked out on the balcony and looked back toward the bridge and the park on the opposite side of the river where the dance was still in progress. Why care what *those* people thought? he asked himself. The civilian world was a joke, a giant self-delusion that had little connection to the realities of nations in conflict.

He remembered a moment of revelation in El Salvador back in the 1980s. A photographer had taken pictures of U.S. advisers carrying weapons in the field and several congressmen had threatened an investigation. The irony was that the El Salvadoran helicopters raking leftist villages with Gatling guns were receiving their coordinates from U.S. AWACS planes high overhead and no media knew anything about it.

Darrel wondered if Amber and her liberal friends at the dance had any idea what was done for them and in their name on the ragged green edges of the American Empire.

But moments of reverie like these were not entirely comforting to Darrel. He also remembered seeing a helicopter gunship coming in low over a rain forest, a molten sun behind it, the downdraft whipping the canopy into a frenzy, then the Gatling guns blowing a series of huts into a pinkish-brown cloud laced with dried thatch. There had been children as well as adult civilians in those huts, and sometimes in the middle of the night he heard the sounds they made before they died.

Greta was making a pitcher of sangria at his bar, although he had not asked her to.

"Still thinking about that spoiled twat?" she said.

"You never told me what you were doing over at Senator Finley's place."

"Mine to know," she said, stirring the ice and red wine with a celery stalk. "But if you insist, I have friends who contribute to his campaign. I suspect you voted for Finley, didn't you?"

"I don't vote. I think politics is a sideshow."

She filled two goblets with sangria, fitted orange slices on the rims, and handed him one. "Here's to all the jerks who take sideshows seriously," she said, and clinked his goblet.

"I don't figure you."

"What's to figure?" she said. She drank from her goblet, then set it down and slipped her arms around his waist. He felt her stomach touch his loins like an electric current.

Later, after they had made love in his roll-away bed, she put on her panties and walked without her top to the bar and came back to the bed with their drinks. She had few wrinkles in her skin, no stretch marks, and her muscle tone was extraordinary for her age. She drank from her glass, then leaned over him and kissed him wetly on the mouth. "You didn't say anything," she said.

"About what?"

"How you liked it."

"Good. I liked it real good. You're quite a woman."

She tapped him on the lips with a finger and winked. "You're not bad yourself. Next time, though, give a girl a little compliment. Mind if I use your bathroom?" she said.

A moment later he heard the toilet flush and the faucet running. The band was still playing across the river, the sound of the music floating thinly above the roar of the current. He put on his boxer shorts and walked to the balcony. Somewhere in the crowd on the clipped lawn Amber Finley was still dancing with Johnny American Horse, the moon rising above the mountains into a turquoise sky, the two of them blessed with youth, the admiration of their peers, the knowledge that the earth and all its gifts had been created especially for them.

He had never felt so miserable in his life.

After sunset and another pitcher of sangria, Darrel drove Greta back to her bungalow in the Bitterroot Valley. When she unlocked the front door, neither of them could believe what they saw. Every room was a shambles. The furniture was turned upside down, mattresses and upholstery slashed and gutted, drywall torn off the joists, desk and dresser drawers dumped, even all the canned goods in the pantry and frozen food in the icebox raked on the floor.

The alarm had never sounded because the home invader or invaders had come through the roof, first chopping a hole in it, then smashing a dead-bolted attic door into kindling. The level of violence done to the bungalow created in Darrel's mind a perpetrator of immense strength and destructive energies, someone with tendons in his arms and hands like steel cable and with absolutely no sense of mercy or restraint at all.

Greta Lundstrum sat down in a deep chair and wept.

"When was the last time you saw Wyatt Dixon?" Darrel asked.

CHAPTER 10

Sunday morning, Amber Finley woke in Johnny's bed and touched the place where he should have been but felt only the warm, empty space he had occupied. The Jocko Valley was still in shadow, the crest of the hills black-green against the light growing in the sky, the sound of the river loud on the rocks at the foot of the property. She and Johnny had slept with the windows open and the room was cold, and she wished he would come back to bed. In the kitchen she heard pans clanking on the stove and smelled coffee boiling and bacon frying in a skillet.

She raised herself up on her hands and yawned. "Johnny?" she said.

But there was no reply. She glanced down at his pillow, and in the indentation where his head had rested was a small blue-felt box. She picked it up and pried the top back on its spring. Inserted in a satin cushion was a gold ring with a tiny diamond mounted on it.

"I was going to surprise you with some apple flapjacks," he said from the doorway, an apron tied around his hips, a spatula in his hand.

"Oh, it's beautiful, Johnny," she said.

"There's a Methodist minister up at St. Ignatius who says he'll marry us any day we want to set it up."

"Let's do it this week. Let's do it tomorrow."

He sat on the edge of the bed and slipped the ring on her left hand, his eyes lowered so she could not read them. "A couple of things we need to agree on," he said.

"What?" she said, her face clouding.

"Your father has to know about it up front. I need to be there when that happens, too."

"He doesn't control my life. He doesn't have anything to say about it."

"He's still your old man. He believes in what he does. He deserves to be treated with respect, don't you think?"

She found his hand again and pressed it hard, then looked admiringly at her ring. "How'd you pay for it?"

"It's called 'credit.' One other thing. If I go inside, we agree you can divorce me. In fact, I'd insist on it. I don't want to create a jailhouse widow out of my best friend." Johnny had small eyes, and they crinkled at the corners when he grinned.

"Don't talk like that. Billy Bob is a good lawyer. We have a lot of friends who will stand up for you," she said.

He stroked her hair and kissed her brow, then her mouth.

"I haven't brushed my teeth," she said.

He pressed her down on the pillow and kissed her mouth again, then the tops of her breasts and the long taper of her stomach and two red moles just below her navel. She curled her knees into him and held him across the back and put her face in his hair and bit his neck. She could feel her breath quicken and a flush spread through her thighs.

He sat up and took both her wrists in his hands. "I have to tell you something else," he said.

The register in his voice had dropped, and she studied his eyes now because they, like his words, never lied to her. What she saw there made her ball her fists. "Say it, say it, say it," she said.

"My dreams started again. Some of the stuff in them doesn't make good sense. My uncle said my dreams would always be distorted, not clear like Crazy Horse's were, because my mother was Salish and I'm only half Lakota."

"You tear me apart when you talk like this."

His eyes were still looking at her, yet she knew they were not seeing her but instead a vision inside his head. He swallowed and there was a dry click inside his throat. "Someone else is going to be killed, here, at my house. It's a man. I think it could be me. Maybe making you my wife would be a

181

selfish thing on my part."

She put her arms around his neck and pulled him down close to her face. She started to speak, then simply held him as tightly as she could, gripping the hardness of his back, pulling at his apron and his belt buckle, aching to have him inside her before he spoke again and her heart burst.

Monday morning, Seth Masterson sauntered into my office and sat down in front of my desk, his long legs, as always, a problem, a tan rain hat perched on his knee. "How you doin', bud?" he asked.

"I'm just fine, Seth. But Lester Antelope isn't. He's dead. My client Johnny American Horse isn't doing too well, either. Unless I get some help, the D.A. is going to bury him alive."

Seth twisted his head and glanced out the window at the maples puffing in the wind on the courthouse lawn, his expression neutral. "We've got a high-tech snitch in this area, a hacker we could have sent up but who we decided to leave on a short leash to help us out once in a while," he said. "The problem with our snitch is he's a wiseass and thinks he's smarter than we are, so he's not always truthful or forthcoming. You with me?"

"No."

"A couple of Indians came to him with a bunch of floppy disks they couldn't get into.

Our snitch says he couldn't find a way into them, either. We served search warrants on the Indians, but their houses were clean. You recognize the names of these guys?"

He slid his notebook across the desktop. I looked at the two names written on the top page and shook my head.

"They were friends of Lester Antelope," Seth said. "I think they're part of the bunch who broke into Global Research."

"Why is a federal agency interested in a small research lab in the Bitterroot Valley?"

He hesitated a moment. "Global has some federal defense contracts," he said.

"To do what?"

"It's agricultural in nature."

"I've got a problem with the way you do business, Seth," I said. "Guys like me are allowed to know parts of things. A conversation with you amounts to other people answering your questions."

He pulled on his ear. "I didn't make myself clear. I think our snitch got into those disks. I think what he saw there scared the shit out of him. Listen, Billy Bob, those two killers American Horse waxed, Ruggles and Bumper? Don't be deceived. There's more of them out there. If that sounds funny coming from a federal agent, that's the way it is." He wrote a number on the back of his business card and flipped the card on my desk. "That's my number at the Doubletree."

He got up from the chair without saying good-bye and, gentleman that he was, fitted on his rain hat only after he had walked out the front door.

Agricultural in nature?

That evening, Darrel McComb got a visitor at his apartment he did not expect. Romulus Finley rang the bell, then began tapping impatiently with one knuckle on the door before Darrel could reach it.

"You got a few minutes, Detective?" he said.

"Sure," Darrel said, stepping back from the open door.

Finley walked into the center of the room, turning in a circle, nodding approvingly. His cheeks were rosy from the walk up the stairs, his arms and shoulders meaty inside his sports coat. "Nice place. Nice view of the river," he said.

"Would you like coffee or a beer, Senator?"

"A beer would be good. Yeah, that would hit the spot," Finley replied.

He didn't want a glass. He drank out of the can, his big hand covering the design and logo on the aluminum. "I'll cut to it, partner. I've seen your file. You're a man of great experience, a patriot and a soldier on many levels. We communicating here?"

"No, sir."

"Some men serve their country off the

computer. They get no recognition for what they do, even when they lose their lives. You're one of them, just like your friend Rocky Harrigan was."

"What do you know about Rocky, Senator?"

"I know he was brave. Just like you, he didn't like what was happening to this country."

Darrel tried to remain stone-faced, to hide the sense of invasion and manipulation that was churning in his stomach. "Rocky was a good guy. But he and I were regular Army, Senator. Our careers probably wouldn't be that interesting to most folks," he said.

"I respect both your modesty and your privacy, Detective. But I've got a personal problem I don't have any permanent answer for. This Indian man Johnny American Horse belongs in a prison. Instead, he's out on bond and is planning to marry my daughter, who is just about as naive as people get, and that includes Eve thinking she could pick apples in the Garden and outwit both God and the devil."

Finley drank the rest of the beer can empty and crushed it in his hand. "You got any suggestions, son?"

"You said you didn't have any permanent answer to your problem. Could you spell that out?" Darrel said.

"I'm not talking about doing anything illegal. I just want the law enforced and that man out of my daughter's life. I had to take the red-eye back here last night so I could stand in my own goddamn living room and listen to a murderer tell me he was going to marry my daughter. I was with the First Marine Division at the Punch Bowl in the Korean War, Detective. When it's time to clean the barn, it's time to clean the barn. You hearing me on this?"

"Somebody broke into Greta Lundstrum's house in the early a.m. Sunday morning," Darrel said. "I think the break-in at her house is connected to the burglary of a research lab in Stevensville. I think this ex-convict Wyatt Dixon is a player in this, too. Amber might have a lot more serious problems than marrying American Horse."

But Finley was already shaking his head before Darrel could finish. "I'm not interested in a lot of bullshit about ex-convicts and burglaries, because none of it has anything to do with my daughter. Johnny American Horse needs to be gone. The operative word is *gone*, Detective. The man who can make that happen is a man to whom I'll owe a mighty big debt. I'll let myself out. Thanks for the beer."

Finley clapped Darrel on the shoulder and went back out the door, not a strand of sandy hair out of place on his head.

De nada, you hypocritical sonofabitch, Darrel thought.

That same evening we had a sunshower, then the rain quit and the sun was gold on the hills, and I drove up to the north end of our acreage, with a half-dozen poplar trees in the bed of my pickup, and began digging holes for them along the fenceline. A white-tailed doe with a new fawn watched me from the sunlight, and down the meadow, deep in the shade, I could hear our horses blowing in the soggy grass by an irrigation ditch.

I cut the burlap from the root balls of the poplars and began dropping them into the holes I had dug. I looked up from my work when I heard a horse nicker in the arroyo above me. The sun had dipped right into a notch in the mountain, and a hot red glow shone down through the dead and collapsed trees in the arroyo. A rider mounted on an Appaloosa gelding with gray and white spots on its rump moved down through the trees, the Appaloosa's shoes barely sounding on the soft carpet of humus and rotted deadfall.

The rider was hatless, bare-chested, riding without a saddle, his silky red hair in his eyes, his skin as smooth as tallow, a huge green deerfly perched on his shoulder.

"Howdy doodie, Brother Holland?" Wyatt Dixon said. "Had my horse over to the vet'inary in the next hollow, then thought I'd take him for a ride up your ridge. Also wanted to give you a report on my reconnoitering efforts." He popped the deerfly off his shoulder with one finger.

"Reconnoitering efforts?"

Wyatt lifted one booted leg over the horse's withers and slid to the ground as smoothly as water sliding down a rock. His chest had small nipples and his underarms were shaved, his lats wedging out like the base of an inverted stump. He used one hand to pick up a poplar tree by the trunk, one whose root ball must have weighed a hundred pounds. He dropped it into a hole and kicked dirt on top of it. "We got us a client-attorney relationship, counselor?"

"No."

"How about I give you a one-dollar bill? That makes it legal, don't it?"

"I don't think that's a good idea, Wyatt. Sometimes the more technicalities you get into, the more problems you have."

"With my record, I guess I cain't blame you for not trusting me. But I got to say I feel a little let down." He pulled on his nose, his jaw hooked forward, his colorless eyes fixed on nothing. "Through my research activities, which I ain't gonna describe, I come up with a couple of names."

He handed me a piece of folded notebook paper. But I didn't read it. I folded it again and stuck it inside the band of my hat. He watched me curiously.

"Are these the Indians who broke into a

research lab?" I asked.

"They're both white men. One is a freelance shooter, does five-grand hits out of Miami. The other one is some kind of child-molester pervert from San Fran. I heard about him in Quentin. He'd do a yard job on a man for thirty bucks. I don't know what either one of them looks like. That's the problem."

"Why?"

"They're already here. At least that's what my reconnoitering seems to indicate. This plainclothes cop, Darrel McComb? He come to see you?"

"No."

"He left his business card at my house. Makes me uneasy when a man bird-dogs my house." Wyatt rubbed his shoulder, found a pimple, and popped it. He seemed to think a long time. But the only color in his eyes was in the pupils, so that his eyes took on no cast, no more than clear glass could. "Brother Holland?"

"What?"

"You wouldn't try to slicker me on this deal, would you? 'Cause of deeds past? Get me to doing scutwork for you, busting the law, ripping folks' ass, then when you was finished with me, drive an eighteen-wheeler up my cheeks?"

"If I wanted to get even with you, Wyatt, I'd hit you in the head with this posthole digger and bury you right here."

He picked up his horse's reins and flipped them back and forth across his knuckles. The curvature of his shoulders and spine was like a question mark. "No, you wouldn't," he said.

"What makes you so sure?"

"You converted to a papist, but you're still a river-baptized man. I got the Indian sign on you, counselor."

"I don't know if I like your tone."

"Them people painted acid on my cinch at the rodeo and liked to got me killed. So that gives you and me what's called a shared agenda." He stepped on a rock and mounted his horse. "I done changed my ways, Brother Holland, but the man ain't been born who can use me and walk away from it. Tell Miss Temple I said howdy doodie."

He kicked his horse in the sides and leaned forward with it as it ascended the arroyo, disappearing through the deadfall into the sun's last red rays.

Back at the house I removed the scrap of notebook paper he had given me from my hatband and read the two names penciled on it: L. W. Peeples and Tex Barker. There was a third name, Mabus, written in the corner, at an angle, a notation that I suspected had been made there at another time and was unrelated to the issue of the two hired killers.

"What are you looking at?" Temple said.

We were in the living room, and outside I could see snow crystals blowing in the light from the gallery. I told her about Wyatt Dixon's visit.

"I can't find words to describe my feelings on this. This man is out of the abyss, Billy Bob," she said.

"I'll get rid of him."

"When?"

"Can you run these two names through NCIC?"

"You know I can. How are you going to get rid of Dixon?"

"I'll figure a way. I give you my word," I replied, refusing to meet her eyes.

But by next morning I still had no plan for getting Wyatt Dixon out of our lives, or at least off our property and away from my office. Temple went through her San Antonio contact and ran the two names Wyatt had given me through the computer at the National Crime Information Center. She called me at noon.

"There's nothing on these guys," she said.

"No arrests at all?"

"The names don't correlate with any particular individual. Can you imagine how many offenders have the nickname Tex?"

"How about the other guy — Peeples?"

"Yeah, there're plenty of them. But none with the initials L.W. Billy Bob, do you actually believe a basket case like Wyatt Dixon is a credible source of information?"

The rest of the afternoon I tried to think of a solution to my situation with Wyatt. Lawyers don't ask witnesses questions they themselves don't know the answer to; wise men don't make deals with the devil; and sane people don't unscrew the head of a man like Wyatt Dixon and spit in it. Why had I been so foolish?

By 5 p.m. my head was pounding. There was only one way out of my problem, and the thought of doing what I had to do made sweat run down my sides.

I drove through the sawmill town of Bonner and on up the Blackfoot, then parked on the roadside across the river from Wyatt's property. When I crossed the swing bridge, the water down below was roaring with sound, pink and green in the sunset, braiding around rocks that steamed with mist. Wyatt's truck was parked by the half-destroyed house in which he lived, but I saw no sign of him in the yard or down by the riverbank. No lights burned inside the house.

I walked under a birch tree and stood in front of the ruined first floor and called out his name. But there was no answer. I threw a rock on the tin roof. A stone barbecue pit was smoking by the side of the house, a steak dripping fat into the coals. I threw another rock on the roof.

"Why not knock on the door like a white man?" a voice said from above.

I looked up into the birch tree. Wyatt sat on a thick limb, his back against the trunk, eating from a carton of peach ice cream.

"I came here to make a confession to you," I said.

"I look like a papist minister?"

"That threatening note you found in your mailbox?" I was looking almost straight up in the tree, my vertebrae and neck tendons starting to stress. But that was not the real cause of my discomfort. I could actually feel my heart hitting against my ribs. "It was a fake. I wrote it. Your cinch breaking at the rodeo was an accident. I was in the stands and saw you get stomped and decided to make use of the situation."

He continued to spoon ice cream out of the carton and put it in his mouth, his eyes hooded, his mouth as cold-looking as a slit in a side of frozen meat.

"I was playing with your head, Wyatt. I showed you a lack of respect, and for that I'm here to apologize," I said. "But I'm also asking you not to come around us anymore. We've got to have that understanding."

The only sound was the wind puffing in the tree and the water coursing along the riverbank, as steady as the sustained hum of a sewing machine. I swallowed as I waited for him to speak, then tried to work the crick

193

out of my neck. I heard him drop the spoon into the empty carton.

"There's a heifer herebouts I punched a time or two, and I don't mean put my brand on, either," he said. "The house she lives in got tore up pretty bad during my reconnoitering."

"Hold on a minute. As an officer of the court, I have to report any crimes I have knowledge of, outside of those confessed to me by a client."

"Work out your own goddamn problems, counselor. Right now I'm having thoughts that tell me it's time for my chemical cocktail or I might do something both of us is gonna regret." He dropped to the ground suddenly and was standing in front of me, his breath cold in my face, the veins in his neck like purple spiderweb. "That detective, Darrel McComb, has got me figured for the break-in at that woman's house. That means she's got me figured for it. That means them two killers got me figured for it. You starting to get the picture?"

I slipped my hands in my back pockets and stepped back from him. "In the past you did great injury to my wife," I said. "As a Christian, I'm supposed to forgive you for it. I don't know if I've done that, but I've tried to put it aside. I'm asking you to do the same. If you don't, one of us is going to end up in long-term refrigeration."

He wiped ice cream off his mouth with his

wrist and looked at it. "Ain't no man uses me, Brother Holland."

"I believe you. Do what you have to do. I can't change it."

I walked all the way to the swing bridge before I looked back at him. He had not moved. He was staring at the ground, his thumbs hooked in the pockets of his jeans, his back at a crooked angle. I walked back toward him and he heard my footsteps in the grass. He turned, the colorless, glasslike quality of his eyes tinted with the redness of the sun.

"Bible says, 'Don't tempt the Lord thy God.' Same warning applies to some men," he said.

"The name 'Mabus' was written on the notepaper you gave me. What does it mean?"

"It was wrote down on several places inside the house that got reconnoitered. But let's stick with the subject at hand. Why'd you run a game on me, counselor? Why'd you go and do that to both of us?"

For just a moment I thought I saw a genuine look of sadness in his face.

I hated violence. Or at least I told myself I did. My family history was filled with it. My great-grandfather was Sam Morgan Holland, an ex–Confederate soldier and gunfighter and finally a saddle preacher who shot between five and nine men. My father died in a pipeline blowout while doing a repair weld, and his death may have been deliberately caused by a man who envied and hated him and opened a valve at a pump station to ensure that gas would be inside the pipe when the electric arc struck it.

As Texas Rangers, L. Q. Navarro and I had waged a private war against drug mules in northern Mexico. We never shot down an unarmed man or refused him quarter when he walked toward us with his hands on his head. But the night ambushes we set up were guaranteed to result in firefights and not negotiations. This particular group of drug transporters, or at least their compatriots, tortured a friend of ours to death, a DEA agent who was one of the finest men I ever knew. We trapped them in adobe huts, mesquite thickets, riverbottoms, and arroyos thick with cactus, and dawn would find us inserting playing cards emblazoned with the shield of the Texas Rangers into the mouths of the dead.

But no matter what the war advocates of our times tell us, no violent excursion ends well. L. Q. Navarro paid with his life for our grandiose schemes, and I still feared sleep and the images that dwelt in my unconscious. That night I sat by myself in the living room until 3 a.m. The valley was dark, the fir trees on the mountains shaggy in the starlight. I could hear deer or elk clatter against our rail fence, a rock tumble from the hillside, a pinecone ping on the barn's metal roof. Was Wyatt out there? I doubted it, not tonight.

But it was only a matter of time, I thought. Men such as Wyatt Dixon were driven by ego and a visceral pride in themselves. In fact, their perception of themselves was actually their only possession. I had just managed to cheapen Wyatt's image of himself, and I knew one day soon the bill would come due.

At the time I did not know there were other people in the area who were even more foolish and reckless than I, a bunch who had just embarked on the worst mistake in their lives.

CHAPTER 11

The next morning started off in earnest with Darrel McComb in my office, a martial light in his face. His cheeks were bladed with color, his crew cut stiff as hog bristles, his suit freshly pressed, his shoes spit-shined and gleaming.

"You look like a man in motion, Darrel," I said.

"What were you doing at Wyatt Dixon's place yesterday?"

"You've got Dixon under surveillance?"

"Duh," he answered.

"It's none of your business what I was doing there."

"Somebody tossed Greta Lundstrum's house. Somebody who could tear two-by-four joists in half with his hands. Sound like anybody you know?"

"If you think Dixon is a viable suspect, go talk to him. Right now I'm pretty busy."

"What was he looking for?"

I could tell he didn't expect an answer, but I surprised him and myself as well. "I think a couple of new shooters are in the area." I wrote down the names Dixon had given me and shoved them across the desk. "Temple came up empty on these guys. Maybe you'll do better."

"You're running some type of police investigation on your own?"

"I didn't say that. And I don't know anything about Dixon breaking into a house, either. If I were you, I'd be careful, Darrel."

"About what?"

"I'm not sure what kind of work you used to do for the G, but I suspect it was down in the basement, off the computer, and genuinely nasty. If I know that, other people do, too. My guess is they're not happy you know their secrets or how they operate."

"I've known some prissy lawyers in my career, but you've got your own zip code, Holland. You got these names from Dixon, didn't you?"

"Maybe."

"What makes you think you have some kind of privileged status in this case? If I catch you holding back information in a homicide investigation, I'll do everything in my power to have you disbarred. Who the hell do you think you are?"

"I can sympathize with your situation, Darrel. You don't get a lot of help. But you beat up a friend of mine with a blackjack. It was a lousy thing to do. So don't be pointing your finger in my face."

I saw his jawbone tighten. He looked sideways, out the window. "So maybe I'd change that, I mean about American Horse."

He waited for me to speak. When I didn't, he opened the door to let himself out.

"Darrel?" I said.

"What?"

"Does the name 'Mabus' mean anything to you?"

"No." He looked hard at me. "Why? Who is he?"

"Probably no one important. Forget I mentioned it," I replied.

"Were you really an assistant U.S. attorney?" he said.

All morning Darrel McComb remained agitated and angry. He was convinced now that Wyatt Dixon had broken into Greta Lundstrum's bungalow and that Dixon had taken information of some kind from the house and was sharing it with an attorney. Now, through the attorney, Darrel had obtained the names of two men who were possibly hired gunmen recently arrived in the area. He started to go into the sheriff's office and tell him of everything he had discovered, then realized he would also have to tell the sheriff he was in the sack with a woman he was using as a confidential informant, one who was perhaps involved with criminal activity.

Darrel had arranged a supper date with Greta that evening. And once again he knew his interests in her were far from purely professional. His memories of their tryst Saturday night caused sexual stirrings in him that made him wonder if part of him wasn't still locked in adolescence. He was also starting to experience another problem, one that was like a sixteen-penny nail driven into his skull. He felt he had betrayed Amber by sleeping with Greta. It made no sense at all. Amber treated him as though he were a moral cretin, a bumbling loser she could dress down at a public dance. To get rid of his own guilt feelings, he let himself imagine Amber in bed with Johnny American Horse, her knees spread on top of him, Johnny's hands cupped on her breasts, her mouth open and her eyes sealed with her passion. Then he felt such rage at the vision in his head he smashed his fist into a locker door while other cops stared at him, bewildered at his behavior.

He tried to eat lunch in a café downtown but couldn't finish his food. He returned to the department, checked out a cruiser, and headed for Stevensville. At first Greta had been devastated by the damage done to her home, but she had quickly regained control of herself, substituting anger and resolve for loss and helplessness. In fact, Darrel was impressed. She had moved into a motel, put someone else in charge at her office, and hired carpenters, roofers, drywallers, and painters to repair her house. She worked side by side with them, firing a nailgun into studs, rolling paint onto drywall, rope-pulling bales of shingles onto the roof. The workmen showed up at 7 a.m., called her "ma'am," and did not use profanity within earshot of her.

When he pulled into the driveway she was on the roof, in white painter's pants, a cute white cap on her head. She climbed down the ladder, a hammer swinging from a cloth loop on her side. "How you doin', handsome?" she said.

"Thought I'd check out how it's going, maybe update you on a couple of things I found out," he replied.

But she seemed uninterested. She tucked a strand of hair in her cap and watched a carpenter running an electric saw through a board. Then she turned back at him and smiled. "Want to have some lunch and maybe a little rest break?" she said.

He felt his loins tingle, his hand close on the steering wheel, and again wondered who was controlling whom.

"I already ate. I'm on the clock, anyway," he said.

"Good, that makes two of us. I have to be back here by three. Follow me to my motel. There's a restaurant next door where you can park the cruiser. I'm in room six."

She pinched his chin, got in her SUV, and drove off.

He waited five minutes, filling out the log for the cruiser, then followed her. He parked on the far side of the restaurant, bought a roll of breath mints from the cashier, used the restroom, and exited the building by the same door he had entered. He cut behind the building, found Greta's room on the back side of the motel, and knocked on the door.

She opened it on the chain, and through the crack he could see she already had her shirt off. She slipped the chain and let him in, then rechained the door and set the night lock. The curtains were closed, the air-conditioning unit turned on full blast, the room as frigid and dark as the interior of an icehouse. She worked her painter's pants off and kicked them into a corner. "Come on, honey bunny, the clock's ticking," she said.

He couldn't quite believe the facility and level of intensity with which she entered love-making — almost like a prostitute, but with an obvious and unembarrassed joy. She came before he did, then mounted him and came a second time with him, collapsing next to him, laughing, biting his ear.

"That one put me on the moon," she said.

"I hear that a lot," he said.

"Don't take a compliment lightly," she said, and hit him playfully with her knee. Then, before he could reply, she was in the shower.

Was she jerking him around as badly as he was beginning to think? Maybe it was time to find out. She came out of the bathroom, blotting at her hair with a folded towel, another towel wrapped around her. She touched at a red swelling under her arm, examining it, then saw him watching her and lowered her arm.

"Ever hear of two guys by the names of L. W. Peeples and Tex Barker?" he asked.

She faced the opposite direction, dropped her towel, and began putting on her undergarments. "No, who are they?" she said.

"Their names have turned up in the B&E investigation on your house."

She was hooking up her bra now and he could see her face.

"These were the men who broke in?" she said.

"No, a source in the investigation says these names were written down someplace in your house. The perpetrator or perpetrators was after names and information, not money or jewelry. That's what all this seems to be about, Greta — information. What do you say about that?"

She bent over and began putting on her painter's pants. She lifted her eyes into his. "I say I think that's the dumbest thing I ever heard."

"You don't know anybody named L. W. Peeples or Tex Barker?"

"What did I just tell you?"

Her eyes were unblinking, her indignation convincing.

"How about somebody named Mabus?" he asked.

She buttoned her painter's pants, her face lowered now, her jaws flexing with the effort to fasten a button. She reached over to pick up her shirt from a chair, and in the side of her eye he saw the bright glimmer of fear. "You *do* know somebody named Mabus?" he said.

"I've heard his name mentioned in business conversations. I don't know how he could have anything to do with the destruction of my house."

"I think Wyatt Dixon had the name of this guy in his possession. Why would a hayseed like Dixon be interested in it?"

"I'm sure I don't know, Darrel."

She tried to look abstract and uninterested, but he could see the prickles in her throat.

"I like you a lot, Greta," he said, almost surprised at the genuineness in his statement. "I think you're in trouble and can't tell anybody about it. Sometimes people just get in over their heads. It's like making a wrong turn in a bad neighborhood. You don't know how you got there, but suddenly you're drowning in a world of hurt. If you can be square with me, maybe we can get you out of this."

"Perhaps you mean well, but this scenario you're describing is comic opera. Really, I mean it. You're a nice guy, but —" She picked up her cute white hat and placed it on her head. "You're looking at a Maryland country girl, Darrel. There's no mystery here. Just an upper South gal trying to make it out here in the Wild West."

He was sitting on the bed in his trousers and strap undershirt, his shoulders rounded. Her denial filled him with a sense of depression like a chemical assault on his system. It was always ordinary people who got in the gravest trouble with the law, he thought. In a peculiar way they retained their innocent belief in a benevolent society that was created especially for them, right up to the time they shuffled off on a wrist chain and entered the belly of the beast.

"Why so glum?" she asked.

"No reason. Thanks for the nooner."

She wagged a finger at him. "I like you a lot, Darrel, but I don't appreciate coarseness. My father was a minister and I grew up in a good home," she said.

Late the next evening two men pulled up in front of a bar on the lower end of the Blackfoot River, not far from the confluence it formed with the Clark Fork. Their pickup truck had an Idaho tag, and fishing rods were propped up in the bed of the truck. The men stood outside the truck, drinking beer from cans, surveying the stilt houses on the riverbank, the independent grocery store across the state road, kids jumping from an abandoned steel bridge into the river, the smoke from the sawmill drifting up the walls of the Blackfoot Canyon. The evening light was a greenish-yellow, the air warm and cool at the same time, the bloom from cotton-wood trees floating on the breeze.

One man was truncated, his muscular arms too short for his torso. He had a high fore-head, receding hairline, and eyes that were set too low in his face. He wore heavy shoes with thick heels and double soles, a wide leather belt through the loops of his jeans, a faded purple T-shirt with a winged dragon printed on it, and a nylon vest that still had a sales tag on it. There were furrows in his brow, as though he were frowning, but in reality a worried look was his natural expression.

His companion was tall and had a formless posture and skin that was milky and dotted with moles. He wore an old fedora, a dark shirt that hung outside his pants, and leather-laced alpine trail shoes that were dusty from wear. He finished his beer and leaned against a headlight on the truck, his chest slightly caved, his stomach protruding over his belt. He watched a young woman pull her laundry from a coin-operated machine, next door to the bar. When the woman looked up and realized she was being stared at, he tipped his hat to her and shifted his attention elsewhere.

The two men went inside the bar and

ordered hamburgers and fries and cups of coffee. While they waited for their food, they took turns walking to the front door and glancing outside.

"You boys expecting somebody?" the bartender said.

"No, can't say we are," the taller man said. He let his eyes linger on the bartender's until the bartender looked away. "We were wondering if it's too late in the day to get on the stream. I hear the salmon flies are hatching."

"There's still a few hatching out," the bartender said.

"That's what I thought," the taller man said, nodding, looking at the door.

"Your food's ready," the bartender said.

The men ate in silence, sometimes gazing at the massive elk head mounted over the front entrance or at someone playing the pinball machine. The truncated man used the pay phone, then sat back down and finished his coffee. "You know a cowboy name of Wyatt Dixon?" he asked the bartender.

"He comes in for his beer," the bartender replied. He was a dark-haired, broad-chested man who had been a gypo — an independent or wandering logger — before he had suffered a heart attack, and the backs of his broad hands were laced with boomer-chain scars. Now he served drinks in a saloon and wore a waxed mustache for the benefit of tourists.

"He comes in on Thursday nights?" the truncated man said.

The bartender wiped the bar idly, then propped his arms on it, his gaze fixed on nothing. "Wyatt don't bother anybody. Least not here he don't. If you got the wrong kind of business with him, you take it somewhere else," he said.

The man in the fedora put a toothpick in his mouth. "We owe him some money for some rough stock. That's why we asked if he came in here. Otherwise we wouldn't be troubling you. Can you relate to that?" he said.

"The two burgers and the coffee are eleven dollars," the bartender said.

When the two fishermen left, the bartender walked to the front window, studied their license tag, and wrote the number in pencil on the doorjamb. Then he rubbed the number out with the palm of his hand and marked off the whole affair as none of his business.

Temple was the best investigator I ever knew. When she could not find information using conventional means, she would spend hours or days on the Internet, in libraries and county clerks' offices, or on the telephone cajoling information out of various law enforcement agencies. I should have known she would not rest until she found out exactly who Tex Barker and L. W. Peeples were.

The same evening the two fishermen had visited the bar on the Blackfoot, Temple got off the phone in our home office and came into the living room, a clipboard in her hand. She blew her breath upward to remove a strand of hair from her eyes. "Don't trust computers," she said.

"What have you got?" I said.

"Wyatt Dixon told you he heard about one of these guys while he was in San Quentin? Something about a guy who'd do a yard job on another inmate for thirty dollars, right? But the computer search at the NCIC didn't pick up the names 'Barker' and 'Peeples' as Quentin graduates, at least not during the time frame Dixon was there.

"So I broadened the search through the entirety of the California system. A guy named Jeff Barker was in Soledad and Atascadero during the same period Dixon was at Quentin. So I called up Soledad and talked to a psychologist there who remembered him. Barker's nickname was Tex. He's not from Texas, though. He got his nickname because he loves Tex-Mex food and was always smuggling it into his cell and heating it up on a stinger and blowing the circuit breaker on the cell block.

"Same computer problem finding L. W. Peeples. Because there is no L. W. Peeples. But a guy named Lynwood Peeples, from Opa Locka, Florida, *was* in the computer. As it turned out, Lynwood was a cellmate of Barker in Soledad."

"You always amaze me," I said.

"Why?" she said, amused, blowing her breath up into her face again.

She was sitting on the couch, across from me, her hair lit by a floor lamp. I sat down next to her and put my arm around her. Her shoulders felt smooth and firm, her upper arms taut from the daily kick-boxer workouts she did on the heavy bag hanging in the barn. I kissed the back of her neck.

"Better listen to what else I found out about these two," she said.

"Can it wait?"

"No, these guys are real assholes. Barker was a suspect in the rape of a couple of children. While he was in Soledad, the blacks were using white guys who had a short-eyes jacket for bars of soap, so he did some yard hits with an ice pick for both the Mexican Mafia and the Aryan Brotherhood. He's been out four years now, with no arrests, which is unusual for a guy whose sheet goes back two decades.

"Lynwood Peeples grew up on a horse farm in northern Dade County. He hung a lot of paper and got caught doping a quarter horse at a summer track in California. I called Miami-Dade P.D. and talked to a homicide cop who said Peeples probably jobs out for the Mob, but they're not sure. Get this. When he was seventeen, he married a fifteen-year-old girl from Georgia. Two years later, what was left of her body showed up in the Everglades."

"Peeples did it?"

"It's anybody's guess. He reported her missing and claimed she was always running off with migrant farmworkers down at Florida City. The body was so decomposed and eaten by crabs the coroner couldn't even determine the cause of death."

Outside, the top of the sky was still lit, the valley floor dark, the hillsides streaked with shadows made by the trees. Our windows were open and I could hear our horses blowing in the pasture and smell the odor of wet grass and water coursing through the irrigation ditches.

I wondered how men such as these could come into our midst, here in a verdant world that in some ways was little different from the way Earth must have looked on the sixth day of creation.

"Does either of these guys have a military background?" I asked.

She glanced through her notes and several fax sheets attached to her clipboard. "None that I could find. Why?"

"The two killers who went after Johnny American Horse were ex-soldiers. But Johnny turned the pair of them into lunch meat. I think whoever is hiring these guys decided to

212

reach down into the bottom of the septic tank for the real article."

Temple set the clipboard beside her, her eyes straight ahead. I heard her exhale her breath. "You think they're coming after us?" she asked.

"We're no threat to them. They'll figure that out," I said, my voice tight with my lie.

"I'm going to bed," she said.

She got up and walked toward the dining room. Then I heard her pause in the doorway. "You coming?" she said.

But I didn't get up from the couch. "I think I've gotten us into a bad one, Temple," I said.

"If they come here, they'll wish they hadn't. Come on, Ranger. I can't fall asleep by myself," she said.

The dawn broke cool and misty on the Blackfoot, the sky crackling with electricity from an impending storm, the river green and swollen with rain. Smoke flattened off the chimney of Wyatt Dixon's house and a light burned in the kitchen. Wyatt came outside in only jeans and a T-shirt, notched an apple in half while he watched the sun's glow spread on the mountain crests, then fed half the apple off the flat of his hand to his Appaloosa and ate the other half himself. His T-shirt was printed with the words RODEO NAKED — YOUR CHEEKS NEED THE COLOR.

He heard rocks toppling down the hillside behind him, but when he looked up through the fir trees he saw two mountain sheep working their way up an arroyo and he paid no more attention to the sounds they made. A moment later someone started a vehicle on the dirt road that curved away around a wooded bend. Wyatt heard the transmission clank into gear, then the tires clicking on the gravel as the vehicle headed in the opposite direction. He went back inside, fired his woodstove, poured coffee grinds and water into a tin pot, and set the pot to boil.

Down the road someone was having a fight. He heard a woman shout, then a car or truck door slam, followed by more shouting. Enough was enough. He opened the kitchen window and stuck his head out. "Shut up that goddamn racket!" he yelled.

It was warm and snug in the kitchen, the iron lids on his stove etched with light from the firebox. The rest of the lower floor had been destroyed by river ice, but the kitchen had been built on higher ground and the glass was still in the windows, the shelves, icebox, and chimney intact. He heated a skillet, then poured flapjack batter into it and broke eggs on the side. He removed a jar of jam and a stick of butter and a loaf of bread from the icebox, toasted the bread in a separate skillet, and sat down to eat.

He looked up and saw a fat Indian woman

with braids staring at him through the window. Before he could get up from the chair, she had gone around to the front of the house. A moment later, she was pounding on the door with her fist.

"Nobody home! Get out of here!" he yelled.

"Help me!" she cried.

He walked through the clutter in the front of the house and jerked open the door. "Was you the woman yelling her head off down the road?" he said.

She smelled of sweat, talcum powder, river damp, and alcohol, and her dress looked like a burlap tent fitted over a haystack. Her left eye was swollen and watery, as though it had been stung by a bee. "My husband says he's gonna kill me and my baby. Call the police," she said.

"See any phone wires going to this house?" Wyatt said.

"He's got a knife. He took the car keys and run up the hill," she said.

Wyatt walked out onto the grass. He gazed up the hill and at the trees and at the birds singing in them and at the steam rising off the river. Dry thunder rippled across the sky. He watched his Appaloosa in the railed lot in back of the house. The Appaloosa was eating grass through the fence, tearing it out in divots. "Where's the baby at?" Wyatt said.

"In my car. I ran away. I was scared," she said.

"Your baby is in the car and your old man is up on that hill and you're here?"

"Yes, sir."

"I ain't no 'sir.' I tell you what. I got to take a shower. Bring your baby to the house and I'll drive y'all into Missoula. I'll leave the door unlocked. In the meantime, I don't want to hear no more yelling or carrying on out here."

He closed the door in her face.

The woman walked back down the road and around the bend the road made between two wooded hills. Wyatt stood among the water-damaged furniture in his living room, tossing a cell phone and catching it in his palm. She was a half-breed, he thought, one he had seen somewhere before. A truck stop outside Billings or Bozeman? He wasn't sure. Truckers called them pavement princesses. This one looked more like Native America's answer to the Bride of Frankenstein, he thought.

But the important fact was that she hadn't asked him if he had a cell phone, even though it had been sticking out of his jeans pocket in full view. He flipped open his cell and brought up the numbers he kept in the memory bank. He looked at my number, pushed the dial button, then thought about it a moment and killed the call. He slipped the cell back in his pocket and went upstairs to the shower.

He turned on the water and put his hand inside the spray until steam began to drift out the open window. He pulled off his T-shirt and hung it on the outside doorknob, brushed his teeth in the basin, and spit. When he looked into the mirror, his own face reminded him of the edge of a hatchet. Through the window he heard his Appaloosa nicker in the lot.

The two killers, whose names were Tex Barker and Lynwood Peeples, worked their way down the slope through fir trees until they hit the dirt road. They moved quickly through the blueness of the dawn, into the lee of the house, flattening themselves against the side wall so they would not be seen from a window. They could hear the shower running upstairs and see steam floating through a screened window into the wind. They began working their way toward the back door while Wyatt Dixon's Appaloosa spooked in circles.

When they entered the kitchen, the firebox in the stove was glowing, the circular iron lids immaculately clean with heat. A plate of flapjacks, eggs, and toast and a full pot of coffee sat on the table. The shorter man, Tex Barker, whose gnarled brow was too long for the rest of his face, snapped on a stun gun, and an electric thread danced between the two prongs on the end. His partner,

Lynwood, carried a .22 Ruger semiautomatic in one hand and in the other a cloth bag framed with wood hasps and a wood handle, one similar in design to a nineteenth-century carpetbag. The two men began walking up the stairs toward the sounds of water drumming on the sides of a tin shower stall.

At the top of the stairs they could see a T-shirt hanging on the outside knob of a door that was half opened on the bathroom. Tex Barker was in the lead, the stun gun tingling with power in his palm. Then Barker felt his partner grab him by the back of his belt. He turned and stared at him.

"His food's getting cold on the table. Something's wrong," Lynwood whispered.

"What did you say?" Tex asked.

Lynwood was starting to back down the stairs, his cloth bag rubbing heavily against the wall.

"No. We take him," Tex said hoarsely.

But Lynwood wasn't listening. *Force the play, just do it,* Barker thought, and charged ahead to the top of the stairs, his stubby thighs knotting like a dwarf's.

"Howdy doodie, boys?" Wyatt Dixon said, stepping out from a bedroom doorway and swinging a cast-iron skillet squarely into the center of Tex Barker's face.

Barker crashed backwards into his partner, his nose broken and streaming blood. Lynwood Peeples tried to raise the Ruger and fire, but the iron skillet came down on his forearm, snapping something inside, and he felt his fingers straighten like useless sticks and heard the gun clatter to the foot of the stairs. Wyatt swung the skillet into Peeples's mouth, splitting his lip, then down on the crown of his skull and the back of his neck. Peeples and Barker both rolled to the bottom of the stairwell, but Wyatt followed them down and swung again, this time catching Peeples on the elbow when he tried to protect his face with his arm.

Each blow snapped off teeth at the gumline, sent bruises all the way into the bone, slung blood on the walls. With one hand Wyatt picked up Peeples by his collar and shoved his face down on a stove lid and held it there. Barker was rolled up into a ball, but while Peeples screamed and fought to get loose from Wyatt's grasp, Barker managed to pull a stiletto from his jeans and flick it open. He stabbed the blade deep into Wyatt's thigh, just before the skillet came down again and almost ripped Barker's ear from his head.

Barker fell out the door into the backyard, with Peeples tumbling right on top of him, the side of his face blistered and puckered from his chin to his hairline. Wyatt pushed open the screen and stepped down hard onto the grass, the stiletto embedded almost to the handle in his thigh, his pants leg painted with blood all the way to the heel of his boot. But Wyatt no longer had the skillet in his hand. Instead, he held what looked like an antique rifle, one with a big hammer on it and long-distance, elevated sights. When Peeples tried to get to his feet, Wyatt butt-stroked him alongside the head, then drove the butt of the rifle into his kidney.

And all the while Wyatt's eyes showed neither pain nor anger, like two pieces of glass with a black insect trapped inside each one. At that moment Barker was sure he was about to die. Then he saw Wyatt waver and lose balance temporarily, his eyes close and his mouth form a cone, as though a wave of nausea had suddenly washed through his vitals.

Barker rose to his feet, then pulled Peeples up from the grass by one arm. The two of them hobbled down the road like men who had been broken on the wheel, holding each other erect, streaked with blood, looking behind them, their faces twitching with shock and fear. Wyatt fell against the fence railing of his horse lot and pulled back the hammer on the working replica of his Sharps buffalo rifle. But the mountain crests and the fir trees on the slopes and the cottonwoods along the river tilted sideways, and he fell backward on the ground as though someone had severed all the motors that went to his legs.

He pulled the cell phone from his blue

jeans pocket and pushed the redial button, then lay back in the coolness of the grass, the cell phone against his ear, the sky and the clouds whirling above him.

"Howdy doodie, Brother Holland?" he said after he got me on the line.

"What is it this time, Wyatt?" I said.

"I'm up here on the Blackfoot. Beautiful morning, counselor. But I think I might be bleeding to death," he said, and passed out.

CHAPTER 12

That evening I sat by Wyatt Dixon's bed at St. Pat's Hospital and tried to figure out the strange processes that must have governed his thinking. Had he called me rather than 911 only because my number was automatically activated by the redial button? Or had he factored me into his life as some kind of symbiotic brother-in-arms? And, more essentially, how could a man who was so brave be capable of so much evil? He had perhaps come within fifteen minutes of dying, had been in surgery four hours, and now lay in traction, his thigh encased in plaster, refusing painkillers, because, he explained, "Dope puts un-Christian-like thoughts in my brain cells."

He stonewalled the cops, stating he had no idea who had attacked him or where the attackers had gone. "What I have told you officers is just a picture from the other side of life in this land of the free and home of the brave," he said. "It is like many a sad situation in the world of dim lights, thick smoke, and loud, loud music, where honky-tonk angels and men with broken hearts play. Sirs, I have came often upon these scenes of destruction, and I heard the groans of the dying but I

222

didn't hear nobody pray."

The cops put away their notebooks in disgust and left the room.

Except for Darrel McComb, who stood at the foot of the bed, snapping a piece of gum between his molars. "You a fan of Vern Gosdin and Hank Williams? Don't bother answering that. I just wanted you to be aware I know where all that cornpone crap comes from," Darrel said.

"In my correspondence with President Bush, I have asked him to put aside extra money for lawmen such as yourself. While the rest of us is sleeping safe in our beds, you are out there fighting the criminals that is turning our great country into a dungheap. Even when I was standing dirty and hungry on the punishment barrel in Huntsville Pen, I knowed it was men like you that was protecting the nation from the likes of me. You have kept the Stars and Stripes popping smartly atop every institution in our fine nation, including the jails where this lonely cowboy slept in shackles and chains. I say God bless you, noble sir."

"You listen, you hillbilly moron," Darrel said. "I know you broke into Greta Lundstrum's house. You think you're some kind of one-man intelligence operation? Here's a big flash for you. Meltdowns and ignorant peckerwoods don't get to be intelligence operatives. You got the names of Tex

Barker and Lynwood Peeples out of her house. Those are the guys who buried that shank in your thigh. They were carrying a bagful of tools to torture you with. Is it starting to add up for you now? You've stuck your dork in the wall socket, Gomer. That means you start cooperating with us or we're going to let them recycle you into fish chum."

Wyatt stared at Darrel McComb, his mouth twisting with each word Darrel spoke, his eyes blinking with feigned awe. "You have done convinced me of the fact you are not an ordinary policeman. I am contacting President Bush immediately to see if he can find federal employment for you. I have never seen such a shameful waste of mental talents."

"Who's Mabus?" Darrel asked.

Wyatt started to speak, then was silent. A strange transformation seemed to take place in his face. He looked straight ahead, his eyes thoughtful, his mouth compressed. He raised his right hand off the sheet and ticked a callus with his thumbnail, his eyes uplifted at Darrel now. "I ain't sure who he is. But I got a notion he's a whole lot bigger than any little shithouse operation you got around here. I seen that name wrote inside a —"

"Inside what?" Darrel said.

"I need my chemical cocktail. I'm done talking with you," Wyatt said, his sardonic attitude gone now, his expression sullen.

After Darrel McComb left the room, a nurse brought in a glass containing the orange medicine that smelled as if it had been dipped out of a settling pond at a sewage works. Wyatt drank the glass empty and continued to stare into space.

"You saw the name 'Mabus' written inside what, Wyatt?" I said.

"A pentagram. The woman who wrote it there knows what a pentagram means, too. Her daddy was a preacher."

"The sign of the devil?"

"I ain't got no more to say on it. God, my leg hurts. Them boys who visited me was a pair of mean motor scooters, wasn't they?"

The next afternoon, Saturday, I was Johnny American Horse's best man at his and Amber Finley's wedding on the lawn of a small white woodframe church with a tiny belfry, set against the backdrop of the Mission Mountains, rising like ancient glaciers straight out of the green earth into the clouds. The ceremony was conducted by both a Methodist minister and an Indian shaman who was the great-grandson of the Lakota mystic Black Elk. Amber wore a white dress with frills on it and purple suede cowboy boots, and looked radiant and happy and beautiful in the sunshine. Johnny, conservative as always, wore what was evidently his only suit, one that brought back memories I did not want to entertain on such a fine afternoon. The suit and vest were narrow-cut, dark pin-stripe, just like the suit worn by L. Q. Navarro on the night he died.

Johnny and Amber had sent out no formal invitations, but the churchyard was crowded with their friends — wranglers, feed growers from the Jocko Valley, musicians, log haulers, university professors, hard-core drunks, organic farmers, writers and artists, Indians from the Salish, Northern Cheyenne, Crow, and Blackfeet reservations, and weirded-out, mind-altered people who still believed the year was 1968.

The reception was in a saloon, the dinner a pig and half of a buffalo barbecued over a pit of flaming wood dug in a grove of cotton-woods. The orchestra was a western string band put together by my son, Lucas, and the dance was held on a cement pad under a lilac sky, the snow on the Missions red in the sunset, the music of Bob Wills and Rose Maddox floating out over a countryside knee-deep in alfalfa and pooled with duck ponds.

Everyone important in Amber's life was there. Except for her father, United States Senator Romulus Finley.

Senator Finley was at my office by 8 a.m. Monday. When he didn't find me there, he went to the courthouse, where I was involved in a trial, and caught me in the corridor outside the courtroom. "What in the goddamn hell do you think you're doing, son?" he said, his grip biting into my arm.

"I'd appreciate your taking your hand off my person," I said.

"A murderer just married my daughter, and you helped him do it."

"I'm not going to ask you again," I said.

He released me and took a step back. "I won't put up with this bullshit, Mr. Holland."

"I think you embarrass yourself, sir," I said.

"Say that again?"

"Your daughter is a good person. Why don't you show her a little respect?"

"Son, I'm just about a half inch from busting you between the lights."

"My father was a stringer-bead welder on gaslines all over the Southwest. He was a fine man and called me 'son.' Other men don't."

"Have it your way. As far as I'm concerned, Johnny American Horse is a subversive and a traitor. He's taken advantage of my daughter's naïveté and you, an educated man and officer of the court, have helped him do it. I won't put up with it."

He walked back down the corridor toward the courthouse entrance, his leather soles loud, his meaty shoulders and neck framed against the light outside.

I should have dismissed the insult, even the implied threat, as the expression of wounded pride in a childish man. But there was something about Finley that was hard to abide, a prototypical personality any southerner recognizes — one characterized by a combination of self-satisfaction, stupidity, and a suggestion of imminent violence, all of it glossed over with a veneer of moral and patriotic respectability.

I followed him down the sidewalk through the maples on the courthouse lawn to a steel-gray limousine with charcoal-tinted windows that was parked by the curb. He opened the back door to get in, and on the far side of the leather seat I saw a man in his fifties who had a good-natured face, blond hair that was white on the tips, a smile that was both familiar and likable. His eyes were friendly and warm, his teeth almost perfect. There were gin roses in his face, but they gave his countenance a vulnerability and consequently a greater humanity. I was sure I knew him and at the same time equally sure we had never met.

Romulus Finley started to raise a remonstrative finger at me, but his companion leaned over so he could look at both of us and said, "Now, now, let's don't have this. Mr. Holland, take a ride with us. We'll have coffee at a dandy place on the river."

"Thank you just the same, but I have an issue here with Senator Finley," I replied.

"Whatever it is, we can work it out," Finley's companion replied. He stretched out his arm and handed me a business card that was inserted between two of his fingers. "My home phone is on the back. I'm impressed with your legal reputation. Your father died in a natural gas blowout down in Texas, didn't he? I bet he'd be mighty proud of you today."

"What did you say about my father?"

"Call me," he said. "I'd like to help you cut through some of the problems you're encountering."

He was still smiling at me when Finley got in the limo and closed the door. I stared dumbly at the tinted back window of the limo as it drove away, then looked at the business card in my hand. The name on it was KARSTEN MABUS.

That evening, Temple and I fixed sliced chicken and mayonnaise sandwiches and iced tea and fruit salad for dinner and took it out on the side gallery to eat. The sky was blue above the valley, the sunlight a pale yellow on the hillsides, and hawks floated above the trees up in the saddles. But I couldn't concentrate on either our conversation or the loveliness of the evening. I wiped my mouth with a napkin and pushed away my plate.

"Want to tell me what happened today?" Temple said.

"I had a run-in with Senator Finley. He seems to think I'm responsible for his daughter marrying Johnny American Horse."

"Tell him to grow up."

"I think I did, but I don't remember. I was pretty angry."

"So that's what's been on your mind all day?"

"Finley was with another man. I'd swear I know him but I don't know from where. He gave me his business card."

I took the card out of my shirt pocket and placed it on the pineknot table where she could read it. Unconsciously, I wiped my fingers on my shirt.

"Mabus? He's the CEO of a chemical company?" she said.

"He knew about my father's death on the pipeline."

"How?"

"I don't know. There's something disturbing about this guy."

"You're listening to Wyatt Dixon — that stuff about a pentagram. Dixon's a nutjob, Billy Bob."

"Maybe." I got up from the table and leaned against the railing on the gallery. A string of white-tailed deer were working their way down a switchback trail into the pasture, their summer coats gold in the shadows. "What right does this guy Mabus have to mention my father's death?"

"So tomorrow morning we check him out. Now sit down and eat," she said.

I thought about Johnny and Amber's wedding and how much Johnny, in his pinstripe suit and vest, had reminded me of L. Q. Navarro. "You believe in premonitions?" I said.

"No," she said.

"I don't, either," I said.

The next morning, as I was leaving for work, I found a note under the windshield wiper of my Avalon. It read:

Billy Bob,

Go to Sheep Flats up on the Blackfoot at 9:00 a.m. today. I'll be parked off the dirt track, down in the trees. Drive past my vehicle, then walk back along the riverbank and up the incline to my vehicle. Carry a fishing rod. Do not mention our meeting on either a cell phone or a land line.

I'll wait for you fifteen minutes. If you're not there, I'll assume you're tied up in court. Thanks,

Seth

I drove up into the Blackfoot drainage, crossed a long cement bridge over the river, then turned up a dusty road that climbed high above the river, so that down below, the water looked like a blue ribbon winding through boulders and sloping hills covered with larch and ponderosa and fir trees. I crossed over a rocky point that jutted into space, then coasted down the road into shade and a wooded, parklike area where the remains of a nineteenth-century logging camp had moldered into dark brown pulp.

I saw a Jeep Cherokee parked in the trees and a tall man in a shapeless felt hat leaning against the grille, smoking a pipe, watching the river course over the rocks down below. I did as Seth had asked and drove past the Jeep, then worked my way back on the riverbank through dry boulders and the willows that grew in the shallows, my fly rod over my shoulder.

"Have I got a tap on my phone?" I said.

"Hard to say. My guess is you probably do," he replied.

"I don't care for that, Seth."

"Join the club." He knocked his pipe clean on a rock, then pressed the ashes deep into the soil. "Let me lay it out for you. I gave the Bureau thirty days' notice. This time next month, my wife and I will be on a passenger ship headed up to the Alaskan coast. This fall we'll be hiking in Silver City, New Mexico. I'll officially be an old fart. In the meantime I have to play out this American Horse situation here. You with me so far?"

"I'll try to grab a noun here and there and work with it," I replied. Then I looked at the cast in his eyes and regretted my flippant attitude.

He unzipped a thin vinyl satchel on the Jeep's hood and removed a folder that contained a stack of enlarged mug shots. "You know any of these guys?" he said.

I shuffled through the photos one by one. "No, I've never seen them," I said.

"All of them are either professional intelligence operatives or assassins. I didn't say mobbed-up button men. I said assassins."

"They work for the government?"

"No, guys like me work for the government. These characters work for people *in* the government. At least that's the distinction I've always tried to make. I want you to talk with Amber Finley and Johnny American Horse."

"About what?"

"I believe Amber was with Lester Antelope and the other Indians who creeped that research lab down at Stevensville. The computer files in their possession are going to get each of them killed, in the same way Lester Antelope was killed, in a way nobody even wants to think about. Tell American Horse and the Finley woman to dump whatever they have. Now, not later. They can put it in a paper bag marked 'FBI' and drop it in a mailbox or tie a rock on it and throw it through a window glass in the Federal Building."

"Who's behind this, Seth?"

"That's like asking how original sin got

233

started. I did two tours in Vietnam. I believed in what we were doing there. Then I spent the next thirty-five years picking snakes out of my head. My dad had a great expression. He'd say, 'Son, if everybody agrees on it, it's wrong.'"

Seth's eyes crinkled when he grinned.

I walked back downstream to my car. When I drove back out of the main dirt road, Seth's Jeep was gone. For a moment I thought I saw a flash of light on metal or a pair of binoculars across the river. I stopped my car and stared at the trees on the opposite bank until my eyes burned, then told myself the sunlight was simply dancing on the early morning wetness of the trees and that my eyes and mind were playing tricks on me.

Temple called me at the office later in the day. "Karsten Mabus is the CEO of the parent company that owns Global Research," she said. "He's been in the biotech business for around twenty years. Owns homes in Arlington, Palm Beach, East Hampton, Santa Barbara, and a place he just built out on Highway Twelve. Has a degree in American Studies from Princeton and an MBA from Harvard. He never married, although he appears to be a ladies' man. His estimated worth is over five hundred million."

"How about a military record?"

"None."

"Did he ever live in Texas?"

I heard her leafing through some papers. "He owns a company in Houston and one in Dallas," she said.

"When he mentioned my father's death, he said my father would be mighty proud of me."

"Like he was home folks?" she said.

"That's right."

"According to a feature on him in *The Washington Post*, he was born in Minneapolis and grew up there and in Milwaukee. The article says his father was a hardware store owner and his mother a schoolteacher. Except I couldn't find any records on the family in either city."

"What's his connection to Finley?"

"A friend and campaign contributor, as far as I can see."

"Do you have any idea what Global Research does?"

"They have lots of government contracts. Some of them have to do with genetically altered foods. Some of their other dealings are anybody's guess. They're a high-security outfit. It's amazing their facility was successfully burglarized . . . Did you just hear something on your line?"

"Yeah, I think we're tapped," I said.

"Tapped?" she said.

"Tapped," I said.

That same day Johnny American Horse

235

and two of his workers were putting in a rail fence on a new dude ranch out on Highway 12, not far from the Idaho line, when a panel truck stopped in a rooster tail of dust and the driver, an unshaved man wearing aviator's shades, slacks, and a dirty white shirt, got out and approached Johnny with a grin at the corner of his mouth. "Got some sportsman's hardware to sell before I move out to California," he said.

"Like what?" Johnny said.

The driver threw open the back door of the truck, exposing at least a dozen shotguns and rifles that were laid out on a blanket. "I'll sell them individual or the whole bunch. Dirt cheap, brother. I'll take pretty near any offer," he said.

Johnny shook his head and went back to setting a post in a hole and packing crushed rock around it.

"How about you fellows?" the man asked the two white boys working with Johnny.

"Johnny doesn't pay us that kind of money," one of them replied.

The boys laughed. The driver of the panel truck picked up an AR-15 that was wrapped in an oilcloth, released the magazine, and pulled back the bolt to show the gun was empty. Instead, a shell ejected from the chamber. "Damn, my nephew left a round in there," he said.

Johnny picked the shell out of the dirt and

threw it inside the truck. The man held out the rifle for Johnny to examine it. "Three hundred dollars," he said.

"It's worth six, easy," Johnny said.

"You know your guns." The man tossed the rifle to Johnny.

Johnny caught it in one hand, then walked to the back of the panel truck and set the rifle down on the blanket. "I've said no to you once. Hate to say it again," he said.

"No offense meant. A guy's got to try," the man said.

Johnny and his two employees watched the man drive away, the dust from the truck blowing across a field of timothy. The man stopped at a crossroads where several land surveyors were eating their lunch under a tree and began making the same presentation to them. Johnny lost interest in the gun seller and went back to work.

Two days later, a Thursday, Darrel McComb was in a bad mood. Wyatt Dixon had just checked himself out of the hospital, against medical advice, and the hospital had not informed Darrel, as it had been instructed. Also, Wyatt had continued to stonewall the investigation into the identity of his assailants, speaking in disjointed hillbilly song lyrics, treating the detectives to his idiot's grin and feigning incredulity at the detectives' wisdom.

The nurses and pink ladies puffed his

pillows and brought him soft drinks and out-door magazines from the gift shop and extra desserts from the dining room. In turn, he signed autographs for them as well as the plaster casts of other patients. Darrel tried to explain to the head nurse that Wyatt Dixon was a recidivist whose brain belonged in a jar of alcohol. She replied, "I don't believe that at all. If he's done anything bad, he's already paid his debt to society. Why don't you people leave him alone?"

Later that afternoon Darrel drove up to Dixon's place on the Blackfoot, but no one was at home and Dixon's truck was gone. The neighbor on the opposite side of the river said he believed Wyatt was at a revival up at the Indian reservation.

"Dixon at a revival?" Darrel said.

"That's right."

"This man is a criminal."

"He's a polite man who always tips his hat to my wife. Why don't you flatfeet stop picking on him?" the neighbor said, and slammed the door in Darrel's face.

Darrel drove up to the Indian reservation in the Jocko Valley. It wasn't hard to find the revival. Between a grove of cottonwood trees and a small rodeo arena and pavilion where the annual summer powwows were held, a huge, open-air striped canopy flapped gently in the warm breeze, the mountains blue and jagged in the distance. Darrel parked his unmarked car in the shade of the cottonwoods and watched the people who were arriving for the revival. They were both Indian and white, poor, uneducated, with the distorted physiques of people who ate the wrong food and had the wrong habits. He wondered how people who had already been so badly treated by life could allow what little they had to be taken from them by charlatans.

He could not shake the vague sense of anger that seemed to foul his blood. Why did Wyatt Dixon bother him so much? Because he had beat the system and was back on the street, lauded by people who had no idea of the man's violent history? Yes, that was part of it. But in his heart Darrel knew Wyatt Dixon bothered him for other reasons as well, ones that went to a central dilemma in Darrel's life. Darrel himself, lawman and soldier, had recruited men like Dixon for military and political operations that were shameful and dishonorable in nature. The qualifications for the job had always been simple: the recruits needed only to be disposable and totally devoid of humanity. Darrel had been their mentor, feeding them patriotic Valium when in reality the men Darrel reported to would not spit on them if they were burning to death.

The sky was yellow in the west, filled with dust and rain, the air smelling of mown hay and the watermelons someone was splitting apart on a wood table. The tent was filling now, a preacher mounting a stage above the rows and rows of folding chairs. Then Darrel saw Wyatt Dixon working his way on crutches down the aisle toward a chair an usher was unfolding especially for him. Dixon wore a shirt emblazoned with blue and white stars and steel-colored eagles with thunderbolts in their talons, one dark blue pants leg split up to the hip to expose the plaster cast on his thigh. He was gripping his hat between his fingers and the handle of his crutch, his mouth like a slit in his face.

Darrel got out of the car and took a seat at the back of the tent. Next to him a tall man, wearing sandals and eyeglasses that hung on a velvet cord around his neck, was setting up a tape recorder.

"What's going on?" Darrel asked him.

"I'm a professor at the university. I have permission to be here, if that's what you mean," the tall man replied.

No, that's not what he had meant, but he didn't pursue it. The preacher introduced himself as Elton T. Sneed, then immediately went into a histrionic sermon that Darrel could only associate with an epileptic seizure. But the preacher's performance, the Appalachian accent and heated gasping for breath at the end of each sentence, was nothing compared to what Darrel saw and heard next.

One by one people rose from their seats at the front of the tent and began to rant and shake, their faces lifted skyward, their eyes closed as though they were experiencing orgasm. But the sounds or words coming out of their throats were like none Darrel had ever heard. Wyatt Dixon rose, too, wobbling into the aisle on his crutches, his chin jacked in the air, a staccato stream of unintelligible language rising from his throat louder than anyone else's.

"What is *that?*" Darrel said to the professor from the university.

"You're listening to Aramaic, my friend. Something you can tell your grandchildren about," the professor replied.

"It's an Indian dialect?"

"It goes back nine centuries before the birth of Christ. It's the language Jesus spoke," the professor said.

"Right," Darrel said. "Glad my tax money is going for a good cause out at the university."

Darrel left the tent and went to a concrete building that contained showers and restrooms that were used by campers during tribal powwows. As he relieved himself in a trough, he could hear the tent session breaking up for dinner. If he was going to make a move on Dixon, now was the time. He used his cell phone to call directly into Fay Harback's office, hoping she would be working late, which for her was customary.

"Fay?"

"Yes?" she said.

"I want to bring Dixon in as a material witness."

"Witness to what?"

"The attack on his own person."

"You want to lock up an assault and battery victim?"

"Got any better solutions for dealing with this guy?"

"Wyatt isn't a guy you squeeze, Darrel."

"Wyatt?" he said.

"He's neither a snitch nor a rat, so forget it," she said.

"Whose side are you on?"

"You should try to relax," she replied.

He disconnected the transmission. Had everyone in the courthouse lost their minds? He left the stalls in the cement building and went back outside into the twilight. Wyatt Dixon was laboring across the rough ground, a soft cowboy hat the color of chewing tobacco low on his forehead, a festive group of men and women on each side of him. They were the homeliest people Darrel had ever seen, their faces creased and work-worn, their teeth decayed, their eyesight diminished by injuries and diseases that were never treated. What did they have to be happy about?

But the faces here at the revival were not new ones to him. He had seen them in El Salvador, Guatemala, and northern Nicaragua. He had seen them staring at him out of windows in government jails, shantytowns, and miserable huts on the fringes of large pepper plantations. He had also seen them at the bottom of excavations just before a bulldozer shoved a mountain of dirt down on them.

His depression was coming back. Get rid of morbid thoughts. He remembered George Patton's famous admonition: You don't win wars by giving your life for your country; you win by making the other sonofabitch give his. For Darrel, that meant taking it to them with red-hot tongs. He waited until Wyatt Dixon was inside the entrance of the men's room, then braced him.

"Think you can just walk out of the hospital and say, 'Screw you,' to the sheriff's department?" he said.

"Why, howdy doodie, Detective McComb?" Dixon said, straightening himself on his crutches. "We're fixing to have a potluck dinner. Dinner on the ground and devil in the bush. Want to join us?"

The men who had entered the restroom with Dixon were staring at Darrel as though he were a Martian. He held up his badge so all of them could see it. "This is police business. Get out of here," he said.

But they didn't move. Not until Dixon turned to them and said, "Y'all go 'head on. I'll be there directly."

"Why don't you leave him alone?" somebody in the back of the room said.

"Who said that?" Darrel asked.

But no one answered. Instead, one by one they left the room, their faces filled with hostility, their eyes lingering on his.

"You fool ignorant people, Dixon, but you don't fool me," Darrel said.

"I got twenty-seven thousand dollars in the bank, own my own truck, personal gear, and a prize Appaloosa cutting horse. I'm on the square with the state and the Man on High, and you ain't got bean dip on me, Detective. Seems to me you're flirting with a civil suit. I've already talked to my friend Brother Holland about taking over some of my legal issues."

"Holland is actually your attorney?"

Wyatt didn't reply. His shoulders were hunched atop his crutches, his head tilted at an odd angle. His eyes seemed to be peeling away the skin on Darrel's face now, burrowing into his mind, prying secrets from him Darrel shared with no one. Then Darrel knew why it was he hated Dixon so much. Wyatt knew his past and looked upon him as a fraud. "You think you know everything about me, don't you?" Darrel said.

"You hire men of my kind to hurt folks who get in your way. That's why I don't have no truck with the government. The whole bunch of you are hypocrites," Dixon replied.

"Hear me real good on this, asswipe. People like you have no right to live in this country. You belong in a cage on an ice floe in Antarctica. You're one of those guys who's still dirty after he takes a shower. Both of us know you're up to something. I just haven't figured out what it is."

"Least I ain't up to somebody's windowsill, looking at some young girl's boobs. Now, if you'll step aside, I'm fixing to take a drain that's gonna blow the porcelain off the bowl."

Dixon creaked forward on his crutches toward a stall, his shoulder brushing against Darrel's. Then Darrel had thoughts of a kind that had probably been working in his unconscious all day, like yellow jackets trapped under a glass jar. Strapped to his ankle was a small holster with a hideaway .25 auto in it, all serial numbers acid-burned and ground off on an emery wheel. All he needed to do was say Dixon's name, wait for him to turn around, and use his nine-Mike to pop one into the center of his forehead. It would be a simple matter to fold Dixon's dead hand around the .25 auto.

"Dixon?" he said.

Wyatt stopped and turned slightly, the eagle on his shirt bunching with the twisted motion he made against the armrests of his crutches. "Spit it out. I'm tired of this game playing," he said.

"You're a piece of shit," Darrel said.

"I've answered to worse. If that's all you got to say, I got to urinate," Dixon said.

A shaft of sunlight shone through the air-space between the restroom wall and roof and made Darrel's eyes burn and twitch. The trough against the wall stank of piss and through the open door of a stall he could see a toilet that was up to the rim with brown water. Outside, somebody had set off a string of firecrackers and they popped like lesions splitting on the surface of Darrel's brain. Darrel looked directly into Wyatt's eyes and believed he could actually hear Wyatt laughing at him, as though Wyatt had stolen his soul and wiped his feet on it.

Darrel caught his breath. "I'm taking you in as a material witness. Then I'm going to get a warrant on your place and tear it apart. I'm also going to get your bank accounts frozen. That's just for openers. When I'm fin-ished with you, you'll wish you were still a dirty thought in your father's mind."

Dixon sucked a canine tooth, then turned back toward the urinal. "I don't think you got too many arrows in your quiver, Detec-tive. I'm taking back my recommendation to President Bush. You just don't measure up, boy," he said.

Darrel cupped him by the upper arm and spun him around. He could not quite believe the level of power he felt in Wyatt's arm and he wondered for a moment if he had made an irreversible mistake. But Wyatt didn't resist. Darrel snapped a handcuff on Wyatt's wrist, then locked the other manacle on an iron pipe that was anchored in the cinder-block wall and the cement floor. Wyatt was now helpless, balanced precariously on his crutches.

"I told you I got to urinate," Wyatt said.

"Maybe you can start a new career doing adult diaper endorsements," Darrel said.

He returned to the grove of cottonwood trees and started his car, his heart beating. What had he just done? Made a bust that wouldn't stick, allowed Dixon to treat him with contempt, and jammed himself up with the D.A.'s office. But it was too late to change course now. He had to brass it out or become a worse object of ridicule than he already was.

He drove his car to the restroom area, blowing his horn to discourage Dixon's revivalist friends who had started to reenter the building. He hit the redial button on his cell phone and heard Fay's voice on the other end. "I'm bringing him in. I'll do the paperwork in the morning," he said.

"You're not doing this on my authorization," she said.

"This guy is a menace. Are you going to back my play or not?"

"Come in tomorrow morning and we'll talk. In the meantime, I don't want —"

He snapped the cell phone shut, parked the car, and opened the back door so he could move Dixon quickly into the car and lock him to the D-ring inset in the floor before Dixon's friends could cause more trouble. He entered the restroom, then stared dumbfounded at Wyatt relieving himself in the trough, one manacle hanging from his wrist. The iron pipe to which he had been hooked up lay on the floor like a broken pugil stick, each end festooned with a chunk of concrete or cement.

Wyatt shook himself off and put his equipment back in his pants. Blood was leaking from the gauze and plaster on his thigh. "Best whiz I ever had," he said, his face beaming with visceral satisfaction.

That night, Darrel McComb ended up in a skin joint and got drunker than he had ever been in his life. The early dawn found him on Greta Lundstrum's doorstep, sick and trembling, afraid he would continue drinking through the day but even more afraid that he would get sober and have to look at himself in the hard light of day. The eastern sky was the color of a Tequila Sunrise, the mountains quaking with lightning. He sat on the steps and removed his piece from his clip-on holster and held it in both hands between his legs. He closed his eyes and imagined himself fitting the barrel between his teeth, touching the roof of his mouth, the astringent taste of gun lubricant mixing with his saliva.

Did Valhalla lie on the other side or only a great blackness? His life was a joke, hardly worth sustaining. One round fired upward into the brain would scroll his name on the wall, then it would be over.

Or perhaps he might take a few people with him. Behind him, he heard the door open.

CHAPTER 13

That same Friday morning, as I headed to work, I saw Seth Masterson's Cherokee parked on the side of the dirt road that led from my house onto the state highway. The driver's door was open and Seth was behind the wheel, eating breakfast out of a McDonald's container. The sun had just tipped the mountains on the east side of the valley, and the light looked like a tiny pink flame inside the needles of the ponderosa tree he had parked under.

I pulled behind him and got out.

"You talk to American Horse and the Finley girl about giving up the computer disks they stole from Global Research?" he asked.

"No," I replied.

He nodded, his impatience undisguised. He wiped his mouth with a crumpled paper napkin and dropped it into his plate. "Mind telling me why not?" he said.

"Because I've talked to Johnny about it before. He's not going to give up his friends or tell them what to do."

"Don't tell me those Indians creeped that place without his permission. The girl's dirty, too. You know it, Billy Bob."

"You want to send her and Johnny a message, go do it yourself."

He poured his coffee into the dust and set the empty container on the floorboards of his vehicle. He stared at the coffee soaking into the dirt. "You used to be a good cop. Maybe you ought to rethink who your friends are," he said.

"Sorry you feel that way, Seth."

He shut the door and drove perhaps ten yards down the road, then stopped and got out, the vituperative moment gone. He had put on a tan cap with a green big-mouth bass imprinted on it and the cap's bill darkened the upper half of his face, but I could tell he was smiling. "My wife and I have a cabin west of Walsenburg. Come down sometime and help me deplete the rainbow population," he said.

Around 9 a.m. that same day, Darrel McComb sat in an uncomfortable chair, staring across the desk at Fay Harback, trying to take shallow breaths through his nose so the alcohol deep down in his lungs did not blow into her face. He had showered at Greta's, shaved with her leg razor, and used her toothbrush to scrub the taste of tequila out of his mouth, then had driven at high speed through traffic in order to reach the office with a semblance of punctuality.

But his jaws were nicked, his eyes scorched, and his shirt and suit smelled as though they had been pulled from a dirty clothes hamper.

"You busted Dixon, then turned him loose?" Fay said.

"Not exactly."

"Then explain what exactly you did, please."

"I drove him to the emergency room at St. Pat's and left him with the docs. I told him we wanted better cooperation from him, but he was free to go from the hospital. Look, Fay —"

"No, you look, Darrel. I think you need to go on the desk or get some counseling. It wouldn't hurt if you checked out a Twelve-Step group, either."

"I don't drink."

"Sorry, I forgot that the odor in here is from the rug-cleaning service."

Only two hours earlier, he had entertained thoughts of killing himself and perhaps others as well. Now he sat hunched in a chair like a chastened schoolboy. His shoes were scuffed, one of them untied, crossed on top of the other. He straightened his spine, took out a handkerchief, and blew his nose. At that moment he would have traded ten years of his life for a Vodka Collins. "A university professor was up at the revival. He said Dixon was speaking in the language Jesus used," Darrel said.

Fay propped her elbows on her desk blotter and rested her chin on the backs of her hands. When he looked into her eyes, he saw only pity and sadness there, and he felt a balloon of anger bloom in his chest, squeezing his heart. Weevil-like motes seemed to swim through his vision. "I'm telling you what the professor said. I don't need any skepticism out of your office. I don't need any Twelve-Step meetings, either. I'm a good cop," he said.

"Go home, Darrel."

"This all started with American Horse."

"It started when you almost beat him to death with a blackjack. You want to get some sleep, or do you want me to call the sheriff?"

"The FBI isn't in Missoula to help us. They're here to shut down the investigation. That's how it works. We're little people and we're in somebody's way. Even Wyatt Dixon has that much figured out. I helped kill hundreds of innocent people. They were all Indians. I know how it works out there."

His words sounded as though someone else were speaking them, as though he were in a windowless room full of white noise and a mechanical presence inside himself was playing a tape he allowed himself to hear only in his sleep. He looked at the blank stare on Fay Harback's face, then opened his mouth to clear the popping in his ears.

"Darrel —" she began.

"Leave me alone," he said, knocking the chair askew as he went out the door.

He signed out of the department, claiming a doctor's appointment, went to his apartment, ate six aspirin and one hit of white speed, showered for the second time that morning, and put on fresh clothes. He tried to file and categorize his thoughts, put the previous night into perspective, and somehow get a handle on it; but he couldn't. He had seriously blown out his doors, gotten drunk in a topless bar, and passed out with his face in a puddle of spilled booze.

He remembered a stripper and bouncer putting his coat on for him and helping him into his car, then leaving him alone in the empty parking lot, barely able to start the engine. Greta had taken him in, gotten his gun away from him, then had led him to her bed like a sexual beggar. Knowing full well she was involved with a criminal enterprise and that ultimately she planned to use him, he let her climb on top of him and haul his ashes, even though it was obvious that she could barely abide his breath and the stink of nicotine that rose from his hair and skin.

He took another hit of speed and felt it kick into his system, temporarily giving a brightly lit rectitude to his thoughts and the jittering energies that were beating in his wrists. Before he headed back to the department, he fitted five shells into a cut-down twelve-gauge pump shotgun, wrapped it in a blanket, and placed the shotgun and the box of remaining shells in the trunk of his Honda. If he had been asked to explain why he was carrying his own shotgun in his vehicle, he would not have been able to give a reason, except for the fact that the mountainous horizon circumscribing the valley seemed to tremble with a peculiar malevolence, and on this particular day that bothersome fact needed to be corrected.

He sat in his cubicle at the department and drank coffee, did paperwork, and answered the telephone in routine fashion, his scalp and forehead shiny under the fluorescent lighting. By noon he was sweating, his throat thick, his hands starting to shake. Maybe he should just go to a bar and get drunk again, he thought — but that was too easy. A dramatic event had to happen, something that would change the daily grief that constituted his life, that would make everyone out there understand where this country had gone wrong.

The phone on his desk rang.

The caller was a parolee, a Deer Lodge Pen dimwit and professional snitch by the name of Wilbur Pickett, who lived up the road in Ronan. "There're two guys here who went to a veterinarian to get patched up. The vet is a junkie and was in Atascadero with these guys. Somebody beat the living shit out of them. Maybe one guy's face is fried, like on a stove. You looking for anybody like that, Darrel?" Wilbur said.

Ten minutes later Darrel signed out of the office and was on the way to Ronan, up in the Mission Mountains, up in Indian country.

While these events were occurring, I was at my office, convinced I would probably not see or talk with my friend Seth Masterson again, at least not until he had retired to a cabin and trout stream in southern Colorado. But at 11:14 a.m. I heard his mellifluous voice when I answered the phone. "I left American Horse a message on his machine. His wife just called me on my cell and told me to come out," he said.

"Amber told you to come to their house?"

"That's right. Why?"

"She doesn't tend to get along with authority figures."

"Who's an authority figure? I quit the Bureau after I talked with you this morning. My leave time will take up the slack in my thirty-day notice. You know the greatest thing about quitting a job?"

"No."

"You walk out the glass doors and it's like you never worked there. Then you wonder why you ever did in the first place."

"Why'd you call?"

"To tell you I quit."

An hour later I saw Amber walk past my office window, a full shopping bag hanging from her hand. I went outside and caught her before she got to her car.

"You invited Seth Masterson up to see Johnny?" I said.

"That FBI moke? What are you talking about?" she said.

Darrel floored his Honda up Evaro Hill. His day was improving by the second. He was back on the edge of the envelope again, the green countryside speeding by him, just like when he and Rocky went in low over a Nicaraguan jungle, their kickers scooting crates of C-rats, AK-47s, frags, and ammo out the bay, the parachutes blooming like the tops of white mushrooms above the foliage down below.

As he topped the hill and entered the Indian reservation, he saw a black Jeep Cherokee parked at a filling station island and that FBI drink-of-water Masterson pumping fuel into the tank. Time to check it out, Darrel thought, and swerved in behind him.

Masterson wore shades and a fishing cap. He glanced up at Darrel. "Fine day," he said.

"You bet. Get anywhere on that Global Research break-in?" Darrel said.

"Call the Bureau. I'm off my tether now."

"Seen American Horse recently?"

"Not really. You know how it goes. Some investigations just don't pan out."

"His place is up on the Jocko. Thought you might be headed there."

"All my official duties are over, Detective." Masterson seemed to gaze wistfully at the row of mountains that lined the valley. He tapped the nozzle of the gas hose on his tank and hung it up on the pump. "Have a good one. Think I might flip a dry fly in the riffle this afternoon."

Darrel watched Seth Masterson drive away, the waxed black surfaces of the Cherokee shimmering with heat. Flip a dry fly, my ass, he thought.

When Seth drove across the iron cattle guard onto Johnny's property, he saw horses in the shade by the barn, a half-dozen goats eating knapweed and dandelions in a pasture, a water sprinkler whirling in Johnny's side yard, boxes of petunias and impatiens blooming in the windows of his clapboard house.

He parked his Cherokee and turned off the engine. In the quiet he could hear the humming sound of the Jocko River, the wind in the trees up the slope, classical music from a radio that was propped in an open window. Wash flapped on a clothesline and a calico cat with kittens lay in a cool, scooped-out place in the dirt under the front porch. Seth walked toward the house.

Then he paused. The curtains in the house puffed whitely in the wind and he heard a door slam in the barn. What was it that bothered him? The absence of any movement in the house, although the front door was open and a pickup truck was parked in back? Or was it the hot reflection of the sun on the tin roof, the flicker of a bright object up in the trees, or the sudden flight of birds from the canopy? In the corner of his vision he saw a red pony sprinting through a field of tall grass toward its mother.

In his youth, during a war few cared about anymore, a glimmer of moonlight on a trip wire, a smell of recently eaten fish, a glimpse of a conical-shaped hat in the elephant grass, had made the difference between seeing the sunrise and walking into an ambush that on one occasion was so intense and certain in outcome that Seth had called in a napalm strike on his own position.

Had he survived the war and twenty-seven years as a federal agent only to develop a case of short-timer's nerves while trying to do a good deed? He fixed his collar, as though it were chafing his neck, then continued toward the front porch. When no one responded to his knock at the open door, he walked up the dirt drive, stooped under the wash on the clothes-line, and mounted the back steps. Behind him he thought he heard a dry, metallic *klatch,* not unlike a sound he had heard on night trails in that forgotten war. He turned and stared at the wooded hillside behind the house, momentarily unsure of where he was in time and place, his hand reaching inside his windbreaker.

Darrel had followed the FBI agent up the state highway through the res, until the agent turned on a dirt road that led to Johnny's ranch. At that point it was impossible to continue the tail without being seen. Darrel continued up the state highway another half mile, then caught the service road and doubled back. By the time he approached Johnny's property, Masterson had already arrived.

Darrel turned into a neighbor's pasture, following the edge of a creek that wound from the river back to a split in the hills. A knoll traversed the pasture, effectively concealing his vehicle from Masterson's view. Darrel's hands were damp on the steering wheel, his heart starting to race. He slowed the car so the dust from his wheels would not drift above the knoll. What did he hope to prove by being there? He didn't know.

Like most county or city law officers, he didn't like federal agents. He thought of them as lazy, arrogant, and disdainful of semieducated locals like himself. But that wasn't why he was bird-dogging Masterson. What if Masterson was working with American Horse, using him as a confidential informant? Or what if Masterson was turning dials on American Horse to get at Amber?

Maybe Masterson had a sexual itinerary, Darrel thought. Why not? It wasn't a coincidence that federal sharpshooters had the muscular physiques of actors in porn films.

But in truth Darrel knew his motivations were not that complex. He simply wanted to step inside a white flame and burn his life clean of all the impurities that plagued his soul.

He parked in a grove of aspens and walked up the knoll with his binoculars. American Horse's house was no more than seventy yards away. Through the lenses Darrel watched Masterson knock on the open front door, wait a moment, then disappear around the far side of the house. A moment later Masterson appeared in the backyard, ducking under the washline, removing his shades, dropping them into his shirt pocket. Evidently no one was home and Masterson hadn't figured that out yet. What an idiot, Darrel thought.

Masterson started up the steps, then paused and looked behind him up the wooded slope, as though he had heard a sound that didn't belong among the trees. Through the binoculars Darrel saw a flock of wild turkeys burst from the hillside and fly into Johnny American Horse's backyard.

The wind was blowing from behind Darrel, so that sight and sound did not coordinate. He saw Masterson's hand go toward his belt, then his head lurch back and both hands rise to his throat, as though he had swallowed a large chicken bone. Red flowers seemed to bloom on his tan windbreaker, and it was then that Darrel heard *pop, pop, pop* and saw the puffs of smoke inside the trees on the hillside.

He couldn't believe what he was watching. The shooter was using a semiautomatic of some kind, but the firing was sustained and rapid, the magazine obviously one of large capacity. Blood fountained from Masterson's mouth. He crumpled against the steps and the railing, still fighting to get his weapon free from its holster, his legs peppered with wounds.

Darrel realized the attrition from last night's drunk was not over. He had left his handheld radio at the department and the battery in his cell phone was dead.

Darrel got the cut-down twelve gauge from his car trunk and went over the top of the knoll at a run. He could see Masterson on his side, a semiautomatic in his hand, firing blindly into the trees even while he was being hit. *That* is one macho G-man, he thought. Darrel jumped across a flattened barbed wire fence, his shotgun at port arms, his face breaking with sweat, his lungs aching from the barroom smoke he had inhaled the previous night.

For a moment he thought of cutting into the woods and advancing on the shooter from his flank, but the time loss of working through the tree trunks would probably cost Masterson any chance he had of survival. So he poured it on, his big shoes pounding like elephant's feet across the sod, his sports coat split at the shoulders. He felt more naked than he had ever been in his life as he waited for the redirected fire that could rip through his viscera or explode his brain pan.

But the firing in the trees stopped, either because Masterson had let off at least a dozen rounds from a nine millimeter or because the sniper was reloading.

Darrel charged into the yard, fired two shells loaded with double-ought bucks into the trees, and heard the pattern spread and knock ineffectively over a large area. He tried to hold the shotgun with one hand and lift Masterson to his feet with the other, but Masterson was hurt too badly to stand. Darrel laid the shotgun on the steps, caught Masterson around the stomach, and worked him up on his shoulder as he would a side of beef.

He could hear Masterson's breath wheezing from a sucking chest wound and feel his blood draining on Darrel's arms and back. He started toward the lee of the house, then the shooter fired again, blowing white splinters out of the steps, breaking a window, ricocheting a round off a metal surface inside. Darrel got inside the screened porch, with Masterson draped over him, and pushed a water-stained couch against the plywood that framed the bottom of the enclosure. He huddled behind the couch, his body shielding Masterson's.

He kicked his foot against the door to the mud room, then kicked it again. But the door was bolted and set solidly in the jamb. He and the agent were trapped, and the shooter could now reposition himself and incrementally cut them apart.

Masterson's face was spiderwebbed with blood, his eyes dull with shock, a red froth spraying from his chest wound. Darrel found a piece of cellophane in a garbage sack, tore open Masterson's shirt, and pressed the cellophane against the hole in the agent's chest. He heard air catch wetly in Masterson's throat and go into his lungs. "I'm going to get you home, pal. You hang tough," he said.

But he could not tell if his words registered with Masterson or not.

Darrel's twelve gauge was still angled butt-down on the steps. The agent's nine millimeter lay in the dirt, with probably no more than two or three rounds in it. Darrel slipped his own nine millimeter from his clip-on holster and clicked off the butterfly safety. But his handgun brought him little sense of reassurance. He and

Masterson were boxed in, with no access to electronic communications. At some point the shooter would flank them, take out Darrel with a head shot, and finish the job on Masterson. What kind of cop had Darrel proved to be? What would Rocky do in these circumstances?

Never accept the hand your enemy deals you, Rocky used to say. Bring it to the bad guys and make them reconsider their point of view. Everybody takes the same dirt nap, Rocky used to say. What's the big deal? It's only rock 'n' roll.

A round from the hillside blew stuffing out of the couch and another shattered the glass knob on the door. Darrel breathed hard through his mouth, oxygenating his blood, then crashed through the screen door, gathering the shotgun up from the steps. He saw a man moving up the slope through the trees and realized he'd caught him changing his position. He fired once and saw leaves and small branches topple through a shaft of sunlight. Then Darrel plunged into the treeline, pumping the spent shell out of the chamber, snugging himself against a ponderosa trunk.

He could hear feet running and peeked quickly around the tree, but he saw nothing except the needle-covered floor of the forest, outcroppings of gray rock, and motes of dust spinning in the columns of sunlight that pierced the canopy.

The ground was spongy with lichen, the air

smelling of fern, stone that never saw sunlight, mushrooms, and burned gunpowder. He followed a deer trail that wound laterally along the hillside, through shade and parklike terrain, but he saw no more sign of the shooter. When he retraced his steps, he saw an AR-15 rifle propped against a boulder, the breech locked open on an empty twenty-round magazine. In the distance he could hear a siren pealing down the dirt road.

He walked back down the slope and entered the screened porch. Seth Masterson lay as Darrel had left him, one hand resting on the cellophane patch Darrel had placed on his chest wound. Darrel sat down on the floor, pulling his knees up, the adrenaline gone, his energies drained. Masterson's face seemed to swim in and out of focus. "You were a brave guy, buddy. It was an honor to meet you," he said.

He cupped his hand on Seth's sightless eyes, closing them as he would a doll's, then hung his head like a man who had not slept in years.

CHAPTER 14

During the next few days the federal and county investigations into the murder of Seth Masterson produced evidence that seemed to aim at only one conclusion: Johnny American Horse's odyssey into the Garden of Gethsemane was just beginning.

The AR-15, the civilian equivalent of the military-issue M-16 rifle Darrel McComb had found on the hillside, was stenciled with Johnny American Horse's fingerprints. In addition, the call made to Seth Masterson's cell phone, supposedly by Amber, was traced back to Johnny's house. There was another problem, too — Johnny had no alibi.

He claimed to have been building a chimney of river stones for a rancher, up the Blackfoot, at the time of Seth's murder. But he had been working by himself and he could provide no witness to corroborate his story. His explanation about the presence of his fingerprints on the AR-15 presented other complications. Johnny told both the FBI and the investigators from the sheriff's department of the man who had tried to sell him an AR-15 out of a panel truck. But the two boys who worked for him could not identify the kind of rifle Johnny had been handed by the driver of the truck, and neither of them remembered Johnny picking up an ejected shell from the dirt, which was the only explanation — provided Johnny was innocent — for the fact that a latent on a .223 cartridge fired from the murder weapon was Johnny's.

By Wednesday of the following week he had been questioned at least five times by federal agents. He came into my office just before noon, wearing frayed jeans and a black shirt with silver stripes in it, his coned-up straw hat clenched in his hand, his face pinched with anger.

"You okay?" I said.

"Two agents just rousted me in front of the courthouse. I told this one guy he puts his hand on me again, he'll wish he stayed in college."

"You told that to an FBI agent?"

"I don't know who he was. Just get them away from me."

"Make a stop at the watering hole this morning?"

"So what?"

"It's what your enemies want you to do, Johnny. If you want to really tie the ribbon on the box, punch out a federal agent."

"I told them the truth. A guy tried to sell me the AR-15. Somebody got in my house and used my phone to set up this guy Masterson.

These guys can't figure that out? Nobody's that stupid."

"You're not under arrest. That means they haven't reached any conclusions. Give them a break. Maybe they'll surprise you."

Wrong words. "Why would I kill an FBI agent in my own house? What if Amber had been there? She'd probably be dead too," he said.

"Sit down," I said.

He started to argue again, his eyes hot, a smell like fermented fruit on his breath. But I cut him off. "All this goes back to that research lab Amber and your friends broke into," I said. "Seth Masterson went to your house to try to persuade you and Amber to give up the computer files that were stolen from Global Research. It cost him his life."

"I can't help that," he replied.

I could feel my own temper rising now. "We'll talk later," I said.

"You ever see photographs of Saddam Hussein's mustard gas attacks on the Kurds back in eighty-eight? Our government armed that motherfucker."

"I'm not making the connections here, but I think you're charging at windmills, partner," I said.

"Tell that to the friends of mine who were killed in Iraq."

"Seth was my friend, Johnny. He died

trying to help you. But I don't think you're hearing that."

He wiped at his nose with the backs of his fingers, his eyes narrowing. "Nobody cares," he said.

"Cares about what?"

"What they're doing to the earth, what they're doing to the human race, what they've done to Indian people for three hundred years. You don't see it, Billy Bob. In your way you're part of it."

"I think I've had about all of this I can take in one day," I said.

"I'm letting you off the hook on my bond. A couple of tribal bail bondsmen are taking it over."

"That's the way you want it?" I said.

"Yeah, that's the way I want it," he said.

"Maybe you should seek other counsel while you're at it."

"Maybe that's not a bad idea," he said.

"*Vaya con Dios,*" I said.

It had been a bad way to end a conversation with a man whose causes I admired. But Temple and I had put up our ranch as surety for Johnny's bond, and his cavalier and ungrateful attitude about the risk we had incurred made me wonder about my own sanity. I also wondered if I had become one of those people who needed to hurt both himself and his family in order to convince himself of his own integrity.

Maybe it was time to make a clean break with Johnny and his ongoing self-immolation. I told that to Temple at lunch. "Giving up on water-walkers?" she said.

"I didn't say he was a water-walker."

"Yeah, you did. That's why you won't let go of him, either."

"Watch me," I said.

She chewed a piece of salad, raised her eyebrows, and looked innocently out the window.

But Johnny wasn't the only person for whom events were going out of control. Darrel McComb had to explain why he was following an FBI agent when supposedly he was pursuing a lead on the two men who had assaulted Wyatt Dixon. He also had to explain how he had gotten involved in a firefight, one that had left the agent dead, without calling for backup. Instead of being cited for bravery, he received a formal letter of reprimand in his jacket. He was also put on the desk until Internal Affairs concluded an investigation into the shooting.

But oddly enough, his receiving recrimination rather than commendation seemed to lift a burden from him. I saw him in front of the drugstore on West Broadway that afternoon, eating from a bag of lemon drops while he gazed at a pair of hang gliders floating on the windstream above Mount Sentinel.

"Sorry about your bud," he said.

I nodded and didn't reply.

"Take a lesson from me, Holland," he continued. "If you work your heart out for the G, if you hump a sixty-pound pack and an M-60 in a hundred-degree jungle with ants crawling inside your skivvies, if you're a good cop who has to get by on speed and booze because broken glass is chewing up your guts, you eventually come to a philosophic conclusion about the realities of life out there in Bongo-Bongo Land: We're not only expendable, we're the people nobody even wants to hear about." He smiled and cracked a lemon drop between his molars.

"You mean nobody cares?"

"Yeah," he said.

"It's funny you put it that way, because Johnny American Horse told me the same thing today."

"I got news for American Horse. He's going down for Masterson's homicide. A done deal, my man."

"I don't believe that."

"They've got the weapon, his latents, a phone call to Masterson originating at his house, and his lifetime record of throwing buffalo shit through window fans. You don't believe the U.S. attorney is going to run a meat hook through both of this guy's buns? Wow, why would they do a terrible thing like that?" He laughed out loud.

After the rain and heavy snowmelt in the spring, the weather had turned dry and hot, and fires had started to burn in Idaho. As I drove home from work that evening, the sky was hazy with dust and smelled of smoke, and freshly exposed rocks along Lolo Creek were white and webbed with river trash and the scales of dead insects. When I turned up the road that led to our ranch, locusts flew in clouds from the knapweed in the ditches and the normally beautiful evening seemed as stricken and poisonous as my thoughts.

I wanted to be gone from Johnny for many reasons — his messianic attitudes and his indictment of me as a white person being only a couple of them. From a legal and professional point of view, I was entirely justified in letting him go. I believed Johnny was knowledgeable about what could be considered an ongoing criminal conspiracy involving his wife and the Indians who had broken into Global Research. In the eyes of the Department of Justice these were ecoterrorists, and, as such, short shrift would be given them by the Office of Homeland Security. As an officer of the court, I had ethical obligations with which Johnny was not concerned.

Maybe it was a cheap and self-serving way to think, but any attorney who ends up in front of the bar or in jail because of his client probably deserves his fate.

I cut and watered the grass in the front and back yards, and scattered feed for the wild turkeys that came down from the hills in the evening to drink from the aluminum horse tank by the barn. But I couldn't free myself from my problems of conscience about Johnny American Horse.

Then the phone rang inside and Johnny took me out of the box I had thought myself into — at least temporarily. "You're hiring Brendan Merwood?" I said incredulously.

"He's doing it pro bono," he said.

"Merwood wasn't conceived, he was poured out of a bottle of hair oil."

"So he wheels and deals. He's working for free. I'm not knocking it."

"Why are you doing this?"

"Maybe I don't want to pull you down."

"Merwood doesn't do anything for free, Johnny."

"Ever hear this one: What's the difference between lab rats and lawyers? Lab rats have feelings. Just kidding. See you around."

After he hung up I stared out the side window at the gloaming of the day, the horses in our pasture, the dry lightning that flickered above the hills. Temple came through the door with a bag of groceries. "What's the matter?" she asked.

I told her of Johnny's phone call.

"Maybe you should respect his decision," she said.

"He's doing it because he doesn't want to hurt his friends."

"Let it go, Billy Bob. For just once, stop protecting people from themselves," she said. She began pulling heavy cans of peaches out of the sack and setting them down hard on the kitchen table.

That night I slept without dreaming and woke at first light, rested and empty of thought or concern about the day or all the problems that had beset me the previous evening. Temple had been right, I told myself. It was time to let go of other people's quixotic struggles and to enjoy the day and the work I did and all the fine gifts a cool morning can bring. A doe and her fawn were drinking at the horse tank. A raccoon was scraping sunflower seeds out of the bird feeder on the deck; the trees behind the house were full of birdsong. Life could be a poem, if you'd only let it, I thought. Why live in conflict and endless self-examination?

I kept that mood all the way to the office. I was still confident about my new attitude as I crossed the street to the courthouse. Then I heard the unmistakable sound of someone's rubber-stopped crutches thudding on the sidewalk behind me. "Slow down there, Brother Holland. I'm pounding my vitals to jelly trying to catch up with you," a voice said.

"Don't want to hear it, Wyatt," I said.

But he cut me off at the corner, aiming one crutch at me like a pistol. "Got to have your hep. This is serious, counselor. Ain't many people I can go to on this one," he said.

I knew I would have no peace that day unless I heard him out. I sat down with him on a steel bench under a maple tree. He looked in both directions, his jaw hooked, his eyes perplexed. "I got word them two yardbirds that put a shank in me was up holed up with a vet'inary in Ronan. But when I got up there they'd done flown the coop," he said.

"I'm not real interested in this anymore, Wyatt. Johnny American Horse is using another attorney now," I said.

"Won't change nothing for him. Won't change nothing for me or you, either. You was baptized by immersion. Not only baptized the old-time way, you're an honest-to-God believer. Tell me I'm wrong."

"I don't want to hurt your feelings, Wyatt, but I don't like you talking about my personal life."

"They're gonna come after me with guns and such. With you it's probably gonna be different. They're out there, counselor, probably watching us right now."

"Who?"

"The ones working for this man Mabus."

I tried to read his eyes. Perhaps he was insane, I thought, or he simply spoke out of the demented cultural mind-set that was characteristic of his class, called white trash in the South, a term that has much more to do with pathology than socioeconomic status. But I had come to learn that Dixon was not a stupid man. His lips were parted slightly, like strips of rubber pasted on his face, his empty eyes waiting for me to speak.

"Whatever cause you're trying to enlist me in, I won't be a part of it. You committed a vicious, unforgivable act against my wife. That's never going away," I said.

He let his hands hang between his thighs and stared at the sidewalk. Then he gathered up his crutches and got to his feet. "Tell Miss Temple I'm sorry. And *you* go to hell, counselor," he said.

With that, he stepped off the curb into the traffic, jaywalking across the street to a café, jabbing a crutch into the door of a taxi that had blown its horn at him.

I could afford to pay Lucas's board and tuition at the university, where he had the improbable double major of music and dairy husbandry, but he would not allow it. Instead, he played several gigs a week at nightclubs and sometimes waited tables while carrying eighteen academic hours. His schedule took its toll, and often he was tired and barely able to stay awake when he came to dinner at our house.

But on Friday afternoon he was beaming as he came into my office.

"Win the lottery?" I asked.

"Pert' near," he replied, taking a torn envelope from his back pocket. "I got a full scholarship, all tuition and out-of-state fees paid, plus five hundred dollars a month living expenses."

"How you'd pull that off?"

"Applied for every kind of financial assistance they got. This one just happened to come through."

He handed me the awards letter. It was written on gold-and-silver-embossed stationery and was from a group called the Rocky Mountain Educational Foundation in Denver. "That's great, Lucas," I said.

"I'm taking y'all to dinner. The Golden Corral has got all-you-can-eat fish tonight," he said.

"Sounds swell," I said.

"Want to ask Johnny and Amber? I reckon they're feeling pretty low these days."

"I'm not Johnny's attorney anymore."

"Y'all have a blowup or something?"

"Johnny has his own time zone. I need to stay out of it."

"You used to tell me a guy can have all the friends he wants when he's in tall cotton.

You always said your real friends are the ones who stick with you in hard times. When did you change your mind?"

A week passed and still Johnny had not been charged in the death of Seth Masterson. I busied myself with other cases, fished in the evenings, and thinned out the trees and undergrowth around our house as we entered the fire season.

At sunset the heat rose from the ground and broke up in the wind, but even though the nights were clear and the stars bright, we could smell smoke lingering on the hillsides and see the glow of forest fires burning out of control in Idaho.

On the Fourth of July, Temple and I attended the Indian rodeo and powwow up on the res, ate buffalo burgers, fried bread, and snow cones, and watched hundreds of ceremonial dancers in heavy, feathered regalia perform in ninety-five-degree shade. I was sure I saw Johnny and Amber in the crowd, but when I waved they showed no sign of recognition.

Perhaps it was the heat and dust and the constant pounding by the elders on a giant rawhide drum, but I felt like an interloper at the ceremony, an effete sojourner little different from the tourists whose chief interest was buying Indian jewelry as cheaply as possible. After the dance ended, I tried to catch sight of Johnny and Amber amid the concession stands or by the rough stock pens adjacent to the bucking chutes.

Instead, I saw Wyatt Dixon perched atop a slat fence, his bad leg supported precariously, a solitary crutch balanced on his loins. His bare arms were red with sunburn, his face shaded by a white, lacquered, high-crown hat he wore low on his ears. He looked at me momentarily, then made a snuffing sound in his nose and turned his attention back to a couple of wranglers trying to load a bull onto a cattle truck.

I didn't think Temple had seen him and I made no mention of his presence. But very little escaped her eye. "What's with Dixon?" she said later.

"Nothing."

"Don't lie."

"He came to see me a week ago. He's got some notion I'm a river-baptized crusader or something. He said to tell you he was sorry for what he did."

"You believe this guy's horseshit?"

"No."

"Then don't tell me about it."

We were in the parking area now. The air smelled of livestock and heat and dry manure, and the sun was red and veiled with dust over the western hills. "I can't keep him from coming around," I said.

"I can," she said. "He'll be the deadest

ex-convict in the state of Montana."

"Why are you so angry?"

"Because Dixon can read you like a map. Your causes come before your family. Sometimes you break my heart."

We drove home in silence. I believe it was the worst Fourth of July in my life.

The next morning was Saturday and I got up before Temple did, packed a lunch, and drove up Rock Creek, which is rated by outdoor magazines as one of the ten top trout streams in the United States. But I didn't fish. In fact, I was not even sure why I was there, except for the fact the morning was cool, the woods deep in shadow, the riffle flowing over a smooth, pebbled creekbed streaked with green moss.

Soon I was back into my old, futile habit of trying to think my way out of conflict or worry. There was no doubt that Dixon had set the hook, either consciously or by accident. I was baptized at age nine under a canopy of hardwood trees that were turning to flame against the blue outline of the Ozark Mountains. The preacher who leaned me back under the water had a face like a horse and teeth like barrel slats. The water was spring-fed and cold, and my skin burned as though it had been held over a cool fire. I broke the surface gasping for air and my father wrapped me in his World War II Army shirt, one with an Indian-head Second Division patch on the sleeve, while the preacher clog-danced on a wood platform, Bible in hand, and the congregation thundered out "I Saw the Light."

But perhaps the ritual was less important than what the preacher told me afterwards, or at least as I recall his words: "You done been joined in spirit to God, to earth, to sky, to water and trees. Jesus is your light, your sword and shield. There ain't no place in his kingdom you don't belong. You ain't never got to be afraid again."

But I cannot say my baptism made me a good Christian. I know for certain L. Q. Navarro and I killed at least seven men. I believe they deserved what they got and the world is a better place without them. But my latent desire for violent recourse did not die with them. The Hollands were violent people, going all the way back to our patriarch, Son Holland, who fought against Santa Anna at the Battle of San Jacinto. The penchant in our family for red-black rage and the shedding of blood lay as strong a claim on our souls as a genetic desire for alcohol. Except that drunkards are consumed by their own energies. The Hollands were not.

A helicopter flew by overhead, low over the canopy, filling the canyon with the roar of its blades. I watched it tip upward into the sunlight, climbing abruptly over a wooded hill, then circle back toward me, the pilot as tiny as a bug inside the Plexiglas. Deer and a moose spooked out of the trees, clattering over stone, then the helicopter lifted once again over a hill and was gone.

It was after 8 a.m. I called home on my cell phone, but Temple didn't pick up. A family in a campground was cooking breakfast, and an old man and a young boy who was probably his grandson were fishing in a pool behind a beaver dam, the current cutting around the tops of their waders. The old man helped the boy unhook a rainbow and put it in his creel, then the two of them walked up on the bank and joined their relatives in the campground.

I thought of my own father and mother, both gone now, and the town in the Texas hill country where I had grown up, a place of green rivers, fried-chicken picnics, and downtown streets that still had elevated sidewalks with tethering rings set in them. I fed my packed lunch to a family of red squirrels and walked back toward my truck. The mystics may have found solace in the meditative life, but I think there are days when memory and solitude are not one's friend.

I was only a short distance down the road when a black car with tinted windows cut me off and a second one pulled in behind me. Two men in suits and shades stepped out of the first car and approached both sides of my truck. The one closest to me opened his identification. "Mr. Mabus would like to invite you for coffee or a brunch," he said.

Farther up the road a steel-gray limo was parked in the dappled shade of cottonwood trees. Beyond the trees, I saw the helicopter that had buzzed the creek sitting idly in an open field where the grass was turning yellow, the pilot smoking a cigarette.

"That's a P.I. badge, partner. It doesn't carry a lot of weight on a rural road in western Montana," I said to the man at my window.

"Whatever you say, sir. But Mr. Mabus would like the pleasure of your company," he replied. He was thick-necked, his blond hair neatly combed, his gaze focused down the road so as not to give the impression his eyes were being invasive behind his shades.

"Need you to move your vehicle," I said.

"Yes, sir, we'll gladly do that. Will you first walk over and speak to Mr. Mabus?" He removed his shades and tried to smile. His facial skin was like pig hide, his eyes dead-looking in the same way a barroom bouncer's are.

"All right, brother," I said.

He opened the door for me and continued to hold it while I got out on the road. "You want to take your hat, sir?" he asked.

"No, because I'll be coming right back. Then we'll have this bullshit behind us," I replied.

He smiled again, his eyes unfocused.

But I was making a point to the hired help, a man for whom restraint was built into his paycheck. The very fact that I was approaching Karsten Mabus's limo indicated I was accepting his imperious behavior. He pushed open the back door and waited for me to get in. He was dressed in the soft, earth-tone fabrics of a gentleman rancher or horse breeder, one arm propped across the top of the creamy, rolled leather seat. Two young women in pin-striped suits and white hose sat across from him, their knees close together, their hands folded in their laps. "Please join us for a late breakfast or an early lunch," he said.

"Where do you get off bracing me on the road, Mr. Mabus?" I said.

"I don't believe they did that, did they? It was meant to be an invitation. Congratulations on your son's scholarship," he said.

"How do you know about my boy's scholarship?"

"I contribute to a few educational endowments. The paperwork floats across my desk sometimes."

"You mentioned my father's accidental death on a previous occasion. Frankly, I resent the hell out of your intrusiveness into my family's history."

"Let's clear this up, Mr. Holland. I own several ranch properties in western Montana.

Their worth is somewhere around one hundred million dollars. I plan to subdivide and put the property up for sale over a five-year period. I need a good local attorney to oversee those sales, not someone from New York or Los Angeles — someone like you, a fellow who knows cattle, horses, indigenous grasses, irrigation methods, and land values. These two ladies here looked into your background. That's how I knew about the circumstances of your father's death. My purposes were purely business-oriented and professional. I apologize if I gave you any other impression."

His speech was husky, as though in spite of his wealth he was perhaps a shy man, a bit diffident, but sincere and forthright. "Get in. Please," he said, opening his hand to me.

It was warm inside the cottonwoods, and insects were worrying my neck and eyes, a shaft of sunlight shining into my eyes. I sat down on the leather seat, inside the coolness and leather comfort of the limo. The perfume of the two young women smelled like flowers in a garden. "Can you handle another client?" he said.

"I'm a one-loop operation. You need a firm," I replied.

He laughed. "I like the way you talk, Mr. Holland. I'd rather pay you six percent on those ranch sales than a bunch of fraternity fellows in Denver."

I realized he was offering me a situation worth hundreds of thousands of dollars, if not eventually millions. I started to speak, but he cut me off. "I'll tell you a fairly well known secret. Terrorists will attack us again. Every government official and everyone in federal law enforcement knows it. It will be large scale and aimed at another American city, perhaps several of them. When that happens, half of the West Coast will want to migrate to small towns in Montana, Idaho, and Utah. What do you think the value of this property will be then?"

"I don't know and I don't care. I'm not a speculator, Mr. Mabus. On that note I'm going to thank you for your offer and say good-bye."

"What can I say?" he said, lifting his hands in good-natured surrender. "Have a fine day. I admire your principles. My guess is you're a hell of a guy."

He shut the car door behind me, then rolled down the window on its electric motor and snapped his fingers several times at the men who had stopped my truck. They climbed wordlessly into their vehicles and drove away, the dust from their wheels floating back into my face.

CHAPTER 15

I should have seen it coming, or at least given more consideration to Darrel McComb's prediction about Johnny American Horse's legal fate; but like most people who believe that humankind is basically good and capable of conducting its affairs in a reasonable way, I daily avoided the inescapable conclusion that collective stupidity has often been the norm in the long and sorry history of human progress, and that perhaps the soundest argument for the existence of God is the fact that the human race has survived in spite of itself.

One week after the Fourth of July, charges were filed on Johnny for the shooting death of a federal agent. But when two dozen government lawmen and sharpshooters in bulletproof vests descended on his house, Johnny was gone, literally out the back door, up the hill and into the Mission Mountains, running with a survival knife, a new trade ax he had bought at the powwow, and one arm looped through a backpack.

Government helicopters buzzed the treetops in the high country for four days and agents on horseback threaded their way up rock-strewn ravines, only to find dead campfires, a hand line and fishing hook by a frozen lake, the cleated tracks of alpine shoes through a griz feeding area, a sweat lodge knocked together from fir boughs and blackened stones.

But it was not a safe bet Johnny was in the Missions. There were sightings of him up in the Swans, in the Bitterroots and the Cabinets, even over the Divide in the Bridgers and the Bear Paws.

Amber denied any knowledge of where he might be. She was held forty-eight hours in an isolation cell as a possible accomplice and questioned repeatedly by both FBI and ATF agents while her and Johnny's house was torn apart. While she was being questioned and her home destroyed, her father remained in Washington and made no attempt to contact her or me, even though he knew I still represented her.

Six days after Johnny had hauled freight into the high country, I saw his new counsel, Brendan Merwood, at the café across the street from the courthouse. Brendan was eating steak and eggs at a table by himself, cutting his food neatly, spearing small bites into his mouth with the tines of his fork held upside down. He wore a long-sleeved pale blue shirt, with white cuffs and a rolled white collar. His posture was simian, his big head almost bald, except for the close-cropped hair around his ears and the back of his neck.

The tan he'd worked on dutifully in Hawaii gleamed under the indirect lighting.

"Join me?" he said.

"Thanks, I'm meeting someone," I lied, and sat down at the counter. I picked up a menu and began to read it.

"Too bad you got screwed on that bail deal," he said.

I set the menu down and looked at him in the mirror. He had gone back to eating his food. I turned around on the stool. "Which bail deal?" I said.

"You didn't know? Those Indian bondsmen Johnny hired didn't process their paperwork. If you ask me, they chickened out. His bond is still on you. That must be the shits."

When I got home that afternoon, I could hardly face Temple.

"We'll owe two hundred thousand dollars?" she said.

"If Johnny doesn't appear for trial in the murder of Charlie Ruggles."

"This can't be happening to us."

"I checked with the court. The bond was never transferred. I called these Indian bondsmen five times. Their secretary kept telling me she had given them my messages but they'd been chasing down a bail skip in Butte. I drove up to the res and found one of them in a bar. He denies knowing anything about Johnny's bond or transferring it from us to him."

"Why did Johnny tell you we were off the hook?"

"He thought we were. That bondsman was lying. Somebody got to him."

"I think Johnny fed us to the wolves."

"I doubt if he knows this has happened, Temple."

"How could he? He's camping in the mountains while we're about to lose our home."

She went into the kitchen and started preparing supper. It was 7 p.m. Thursday, the one evening of the week during summer we always saved to attend the open-air dance in the park by the river. This particular evening a bluegrass group was playing, and a late afternoon shower had dropped the temperature ten degrees and filled the air with the smell of flowers and lawn sprinklers striking warm cement. But in the kitchen I heard Temple slam a cabinet door and clang a skillet on the stove, then make a grunting sound as she struggled with a can opener, just before slicing her hand.

I turned off the stove and ran tap water over her hand. In her anger she tried to resist my help, but I held on to her, gathering her against me, pressing my face in her hair, holding her tight, even when she hit me in the back and sides with her fists, the cut on her thumb streaking my shirt with blood.

On Saturday, Lucas came to the house, a torn envelope and a sheet of gold-and-silver-embossed stationery in his hand. "I cain't figure this. Don't them people know how to run their own business?" he said.

I took the letter from his hand and read it, then put it in my back pocket. I tried to keep my face empty. "I'll give them a call Monday," I said.

"How can they give me a scholarship, then take it back because I'm an out-of-state student? My application already said I was from out of state. It's like they're calling me a liar."

"There's a guy around here by the name of Karsten Mabus. He's a donor to this educational foundation. I think he's trying to squeeze me by going through you," I said.

"What's he want from you?"

"It has to do with Johnny American Horse."

"Well, throw that damn letter away. I wouldn't use the sonofabitch's money to wipe my —"

"I'll call Monday."

He studied a distant place on the hill across the road, his thumbs hitched in his pockets, his brow furrowed under the brim of his hat. His cheeks were flushed, his eyes vexed, but I knew his disappointment would not last. Lucas was endowed with both a childlike innocence and a love of his art, and he didn't care two cents for the world's opinion or the material rewards it might offer or deny him.

His face seemed to reach a conclusion in his thought process. "Y'all eat breakfast?" he asked.

"Not yet. How about tanking down some pork chops and buttermilk biscuits with us?"

"Sure I'm not barging in?"

"Not at all."

"Want to wet a line later on?" he said.

"You got it."

I could have learned a lot from Lucas.

Monday morning I called the educational foundation in Denver and tried to extract an explanation from the personnel there for the retraction of Lucas's scholarship. I was put on hold twice, cut off once, and finally told by a man with a sonorous voice that a clerical error had been made, that Lucas was ineligible for the particular award that had been given him, and that he could apply in another category. "We're sorry for the inconvenience," he said.

"That's my son you're jerking around," I said.

"Thank you for your inquiry," he replied, and quietly hung up.

An hour later, I received an office visit from Brendan Merwood. He was a strange man, one I had never understood. His skill as a trial lawyer was well known throughout the Northwest, but he seemed to have no principles whatsoever. He was a glad-hander, a sycophant, and a toady for every meretricious enterprise in the state, as though his own merits and well-earned success as an attorney brought him no sense of validation. Even his pro bono work seemed to be a public exercise in self-flattery. Now, he sat in my office like a battle-scarred feral hog, reeking of aftershave lotion, effusive with so much goodwill that I believed Brendan Merwood was a genuinely frightened man.

"I think you got a bum deal on this bail bond business," he said. "You tried to help Johnny in good faith, and look what happened. Both of you thought he'd be there for trial and never saw this tragedy with the federal agent in the making." He shook his head to show his sense of mystification at the unfairness of the universe. "I just don't think innocent folks should get hurt like this. That's why I want to help."

"What are you trying to tell me, sir?"

"You and I both know this is all connected in some way with ecoterrorism. Somebody is sitting on those materials that were stolen from Global Research. Those materials have got to get back into the right hands — either the government's or the owner's. Are my words getting through here, Billy Bob? Talk to Johnny's wife. She'll listen to you."

"No, she won't."

He crossed his legs and pulled at one knee, as though it were injured, his eyes lifting toward the ceiling. "Once in a while you have to make a concession. You make the concession and you move on. That's how the world works. This is a good community. We don't need all this trouble," he said.

"My wife and I didn't cause it. But somebody is doing his best to destroy us."

"I wouldn't know anything about that. I guess people fight with the weapons that are available to them."

"So do I."

"I've heard about your history in Texas. I don't think that's going to work here, my friend. Believe it or not, I'm on your side," he said.

"I think in your way you probably are. So thank you for coming in, Brendan. Tell the man you work for I'll kill him if he tries to hurt my family."

He shook his finger back and forth. "This conversation is one in which we didn't communicate very well. That's the only memory I'll have of it. If Johnny gets in touch with you, tell him to surrender himself or to call me. I don't want that boy hurt. God's truth on that," he said.

He left my office, shaking his head profoundly.

That afternoon, as I pulled into the dirt drive at Johnny's house, I saw Amber unloading boxes of groceries from her Dakota. I followed her into the back of the house without being invited. She had swept the floors clean of splintered wood and broken glass and had placed a throw rug over the stain where Seth Masterson had died.

"That's a lot of food," I said.

"Not in the mood for it, Billy Bob," she replied.

"Brendan Merwood was in my office this morning. He knows you have the records that were stolen out of Global Research. He wants you to give them up."

"The day Global gets its goods back is the day Johnny gets his death warrant signed. What a life, huh, boss?"

One sack on the table was filled with first-aid supplies.

"You don't think you're being watched or followed?" I said.

"They try. I don't think they do a very good job of it. Did you see those telephone workers by the crossroads? I wonder why they all have the same haircut."

"I wouldn't underestimate them," I said.

But my words were useless. I leaned against the doorjamb and watched her sort out the canned and dried food and medical purchases that she was obviously taking to Johnny. I wondered how long it would be before she was in the crosshairs of a telescopic lens.

"How badly is he hurt?" I asked.

"Bad enough."

"Amber, you need to be aware Temple and I are about to lose our home. Johnny's tribal bondsmen double-crossed him and us."

Her back was turned to me. She paused in her work a moment, as though she were about to speak. Then she wrapped a bottle of hydrogen peroxide in a towel and placed it deep in a cardboard box.

"Did you hear me? Others are being hurt as well as you and Johnny. Seth Masterson got set up and blown into a pile of bloody rags because he tried to save Johnny and you from yourselves."

This time she turned on me. "How serious do you think anthrax is? Or bubonic plague or the Ebola virus? Forget about the fact it's down in the Bitterroot Valley. How do you feel about this stuff being used on human beings?" she said.

"That's what they're messing with at Global?"

"They're the bastards who gave Saddam Hussein part of his biological warfare program."

"Turn over your material to the media. You can do it anonymously."

"It would never see the light of day."

"I tried," I said.

"Yeah, you did. Go burn a candle to yourself. I wish the tribal bondsmen hadn't shafted you. One of them just made a down payment on a new house. Not on the res, either, since he's obviously moving up in life. You got screwed and so did we and so did your friend the FBI agent. I don't have anything else to say, except ta-ta. That's the way it shakes out sometimes."

I went back outside, got in my Avalon, and turned around on the edge of the yard. The air was dry and I could see a smoky sheen rising into the sky from fires that were burning close to Glacier National Park. Amber came out on the porch and waved for me to stop. The anger and self-manufactured cynicism had gone out of her face, replaced by a vulnerability I didn't normally associate with her.

"Do you ever hear from my father?" she said.

"No, I don't."

"He was in town. I thought he might have called."

"Sometimes my answering machine is off when the office is closed."

"He's mad about my marrying Johnny, but he always checks on me through third parties. That's why I was asking," she said.

I wanted to tell her to be careful, to wrap herself in whatever spiritual shield ancient deities could provide her. But how do you caution a fawn about a cigarette a motorist has just flipped from his car window into a patch of yellow grass, or tell a sparrow that winged creatures eventually plummet to earth?

★ ★ ★

That evening Temple and I moved about the house in silence, clicking on the cable news, clicking it off again when the other entered the room, busying ourselves in our self-imposed solitude with inconsequential chores, as though our feigned solemnity were a successful disguise for our depression and mutual resentment.

It was dusk, the valley purple with shadow, when she finally spoke out of more than necessity. "Wyatt Dixon called the house today. He wanted to talk to you."

"About what?"

"I didn't give him a chance to say. I told him I'd report him to the sheriff's office if he called again."

"I'll have a talk with him."

"He's worthless. Let him alone."

She walked down to the barn and turned on the valve that fed the irrigation line to the pasture. In the distance I saw the water burst from the pipe and spray in the wind. Then she came back in the house, showered, and went to bed. I went into the den I used as a home office and sat in the dark with L. Q. Navarro's holstered .45 revolver in my lap. It was a beautiful firearm, blue-black, perfectly balanced, with yellowed ivory grips and a gold-plated trigger guard and hammer. I sometimes wondered if my fondness for holding L.Q.'s revolver wasn't a form of fetish, but actually I didn't care whether it was or not. I loved guns then and I love them now, just as I loved L.Q. and his courage and his manly smell and his confidence that regardless of what we did, we were always on the side of justice.

The moon above the hills was the same pale yellow as the ivory on L.Q.'s revolver. I could hear heavy animals cracking through the underbrush on the slope behind the house and pinecones pinging off the metal roof when the wind gusted hard out of the trees. For a moment I thought I saw L.Q. moving about in the shadows, his jaws slack, his white shirt water-stained from the grave, death's hold on him not up for debate.

In my mind's eye I saw the beer garden strung with paper lanterns where we attended dances in Monterrey; the times he and Temple and I ate Mexican dinners in a sidewalk café by the San Antonio River, only two blocks from the Alamo; the ancient Spanish mission where he was married and I stood as his best man, the same mission where his wife's funeral Mass would be celebrated six months later.

L.Q. and I had lived a violent life, marked by death and memories of nocturnal events that made me doubt our humanity, but it had its moments. I just wished I could reclaim them.

I felt Temple's hand on my shoulder. "I've

acted badly," she said.

Her nightgown was backlit by the moon, and I could see the outline of her body inside it.

"No, you haven't. You warned me about Johnny, but I walked into a buzz saw," I said.

"Your goodness is your weakness. People use it against you. That's why I get mad."

"I don't believe Johnny and Amber meant to hurt us."

"We're not going to lose our home, Billy Bob. We're going to find out who's behind all this and make their lives miserable."

"L.Q. couldn't have said it better."

"What are you doing with his gun?"

"I hear sounds out in the woods. Sometimes I think it's L.Q."

She looked at me strangely. I leaned forward in the leather chair in which I was sitting and dropped L.Q.'s revolver in my desk drawer. "Sometimes I still want the old ways back. I want to round up every greedy shit hog who's feeding off this country and blow them apart," I said.

She sat down on the arm of my chair and pulled my head against her breast and pressed her cheek down on my hair. I could feel her heart beating against my ear.

I didn't know Wyatt Dixon's cell phone number and the next morning I had to drive out to his house in order to talk to him. He was sitting on a rock patterned with the scales of dead hellgrammites, wearing neither shirt nor shoes, flipping a wet fly into the current, watching it float downstream.

"Doin' any good?" I said.

"It's too hot. They're holed up in them pools."

"Why'd you call my wife yesterday?"

"Your office was closed. So I rung you at home. I wasn't trying to bother your wife, if that's why your nose is bent out of joint."

"She doesn't want to hear from you. What does it take to get that across?"

His mouth was hooked down at the corners, his face as absent of emotion as clay. "There's a yard bitch by the name of Wilbur Pickett, lives up at Ronan. I knowed him from some of my past activities before the Man on High got my attention. He says them boys who put that frog-sticker in me told him there's an ex–Texas Ranger herebouts gonna get himself boxed up and shipped to the boneyard. The ex-Ranger and maybe his old woman, too."

"How about giving me Mr. Pickett's address?"

"Mr. Pickett has done caught air for other parts. Primarily 'cause he dimed them two boys with Darrel McComb and they found out about it."

"My wife was mentioned in this threat?"

He retrieved the wet fly out of the riffle

and flicked it out again.

"Asked you a question, partner," I said.

"When you tell a man to repeat himself, you're accusing him of lying. I don't care for it, counselor."

"Who's paying these two guys?"

"I think you know." He set his fly rod down on the rock. Perhaps because of the shade his eyes had taken on the pale blue cast of the sky, but nonetheless they looked like marbles placed inside a death mask. "That name 'Mabus' wrote down inside a pentacle won't go out of my head. I ain't got the education or experience to deal with them kinds of things by myself. The preacher at our congregation ain't an educated man, either. But you and me? That's another matter. Brother Holland, we could crank up the band."

"Deal with what things?"

"Read the Book of John. I made a study of it in Deer Lodge." His eyes clicked sideways and looked into mine.

"Don't call my wife again," I said.

Darrel McComb was in trouble with Fay Harback, but this time he was beginning to enjoy it. In some ways it felt good to be excoriated, to be the one wheel in the machine that didn't automatically lock into gear when a lever was pulled. In fact, for the first time in his life he felt genuinely free.

Fay Harback removed her glasses and looked up at him after reading the document on her desk, a Xerox of a letter Darrel had written and mailed four days earlier. "Darrel, you cannot write to the United States attorney and say the kind of things you say in this letter," she said.

Her tone was not unsympathetic. Actually, Darrel had just realized he liked Fay; he also liked her petite features and small face and the way her mahogany-colored hair lay thickly on the back of her neck. He couldn't remember when he had felt so protective toward her.

"Darrel?" she said.

"Yes?"

"Are you listening?"

"You said I shouldn't take it on myself to write the United States attorney. But why shouldn't I? The First Amendment gives me that right."

"You accused him of misusing his office."

"Not exactly."

She slipped her glasses back on and looked back down at the photocopy. " 'If you'd take the time to examine American Horse's service record, you'd discover he was an expert marksman. The shooter on the hill behind American Horse's house couldn't hit a blimp with a guided missile. Maybe you guys used up the remnants of your brainpower while persecuting Richard Jewell, but this time out

304

I suggest you give up the role of court jesters and not try to railroad another innocent man.' "

"Sounds pretty accurate to me," Darrel said.

"I worry about you."

"Why?"

"I think you're having a nervous breakdown."

"Maybe I was. But not now. Life is great."

"I.A. still has you on the desk?"

"Some guys are cops twenty-four hours a day. What's eight hours?"

"Not a good statement to make to the district attorney."

But he wasn't listening now. Through the window he saw Wyatt Dixon parking himself and his crutches on a bench under the maples, a group of bums and jailhouse riffraff greeting him, shaking his hand, as though he were a celebrity. "Before this is over, I'm going to cool that son of a buck out," Darrel said.

Fay followed Darrel's line of vision to Wyatt sitting on the bench, a silvery shirt stitched with purple roses stretched tightly across his back, a black hat with a red feather in the band perched high on his head. "What I see is a man enjoying the morning and not bothering anyone. And I didn't hear that last remark," she said. "God, you're a fruitcake."

***

But Fay's political correctness and personal denigration of him did not diminish Darrel's mood or the new sense of freedom that had somehow rooted itself in his life.

It took Greta Lundstrum to do that. He had begun the affair believing he was in charge, that he was using her as a means to solve a case no one else wanted to touch. But as time progressed, he wondered more and more about his own sexual dependency and if, in fact, he hadn't developed a genuine affection for Greta. She was an Amazon — in bed, in her business dealings, with men who got in her face. He even wondered if there was not a perverse element in his erotic attachment to her, namely, her masculine qualities, the heated, muscular way in which she made love, the orgasms he could equate only with a volcanic upheaval.

That evening she greeted him at the door in straw sandals, white shorts high up on her thighs, and a nylon shirt whose color changed from copper to magenta.

"You're early. I haven't had time to dress," she said.

"I think you look swell," he replied. Actually, she looked better than swell. Even though she was a bit overweight, her robust posture and strong features gave her simple clothes a kind of working-class elegance, the uplifted heft of her breasts a tribute to her power.

But the protean nature of Greta's personae filled him with conflicting thoughts. At the sink, she sliced the rind on a grapefruit, then ripped it loose from the pink meat with her fingers, rinsing her hands under the faucet as she worked, like a country woman cleaning game. Through the kitchen window he watched her fork the steaks off the grill on the patio, her eyes squinting in the smoke, and he knew this was the exact image of the blue-collar woman a man such as himself was supposed to love and build a home with. Maybe this was the life that was still waiting for him, but if so, why did the thought of it make his scalp constrict?

Was it because he was still infatuated with Amber Finley, now known as Amber American Horse? How did Rocky used to put it? There were three ways for a career noncom to ruin himself: He could fall in love with a whore, an officer's wife, or a rich girl who hated her right-wing father and liked to get arrested at peace demonstrations.

But that was not the source of the tension band that was like an invisible hat cocked on the side of Darrel's head. He wondered if Greta, the Amazon woman in bed, with her thick forearms and broad hands, could be capable of pressing a pillow down on a man's face and holding it there while he struggled for breath and his heart exploded in his chest.

"Why you staring at me, handsome?" she said.

"You a survivor, Greta?" he asked.

She set the steaks and a plate of sliced tomatoes on the dining-room table and thought about his question. "Survivor in which way?" she said.

"I've been in situations where I was scared enough to do whatever it took to stay alive."

"My life's been pretty dull. At least until I met a certain someone," she said.

"I wouldn't hold it against you. I mean, if you got jammed up real bad and had to do something against your conscience."

"You've got a wild imagination, Darrel. But I love you just the same." She pursed her lips and made a kissing sound.

She had never used the word "love" to him before. During dinner he kept trying to read her eyes and sort out the way she always seemed to imply his concerns were unfounded or even irrational. Maybe he'd been a cop too long, he thought.

"Ready for dessert?" she said.

"Yeah, what is it?"

"Go in the bedroom. I'll be along in a minute." She carried the dirty dishes into the kitchen, a glimmer in her eye.

"No games tonight," he said.

"Do what I tell you. You won't be disappointed," she said.

A few minutes later she entered the bedroom

in a black nightgown, carrying a tray with dishes of vanilla ice cream on it, the ice cream covered with a brandy-laced chocolate sauce. Also on the tray was a narrow box wrapped in satin paper and blue ribbon.

"Happy Birthday," she said.

"How'd you know it was my birthday?" he asked.

"I have my ways. Open it."

He sat on the side of the bed and unwrapped the satin paper from a black velvet box. He pushed back the top against the spring.

"That's an expensive watch, Greta," he said.

"You're worth it."

"Thank you."

"Eat your ice cream before it melts."

They made love, with her on top, her breasts hanging close to his face, her energies concentrated and unrelenting, as though she were determined to make this birthday the most memorable in his life. When she finally lifted herself off him, he was exhausted, happy, and totally separated from the dark speculations he'd had about her earlier. He slipped one arm around her, pulling her against him, stroking her hair and skin with his other hand. Then his fingers touched the swollen place under her right arm. It was reddish in color, hard, as though a tangle of wire had been inserted under the skin.

"What's that?" he said.

"A horsefly bit me there," she replied.

"Really? Pretty mean horsefly," he said, his eyes crinkling.

"I'm going to shower. You take a nap," she said, and kissed him on the cheek.

He didn't know how long he slept. He dreamed about an island he'd once visited west of Tahiti. Not far from the beach, a pink reef lay just below the waves, and inside it was a cave surrounded by gossamer fans. As he swam toward the entrance, patches of hot blue floated overhead, like clouds of ink in the groundswell, forming shadows on the ocean floor. Then he realized the shapes were not shadows but the hard-packed, leather-hided bodies of sharks.

He sat up in the bed, unsure of where he was. Outside, the landscape was red, the mountains a dark purple against the heavens. Through the wall, he heard Greta talking to someone on the phone. "Don't call here again, you dumb asshole," she said. "He's here now . . . Well, forget it, you're not getting any more money . . . Fuck you. I can make one call and you and that other sack of shit will be taking a long nap under the Thompson Falls landfill."

Darrel listened to Greta's words, the ugliness in her voice, and looked wanly at the watch in the velvet box on the nightstand. Then he sighed resolutely, lay back on the pillow, and pretended to be asleep when she entered the room.

"I didn't wake you up, did I?" she said.

"No, I slept like a stone."

"You like your watch?"

"It's grand."

"I'm glad. I've never been happier than when we're together," she said. She sat down next to him and took his hand. She traced the scar tissue on his knuckles and the backs of his fingers. "Darrel, I think you're right about Wyatt Dixon. I think it was Dixon who broke into my house and tore it up. He's a hateful, vindictive man. The thought of him coming back here scares me."

"Don't worry, kiddo. We'll take care of Dixon," he said, patting her on the back.

"For sure?" she asked.

"You bet. Don't let him cross your mind." He looked at the time on his new watch. "Wow, I'd better get home."

Later, when he got back to his apartment, he peeled off his clothes, flung them on the floor, and scrubbed himself with a hard-grained soap in the shower. Then he sat in the bottom of the stall for almost an hour, until the hot water tank was empty and his skin was so numb he could not feel the coldness that blazed out of the showerhead.

CHAPTER 16

Wednesday afternoon was hot and dry, hazy with dust and smoke, the highway scattered with ash that looked like the gray wings of dead insects. I was at a civil trial down in Hamilton when Wyatt Dixon called the house again. "Why, howdy doodie? Is the counselor there'bouts?" he said.

"Didn't Billy Bob warn you about calling here?" Temple said.

"Come to think of it, he did. But since he ain't at his office, and since I ain't God and cain't dial up Brother Holland's head, I called his house. What y'all cain't seem to understand is we're all soldiers on the same side. I think this man Mabus works for the devil."

"The fact you're on the street makes me wonder if there shouldn't be a three-day open season on people. I can't change what the court has done, but I can make you a promise —"

"Done heard all that before, Miss Temple, and I ain't interested in hearing no more of it. Tell your husband I'll ring him later. Y'all don't like it, the feeling is mutual. Brother Holland come to my house, making threats,

312

and I ain't gonna abide it. I think my chemical cocktails ain't working too well these days. You can also tell him I'm starting to get tired of pulling y'all's acorns out of the fire."

The connection went dead.

Temple sat in a chair and tried to think about what Dixon had just said. Was he simply trying to provoke her and bait another trap? If so, what was his motivation? Or was he just trying to make her miserable, to live inside her head, to occupy her dreams and force her again and again to reenter the premature grave on which he had stacked stones one by one, while she lay bound and blindfolded, encased inside the hard-packed dirt, a rubber hose inserted in her mouth?

She leaned over in the chair and thought she was going to be sick. She heard rocks clattering on the hillside and knew the sounds were only those of deer or elk working their way down to the pasture. But the image they conjured out of her memory made her press her hands against her ears, then turn up the volume on the television set until the adenoidal voice of a newscaster talking about hog futures filled the house like an old friend.

She had come too far to lose it like this, she told herself. She would not accept the role of victim, not be manipulated by Dixon, not allow him breath inside her head. When

Billy Bob came home, they'd have a talk, maybe go out to dinner, and decide once and for all —

She realized she was repeating the same patterns of behavior about Dixon over and over, somehow expecting different results. Each time Dixon had made contact with them, she had blamed her husband, acting grandiosely, speaking of the violence she would do, but ultimately pushing the problem and its resolution onto someone else.

Had she lost her courage? Worse, had she demeaned her husband in order to hide her own fear? She felt the blood drain from her head and had to sit down again. There was only one way to overcome fear, and that was to confront it. But she tried to shake the thought of confrontation with Dixon out of her head. Don't be a fool, she told herself. You don't enter the cage of a wild animal in order to prove your courage. You don't allow degenerates and sadists to draw you into their maw.

No, you sit like a prisoner in your home, waiting for the phone to ring, flagellating your husband for your inability to deal with your problem.

She put her .38 on the seat of the Tacoma and drove through the tiny mill town of Bonner and on up the Blackfoot toward Wyatt Dixon's house, passing company-owned cottages shaded by birch trees and orange cliffs from which high school kids cannonballed into the river.

Up ahead, on the left, she saw the swing bridge spanning the Blackfoot and Dixon's ruined house perched up on a green slope. But she decided to cross the river farther down, on the vehicle bridge, and use the back road to approach the house so her truck and her revolver would both be close by when she confronted him, since she had already resolved she would do so unarmed.

A tractor-trailer boomed down with ponderosa logs roared past her in the opposite lane, blowing dust and the smell of pine rosin and diesel smoke through her window. She crossed the river on a two-lane bridge into trees and drove down a dirt road that wound along the bottom of a hill whose sides were slashed with rock slides. Ahead she could see smoke blowing down the canyon from the sawmill, the sun's reflection like hammered bronze on the river's surface, and the roof of Dixon's house, the pipe from a woodstove wisping in the breeze.

Maybe he won't be home, she told herself, then felt a rush of shame at the fearful content of her thought processes. The .38 vibrated next to her on the seat, and she touched it and pushed it against the backrest so it wouldn't fall on the floor. The left front tire hit a rock, lurching the truck frame toward the road's edge, forcing her to grab the steering wheel with both hands. In her rearview mirror she saw small yellow rocks cascading off the road into a green pool down below.

She came over a rise and looked down the road into the twilight and saw Wyatt Dixon in his yard, shirtless, one thigh still in a cast, dipping a sponge into a water bucket and wiping down an Appaloosa whose rump was blanketed with gray and white spots.

Dixon seemed to turn and look at her just as she came over the rise, frozen in time and place, as though in a sepia-tinted photograph, his skin as smooth as melted candle wax, his face slightly bemused, a dusty shaft of sunlight causing him to squint one eye. In that moment he seemed to become flesh and blood, no longer a phantom, no longer larger than life. Her fear and self-doubt seemed to die in her chest like a fever that has run its course, and the wind off the river was suddenly cool and sweet-smelling in her face, the world once more a place of birch and fir trees and aspens and wild roses on a riverbank. Wyatt Dixon was only a man — a pitiful, malformed creature whose mother had killed his father for the years of drunkenness and abuse he had visited upon her and then for extra measure tried to kill Wyatt, age thirteen, with a hay fork. How could anyone fear a man who had probably been born only because his mother couldn't afford an abortion?

She rolled down the incline toward the back of Dixon's rented property, touching the brakes, wondering if she should park by the back shed or simply pull boldly into his yard.

Except the brake pedal had no resistance under her foot and it sank to the floor as though it had been disconnected from its own mechanical apparatus. Suddenly Temple was speeding down the incline, while in front of her a jagged rock the size of a watermelon waited for the tie rod on her left front tire. She heard metal snap, felt the steering wheel twist crazily in her hands, then, as in a dream, saw the front of the truck dip over the edge of the road and take her with it, plummeting through space, upside down, into a green pool whose surface was swirling with dirty white froth from a beaver dam.

The air bag exploded against her chest, pinning her against the seat, but she got her fingers on the window levers and was able to close both windows before the cab filled.

Water pin-holed through the floor and dashboard, and river gravel crunched against the windows as the truck's weight settled to the bottom of the pool. The crown of her skull was jammed into the headliner, and while the truck's engine boiled like a woodstove in the current, she could feel water rising to her brow and she knew in that moment that she would die upside down, like Peter on his inverted cross, alone and abandoned, in her case twice condemned to incremental suffocation inside a premature grave, and she wondered what wickedness she could have done in this life to deserve such a fate.

She struck at the air bag with both hands and jerked impotently at the safety strap, then gave up and strained her head upward as the water crept over her eyes and into her nose. In high school, on a dare, she had held her breath for almost two minutes in a swimming pool. She wondered if she could do that now and, if she could, if it was actually worth the effort. She had become an expert in dying an inch at a time inside a place where no one could see or hear her. Inside that dark place, death didn't come by stealth or a sudden rending of the heart. Suffocation was an animal trying to claw its way to light; it was muriatic acid setting the lungs aflame, shards of glass slicing through pink tissue; it was a steel saw cutting through the sternum while the victim was denied the right to scream.

For the first time in years she wanted to weep, to find the revolver that lay somewhere on the headliner and put a bullet into her brain.

She saw a shirtless man plunge through the river's surface, clutching a gunny sack with a huge rock twisted inside it, air bubbles chaining out of the plaster cast on his thigh.

A cloud of sand mushroomed around him when he struck the silt at the bottom of the pool. In his right hand Temple saw a bowie knife, one with a blood groove and a point that had been sharpened into a sliver of ice on a whetstone.

He stuck the bowie knife in the sand and tried to pull the door open with one hand while holding the rock in the other. But the door was wedged hard into the river bottom, and each time he tugged on it, he lost purchase and his feet floated out from under him.

He let go of the rock, grabbed the frame of the truck with both hands, and drove one boot through the window glass, releasing a torrent of water into the cab. Then his hands were inside the rim of the window, lifting the cab free of the sand.

He got his arm inside the window, drove the knife into the air bag, and sliced the safety strap off her chest. The cab filled in seconds. Temple could see Wyatt Dixon's face inches from hers, his face dilating from lack of air. He tore the door loose from the frame, scraping it back in a shower of sand, then grabbed her with both hands and ripped her from behind the steering wheel.

The eight feet to the surface was like eight miles, then she seemed to soar through wet cellophane and fractured light into wind and trees and air that was as cold and pure as bottled oxygen. She treaded water and turned in a circle, expecting to see Wyatt Dixon, but she saw only a long, bronze-hammered riffle coursing down the center of the river, gray boulders etched with the skeletons of hell-grammites, and the eroded caverns under the bank that hummed with a sound like a muted sewing machine.

She ducked under the surface again and saw Dixon fighting to free his cast from where it had snagged on the edge of a beaver dam. But his situation made no sense: Why had he floated into the dam, rather than rising straight to the surface as she had? She dove down to the dam, but before she reached him he cracked the cast loose from his thigh and pushed himself toward the bank, where he was able to get one foot on the bottom and break the surface with his chin.

He crawled up on shore twenty yards down from her, vomiting water on the rocks, trembling like a dog trying to pass broken glass. She walked up beside him and sat down on a boulder, exhausted, out of breath, prickling with cold in the wind.

His face lifted up at hers, blood and water networking down his thigh, his back and side half-mooned by an old scar. "Tell you what, Miss Temple, next time you come calling, how about using the goddamn swing bridge?" he said.

"Why didn't you swim up with me?" she said.

"Ain't never learned how. My cell is up at the house. Can you put in a 911 for me? I think I done tore my stitches again."

Temple went to the hospital for an examination, but she had no water in the her lungs and came home with me that night. Wyatt Dixon had to go back into surgery. When I visited him the next morning, his leg was in traction, a fresh white cast on his thigh.

"What you did took a special kind of courage," I said.

"Your thanks is appreciated, but I didn't have no idea who was in that truck."

"You know my truck, Wyatt, and you saw my wife through the windshield before the truck went into the drink. Temple and I had a talk last night, and we wanted to tell you we consider the slate wiped clean."

He rolled a fish-and-game magazine into a telescopic tube and stared through it at Mount Sentinel. "You gonna be my official lawyer?"

"I'll think about it. Why'd you call me yesterday?" I asked.

"Except for running a little weed and boosting a few cars when I was a kid, I was never a criminal in the reg'lar sense. But I done enough time in enough joints to know everything that goes on in a criminal mind.

You and me been going at all this stuff all wrong, Brother Holland."

"How's that?"

"From my reconnoitering efforts and hands-on intelligence gathering, I've figured out Greta Lundstrum probably has done got a whole shithouse of grief dropped on her by parties known or unknown. She was running the security system for that research lab that got busted into, and the guy who owns it, this fellow Karsten Mabus, wants his goods back. So it was her brought all these magpies into Missoula and got Lester Antelope killed and a shank stuck in my leg. Being that I stuck something in Miss Greta on a couple of occasions, my injury probably give her a special pleasure."

"For a guy with no badge, you're not half bad, Wyatt," I said.

"You ain't hearing me, counselor. Them people want their goods. They tortured Antelope but didn't get what they wanted. They're gonna come after you next, 'cause they think you're hooked up with the Indians. When that don't work, they're gonna have to decide if they're gonna keep using American Horse's wife as bait or go after her personally."

"Amber as bait?"

"Why you think they ain't grabbed holt of her already? They're using her to get to American Horse. My bet is them government motherfuckers got their hand in this somewhere, too."

"The Feds don't work that way."

He laughed and studied the mountain through his rolled magazine.

That afternoon, Darrel McComb came into my office, twirling a porkpie hat impatiently on his finger. "You think Dixon is a hero?" he said.

"He saved my wife's life."

"Maybe he was behind her accident, too."

I waited for him to go on, but he didn't. I set down the pen I was writing with. "I don't have anything else to do. I'll bite," I said.

"Our mechanic says somebody punched a hole in your brake line."

"You're sure. It wasn't hit by a rock or —"

"It was a clean cut, about a quarter way through the line. The mechanic says maybe it was done with wire cutters or tin snips."

My mouth felt dry, my stomach sick. "It wasn't Dixon," I said.

"Why not?"

I could feel anger rising in me at his deliberate obtuseness, his 1950s crew cut, his small, downturned mouth, his jockstrap aggressiveness. "The man can't swim, but he dove in the river and almost got himself killed. On another subject, what's the nature of your relationship with Greta Lundstrum, anyway?" I said.

"My *relationship?*"

"You two seem to be an item. Bad timing,

if you ask me. You know, conflict of interest, sleeping with the enemy, that sort of thing?"

"You want to repeat that more slowly?"

"I think she hired the guys who attacked Dixon. I think you know it, too."

"You're out of line."

"The same people who killed Lester Antelope probably sabotaged my truck. But for some reason you've got a perpetual hard-on about Dixon. Maybe you ought to get your priorities straight."

"I heard you accidentally shot and killed your partner down on the border. That's too bad. I guess carrying something like that around could make anybody a full-time asshole," he said.

It had been pointless and self-defeating to take my anger out on Darrel McComb. I'd come to appreciate the fact that he was a better cop than he was given credit for, and in all probability he would eventually home in on the people who had murdered Lester Antelope. But in the meantime I had no idea how or when the brake-fluid line on my truck had been cut, and I had no investigative authority to depend on except McComb. That evening, I examined the floor of the garage where my truck had been parked. There was a single drip line across the cement where Temple had backed onto the driveway, which indicated that the damage to the truck had been done inside the garage, perhaps during the day, while we were at work.

The intruder had no way of knowing who would drive the truck later or the kind of accident, if any, the perforated brake line would cause. It was meant, in almost arbitrary fashion, as either a warning or a mortal distraction, whichever came first. The intent was obviously to change our behavior.

I believed the network of assassins or mercenaries responsible for Seth Masterson's and Lester Antelope's deaths were becoming better at what they did. They wouldn't repeat their mistakes or misjudge their adversaries as they had Johnny, Wyatt Dixon, and even Lester Antelope, who had put up a ferocious fight before he died. I believed they would soon abduct another victim, take that person to a remote location, allow him or her to consider the possibility that not all of us are descended from the same tree, and this time extract the information they needed.

My guess was their interrogations were not aimed at pliant subjects. They would choose someone whose principles were such that the subject's surrendering of them under ordeal would leave no doubt as to their validity. The images that swam before my eyes were like those in crude medieval drawings depicting the fate of those who suffered at the king's pleasure. In terms of evil, I had come to think of Wyatt Dixon as an amateur.

That evening I drove west on Highway 12, along Lolo Creek, through mountains and patches of meadowland that were a dark green from evening shade and the wheel lines spraying creekwater above the alfalfa. It was the same route Meriwether Lewis, William Rogers Clark, and the young Indian woman Sacagawea had taken to Oregon, and Lolo Peak was still blue and massive and snowcapped against the sky, just as it was two centuries ago when a million-acre fire could burn and extinguish itself without one human being ever witnessing the event.

But the fires on the far side of Lolo Pass were eating huge tracts of forest now and incinerating homesteads, and I could see their glow beyond the mountains as I turned off the highway into a manicured ranch set back in domed-shaped hills that reminded me of women's breasts. The railed fences were painted white, as were the horse barns, which looked more like Kentucky breeding stables than structures on a working Montana ranch. But the main house was even more incongruent with its surroundings than the displaced barns and hot-walker rings. The house was not simply large; its size was far greater than any individual or group of individuals could possibly make use of in a lifetime.

It was built of cedar and river stone, with cathedral ceilings, the windows orange in the sunset, as though the season were fall rather than summer, the galleries strung with baskets of chrysanthemums rather than petunias. But the alpine design was out of kilter. Shaved and lacquered ponderosa had been used as columns on the front porch, in imitation of Jefferson's architectural experiments, so that the entrance looked like the gaping mouth of a man with wood teeth.

There were other aspects of Karsten Mabus's home that were even more unusual. A sweathouse constructed of dark stone, dripping with moisture, stood not far from a swimming pool shaped with undulating curves that were obviously meant to suggest the outline of a woman. Bronze dolphins mounted on stanchions ringed the pool, along with palm, bottlebrush, and banana trees that grew in redwood tubs. The pool was sky-blue, coated with steam, and at the far end a white-jacketed waiter with oiled black hair stood behind an array of liquor bottles and colored drink glasses clinking with light.

As I got out of my car a young woman, absolutely naked, walked out of the steamhouse, her skin threaded with sweat, and dove into the pool. Then two others emerged from the steamhouse, also naked, pushing back the hair on their heads, and dove into the pool, too. The three of them swam in tandem to the far end, taking long strokes, breathing effortlessly to one side like professional swimmers, the water sliding across their tanned buttocks. They paused under the diving platform, grasping the tile trough, while the waiter stooped down and placed three frothy pink drinks before them. They did not speak to one another or to the waiter, as though each of them was involved in a solipsistic activity that had no connection to anyone else.

If Karsten Mabus employed security personnel on the grounds, neither their dress nor their functions showed it. Gardeners and ranch hands came and went; a carpenter hammered nails on a roof; a maid carried jars of sun tea from a picnic table into the kitchen. I had no appointment, nor had I called before coming to his house. But he met me at the door as though I were not only expected but welcome.

"You're taking me up on my offer?" he said.

"To sell ranch properties? No, sir."

"Doesn't matter. Come in, come in." He closed the door behind me, his hand on my arm. "You've given me an excuse to get rid of my current guest."

Inside the huge living room, under a vaulted ceiling, sat a gelatinous pile of a man in a white suit. His head was large and bald, marked with soft blue depressions, like those in a premature baby. His lips were the color of old liver, his skin so pale he looked as though the blood had been drained from his veins. I could hear his lungs wheezing under the massive weight on his chest. "I'll be with you in just a minute, Emile," Mabus said to him.

Mabus picked up a whiskey and soda from a table and walked me into a mahogany-paneled hallway that led deep into the house's interior. "I'll give you the whole tour in a minute. Let me get rid of this fellow first. In the meantime, entertain yourself with anything you want back here," he said.

"I need to talk to you now, Mr. Mabus."

"You will, you will. Did you see those three lovelies splashing about in the pool? Like to meet one of them?" he said.

He held his eyes on mine, suppressing a grin, then suddenly broke into a laugh. He smacked me on the arm. "I had you going, didn't I? Those are Emile's unholy trinity. Their collective IQ is less than their thong size, that is, when they wear one. If you think they're an embarrassment in the pool, how would you like to have them walking around in your house? At a formal dinner with the Vice President of the United States," he said.

He laughed so hard he had to hold on to my shoulder.

Then he was gone, back with his guest, standing over him, the two of them chatting in front of the dead fireplace, sharing drinks from a decanter of whiskey, the mountainous world outside little more than a backdrop for their conversation.

The labyrinthine interior of the house seemed to dwarf its own contents, which included a bowling alley, a handball court, a playroom for children (the walls garish with cartoon art), a swimming pool divided by a volleyball net, an exercise room, and a library tiered to the ceiling with shelves of leather-bound, gold-embossed books and classics that had been purchased in sets.

But I couldn't find a bathroom. A side door in the library gave onto a darkened bedroom, one that upon first glance appeared windowless. I used the half bath inside it, washed my hands, and came back out, not looking in a deliberate way at the decor in a room whose privacy I was violating. But this room was different from the others, its sybaritic ambiance unmistakable.

The walls were covered with red and black velvet stamped with silver designs of nymphs, mermaids, satyrs, and, on the ceiling, a depiction of Leda being raped by the Swan. The water bed and the pillows on it were sheathed in black satin. In the center of one wall was an abbreviated red velvet curtain that seemed to have no purpose. I parted the curtain slightly and looked through a fixed glass window onto a recessed boxing ring and a cockfighting pit.

When I returned to the living room,

Karsten Mabus was saying good-bye to his guest at the door. The gelatinous man who seemed to have no blood under his skin looked at the light in the sky the way ordinary people look for impending rain, then put on a straw hat and shook hands before walking toward the pool to gather his companions. I would have sworn Mabus and his friend were speaking in a Middle Eastern language, but perhaps it was my imagination.

"Let me get you a drink, Mr. Holland," he said.

"No, thanks. I'll make this quick. Someone has created some serious problems for my family. My son received a scholarship which he sorely needed, only to discover he wasn't eligible. Then I got stung on a bail deal for two hundred thousand dollars. Yesterday the brake-fluid line on my truck was cut and my wife almost died in the Blackfoot River."

"I'm sorry to hear all this. Sit down."

"I'll stand, thanks. My purpose is to tell you neither my wife, my son, nor I have anything you want or need. We don't know the whereabouts of the files stolen from Global Research or even who stole them. We are of no value to you or people who might work for you."

He listened respectfully, nodding, taking a sip from his whiskey and soda before setting it down. He held his eyes on me, then began. "The research facility I own here is involved with genetically enhanced food production. Nothing else, sir. Our goal is to end starvation in the Third World. But for some reason probably known only to God, a bunch of fanatics have targeted my company as the source of all evil in the world. I don't begrudge them their point of view, but I'd at least like to have a dialogue with them before they decide to burglarize my businesses and characterize me as the Antichrist."

"Leave us alone, Mr. Mabus."

He sat down on a couch even though I was still standing, his eyes searching the air as though he could not find the proper words to express his frustration.

"Long ago I stopped trying to sort out all the ethical complications that accompany the operation of a national or global enterprise," he said. "Today, my standard is simple: I protect myself from my enemies and try to do the greatest good for the greatest number of people possible and make an acceptable profit at the same time. Occasionally, that means doing business with people like Emile Asahari. You know who he is, don't you?"

"No," I replied.

"The third biggest independent arms dealer in the world. He provided over two million Chinese-manufactured AK-47 rifles to rival factions all over the Mideast. On one occasion, when he thought a particular regional war wasn't being prosecuted vigorously enough, he paid a bounty for human ears. His business boomed. *Sixty Minutes* did a special on him."

"Not interested."

"You should be. Emile gets along very well with a lot of people in our government."

"I had my say, Mr. Mabus."

"You went in the little bedroom off the library, didn't you? Don't bother explaining. You went in there to use the bathroom. Your hands are still a little wet." He jabbed his finger at me, his face breaking into a grin. "Got you again, didn't I?"

"You sure did."

He got up from the couch. "That bedroom looks like it was transported from a Marseilles whorehouse." He started laughing. "But the house came like that. It was built for a notorious Hollywood sex freak who blew out his doors with speed he cooked down from diet pills. Come on, lighten up. The guy screwed every starlet in the business, then canceled his own ticket because his stomach was so big he couldn't see his schlong." He laughed until he had to wipe his eyes. "Anyway, that bedroom is scheduled to be remodeled next week. In the meantime, don't leave here thinking you've just visited a theme park for sex addicts. I'm a decent guy. In fact, you may be looking at the next governor of Montana."

When I left, he was laughing so hard he could barely catch his breath. As I drove back toward the highway in the fading light, the wheel lines blowing haloes of water spray above Karsten Mabus's pastures, I had to conclude that he was perhaps the most engaging man I had ever met. I also believed absolutely nothing he had told me.

That night, while we slept, someone cinched a vinyl garbage bag over the head of my buckskin gelding and let him run himself to death in the darkness.

CHAPTER 17

I reported the gelding's death to Darrel McComb in the morning. He looked wired, distracted, his hands too busy on top of his desk. "You don't have any idea who did it? An angry client, maybe some guy you defended on a traffic ticket who ended up in Deer Lodge?" he said.

"You think this is funny?"

"I'm on the desk, if you haven't noticed. I can't do anything for you."

"You're a good cop, Darrel. You're the one guy in here who *can* help me."

He twisted a pencil between his fingers. Two wire baskets filled with traffic reports and time sheets rested on his desk. He wore a starched white collar that was biting into his neck. He pulled at his collar and glanced through the opening in his cubicle. "Romulus Finley wanted me to get rid of Johnny American Horse for him. I thought it was because he wanted Johnny out of Amber's life. Now I'm not so sure."

"Get rid of him?"

"You heard me."

"Go back over that. You're not sure about what?"

"I thought Finley was bent out of joint because his daughter was the regular hump for an Indian. But I think the real deal is the break-in at Global Research. I got played on that, too."

"By whom?"

"My own Johnson. I'm going to lock it in a vault."

"Greta Lundstrum played you?"

"No, guys like me get to sleep with Sharon Stone. You really blow my head, Holland."

I went down to the Federal Building on East Broadway and tried to talk to either an FBI or an ATF agent and got nowhere. But I wasn't surprised. All the personnel there knew I had been Johnny American Horse's attorney, and right now, in their mind, he was not only the man who had killed Seth Masterson, he was taking on the supernatural properties of a mythological hero at their expense.

There were many stories about Johnny's elusiveness. He was seen everywhere and nowhere. Some speculated he had died from a fall or hypothermia high up in the Missions or from drowning in the Tongue River Reservoir. A trucker said an Indian fitting Johnny's description had hitched a ride with him over Lookout Pass into the old mining-and-brothel town of Wallace, Idaho, then hooked up with a gang of bikers on their way to Sturgis, South Dakota — in the opposite direction. A rancher who raised buffalo as commercial beef by West Yellowstone, hundreds of miles away, claimed he'd seen wolves tearing apart a cow in his pasture. When he drove his truck at them in the darkness, blowing his horn, a man in a loincloth, his body streaked with blood, had separated himself from the wolf pack and raced into the woods, a torn haunch over his shoulder.

That same night a bartender in Missoula swore Johnny came into his saloon, drank for an hour, settled his tab, and left in a taxicab.

It was obvious the Feds were tracking Amber's movements in order to find her husband. She showed up in Lame Deer, on the Northern Cheyenne Reservation, buying canned goods, dried beef, cases of diet soda, a secondhand saddle, coils of rope, rifle ammunition, and a set of animal traps. She drove her Dakota all over the Custer National Forest, pulling perhaps a dozen agents out of the Billings area with her. Meanwhile, one hundred miles away, Johnny walked out of the bulrushes on the Little Big Horn River, ate lunch with an Indian farm family in Garryowen, then swung up on a freight train headed back west over the Grand Divide.

My favorite story about Johnny and the authorities' pursuit of him involves a Crow Indian named Half Yellow Face, who was a descendant of one of Custer's scouts at the Little Big Horn. Half Yellow Face was a seasonal firefighter and packer for the U.S. Forest Service who could look at a hoof scratch on a dry rock and tell you the size and weight of the animal that had put it there and exactly where it had gone. Johnny had been spotted at the head of a canyon in the Bob Marshall Wilderness, then bottled up and sealed off by federal agents and Flathead County sheriff's deputies. Half Yellow Face was helicoptered in by the FBI to ferret out Johnny's hiding place, although he was not told the name of the man he was supposed to find. The road leading into the canyon was lined with government vehicles, the blades of helicopters thropping overhead, agents with scoped rifles and caps inverted on their heads resting by the roadside.

Half Yellow Face was six foot seven inches tall, had haunted, recessed eyes, had done time in both Vietnam and Deer Lodge Pen, and towered over the government men around him. "This guy got loose from a federal pen?" he said.

"His name is Johnny American Horse. He's wanted on a murder warrant. You don't watch the news?" an FBI agent said.

Half Yellow Face stared at his feet, cleared his mouth, and spat, grinding the saliva into the dust with his boot. He stared up at the gray cliffs that rose straight into a sky sealed with smoke and rain clouds. The only access to the head of the canyon was a dry streambed cluttered with slag. On one bank,

338

among cottonwoods, were the remains of a deer that had been killed by either a cougar or a grizzly, the desiccated hide as taut as a lampshade on its ribs.

"You ain't gonna catch him," Half Yellow Face said.

"He's got no back door up there. If he comes out from under the canopy, our choppers are going to grease him all over the rocks," the agent said.

"American Horse has medicine. He don't need doors. I'm going back home."

"Sounds like you guys are old buddies at the bar. I thought the Crows didn't have much use for the Sioux," the agent said.

" 'Crow' is the white man's word for us. I'm a member of the Absarokee. That means 'Children of the Large Beaked Bird.' The Absarokee lived in the sky until the white man penned them up. American Horse can turn himself into a hoofed or winged creature. You ain't gonna see him."

"I'll make a note of that and fax Washington right away," the agent said.

Ten minutes later, as the sun disappeared beyond the mountains and the temperature dropped precipitously, the sheriff's deputies and government agents along the road heard the popping sounds of large-caliber ammunition up on the cliffs. They took cover in the trees while a helicopter roared over the canyon, searchlights on, sharpshooters positioned in the doors.

The sound of firing went on intermittently for five minutes. The helicopter reported campfire smoke in the trees at the top of the canyon, and federal agents and county lawmen worked their way up the streambed, clattering over the slag, crouching each time a round popped on top of the cliff. Finally they lifted one another nine feet up a sheer stone wall onto the pine needle floor of the forest and crawled through timber shaggy with moss to Johnny's campsite.

Inside a clearing, a big steel skillet sat in a campfire that had crumpled into ash. Empty .308 casings that had been dumped into the skillet and left to explode as the skillet heated stuck out of the ash like brass teeth. The wind blew through the clearing and feathered the smoke in the trees. From the cliff the agents could see their vehicles parked on the canyon road, their tires flat, the valve stems slashed off with a trade ax.

The farthest vehicle from the cliff, a U.S. Forest Service crew bus, had been moved and parked at an angle across the road and was now burning brightly in the dusk. Johnny was nowhere in sight. No one could explain how he had descended from the mountain and circled behind his pursuers. He had not stolen a vehicle, nor did he leave any scent for bloodhounds on the vehicles he had vandalized.

The agents and country deputies watched a

solitary blue heron fly the length of the road, then lift on extended wings in the sunset and soar toward the wetlands in the Swan River drainage. The country deputies, most of whom had lived all their lives in that area, said herons did not fly into the high country and could offer no explanation for the blue heron's presence in the canyon.

That night Half Yellow Face burned wet sage on a rock behind a bar in Seeley Lake and sang the loon's song to the wind, sure in his heart that Johnny American Horse, wherever he was, could hear the Children of the Large Beaked Bird talking to him.

The FBI men were not interested in the attempt on my wife's life or the cruel death imposed on my buckskin gelding, but I didn't fault them for it. They had their own problems, and I was not reporting the commission of a federal crime. But I did resent their bureaucratic single-mindedness, which in this instance I believed masked political convenience. They did not want to consider the possibility that a large conspiracy was at work to hide the history of Global Research, Inc.

When I left the Federal Building I felt like a man who had just filed a report on an alien abduction. Back home, I sat by myself a long time in the backyard, then went inside and returned with L.Q.'s revolver, a box of shells, a pair of ear guards, and two empty peach cans. At twenty-five yards I blew the cans skittering across the arroyo, banging them off rocks, knocking them in the air, twice hitting them on the fly. I loaded and reloaded and continued firing until my palm tingled and the grass was littered with shell casings.

I did not allow my thoughts to dwell on either my actions or the strange sense of serenity I experienced when I felt the heavy weight of L.Q.'s revolver in my hand. I cleaned the revolver with a bore brush and an oil rag, reloaded the chambers, and put it back in my desk drawer. Through the window I watched the light die in the valley and the flames on Black Mountain, just north of us, gusting three hundred feet into the sky.

Saturday morning, Darrel McComb made several entries in his home computer, all of them indicating his inability to deal with Greta Lundstrum's treachery. Over and over he relived his birthday celebration at her house, the dessert she had prepared especially for him, the fine watch she had given him, the way she had made love to him and then talked secretly on the phone about him with a dirt bag after she thought he was asleep.

How bad could one guy get taken?

But he didn't know what to do about it.

She had used him for a dildo, pumped him for information, and helped him paint himself into a corner so he couldn't explain the nature of his problem to either the D.A. or the sheriff without admitting he was a professional idiot.

It was a collection of pocket gophers that gave Darrel a plan. Darrel had bought a five-acre lot up on the Swan River years before hoping eventually to build a cabin there. The grass was tall and emerald-green in the spring, interspersed with Indian paintbrush, lupine, and harebells, shaded by cottonwoods and birch trees, a virtual fairyland. Then a family of pocket gophers moved in, burrowing under the sod, eating the root systems, covering the terrain with barren, serpentine mounds that looked like calcified scar tissue.

Darrel had thought the problem could be easily handled. A rodent was a rodent, food for owls and coyotes, hardly worth the price of a .22 round. He sprayed pesticides and dropped strychnine down their holes and saw no effect. So he called the county agent and was told to cover all the holes around the burrow except one, then flood the burrow with a garden hose. Darrel pumped enough water into the ground to float Noah's Ark and managed to push one gopher to the surface. He flattened it with a shovel. In the morning, fresh dirt piles exploded all over the lot.

He moved on with exhaust fumes that he piped from his car into the ground. He could smell the carbon monoxide rising from the dirt mounds, even hear tiny feet running under the sod. But at sunrise the next day fresh piles stood at the entrance of every burrow and not one dead gopher lay in sight.

Darrel drove to a fireworks stand in Seeley Lake and loaded up with M-80s, cherry bombs, Roman candles, and devil-chasers, which fired like rockets down the passage-ways and exploded deep inside the burrows. The upshot was that he set his own field on fire.

Darrel upped the stakes with gopher bombs that looked like half-sized sticks of dynamite, a combination of sulfur and sodium nitrate that created curds of thick yellow smoke and an unbearable stench. He spaded open the burrows, lit the fuses, then packed the dirt tightly on top of the openings and stood back to watch his handiwork. He could hear the bombs burning underground and the roots of the grass and wildflowers frying in the heat, and see tongues of sulfurous smoke rising out of the sod all over the field.

The next day, he saw no sign of gopher ac-tivity. With a happy heart he strung water hoses and sprinklers over his property, raked grass seed into the serpentine lines of sterile dirt and rock that now networked his entire lot, and drove home whistling a song.

When he returned the following week, he couldn't believe his eyes. The combination of chemical, igneous, and rodent damage was incredible. Grass that had not been eaten at the roots had been cooked by the rockets, firecrackers, and sulfur bombs. The grass was yellow or dying, the field pocked with collapsed areas larger than his car, his well water contaminated. He saw a solitary gopher sitting on the edge of its hole and emptied the magazine of his nine millimeter at it. Some of the bullets ricocheted off a rock and hit a neighbor's truck across the river.

The following week, Darrel determined the flaw in his strategy. He had waged a war of aggression and superior force against a wily creature that had survived millions of years by using its wits to outsmart both primitive and modern man. Power and success had their origins in guile and deception, not in force and weaponry. How had the famous North Vietnamese general Giap once put it? He had defeated the French not with the gun but with the shovel. Darrel had tried to defeat the gopher with the gun.

What was the answer?

Give the gopher what it wanted.

Darrel fixed a huge salad of scallions and the tender root systems of alfalfa and Canadian bluegrass. He wore rubber gloves so as not to get his scent on the salad, then soaked it overnight in poison. The next morning he packed the salad down the burrows of every pocket gopher on the property. His gopher problem disappeared.

Give your enemies what they want, he told himself. With Greta and her friends, that was easy.

Greta wanted Wyatt Dixon dead and the goods from the Global Research robbery back in the company's possession.

Before he went to her house that afternoon, he gargled with whiskey, swallowing none of it, and dabbed some on his cheeks and shirt. When she opened the door, she caught a load of his breath and said, "I thought you'd given up getting hammered for a while."

"What's a guy going to do on a Saturday afternoon?"

"Come in and I'll show you," she said, pulling him by the arm.

He feigned a smile and sat down heavily in a chair. "Got a cold beer? I smell like a smoked ham. The fire on Black Mountain blew out last night," he said.

She unscrewed the cap on a long-necked bottle and handed it to him. "Want to take a shower?" she said.

"Got to work tonight. I think I'll be scrubbing a couple of your problems off the blackboard."

"Like what?"

"Know why the Feds haven't found the

goods from the Global Research break-in?"

"The Feds are bozos?"

"No, they're smart guys. At least most of the time. They just didn't figure Wyatt Dixon as a serious player. They marked him off as a psycho because he writes letters to the President." He upended his beer and smiled at her over the top of the bottle.

She sat down in a chair across from him. She wore a white dress with purple and green flowers printed on it, a silver chain around her neck. Her hair was brushed in thick swirls, her cheeks ruddy. Once again she made him think of a country woman, someone who could knead bread dough, grind up hamburger, and handle a windstorm blowing her wash all over the lawn.

"Darrel, I've got a lot at stake in this. Don't be clever or tease me," she said. Her eyes were green and sincere, and they never blinked when she spoke.

"The Indians had the stuff from Global Research stashed in a barn up by Johnny American Horse's spread," he said. "Wyatt Dixon is con-wise and was onto these guys from the jump. That's why he was following Amber Finley around. He found their stash and moved it to an old potato cellar behind his house on the Blackfoot. I'm going to take him down tonight. Dixon's going to do the big exit on this one."

"Say that last part again."

"Tonight he gets his ticket punched. No transfers. Next stop, a long cylinder where he gets turned into a shoe box full of ashes." Darrel laughed, watching her.

"That sounds mean," she said.

He studied her face, the expression in her eyes, the pulse in her throat. "It doesn't have to be that way. I thought it was what you wanted," he said, his heart regaining a sense of hope he had all but abandoned.

There was a long silence. She turned from him and gazed out the window, biting down on the corner of her lip. She cleared her throat. "I don't tell other people what they should do," she said.

So much for pangs of conscience, he thought.

Then he pulled the string on her.

"The stuff from Global Research will have to go into an evidence locker for a while. But eventually it'll get back to the owners," he said.

Her expression clouded. She took his empty beer bottle from his hand and went to the kitchen to get him a fresh one. When she returned, her eyes were flat. "You don't want to do something before you work?" she said.

"The highway is clogged with fire trucks. I'd better go."

"You said, '*I'm* going to take him down.' Don't you have to use backup?" she said.

"Did I tell you I was an M.P. in the Army?"

"No."

"Know what an instructor told me off the record in M.P. school?"

"No," she said, one hand on her hip, looking down at him curiously.

"When you escort a prisoner and a situation goes south, you bring back only one story. Isn't that a howl?"

Wyatt Dixon did not dream in color, nor upon waking did he remember stories from his sleep or events that fell into any narrative sequence. His dreams were stark, in black and white, composed of indistinct shards, dis-embodied faces carved out of wood, voices that had no source, perhaps a bull exploding like a piece of black lightning from a bucking chute, or sometimes a razor strop hanging like a punctuation mark in the back of a closet.

In his dreams he both saw and smelled his father, an unshaved, jug-headed man whose overalls hung like rags on his body. The father did not speak in the dream; he simply stared, one eye squinting with an unrelieved anger that seemed to have no cause. But his hands were remarkably fast, a blur of light capable of delivering blows before Wyatt ever saw them coming.

When Wyatt woke from dreams about his father, he would sit for a long time on the side of the bed, his skin insentient, a sound in his ears like wind blowing in a cave. On this particular night he woke to his father's presence in the room, as palpable as the smell of field sweat and smoke from a stump fire and fresh dirt peeled back over the point of a plowshare. His father stood in silhouette against the window, a revolver hanging from his hand.

"You wasn't worth the busted rubber that got you born," the father said.

Wyatt sat on the side of the bed. He wore no shirt and the cold from the river had invaded the room. "What are you doing here, Pap?" he said.

The figure stepped out of the moonlight, the revolver still pointed at the floor. "There are men coming to kill you. I suspect they'll try to take me out at the same time. Do I have to hook you up again?"

Wyatt focused on the face looming above him and saw his father's image disappear and another take its place. "How'd you get in, McComb?"

"It was pretty hard. I had to slip the lock with a credit card. Why don't you invest three bucks in a dead bolt?"

"You said some men is coming here to kill me."

"Old friends of yours." McComb touched Wyatt's cast with the barrel of his revolver.

"Take this dogshit of yours somewheres else."

"What makes you think you got a vote in this?" Darrel asked.

Wyatt picked up a jelly glass partially filled with his chemical cocktail. He upended the glass, gargled, and swallowed. He licked the dirty residue from the inside of the glass, then set the glass back on the nightstand. "You ain't no different from me, McComb. Anything I done, you done it twicet over. Except you hid behind the government and done it against a bunch of pitiful Indians down in Central America."

Even in the dark Wyatt could see Darrel's hand tighten on the grips of his revolver. "You're a stupid, ignorant man. Question is, what do I do with you?" Darrel said. "Reason doesn't work and neither do threats. Know why? Because guys like you wait all their lives for somebody else to snuff their wick. Every one of you knows your parents hated you from the first day your mother didn't have the monthlies."

Wyatt sat very still in the gloom, his hands flat on his thighs. Darrel waited for him to reply, but he didn't. Wyatt's eyes stared into space, the pupils like drops of black ink. A train whistle echoed along the canyon walls.

"Did you hear what I said?" Darrel asked.

"My chemical cocktails ain't working no more," Wyatt said.

"Say again?"

Wyatt continued to stare at nothing, his hooked jaw and Roman profile as immobile and chiseled as a statue's. Darrel shook his

351

head in exasperation, then heard rocks sliding on the hillside behind the house. He went to the back window and looked out at the trees and at the shadows they made in the moonlight. The potato cellar he had told Greta about was cut back into the face of the hill, shored up with pine logs, covered with a slat door. Pieces of gravel or dirt bounced down the hillside above the cellar and fell into the yard. Darrel strained his eyes at the shaggy outlines of the fir trees and saw the shape of a man move through a patch of moonlight, then disappear. He looked over his shoulder at Wyatt.

"They're coming. You stay out of the way," he said.

"That was you said I wasn't worth the broken rubber that got me born?" Wyatt asked.

"What?" Darrel said.

If Wyatt answered, Darrel did not hear him. Up on the hill a second shape, then a third, moved across the illuminated spot in the trees. His cut-down twelve-gauge pump was in the kitchen, along with a high-powered flashlight. He had a full magazine in his nine-Mike and five shells loaded with double-ought buckshot in the pump, enough to make everyone's evening an interesting event. But he wondered at his own recklessness and whether his words to Dixon about repressed suicidal intentions were not better directed at himself.

He stepped back from the window. "If I don't walk out of this, get on your cell and call for the meat wagon." He flipped his credit card on Wyatt's bed. "Then buy yourself a dinner on me."

He turned back toward the window. He thought he heard someone sliding down the slope through slag, perhaps fighting to catch his balance. A fine mist, mixed with smoke, had drifted into the canyon, and the moonlight inside it gave off a sulfurous yellow glow. The floor creaked behind him. He turned curiously, having already forgotten about Wyatt Dixon and his exchange with him.

Wyatt stood shirtless and barefoot in the center of the room, wearing only a pair of jeans, one leg split to accommodate his cast, a Sharps buffalo rifle held at port arms. His mouth made Darrel think of the square teeth carved in the face of a Halloween pumpkin.

"Ain't no man uses me, Detective. Ain't no man comes in my home and wipes his feet on me, either," Wyatt said.

He butt-stroked Darrel so hard across the jaw Darrel's partial bridge flew from his mouth, his head snapping back into the wall. Then the floor came up and hit him in the face. He felt the room, the house, and the ground it stood on float away like a wood chip on the river's surface.

Wyatt filled his hand from a box of fifty-caliber shells, stuffed them in his pocket, and shuffled through the kitchen and out the back door. Smoke or ground fog or a mixture of both had rolled off the river into the yard and hung as thick as wet cotton in the trees. He could make out three men at the opening of the potato cellar. He thought he saw two more, up on the hillside, where the old railroad bed used to be, before the tracks had been torn up and hauled away for scrap. What had McComb said? They were coming to pop Wyatt and take out McComb for extra measure. But why were they at the potato cellar? It contained nothing but a set of studded snow tires for his truck. It made no sense.

But the two men on the railroad bed did. They were going to flank the house or pop Wyatt when he moved into the backyard. He went back through the house, out the front, and circled around the side, deep inside the shadows, out of the moonlight.

A rusted tractor, spiked with weeds, its engine stripped for parts, was parked by the back corner of the house, a perfect shield between himself and the men up on the hill and the three using a pair of bolt cutters on the lock and chain strung across the potato cellar door.

The tractor had been used to drag logs off the hillside, and the owner had welded a steel cab over the seat in the event the tractor ever rolled. Wyatt positioned himself at the edge of the cab, took aim across the hood, and clicked back the hammer on the Sharps.

"What do you collection of pissants think you're doin'?" he said.

Two of the figures automatically crouched down and one ran into the undergrowth at the base of the hill. One of the crouching men shined a flashlight on the tractor, then he and the man next to him opened up, the fire from their pistol barrels slashing into the dark, the rounds whanging and sparking off the tractor. Wyatt squeezed the trigger on the Sharps and felt the rifle's weight heave into his shoulder. One of the men by the cellar was propelled backwards as though he had been jerked on a wire.

Wyatt worked the lever under the Sharps, ejecting the spent casing, fitted another cartridge into the chamber, and closed the breech. He took aim at one of the men up on the hill and squeezed the trigger. The bullet struck a boulder and whined away into trees. Wyatt sank to one knee and reloaded just as a man broke from the brush and ran up a deer trail into the timber. Wyatt swung his sights on the man's back, pulled the trigger, and saw the man crash against a ponderosa trunk.

Wyatt's eardrums were numb from the explosions of the fifty-caliber rounds and he could no longer hear the men running through the slag or the trees. The first man he hit had stayed down, but the second one was being lifted to his feet by the two men Wyatt had seen on the abandoned railroad bed. Wyatt stood erect, trying to keep his weight off his bad leg, worked the lever on the Sharps, and fumbled another round into the chamber.

But the home invaders were gone, except for a man with five days of unshaved whiskers and hair like black snakes who lay slumped against the door of the potato cellar, a hole as big as a thumb in his sternum. Wyatt picked up the man's wrist and felt for a pulse, then set the man's hand back in his lap. In the center of the man's forearm was a red welt, like wire that had been threaded into a design under the skin. Wyatt touched it with his fingertips, felt the hardness in the tissue, then wiped his fingers clean in the dirt.

He stood erect by pressing his weight down on the rifle butt and limped back toward the kitchen door.

Darrel McComb stepped outside, holding his jaw. "Where are they?" he said.

"Gone, except for that one yonder. Sunk one in a second man, but my aim was off."

"I could lie and mess you up, Gomer. But I'm letting this slide for now. What happens down the road is another matter," he said.

"You a student of Scripture?"

Darrel waited for him to go on.

"Take a look at the mark on that fellow's right arm," Wyatt said.

McComb squatted down by the cellar door and clicked on a penlight, moving it back and forth in the darkness. "What mark?" he said.

Wyatt limped back to where the dead man lay. The blood had already settled in the lower regions of the body and the face had turned unnaturally white, the eyes fixed and half-lidded. "Shine the light again?" Wyatt said.

He studied the dead man's forearm, then touched the skin gingerly with the balls of his fingers. He held on to the rifle with two hands and pushed himself to his feet.

"Where you going?" Darrel said.

"To sleep."

"There's nothing on the guy's arm. Why'd you tell me to look at it?" Darrel said.

"He was carrying the mark of the beast. But it ain't there now. They don't take it with them when they die. Don't bust in my house again, McComb. Next time I'll take your head off."

CHAPTER 18

The dead man had been a Marine Corps veteran and inveterate gambler from Elko, Nevada. He had no criminal record, but he had gone into debt to moneylenders in Vegas and disappeared from the computer five years before. The insides of his arms and thighs were laced with scar tissue from repeated hypodermic injections. The most recent ones were infected.

The investigation into the homicide behind Wyatt's house cleared Wyatt of any culpability, but not Darrel McComb. He was suspended from the department without pay, pending a determination by Internal Affairs regarding the general deterioration of both his private and professional life. He had now shown up in the middle of two firefights without adequate explanation, been witness to the death of a federal agent he was following without authorization, and broken into the house of an ex-felon. To make matters worse, Darrel had been on the premises while the ex-felon killed a man. One of the investigators from Internal Affairs, dead serious, asked Darrel if he had been recently tested for syphilis of the brain. Humorous insiders at the courthouse suggested that Darrel resign his job now and consider a career as a mortician's assistant in a town that had never heard of him.

The following week I saw him on a steel bench on the walk by the river, feeding pigeons from a bag of caramel popcorn. In his scuffed, boxlike shoes, white socks, ill-fitting dark suit, and pale blue necktie printed with trout flies, he was probably the saddest-looking plainclothes cop I'd ever seen.

"Wyatt Dixon told me everything that happened," I said.

"So?" he replied.

"If you'd been a little creative in your report, you could have skated and jammed up Dixon at the same time. I think you're a stand-up guy, Darrel."

"Fay Harback ratted me out with Internal Affairs."

"Doesn't seem like Fay's style."

"Yeah? Well, she dimed me good. Those I.A. guys think I'm having a nervous break-down. They say it's been a concern to the D.A.'s office for months. Ever try proving to people you're not nuts?"

"Why were those guys trying to break into Wyatt Dixon's potato cellar?"

"I spread the word the goods from the Global Research robbery were in there."

"Through Greta Lundstrum?"

"Maybe."

"You told the sheriff all this?"

"I don't trust anyone in that courthouse. You want justice, you got to get it yourself." He felt the inside of his swollen jaw with his tongue, his eyes slitted.

"Why do you hate Wyatt Dixon?" I asked.

"It's enough I hate him. He's a psycho. What do you care, anyway?"

"Sometimes we hate the people who remind us most of ourselves. It can flat eat you up."

He nodded his head. "You a churchgoing man?" he asked.

"I guess."

"Keep doing that. It looks good on you," he said. He dumped his popcorn on the cement, then walked across the lawn of a Holiday Inn to a cul-de-sac where his car was illegally parked.

Johnny American Horse was hurt. He had been hurt several times while federal agents and county lawmen chased him across the state — abrasions, sprains, and cuts from falls — but this time it was serious and he had lost the medical supplies Amber had sent him. Up in the Bob Marshall Wilderness a sharpshooter's round had ricocheted off a boulder and driven a stone splinter deep into his left forearm. He had removed the splinter, bled the wound, and washed it clean in a stream, but two days later the edges of the hole were red and tender, a tiny pearl of infection in the center. He gashed the wound open with the point of his survival knife, an electrical current climbing instantly into his armpit, then heated the knife blade in his campfire and stuck the point inside his flesh.

He passed out and fell backwards into a patch of moss under a fir tree. When he woke in the morning, western bluebirds filled the branches, their breasts as orange as new rust in the sunrise. He made a poultice of birch bark, wrapped it on his arm with a leather bootlace, and walked higher up on the mountain, out of the smoke of forest fires, into strips of snow among fir trees.

Fever took him the next day, although he wasn't sure if it came from infection in his arm or bad water in a slough. He wandered deeper into the Bob Marshall, climbing to the top of the Grand Divide, from which he could see Marias Pass and the ancient home of the Blackfoot Indians. Farther east, beyond the roll of the plains, was the home of the Crow, the Northern Cheyenne, and the Oglala Sioux. The Blackfeet called the place he stood on the Backbone of the World. Somewhere in the distance, beyond the vastness of the landscape below him, was a place called the Sand Hills, where the dead went to live with the buffalo and the grandfathers who watched over the four corners of the universe. Far to the east, it was raining on the hills, and clouds veined with lightning moved across the sky like bison flecked with St. Elmo's fire.

In that moment Johnny American Horse knew he would never be alone.

Canned food, a GI mess kit, and a canteen filled with apricot brandy, even a GI can opener tied on a thong to an obsidian arrowpoint, had been left for him under rocks or hung in trees by other Indians, all of whom knew Amber and told her where Johnny was and where he was going. But the living were not the only friends Johnny had. Perhaps because of his fever, or perhaps not, he believed his odyssey across the Backbone of the World had intersected the Ghost Trail.

On it he saw the spirits of Red Cloud, Crazy Horse, and the holy man Black Elk. But there were others on the Ghost Trail who had no names. Heavy Runner's band, who had been massacred on the Marias River by the U.S. Army in 1871, still lived inside the morning fog and looked at him with hollow eyes from inside the trees. The hundreds of Blackfoot men, women, and children who had died of smallpox and were supposedly buried in a pit on Ghost Ridge outside Browning sat on rocks high overhead, beckoning, their agency-issue clothes hanging in rags.

When he passed them by and waved farewell, they did not appear to him again. Instead, a lone Indian woman materialized on a ledge, inside a mist, above a stream that boiled over rocks. She wore beaded moccasins and a white buckskin dress fringed with purple glass beads, eagle feathers tied to her braids. He did not have to ask who she was. For years she had been seen not only by Indians but by the military personnel who guarded the intercontinental missile silos positioned along the eastern slope of the northern Rockies. Soldiers standing sentry swore they had seen her inside secured areas that no un-authorized person could have entered, her dress glowing in the darkness, her large eyes filled with an indescribable sadness.

Once, when Johnny had lost his coat crossing a stream, she pointed to a cave behind a cluster of box elder. Inside it, he found a blanket pack rats had made a nest in and six cans of condensed milk. When he slipped on the edge of a crevasse and almost fell three hundred feet onto rocks, she appeared on the cliff and moved a ponderosa branch aside so he could see handholds cut into the stone by Blackfeet hundreds of years ago.

He circled back through the Bob Marshall, crossed the middle fork of the Flathead River, and kept going south toward the Swan Peaks, his arm throbbing, his fever like a warm friend inside his clothes. He no longer thought in terms of calendar days. In fact, he began to think of time as a self-contained entity that could not be compartmentalized. The present disappeared inside morning fog or the misty haze of smoke and rain that lay on the mountains at sunset, smudged out as though by a giant thumb, leaving only the woods, the creeks, the peaks against the sky, then suddenly a trapper's log cabin hidden in a hollow, flint tools washed loose from a hill by snowmelt, a rusted ax head buried deep in a tree trunk, a rocker box standing starkly in a dry streambed, tepee rings on a shady knoll, a turkey track carved on a flat rock, pointing to the North Star.

He followed a trail used by grizzlies along the crest of the Flathead Range. To the west he could see Swan Lake, like a giant blue teardrop, and the Swan Peaks rising gray and steel-colored and cold into the clouds. At night, the Indian woman in the buckskin dress lit his way, the incandescence of her dress moving ahead of him in the trees.

It rained on the canopy, but he could not feel the water on his skin. Sometimes he had to stop and rest, his head reeling from the thin air, the wound in his arm tightening against the poultice wrapped around it. Up ahead, the Indian woman waited for him in the evening shadows. Somehow he had lost his backpack and his food and cans of condensed milk, although he could not remember slipping the straps from his shoulders. He took a swallow of the apricot brandy from his canteen, but the liquor was like diesel fuel on his empty stomach, and he vomited on the ground.

He saw the Indian woman walk toward him, her cupped hand extended. He opened his palm without being told and she filled it with huckleberries.

"Thank you. You're a kind woman. But you haven't told me your name," he said.

There was no smoke in the wind that gusted up the trail, and he could smell the odor of wet leaves on her skin and rain in her hair. She spoke to him in the Blackfoot language, but he could not understand what she was saying. She pointed to the south, at the Swan Peaks, and touched his shoulder, indicating that he must follow her now, that he must not sleep until he was in a safer place.

"We're safe on the trail. There's no one up here," he told her.

But she ignored his words and beckoned for him to follow, an urgency growing in her face.

Around the next bend she left the trail, mounting the hillside, and set her hand on a dome-shaped, lichen-encrusted boulder protruding from the soil. Behind it was a deep depression filled with trees that had rotted into dark brown humus and a burrow that a bear had dug for a winter den. Johnny crawled inside the den, took off his canteen, trade ax, and knife, and laid his head down on a thick pile of animal-smelling moss just as a helicopter roared by overhead, its searchlights vectoring down into the forest.

The next morning he thought someone might have shot at him, but he couldn't be sure. Dry thunder had been echoing in the canyons, and a violent gust of wind could snap a tree limb as loudly as a rifle shot. But the second time he heard a popping sound, he also saw pulp fly from the trunk of a dead larch. He left the trail, zigzagging through the forest, not stopping until he had crested a hill. He slid at least two hundred feet down an arroyo into a streambed, next to a row of nineteenth-century sluice boxes strung out on the rocks like a miniature wrecked train.

That night he came out of the mountains into a wet glade spiked with cattails, where he watched a cinnamon bear and two cubs cornering and swatting fish out of a slough. He crossed the glade, following the Indian woman, whose moccasined feet left soft green depressions in the reeds she walked through. He entered mountains again, where he found a cairn with a deer antler protruding from the top of the pile. Under the rocks were cans of sardines and boned chicken, a package of nuts and dried fruit, a box of Hershey bars, toothpaste and a brush, aspirin, bandages, iodine, and a bottle of hydrogen peroxide. He pulled the poultice from his arm and a smell like rotten eggs rose into his face. He poured the disinfectant onto the wound and watched it boil in the moonlight, then washed it clean with brandy from his canteen. In the distance he could see a ranch house surrounded by a rick fence, inside of which were red horses racing through a meadow, under the moon.

He lay back in the grass to sleep, but the Indian woman squatted next to him and looked entreatingly into his face.

"What is it?" he said.

She placed her hand on the disturbed pile of stones. As she did, a white light shone through the pile as though it emanated from the earth rather than her palm. Crumpled between two pieces of slag was a letter inside a Ziploc bag. It was written in longhand, and it read:

Dear Johnny,

The FBI have doubled their surveillance on me and I can't get to the materials to move them. People being what they are, I'm afraid it's a matter of time before someone gives us up. But even if we fail, I will always love you and be proud of what we have done together. Lester Antelope gave his life and died bravely for our cause. I only hope I can be as brave as he.

Your gal with "The Eight-Thirty Blues," Amber

How long had it been since they had

danced to "The Eight-Thirty Blues" under the stars at the Thursday evening concert on the river? It seemed a lifetime ago. He put the letter inside his shirt and fell asleep in the grass. Through the ground he could hear the drone of automobiles on a highway.

He woke just before dawn, the mountains like a black bowl around him, the sky and stars swept clean of smoke and dust, the air dense with the smell of ozone and distant rain. He ate a can of boned chicken, washed his face in a stream, and brushed his teeth. He started to examine the wound in his arm for infection, but the bandage was still clean and taped solidly in place, and he felt no pain when he touched its surfaces. He decided to let well enough alone.

Just as the light went out of the sky and the stars faded into the morning, he thought he saw the Indian woman among a grove of cottonwoods farther down the stream, waiting for him. But when he approached her, the wind gusted through the trees, and a large doe clattered out of the grove and churned up the hillside. Then it stopped and stared back at him.

"It's only me," he said.

He thought the wind would gust again and change the animal's shape back into that of the Indian woman. Instead, the doe flipped its tail in the air, exposing the white fur underneath, and galloped away, two spotted fawns running behind its hooves.

It was evening and the sun had gone all the way across the sky when Johnny came out of the mountains onto the highway and the world of truck stops, tourist cabins, and cracker-box real estate offices knocked together from fresh-planked pine. In a general store he bought a denim shirt, new jeans, socks, underwear, a razor, and soap. He shaved and changed into his fresh clothes in a filling station restroom, then looked into the mirror and went back to the general store and bought a straw hat that he pushed down low on his head.

A highway patrol car passed him as he walked toward a truck stop where a half-dozen tractor-trailers were parked. He used the outside mirror on a parked pickup truck to watch the patrol car disappear up the road, then bought a fried pie and ate it on a wood bench in the shade of the café. Through the trees on the opposite side of the road he could see a blue lake and a man in a red canoe fishing in the shadow of a cliff. The wind was cool and surprisingly free of smoke, the sky streaked with lavender horse-tails in the south. Again he thought he smelled rain.

Above him, a piece of paper flapped from the thumbtack that held it to a message board.

The sheet of paper had been rained on and

sun-dried and was curled around the edges, but he could clearly see the bold lettering printed across the top: HAVE YOU SEEN THIS MAN?

The picture under the caption was an enlargement of a mug shot taken in the early morning hours at the Missoula County Jail. Johnny looked at the face in the photo — the eyes half-lidded, the jaws slack with booze — and hardly recognized himself.

A couple of log truck drivers came out of the café. One of them sniffed the air and looked at Johnny, his face disjointed. Johnny lifted his eyes into the driver's and held them there.

"You doin' all right, buddy?" the driver asked.

"Yeah, I'm all right. How 'bout you?" Johnny said.

The driver didn't answer. He and his friend got into their rigs and pulled onto the highway.

Why had the man stared at him like that? An attendant at the gas pumps was using the pay phone, looking briefly in Johnny's direction. When Johnny stood up from the bench, threadworms swam in front of his eyes. He walked into the side lot of the truck stop and approached a driver standing by a rig boomed down with ponderosa logs, the engine hammering under the hood.

"Going toward Missoula?" Johnny said.

"I might be," the driver replied. He was a

short, hard-boned man with olive skin and a colorless cloth cap pulled down tightly on his scalp. He wore laced boots, black jeans, and a long-sleeved khaki shirt that was sweat-ringed at the armpits and flecked with black ash from a grass fire. He had a cold and was blowing his nose into a bandanna.

"I'd appreciate a ride," Johnny said.

The driver's eyes ran over Johnny's person, lingering in places they shouldn't have. "Climb in," he said.

When Johnny pulled himself into the cab, he felt as though the tissue in his body were being separated from his bones. The trees along the road, the blue lake, and the fisherman in the red canoe seemed to spin around the truck's cab. As the truck drove south and crossed a stream strewn with white rocks, he thought he saw the Indian woman looking back at him from a stand of aspen trees. He raised his hand to wave at her, then realized the driver was staring at him.

The driver's ears were filmed with soot, and the initials "K.K.K." were inked across the top of his right wrist.

"You in the Klan?" Johnny said.

"I put that tattoo on me when I was a kid. Wish I could take it off, but looks like I'm stuck with it."

"You ought to take it off."

"Yeah?"

"Yeah," Johnny said.

Then his head sagged on his chest and he felt himself dropping away inside the steady motion of the rig, the whir of the tires on the asphalt, and the predictable vibration of the logs under the boomer chains. He didn't know how long he slept, but he dreamed he was drunk, stumbling on a street, trying to hold on to a parking meter while passersby looked at him with a mixture of pity and revulsion. A terrible odor rose into his nostrils, but not one of vomit or jailhouse stink. It was infinitely worse — a fetid, salty stench like whorehouse copulation, a rat trapped in a wall, an owl incinerated in a chimney. In the dream he was still on the street, incapable of caring for himself, but all the passersby had fled and he was left alone against a backdrop of skeletal trees, deserted houses, and a white sun that was crumpling the sky into a carbonized sheet of blackened paper.

When he woke, he was by himself in the cab, parked by a motel with pink doors and green neon scrolled around the office. The summer light still hung in the sky, but the hills were dark, and he could see the glow of Missoula behind him. They had already driven through town and were not far from the reservation. What had happened? He took two swallows of brandy from his canteen, then drank again and felt the world begin to come back into focus. The truck driver was inside the motel office, counting the change the clerk had just given him. The driver crossed the lot and opened the cab door.

"Why are we stopped at the motel? Why didn't you put me down in Missoula?" Johnny said.

The driver's mouth looked small, his jaws fragile and too thin for the rest of his face. He glanced back at the office. "I tried to. You told me you wanted to go to the cemetery," he said.

"I don't remember that."

"Sorry, fellow, but I can't have that smell in my cab no more. I paid for your room. If I was you, I'd get ahold of a doctor."

"You damn queer," Johnny said.

"What did you call me?"

"You're a queer or with the G," Johnny said.

"Get out of my rig."

Johnny stepped out of the cab, almost falling, and ran across a field and up an arroyo, his survival knife, canned food, medical supplies, and trade ax swinging inside the cloth sack in his hand. He ran until he collapsed behind a barn on a deserted ranch, high up in a vernal cup between two mountains. He lay on his back in the grass and mushrooms, panting, the stars hot and bright in the sky, his bandaged arm throbbing. When he removed the wrappings from his wound, he could hardly believe what he saw.

Johnny fished in his tote sack for his bottles of peroxide and iodine, but all he felt at the bottom of the sack was wetness and broken glass. He upended the canteen and drank until his throat constricted, with no sense of caution or restraint; he felt his heart slow and the brandy's warmth settle in his stomach and spread through his limbs like an old friend. Then he filled his jaw with aspirin, found a shovel in the barn, and began walking.

He tripped over tangles of fence wire and in a creekbed was struck in the face by flying bats. He was up in the Jocko Valley now, back on the reservation — drunk, sick, his left forearm the color and texture of a pomegranate swollen with rot, its skin about to split. What had happened to the Indian woman? Why had she deserted him? Why had his power been taken from him?

But maybe the power he believed had been passed down to him from Crazy Horse was just another sham, a cheap illusion that provided an excuse for his personal failure and gave importance to a worthless alcoholic existence. Maybe he was exactly what most white people had always thought — another drunk Indian, a feathered joke dancing at powwows for the entertainment of tourists, a pitiful rumdum who got out of jail on Monday mornings and headed for any bar where he still had a tab.

An alcohol and drug abuse counselor at the V.A. had told Johnny there was a good chance he would end up a wetbrain. A day would come, the counselor said, when Johnny would experience a chemically induced seizure from which he would not recover. He would stumble along the streets, talking to himself, sometimes raging at strangers, his body crawling with stink, and never be aware that a change had taken place in his life.

Maybe that had already happened. Why had he insulted the truck driver who had tried to help him? More important, if indeed he had power, why had the Indian woman deserted him when he needed her most?

He sat down on a promontory that jutted out of a hill overlooking the Jocko Valley. He had thought the forest fires were out, or at least contained, but his perception had been an illusion, as perhaps all his other perceptions had been. Ash was drifting down on the trees like snowflakes, and in the west, beyond the crests of the mountains, he could see the reflections of fires in the clouds, even though he could not see the flames themselves. He remembered the truck driver who had given him a lift and remembered the soot on his skin and the smell of smoke in his clothes. The driver had been a strange man, his truck unmarked by a logo, with no identifiable license plate that Johnny could remember.

He pushed himself up on the shovel he

had stolen out of the barn. When he looked up at the sky, the treetops and stars were spinning. He squeezed his eyes shut and tried to see the driver's face again. Did Death drive a truck and have a perverse gleam in his eye?

He stumbled down the hill toward his destination, no longer sure of either his sanity or the breath he drew. But of one conclusion he was certain — he would not arrive at his destination without help.

One of the bondsmen who had betrayed him lived on a small ranch, back against the hills, where he grew feed on thirty acres he had acquired by marrying a white woman. Parked in the dirt driveway was a patrol car used by the tribal police. The two-story clapboard house was dark, the keys in the ignition of the car.

Johnny threw his tote sack and shovel inside, started the engine, and drove without headlights through the back of the property and up the hill toward the headwaters of the Jocko River.

The cemetery that Lester Antelope had used to hide the goods from the Global Research break-in was located two hundred yards off the road, in a swampy notch fed by springs that leaked from green and yellow rocks. The cemetery was an environmental disaster created by the founder of a right-wing cult that had been run out of Sanders County, an area that normally gave refuge to groups as extreme as the Aryan Nation and Christian Identity. For Christmas, the cult's founder had given his wife a coffin; after his divorce, he published her phone number and address in *Screw* magazine.

His eccentricities also included his demand that all deceased cult members and their loved ones be buried in his cemetery and that none of them be embalmed.

Johnny kicked aside a plastic cross on a grave and pushed his shovel into a lichen carpet dotted with poisonous mushrooms. He peeled back layer upon layer of humus and soil that was thick with worms and white slugs. The smell was not bad at first, but two feet down it struck his face — an odor that was like sewer gas, feces, and decomposing fish roe, the same odor he had smelled in the truck driver's cab. He tied a bandanna over his nose and mouth and worked faster, flinging dirt and pieces of cloth and bone from the hole, until the shovel clanked against a metal box. He grabbed it by the handle, ripped it loose from the soil, and heaved it up into the leaves and pine needles, his eyes watering, the cloth of his bandanna sucked into his mouth.

Johnny heard a helicopter somewhere above the mountains, then the thropping of the blades drew closer, echoing off canyon walls behind him, searchlights piercing the treetops. He froze in the cemetery, his face tilted at the ground so it wouldn't reflect light, his body contorted into a stick.

The downdraft of the helicopter roared over him, swirling pine needles off the ground, then was gone as quickly as it had come. Johnny dragged the box to the patrol car, shoved it into the backseat, and headed back down the road in the dark, his lights off.

He drove back through Missoula and caught the highway into the Bitterroots, passing a city police car parked on the shoulder. At Lolo, he turned west just as emergency lights appeared in his rearview mirror and a helicopter zoomed by overhead. He passed the dirt road we lived on and turned up a drainage between low hills, then cut across a field and bounced up a log road that climbed steadily through fir and pine trees and burned snags left by an old fire. He drove over the crest of the mountain into heavy timber, his headlights off now, the log road strewn with broken rock. Down below he could see our house and the pasture in the moonlight.

He stopped the stolen patrol car, pulled the lockbox from the backseat, and flung it down the side of the mountain into the trees.

Then he continued up the log road, back toward Missoula, or wherever the road went, the sides of the vehicle sparking off boulders, the frame bouncing on the springs, rocks exploding against the oil pan, tree limbs smacking across the windshield.

The oil and heat indicators were lit on the dashboard, and he could hear piston rods knocking in the engine. From both north and south he saw helicopters headed toward him, their searchlights blazing.

He twisted the wheel on his vehicle and drove off the shoulder of the log road, crashing down the mountain through the undergrowth, pine seedlings whipping under the frame. The helicopters followed him down, flooding the woods with a white brilliance that left no place to hide. His vehicle went over a log, shattering the drive shaft, spun in a circle, and dead-ended against a boulder.

He opened the door and fell onto the ground, dragging his tote sack with him. He could see the heavy, armor-vested, helmeted shapes of his pursuers moving up the hill toward him.

He crawled away in the trees, his tote sack wrapped around his right wrist. His left arm was on fire, his heart hammering in his ears. Once again, he smelled the odor of a grave on his clothes and skin.

So this is how it plays out, he thought. You get popped at point-blank range in the woods or wrapped in chains and returned to jail, one of a series you'll never leave. Either way, you're about to be brought out of the mountains like a gutted animal hung from a stick, a lesson for all those who would imitate you.

Maybe it was time to let the other side pay some dues, he thought. He estimated he could get two, perhaps three, and with luck maybe even four of his pursuers before he went down himself. Why not? They had seen only his back while they had chased him all over the state. Johnny would never get the people who had killed Lester Antelope, but he could take several of this bunch as surrogates. They wouldn't be expecting a street drunk to come at them with only a knife and trade ax. Time to paint the trees, fellows.

Besides, what did he have to lose? His power was gone. The Indian woman had left him at the highway, where the woods ended and the white man's world began. The Indian way of life was dead, and Johnny American Horse and those like him were self-deluded fools to believe otherwise.

He blackened his face and hands with dirt, then reached inside his tote sack for a weapon. But his hand found only canned goods and broken glass. He dumped the sack's contents on the ground. His knife and trade ax were gone.

A circle of flashlights shone in his face, then someone racked a shell into the chamber of a cut-down ten gauge. Johnny sat back against a tree, his bad arm in his lap. Red circles of light burned into his eyes and receded into his brain.

"Squeeze it off and be done with it," he said.

"Are you kidding? Those shells are expensive. Hold up your wrist, Running Man Who Thinks with Forked Brain," an FBI agent said.

The other agents laughed and lit cigarettes and talked about the National League pennant race. How about those Atlanta Braves?

In the predawn darkness, Amber thought she was having a dream about a violent wind, then she realized the sounds surrounding her were real. The house shook, the doors rattled against the locks, and a glass pitcher on a kitchen windowsill shattered in the sink. She looked out her bedroom window and saw lightning in the clouds, like streaks of gold inside pewter. The air was filled with pine needles blowing from the trees on the hillsides, then the front screen door sprung back on its hinges and snapped back into place as loudly as a pistol report.

She got up from her bed and began closing windows, sure that the rain everyone had prayed for was about to drench the countryside. When she entered the living room she saw a yellow glow flickering on the porch, like the flame given off by a guttering candle. Then the entire yard filled with a warm yellow radiance, burning away the shadows, reaching all the way back to the barn, carving the horses out of the darkness.

Amber pulled open the door, thinking she was about to see her first instance of ball lightning. Instead, the yellow light constricted upon itself, forming an envelope around an Indian woman wearing a white buckskin dress fringed with purple glass beads that were shaped like teardrops. The wind ripped through the house, blowing pictures off the walls, spinning the Rolodex on the telephone stand.

"Who are you?" Amber asked.

The Indian woman didn't answer. She pointed toward the south, in the direction of the Bitterroot Mountains.

"Please tell me who you are," Amber repeated, stepping out on the porch. Her bare foot came down on a cold, sharp-edged object. She stepped backwards and looked down at Johnny's trade ax and, next to it, his survival knife.

"Where did you get these? Why did you bring them here?" Amber asked.

The Indian woman's shape broke into hundreds of fireflies and disappeared. When Amber went back in the house, one of the Rolodex cards had been torn from the spindle and lay on the floor. The names on it were those of William Robert and Temple Holland.

CHAPTER 19

The next day was Saturday. Johnny was in St. Pat's Hospital, under arrest, his arm pumped full of antibiotics, but I was not allowed to see him, since I was no longer his attorney. Amber came out to the house that afternoon and told me of the Indian woman who supposedly had left Johnny's survival knife and trade ax at her door. I tried to listen without letting my feelings show, but I could not help but believe her bizarre account hid an element in Johnny's story she didn't want to share.

"The Indian woman saved Johnny's life. If he'd attacked the agents, they would have killed him," she said. "Johnny thought she'd deserted him, that he'd lost his power."

"I think somebody found Johnny's weapons along his route, recognized them as his, and returned them to your house. I also think there's something you're not telling me."

We were in the living room and through the front window I could see ash drifting in the sunlight. Amber walked in a circle, tapped her knuckles on the stonework in the fireplace, and stared at the hillside and the wind ruffling the trees. "I think Johnny might have thrown the Global Research stuff up there on the ridgeline someplace," she said.

"Pardon?"

"He's not sure where he threw it. He was almost delirious. It could be anywhere. What was he supposed to do, let the Feds nail him with it?"

"He hid materials from a burglary on our property?"

"He didn't hide it, he just got rid of it. In the dark. He didn't know where he was. Maybe it's not on your property. Why don't you worry about someone except yourself for a change?"

"I hate to say this, but I don't think anyone, and I mean *anyone*, can afford knowing you and Johnny. I'd probably tell other people about this, but I think they'd recommend I have a lobotomy."

"He tried to protect you. That's why he fired you and hired that piece of shit Brendan Merwood. That's why he tried to get his bail transferred to those worthless tribal bondsmen."

"I don't care how you do it, but you get that stuff off our land."

"I don't know where it is or I would. So stick your self-righteous attitude up your ass, Billy Bob."

She slammed out of the house. For the first time in my relationship with Amber, I felt a degree of sympathy for her father.

★ ★ ★

An hour later Wyatt drove his skinned-up, slat-sided truck across the cattle guard and parked in front of the house, his arm cocked on the driver's window, an empty horse trailer bouncing behind him. "Just dropped my Appaloosa off to get his teeth floated and thought I'd see what you was up to," he said. "You seen all them FBI and ATF agents up on your ridge?"

"No," I said, glancing involuntarily up the hill behind our house.

"They must have strung a half mile of crime scene tape through them woods. Ain't that where American Horse got busted last night?"

"What do you want, Wyatt?"

He got out of his truck on his crutches and propped his butt against one fender, then began paring his fingernails with a toothpick. "Them boys that shanked me in the leg? A buddy of mine seen them in Hamilton yesterday. That means they still aim to take me out, or else they'd be to hell and gone down the road by now, know what I mean?"

"What do you want me to do about it?"

"Ain't many I can talk to. Ain't many gonna understand. But you and me share the same kind of upbringing. You growed up in a church where the preacher preached hell so hot you could feel the fire climbing up

385

through the floor. It was a three-ring circus, with folks talking in tongues, drinking poisons, sticking their hands in a boxful of snakes. Tell me I'm wrong."

"You're wrong," I lied.

He kept his eyes on his nails. "The man I killed behind my house with my Sharps had the mark of the devil on his arm."

"I don't want to hear this."

"I seen it. I touched his skin. I ain't a drunk or an addict, counselor. I ain't crazy, either, at least not no more. Them people is acolytes of Satan himself."

How do you talk to a man for whom the devil is more real than God? But I tried. "Isn't there enough evil in human beings without looking for the devil as the cause of our problems? You're a smart man, Wyatt. Why not deal with the world as it is and not get lost in the next one?"

"You're a naive fellow, Brother Holland."

"Oh?"

"One child gets the daylights slapped out of him for messing his diapers and grows up picking cotton from cain't-see to cain't-see in a hunnerd-degree heat, but he don't turn out much worse on a personal basis than a rich kid whose daddy give him everything he wanted.

"But maybe right down the road there's another kid, with ordinary folks, maybe a little shiftless but ordinary just the same —"

"Wyatt —" I said, holding my hand up for him to discontinue.

"No, you hear me out. That same kid grows up cruel to the bone. He don't enjoy sex unless he's hurting someone while he's doing it, and when he finally gets to the joint, he lets everybody know he's the huckleberry who'll bust a shank off in your back for a deck of smokes. Worse, he ain't got no fear of God 'cause he murdered all the light in his soul. That's the ones got the mark of the beast on them, counselor. I been jailing with them since I was fifteen years old."

His description of a sociopath was possibly the most credible I had ever heard, and I wondered if it came from self-knowledge rather than his experience. Then I realized he had read the question in my eyes.

"I ain't one of them kind. Least I don't think I am. But you never know, do you?" he said.

He opened the driver's door to his truck and threw his crutches inside.

"What's your purpose here, Wyatt? Do you just want to be a source of worry and irritation and grief? Is that why you come here?"

"Maybe you and American Horse both owe me. I got confidence in you. You'll figure it out directly. Lordy, you got a nice place here," he said, surveying the house and the deep green of our pasture under the pall of yellow smoke that hung over it.

★ ★ ★

Just before the sun slipped in a red orb
behind the ridgeline, an FBI agent named
Francis Broussard served a search warrant on
our property. He was a trim, rosy-cheeked,
olive-skinned man, with a fresh haircut, a
dimple in his chin, and a Cajun accent.
"We'll be working our way over the top of
the mountain and into your backyard. We'll
try to get out of your way as soon as we
can," he said.

"Mind telling me what you're looking for?"
I asked.

"I think you know. Yes indeedy, I surely
do," he said.

"Yes indeedy?"

"Come on up the hill and help us out. I'll
make note of your cooperation in my report.
That might give you greater credibility later."

"I'm glad to know y'all are in a light-
hearted mood."

He held a clipboard in one hand and wore
a blue windbreaker with the abbreviation for
his agency in bright gold letters on the back.
He gazed abstractly at the haze on our pasture and the purple shadows spreading across
the valley floor.

"Is there something else you need?" I said.

"Yeah, I hate to ask you this. But could I
use your bathroom?" he replied.

For the next hour, Broussard and the
agents under his supervision fanned across

the hillside and worked their way down through the timber toward the house and the barn. The wind began to blow out of the east, clearing the ash from the sky but feeding the fires that were raging on the Idaho line. When I stood in our front yard, I could see streamers of sparks rising in the west and twisting columns of smoke that were filled with light, almost like waterspouts on the ocean. Then I heard an agent shout to his colleagues up on the hillside.

I saddled my Morgan, whose name was Beau, and rode him onto one of the switchback deer trails that zigzagged up to the ridgeline behind the house. The fir and larch trees looked mossy and shapeless in the evening shade. Up ahead I could see a dozen FBI and ATF agents shining their flashlights across rocks and deadfalls and arroyos that were littered with leaves and pine needles and the detritus from years of snowmelt. Even though the tips of the trees were bending in the wind, smoke was trapped under the canopy, the air was dense and acidic, and I was starting to sweat inside my clothes.

With the exception of the agent in charge, Francis Broussard, none of the agents even bothered to look at me, which told me they had already found what they were searching for and hence my presence was of no interest to them.

"Glad you dropped up to see us, Mr. Holland," Broussard said. "See that broken place in the deadfall? Something heavy, with hard edges, probably metal ones, bounced down the hill and crashed right through a bear's lair. Pretty interesting, huh?"

"You bet," I said.

"Except whatever came crashing down the hill is no longer here. Know why not?" he said.

"You got me."

"Somebody hauled it out, probably with a rope and a horse. Step down here, if you don't mind."

I swung down from the saddle and looked at a torn area of broken leaves and dirt on the edge of the deadfall, where he was now shining his flashlight.

"See the hoofprints and the drag marks going back up toward the log road? I bet somebody had a rope looped around a big, heavy metal box and towed it up the hill there. What do you think, Mr. Holland?" he said.

"I'm probably not qualified to make an observation, Mr. Broussard."

"Notice anything unusual about those hoofprints?"

"Was never much of a tracker."

"The horse wasn't wearing shoes. What's that tell you, Mr. Holland?"

"Nothing."

"The horse we're talking about has hard feet. Like an Appaloosa might have. You own an Appaloosa, Mr. Holland?"

"Two of them. But the last time I looked, they were both shoed."

"I'll take your word for it. Know why anybody might want to drag a heavy metal box up the hillside?"

"When you find out, let me know."

"You don't like us much, do you?"

"I like you fine. I just don't like some of the causes you serve."

"You were a Texas Ranger and an assistant U.S. attorney?"

"That's right."

"Ever listen to that shock jock on the radio, guy was a disgraced FBI agent, did a federal bit for a B and E, always putting down the government?"

"Yeah, I've heard him," I replied.

Broussard's eyes looked straight into mine for a beat. "He's an interesting study," he said. He clicked off his flashlight and walked up the hill, his back to me.

A gust of wind blew through the tree trunks. The sweat on my face felt as cold as ice water.

But I didn't have time to worry about Francis Broussard's condemnation. Somebody riding an unshod horse had rope-dragged the goods from the Global Research burglary off our property. It had to be someone who had access to the ridgeline, someone perhaps riding an Appaloosa, a breed known for its hard feet. The only candidate that came to mind was Wyatt Dixon. He used a farrier and veterinary service in the drainage just over the hill from us, and he had a way of finding excuses to wander onto our property. Could he have seen Johnny's flight up the mountain and followed him?

I went back into the house and told Temple of my conversation up the hillside with Francis Broussard and the removal of the metal box.

"Well, maybe it's over, then," she said.

"I think Dixon took it."

"Who cares?"

"You've got a point," I said.

I began fixing a cold supper for both of us. I opened a bottle of wine and poured Temple a glass and one for myself.

"I think I'll just have some Talking Rain to drink," she said.

"You feel all right?" I asked.

"Yeah, I'm fine."

"On Saturday night you always have a glass of wine."

"I'm just not in the mood. Want to take a walk? We can eat when we come back."

"Sure," I said.

I put the food back in the refrigerator and followed her outside. The valley was dark now, the sky still blue, the evening star twinkling in the smoke to the west. I heard the phone ring inside. "I'll be right back," I said.

I picked up the phone receiver in the hallway. Through the front window I could see Temple waiting for me in the yard, the gallery light shining on her hair, one knuckle pressed against her chin, her face lost in thought.

"Hello?" I said into the receiver.

"Hey, glad we caught you at home, dickwad," a voice said.

I checked my caller ID. The call number was blocked. "Say it," I said.

"You got other people's property. That's not nice."

"You're wrong."

"The Indian dumped a lockbox on your property. It's not there now. Where do you think it went? It grew wings and flew up in a fucking tree?"

The accent was eastern seaboard, maybe Jersey or Rhode Island, the question mark at the end of a sentence as barbed as a fishhook.

"You got a line into the Feds?" I asked.

"What we got a line into is your old lady's womb. Want your baby to get born? If not, we got a guy does beautiful work with a coat hanger."

"What?"

"There's nothing about your life we don't

got. That includes your old lady's medical records. Deliver our goods and you don't got a problem. Think I'm blowing gas? When you get off the phone, ask your son what kind of day he's had."

"You listen, you motherfucker —"

"We'll be in touch. Buy better rubbers or stay out of other people's business," he said.

The line went dead.

I went outside, my hands shaking so badly I had to put them in my pockets.

"What happened?" Temple said.

"A guy just threatened you. He said you're going to have a baby. What's he talking about?"

I saw the blood drain in her face. "I just found out yesterday. I'm pregnant. I was going to tell you tonight. I didn't know how you were going to take it."

"How I was going to take it? You thought I didn't want a child of our own?"

"How am I supposed to know? Half the time, we're worrying about every person on the planet except ourselves."

"That's not true."

"Yes, it is. And it's because of your goddamn guilt over shooting L.Q. Navarro. It's always your goddamn guilt and the obsessions you drag like a junkyard with you from one day to the next."

I couldn't speak. My words were like fish bone in my throat. I felt my heart twist as though someone had inserted a cold hand into my chest. I went back into the house, my ears ringing. I could hear her feet coming hard behind me.

"Who was it that called?"

"A piece of human garbage who said he was going to use a coat hanger on you. A man who's done something to Lucas."

"Lucas?"

"Yeah, one of the people I evidently don't have time to care about," I said, hardly able to punch his number into the telephone.

She sat down in the living room, her hands clasped together, pushed down between her thighs. "Don't let them do this to us, Billy Bob," she said.

But they already had.

On Saturdays, Lucas sometimes swam or shot hoops at the university gym. That afternoon he had changed into his workout clothes, stuffed his gym bag in a locker, snapped his combination lock on it, and joined a basketball game on the court. Sunlight flooded through the high windows, and the slap and squeak of basketballs and the slam dunks through the steel hoops echoed in the cavernous building like a testimonial to all that is good and wholesome in traditional America.

Then the ear-splitting cacophony of the fire alarm rose into the rafters. The building was evacuated in minutes. Lucas stood among a crowd of students in gym clothes and wet swimsuits and watched firemen, campus and city cops, and a bomb-squad unit with leashed dogs stream inside, some of them carrying fire protection shields on their forearms.

A half hour passed and the emergency personnel began exiting the building. A false alarm, everyone said. Wow, what a drag. What some guys will do for a few kicks. How about that for sick?

But something wasn't right. City cops and campus cops had crossed the street onto the shady lawn where the students were standing. The cops circled behind the crowd, forming a gray-and-blue cordon through which no one could leave.

"Women students can go, everybody else back inside! Women students can go, everybody else back inside!" a cop wearing a cap and bars on his collar was saying.

"I'm bisexual. How about me?" a kid next to Lucas shouted.

The crowd laughed; the cops didn't.

The male students filed back into the gym and stood listlessly on the polished floor, one or two of them picking up basketballs, arching them through the air, twanging them off steel hoops. Ten minutes later two older men in suits and ties, university administrators of some kind, joined the cops, then cops, students, and administrators went into the men's dressing room. Someone clanged shut and locked a metal door behind them.

As Lucas looked into the rectangular depth of the room, the rigidity of the lines, the tea-colored light, he felt as though he were staring into the interior of a coffin. It was the same strange emotion that had invaded his system and poisoned his blood as a child after his mother had died and he had been left in the care of a harsh, inept stepfather who believed joy was an illusion and brotherhood a sucker's game.

At the far end of the room a cop had pulled up a choke chain on a bomb-sniffing German shepherd. Every locker on either side of the dressing benches was closed, except one. The shaft on the combination lock had been snapped in half by bolt cutters and all the locker's contents raked out on the floor. Lucas swallowed as he recognized his Wrangler jeans with the wide belt and Indian-head buckle threaded through the loops, his beat-up Acme cowboy boots, his snap-button checkered shirt, his gym bag that he had packed with a towel, soap, fresh underwear, and socks.

But items that didn't belong to him were there, too: a string of Chinese firecrackers, an open manila envelope with a sheaf of papers protruding from it, and a Ziploc bag fat as a softball from its shredded green contents.

One of the administrators, a man with meringue hair and tiny veins in his soft cheeks, was holding a hand-tooled wallet in his palm. He opened it and studied a celluloid window inside. "Which of you is Lucas Smothers?" he asked.

"I am," Lucas said.

"You want to explain this?" the administrator with meringue hair said, nodding at the piled items on the floor.

"That wallet and those clothes and that gym bag are my stuff. I don't know where them other things come from, if that's what you're asking me," Lucas said.

"Son, how can part of these things be yours and part not be yours, when all of them were in the same locker?" the administrator said.

Unconsciously, Lucas shifted his weight from one foot to the other, the same way he had done when his stepfather hurled accusations at him, totally irrational ones, that he couldn't answer. "Why would I have firecrackers in my locker?" Lucas said. Then he realized he had stepped into the old trap of defending himself, legitimizing his accuser.

"How about the baggie here? You wouldn't be a user or purveyor of marijuana, would you, Mr. Smothers?"

"A pur—" he began, unable to process the word.

Everyone was looking at him now. His skin felt tight against his face, his body shrunken inside his sweat-stained clothes. Don't lose your temper, don't smart off, just don't say anything, he told himself.

"I ain't never used dope. The person who says I have is a dadburned liar," he said.

"Frankly, I don't care if you use dope or not, Mr. Smothers, because you're not going to be around here very long. Know what's in that envelope?"

"No, 'cause I ain't ever seen it before."

"They're stolen LSATs and the answer sheets that go with them. How much you get for these, son?"

Lucas could feel his eyes watering, the room morphing, the faces around him distorting, going out of shape. "I didn't steal no LSATs or whatever they are. I didn't carry no reefer in here, either. I work two or three jobs —"

He couldn't finish his statement. All the correct grammar he had learned in composition courses had disappeared and he was once again the kid in strap overalls standing in the principal's office of a rural junior high school, in trouble, tongue-tied, his cheeks pooled with color, the years of his stepfather's belittling remarks thundering in his head.

"Go wash your face, then accompany these officers. There's a price to pay when you break the law. My advice is you own up to your problems here and get them behind you," the administrator with meringue hair said.

Lucas stared at nothing. The room was silent, the faces of everyone around him now indistinct, somehow separate and no longer a part of his life. Outside, he could hear people whocking the ball back and forth on a tennis court.

"What are you doing?" the administrator said.

Lucas stepped out of his tennis shoes and peeled off his T-shirt, gym shorts, and jockstrap, then stood naked and raw with stink in the middle of the room, taller than anyone around him, his gaze now turned inward. "Gonna take a shower and put on fresh clothes," he said. "Then when I get to the jailhouse I'm gonna call Billy Bob Holland and tell him to sue y'all. How you like them apples, sports fans?"

He smiled at his own question, his head tilted quizzically, his eyes squeezed shut.

Lucas's heart was always bigger than the adversity the world handed him, but as I sat with him in his jail cell that night I had a hard time participating in the optimism and indifference Lucas always used as a shield when he was badly hurt. In all probability he would be charged with possession of stolen property and narcotics. If he was really unlucky, the latter charge would include intent to distribute. Bail would not be set until Monday morning, which meant he would have to stay in jail through the weekend. Suspension from the university was a foregone conclusion.

"So what? My summer courses are over. We'll get all this straightened out by fall. This don't bother me," he said.

The stainless-steel toilet attached to the wall gurgled when somebody in another cell flushed his. I was sitting on the edge of Lucas's bunk, looking at the tips of my boots, unsure of what to say, reluctant to rob him of his courage. He got up and walked to the bars, shirtless, his back like an inverted triangle, his shoulders wide and knobby.

"I still cain't quite put it all together, though. Can you figure it out?" he said, smiling halfheartedly, trying not to give recognition to the cunning of the people who had undone him.

"Some pretty slick guys opened your locker, planted the dope and stolen exams and firecrackers inside, then called in a bomb threat. They knew the cops would search the gym with explosive-sniffing dogs. The gunpowder in the firecrackers brought the dogs straight to your locker."

"These are the same guys who jerked me around on the scholarship?"

"The same guys," I replied.

"What do they want?"

"They think I have some records that were stolen from a biotech research lab. A guy called me this evening and told me he knew Temple was pregnant. He said a friend of his might abort the baby with a coat hanger."

"Y'all gonna have a baby?" he said, the evil represented by the phone caller not even registering on his consciousness.

"Yeah, she was going to tell me tonight."

"Man, that's great. Wow, I cain't believe it. I'm gonna have me a little baby brother or baby sister. Way to go, Billy Bob, you son of a gun," he said, his whole face lit by his grin.

CHAPTER 20

I slept little either that night or the next. Early Monday morning, I tracked down Special Agent Francis Broussard at the Federal Building on East Broadway. He was standing over a desk in a small office, sorting papers in piles from a manila folder, his back to me, when I tapped on the jamb of the doorway. He looked at me peculiarly. "You all right there?" he said.

"No, my son's in the can on bogus charges and an anonymous caller threatened to mutilate my wife and unborn child with a coat hanger," I said.

"Is this connected with American Horse?"

"What do you think?"

"How about changing your tone of voice?"

"Know a guy name of Karsten Mabus?"

"Do I know who he is? Yeah, who doesn't?"

"You damn well better do something about him."

"Why don't you go get a cup of coffee and a couple of aspirin and come back when you're feeling better, Mr. Holland?"

"Ever been a victim of a violent crime, Mr. Broussard?"

"That's the last personal statement you're

going to make to me this morning."

"I think Wyatt Dixon has the goods stolen from Global Research. He rides an Appaloosa. He has strange biblical convictions about our man Karsten Mabus."

"The cowboy clown with horse pucky between his ears who writes letters to the President? He's the source of all our trouble?"

"Excuse me for saying this, but you're starting to piss me off."

"Which means, if you don't get what you want here today, you're going to kick some ass on your own? My advice, Mr. Holland, is you clean those thoughts out of your head, take care of your son, and stay out of federal business."

"What bothers me, Mr. Broussard, is I think you bastards have probably used the Patriot Act to tap my phones. That means you already know about the threat to my wife and our unborn child but you're pretending otherwise. If I had the goods from Global Research, I'd turn them over to y'all or return them to the owner. But I can't do that, so I'm stuck. What would you do if you were in my shoes?"

"Start my life over, to be honest."

"Care to walk outside and talk about this more specifically? I'll try not to make it too personal."

"Stay out of the line of fire, Mr. Holland. And take your histrionics out of my office," he said.

At 11 a.m. I got Lucas out of jail on a five-thousand-dollar bond, then drove up to Wyatt's place on the Blackfoot River. His truck was gone, but his Appaloosa was in the lot behind the house, nosing through a curlicue of fresh hay Wyatt had dumped on the ground. I climbed through the fence and lifted one of the Appaloosa's hooves. There were small nailholes where the hoof had probably once held a composite shoe, but there were no shoes on the animal now. I had no doubt it was Wyatt who had found and rope-dragged Johnny American Horse's lockbox off the hillside behind our house.

I heard a junker car misfiring up the dirt road, dust and oil smoke spiraling back from the frame. The driver, a tattooed man wearing a strap undershirt, with body hair as thick as monkey fur, braked to a stop in the yard. "What are you doing with Wyatt's horse?" he said.

"Looking at his feet. Who are you?" I said.

"The neighbor. You another one of them federal men?"

"I'm Wyatt's lawyer. Which federal men?"

"They was here yesterday, looking at that animal's feet, just like you. What's this with the feet?"

"There's a lot of fetishism going around."

"What?"

"Where's Wyatt?"

"He left here with the pastor from his church. I think they was going up to the res. What's your name?"

"If Wyatt's got any complaint about people trespassing on his land, tell him to call Francis Broussard at the Federal Building. Got that? Francis Broussard is the man to talk to. Francis Broussard would love to hear from Wyatt."

It was midafternoon when I got up to the res. The sky was yellow with smoke, and I could see Forest Service slurry bombers coming in low on a hillside, laying fire retardant in a frozen pink spray across the canopy. Wyatt's church building was an ancient brick-and-wood schoolhouse, one with dark-stained gables, not far from the Jocko River. Someone had run a dozer into the yard and pushed the rusted wrecks of cars that had sat there for years into a huge metallic junkpile, leaving behind road-size scars in the soft green sod.

The church was empty, but down by the riverside a rock sweathouse was leaking with both steam and chants in a consonant-heavy language I had heard only two or three times in my life. I wanted to be kind in my attitude toward the members of Wyatt Dixon's church, but as a person raised in the rural South I'd known many like them, and as a child they had filled me with fear. The severity of their views, the ferocity of their passion, the absolutism that characterized their thinking were such that I always felt they had one foot in the next world and were heedless of this one. I also believed that, given the opportunity, they would destroy the earth rather than let it be governed by a creed other than their own.

Moreover, Wyatt's church had a singular reputation for inclusion of brain-singed mercenaries and war veterans who stayed off the computer and moved about like gypsy moths through the mountains and rain forests of the Pacific Northwest. Some of them were harmless Libertarians or survivalists trying to recreate a nineteenth-century frontier ethos; but others were tormented men who could not purge their dreams of memories that no human being should have to carry.

I pulled aside the tarp that hung over the truncated door in the rock house, squatted down, and stepped inside. The heat and steam and astringent odor of male sweat covered my face like a wet cloth. In one corner the pastor sat on a stool in an oversized pair of black swim trunks, his skin as pink as a baby pig's, his face smiling, a jolly, innocent man among men whose backgrounds had nothing in common with his own. Wyatt sat across from him on an old rug, wearing only a jockstrap, his knees pulled up in front of him, drops of sweat as big as dimes sliding down his face. But it was the three other men in the rock house who bothered me.

Perhaps I had been away too long from hands-on involvement with law enforcement and the realities of the criminal world. Perhaps I had become too much like the ordinary citizen who sees criminals only when they are in custody — free of drugs and booze, showered, clean-shaven, their hair freshly barbered, their tattoos hidden by buttoned collars and conservative neckties and long-sleeve shirts. It had been a temptation to think of Wyatt as a slightly fried, engaging, hillbilly eccentric; but one look at his sweathouse friends was a quick reminder that his jailhouse past and criminal frame of reference were not abstractions.

One man was totally naked, head shaved, perhaps six and a half feet tall, snake-belly white, the edges of his eyes tattooed with blue teardrops. An Indian sat next to him, his braids, sopping with moisture, tied on top of his scalp, his chest pocked with two lead-gray circular scars that looked like bullet wounds, his arms scrolled from wrist to armpit with jailhouse art that convicts call "sleeves."

The third man had the flawless gray proportions of a granite sculpture, his abs recessed, elongated like strips of stone below the curvature of his chest, his phallus huge, his eyes dancing with an inquisitional light as though my casual glance at him were a personal challenge to his manhood.

"See you outside, Wyatt?" I said.

"This is a prayer meeting. Can it wait?" he replied.

"No," I said, and stepped back outside, my shirt peppered with moisture.

He followed me, standing up on a pair of walking canes, but before I could speak he lumbered into the Jocko and sat down chest-deep in the current, holding on to a boulder with each arm while the ice-cold water boiled over his skin. Then he hobbled back up on the bank and began pulling on his clothes, one eye squinting at me. "You got a beef about something?" he asked.

"I'm taking your weight," I said.

"For what?"

"You found the goods from the Global Research robbery. But some guys think I've got them and they're coming down on my family to get them back."

"Sorry to hear that."

"I'm in a bad mood, Wyatt. I don't have a lot to lose at this point, get my meaning? You think you're about to make the big score with the Global goods? Is that why you're hanging with the Deer Lodge alumni in there?"

"I wouldn't say that too loud if I was you."

"You turn the goods over to the Feds or Karsten Mabus's people, I don't care which."

"I thought you was a smart man, but I'm

revising my opinion downward. I got a buddy to bust into them files. The day that Mabus fellow gets them files back, I'm a dead man and so are you."

"Call *The Washington Post* or *The New York Times*. I'll help you."

"Yeah, they'll run with that one — stolen goods turned over to them by an ex-con with a homicide in his jacket and a lawman who killed his best friend."

"Nobody can accuse you of an excess of sentiment," I said.

He tucked his shirt into his jeans, his mouth twisted into a button. "I'm always on the receiving end of your insults, counselor. It gets to be a drag."

"What's in those files?" I said.

"Stuff about anthrax, Ebola virus, mustard gas, the Black Death. I done told you before, I ain't got the education or the experience to deal with a man like Mabus. But the two of us can come up with a plan. It takes smarts to whip the devil."

"Let's keep it simple and save the Bible lessons for your study group in there. You dump the goods. End of story."

"No, you listen to me," he said, pointing a finger at my face. "Them three ex–fellow travelers of the Lost Highway in the sweat lodge? The Indian took two rounds from a .357 Mag and crawled a half mile in a hunnerd-degree desert to kill the man done it

410

to him. The tall fellow who looks like a big Q-Tip done hits for the Aryan Brotherhood in Quentin and Folsom. Each one of them teardrops tattooed on his eyes is for a man he done for free, just a favor for the AB. The iron man you seen in there, one with the crazy look in his eyes, has done committed crimes both inside and outside you don't want to even know about.

"What I'm saying to you is men like that, men like me, ain't no threat to the likes of a Karsten Mabus. A man like you is. If I had your education, I'd own this whole fucking state."

"You're mistaken, Wyatt."

He picked up his canes and stared at the river, the trees bending in the breeze on the hillside, the smoke that mushroomed into the sky as yellow as sulfur. His eyes looked prosthetic, impossible to read, the crow's-feet at the edges like artistic brushstrokes that were intended to give his face the human dimension it lacked. "When I first come out of the pen, I wanted to hurt you for what you done to me," he said.

"Let's stick to the subject," I said.

"Not hurt you like you think. I wanted to get close to you and bring you down to where I was, make you into the very kind of man you hated. I figured that was about the worst thing I could do to anybody on earth. Anyway, that was then, this is now. It's gonna take the two of us to shovel Karsten Mabus's grits in the stove. Get used to the idea."

"I dimed you with the Feds this morning."

"You're too late. They tore my place apart yesterday. They ain't found squat on a rock, either."

I gave up. He was impervious to both my questions and insults, even my admission that I had informed on him. But there was still one other question I had to ask him. "Were y'all talking in tongues earlier?"

"Why you want to know?"

"Because I think you're psychotic. That and the fact you're injured is the only reason I don't break your jaw."

"You done let me down, Brother Holland. I figured you for more sand. Anyway, time for my chemical cocktail," he said. He fitted on a peaked, slope-brimmed hat and hobbled toward the church on his canes, the pupils in his eyes like broken drops of India ink.

CHAPTER 21

Darrel McComb did not know how he would do it, but one way or another he was going to get even. The Feds had treated him like the best-dressed man of 1951, Greta Lundstrum had played him, his own department had dumped him, Fay Harback had dimed him with I.A., and a jailhouse dickwad like Wyatt Dixon had sucker-dropped him with a replica of an antique rifle.

In addition, he'd almost been killed trying to save Seth Masterson's life, and the upshot had been an official reprimand and a departmental suspension. The ultimate irony was that he was probably the only cop in Missoula County who knew the score on the Global Research break-in. Or at least he knew most of the score. There was one element about the break-in and its aftermath that he didn't like to think about, primarily because even consideration of the idea put him in a league with a psycho-ceramic like Dixon.

Greta had set him up the night a hit team had descended on Dixon's place; she had not only known he would be on the premises, she knew there was a good chance he would be taken out along with Wyatt. But instead, the lowlifes had walked into a firestorm. In fact, Darrel had to give Dixon credit; when it came to inflicting carnage on the enemy, Dixon had no peer. What troubled Darrel was not Dixon's humiliation of him but instead the possibility that Dixon's perverse religious views had credibility.

On two occasions Darrel had noticed a red mark underneath Greta's right arm, one she had tried to dismiss as a horsefly bite, an explanation that in itself was a problem: Greta wasn't a horsewoman and had no interest in animals or being around them.

Blow it off. Maybe she found a lump she doesn't want to talk about, he told himself. He wondered if he was starting to lose his sanity or, more specifically, if his own head hadn't become a dark box where his worst enemies were his own thoughts.

Keep the lines straight, he thought. Dixon was nuts, Greta was a Judas, and the judicial system in this country sucked. That's all he had to remember: meltdowns were meltdowns, women screwed you in more ways than one, the system copped pud, and good guys like Rocky Harrigan led us away from ourselves.

But the bump under her arm wasn't put there by a horsefly. The lie wasn't even close. He had touched the swollen place while they made love; it was hard, configured like a midsized, calcified boil. Why hadn't she gone to a doctor and had it treated?

He had deliberately not confronted Greta about her betrayal. He still believed she was an amateur, and as such he had known her defenses and denial and explanations would be in place in the immediate aftermath of her treachery. But silence and unpredictability unnerved amateurs far more than confrontation did. You waited and let them think they had skated, then you dropped the whole junkyard on their heads. Usually, they crumpled like a piece of paper thrown on hot coals.

On the evening of the same Monday I had gone to see Wyatt at his church, Darrel dropped in on Greta at her bungalow without notice.

She opened the door, her hair unbrushed, her face stark, without makeup, her big eyes unblinking, her level of discomfort crawling on her skin.

"Where have you been, stranger?" she asked, her smile like a rip in a clay mask.

"Hanging out, watching a lot of baseball, staying out of the smoke. See, I'm suspended without pay, which is the same as being fired, so I got a lot of time on my hands and I thought I'd drive down and check out how things are with you. So how's it goin'?"

He walked into the living room without being invited.

"I was starting to get a little worried about you," she said. "I called a couple of times but your message machine must have been off. You been all right?"

He let the lie about his message machine pass. "I'm doing good. Got a beer? Why don't we play some music and slap some steaks on the grill? You're not doing anything else, are you, Greta?"

"I've got hamburger. I can chop some onions in it, the way you like it. I can fix a salad. Is that okay?" She didn't know what to do with either her hands or her eyes. She coughed into her palm and waited.

"Wow, that smoke is something else, isn't it?" he said. "My lungs feel like I've been smoking three packs of cigarettes a day. Hey, hamburger would be great."

He put a CD compilation of 1940s swing music on her stereo and sat in a deep chair and gazed out the side window at the mountains while she began preparing dinner in the kitchen. Greta was a middle-class bumbler who'd strayed into the criminal world, and Darrel knew that by the end of the evening he would have everything from her he wanted. But he had to wonder at his own coldness and the ease and confident sense of calculation he felt as he went about dismantling the life of a woman he had not only slept with but had formed a strange affection for.

But that was the breaks, he told himself. She was about to join that four percent of the criminal population who actually paid for their crimes. Like most amateurs, she probably never believed a day would come when she would have to stand in front of a judge, her life in tatters, her bank accounts emptied by defense lawyers, and listen mutely while the judge told her she had just become a bar of soap.

If they did the crime, they stacked the time, Darrel told himself. Why beat up on himself about it? But he could not deny the rush of satisfaction he felt when he took down perps, any of them, not just Greta, blowing apart their shoddy defenses, exposing their lies, making them see for just a moment their own pathos and inadequacy. Sure, they were scapegoats, surrogates for all the grimebags and degenerates who skated, but that's what scapegoats were for, he thought. Were it not for the scapegoats, the job would be intolerable.

Darrel could not count the number of unresolved cases in his career. In fact, often the worst of them never got to be "cases," because they existed in a category of moral failure over which criminal law had little governance or application.

He remembered seven years back when he had investigated a one-car fatality accident by Alberton Gorge. The driver, a man who worked in a Spokane bookstore, was returning home from a funeral in Minnesota. On an empty highway at dusk, his compact hit a guardrail, gashing open the gas tank. The compact seemed to right itself momentarily, then a flame twisted from under the frame and a ball of light mushroomed out of the windows.

The weather had been good, the road dry, and the highway patrol concluded that the driver had fallen asleep at the wheel. But the driver's wife would not accept the highway patrol's explanation. Her husband had a perfect driving record, she said. He was a conservative, abstemious man who never drove when he was tired, never broke traffic regulations, and was always conscious of the safety of others. There could have been no mechanical failure, either; his car was new and the maintenance on it was done by her brother, a mechanic. Darrel believed her.

Darrel had the widow send him all her husband's credit card records, and he re-created each step of the husband's trip from Spokane to the funeral service in St. Paul and back home again. The dead man and his wife were people of humble means, and it was obvious the husband did everything in his power not to spend an excess of money on himself, hence his decision to drive the thousands of miles to attend an uncle's funeral rather than fly without discount reservations. He bought gas at off-brand filling stations, stayed at the Econo Lodge and Motel 8, and evidently ate at cash-basis fast-food restaurants, since the credit card records showed almost no purchases for food.

Darrel began calling each motel along the husband's return route. But no one could offer any personal information about the bookseller from Spokane, other than the computerized record that showed the time and date of his check-in. Then a casual addendum in a conversation with a desk clerk in eastern Montana opened up another scenario and suddenly gave a face, an identity, and a sad kind of history to a man who was about to be written off as the cause of his own death.

"Yeah, he checked in on a Saturday afternoon two weeks ago. It was colder than hell. Wind must have been blowing forty miles an hour," the clerk said. "We were packed to the ceiling, hunting season and all."

"Was he drinking? Was there anything unusual about his behavior? Did he seem sick?" Darrel said.

"Actually, he didn't stay at this motel. When we have an overflow, we register guests at this motel but we send them to the motel across the road. See, we own half of that one with my brother-in-law."

Darrel got the number of the brother-in-law and left a message for him. The next

419

day, the brother-in-law returned the call. "Yeah, I remember him," he said. "He was a nice gentleman, quiet fellow, played with my cat on the counter when he came up to get some soap for the room. He do something wrong?"

"He was involved in a traffic accident. I was just checking out a couple of details for my paperwork. Did he have booze on his breath or seem to be sick?"

"No, I saw him early in the morning, just before he left. I'm sure he wasn't drinking. I felt bad about the room I gave him and offered not to charge him for it, but he said it was no problem."

"Would you explain that in a little more detail."

"A bunch of loudmouth hunters were in the rooms on each side of him. They came in drunk about eleven o'clock, yelling outside the rooms, throwing ice chests around in their trucks, rattling the Coke machine, stuff like that. He must have asked them to be quiet, 'cause I think they beat on his wall or his door. No, that's not exactly right. I know they gave him a bad time. These guys were real assholes. They got up at four in the morning and did it again before they left, I mean slamming doors and hollering at each other, racing their truck engines, like nobody else is on the planet, so I don't think that poor fellow got any sleep at all."

"You got names and addresses for these guys?" Darrel asked.

Over the next few days Darrel called up seven men who had stayed in the rooms close by the bookseller's. Each denied any responsibility for the dead man's sleep deprivation. Three of them hung up on him. If any of them felt any guilt over the bookseller's death, it was not apparent to Darrel. In fact, none of them seemed to even remember the anonymous, faceless man who'd had the bad luck to be sandwiched between their rooms.

In Darrel's opinion, the hunters might not have been the direct cause of the bookseller's death, but they had certainly contributed to it. And that's the way it would end, Darrel thought. The hunters would go back to their jobs, their families, their venison dinners, and their swinging-dick bravado; they'd get laid, knock back shots in loud saloons, slam poker dice down on hardwood bars, see the sunrise with the warmth of a wife and mother next to them, attend churches that were little more than extensions of civic clubs, watch their children grow up, and one day many years from now, just before all the cares of the world became as dross before their eyes, wonder why a vague memory of a Saturday night outside Glendive, Montana, should hover like a chimerical presence next to their beds.

Darrel drove over to Spokane and took the dead man's widow and children to an amusement park in Coeur d'Alene, then at dinner that night told the woman her husband might have swerved his car to avoid hitting a deer, that evidently he was a kind man and instinctively had chosen to cut his wheels toward the shoulder rather than simply slam on the brakes and broadside an animal that had probably frozen in the headlights.

Darrel could not bear to tell her that a collection of dog-pack bullies had robbed her husband of his sleep, forcing him to make the long drive across the state while he was bone-tired in order to be at work on time Monday morning. Also he could not bear to tell her that a prosecutable case against the dog pack was a legal impossibility.

The next weekend Darrel drove to the hometown of the hunters, a windblown, godforsaken place close to the Canadian line, and in an hour had the name of the man who was considered to be their leader. At 2 a.m. he used a pay phone to call the man's house. The wife answered, but at Darrel's insistence she woke her husband and got him on the phone.

"Who the hell is this?" the man said.

"Bang!" Darrel said, and hung up.

Darrel fired a single .44 Magnum round through the front window of the man's auto parts store, listened to the bullet ricochet and break things inside, then drove back to Missoula.

At Christmas, the leader of the hunters received a greeting card inscribed with a single line: "I'm still out here."

"Why so lost in thought tonight?" Greta asked.

"Thinking about you, Greta. Want to dance?" he said.

"The food's almost ready."

"It'll wait. Come on," he said.

He put one arm around her waist and lifted her right hand in the air. Bunny Berrigan's "I Can't Get Started" was playing on the stereo. Darrel pulled Greta against him, pushing her arms around his neck, as though he were going to hug her. But he let his fingers slide up her side, until he felt a knot about five inches below her armpit. The balls of his fingers traced its outline against her shirt. The knot had not grown in size, but it was harder, the configuration more defined.

"Don't," she said.

"It hurts?"

"I told you, it's an insect bite. It got infected."

"Let's take a look at it."

"It's time to eat."

"Take off your shirt."

"Come into the bedroom and I might do that," she said, half smiling.

"The romantic jerk-around is over, Greta. You did me. Know the expression 'First time shame on you, second time shame on me'?

You sicced the lowlifes on me at Dixon's place. I almost got my kite burned, Greta. Problem is, I was onto you and it didn't work. You're in deep shit, girl."

Her face was only inches from his, the dance music still playing. She started to speak, her eyes wide with both fear and shock.

"No, no," he said, touching her lips with one finger. "You don't lie anymore, Greta. While you thought I was asleep, I heard you talking to your trained cretins. So I told you the Global Research goods were at Dixon's place and I was going to take him down. Sure enough, your pals showed up that night, ready to pop both me and the peckerwood. You're a Judas, Greta. For cops, that's a category below drug dealers and pimps. Ever hear of the Contras?"

"Who?" she said, all of it going too fast for her now, her mouth twitching, an ugly smell from the kitchen wrapping itself around her face. "The food's burning. I left the burner on high."

"That's good, because we're not going to be eating it. I was with the Contras in northern Nicaragua, Greta, saw some mean shit go down that I don't like to remember. I was an adviser to Somoza's Rattlesnake Brigade, badass dudes who wired people up to field generators, got fed by the peasants, or burned the ville. But we had a problem — a turncoat was pipelining intel into the Sandinistas. One day out on the trail the lieutenant stops the column and says to him, 'You got to dig a hole, then take a rest, man. We're going give you a good meal, some rum, you want to get laid, there's time for that, too, man. But then you got to rest.'

"The turncoat knows what's about to happen. First he lies, then he lies and he lies and he lies some more, and when that doesn't work, he begs on his knees. My job was to stay out of it, but I didn't want to see the guy get whacked. I kept hoping he'd do the right thing, act dignified, not insult people with his lies. But he was a dumb guy and thought he could lie his way out of it, then he thought he could beg and make people feel sorry for him. Know what that did? It made it easy for everybody else. Someone finally shut him up with an AK, splattered his salad all over a ditch, and nobody could have cared less.

"If the guy had been stand-up and told the truth, if maybe he'd given up the name of his contact, chances are the others would have let him go back to his family. You hearing me on this? Don't lie. Don't degrade your-self. I'm the only person who can save your ass. No, don't look away, don't start crying, either. That stuff belongs on soap operas, not in big-people land, Greta. Why'd you kill Charlie Ruggles? Poor ole Charlie, sawed-off little jarhead gets snuffed by a broad, probably humiliating as hell for him."

He thought she was going to faint. She sank heavily into a chair, her face splotched with color, her green eyes as round as Life Savers. "I had to. I lost control of my life years ago. My second husband was a martial arts instructor who did security work for Karsten Mabus. I went to work for him, too."

"That means you *had* to smother a guy in a hospital bed?"

Her hands were fists, her arms folded across her breasts, her throat as taut as a chunk of sewer pipe. Then the fingers of her left hand seemed to spread protectively over the lump on her side. "Mabus owns people. You can't guess at what it's like," she said.

Her face was uplifted, her eyes fixed on his now. The direction of the conversation was not one Darrel liked. The motivation in most crimes was money. Not sex, not power. It was money. Money could buy you all the sex and power you wanted. A premeditated homicide, in this case holding a pillow down on the face of a potential government witness, was done for money. But Darrel's own questions about the mark or lump or whatever it was on Greta's side would not let go of him.

"Dixon says the crew working for Mabus have the mark of the beast on them. I don't like to even repeat bullshit like that, but what the fuck is he talking about?" he said.

She bent over in the chair, her hands pressed on the sides of her head. "I'm going to be sick," she said.

"Are you in a cult?"

"Cult? You idiot! *Cult?* No one can be that stupid."

Her skin had turned as gray as a cadaver's, her upper lip beaded with moisture. Then she sniffed at the air again, remembering the food on the stove. She ran into the kitchen and shut off the flame under a pan filled with blackened onions and scorched hamburger patties.

"Turn around and look at me," Darrel said.

Instead, she swung the pan at his head. He blocked her arm and food that smelled like it had been dug out of an incinerator splattered all over the walls. But she wasn't finished. She struck at his face and tried to claw his eyes, and he had to pin her arms against her sides and squeeze them against her torso in a bear hug until the tension made her breath seize in her chest and her spine pop.

He saw her mouth open, and he knew what was coming next. He released her, and she ran to the toilet and threw up, then went into the dry heaves on her knees, clenching the edge of the bowl, her back shaking, her skin the color of cardboard.

Darrel sat on the rim of the tub and flushed the toilet for her, then wet a towel and put it in her hand. "Why'd you rat-fuck me, Greta?" he said.

"Because I hate you," she replied.

"For once you're probably telling the truth," he said, his eyes flat, concealing the recognition that her words could still wound him.

He leaned over and raised her shirt, exposing a dry, star-shaped swelling under her arm.

"That looks like a jungle ulcer. We used to get them in Nicaragua," he said.

"Rah-rah for you," she said.

"It's just a skin problem, so now we got that out of the way. You're going to wear a recorder into Karsten Mabus's house, Greta."

"No, I'm not."

"I still don't think you understand my status. I'm effectively canned, in large part because of you. That means we're not using rule books here. You wear a recorder, or I put out the word you're a federal informant. I also stoke up Wyatt Dixon and let him know who sent that collection of killers to his house. Want Wyatt coming around to see you again, Greta?"

"I have melanoma. It's already gone into my organs. You can't hurt me," she said. She tried to hold her eyes on his, but they watered around the edges and she blinked and looked away.

"Good try," he said.

★ ★ ★

Johnny American Horse's window at St. Pat's looked out upon a neighborhood of early-twentieth-century buildings and sidewalks shaded by dense rows of maple trees. The buildings were brick, solidly constructed, undiminished by time, but the porches were made of wood and the cracked paint on them gave the dwellings a look of weathered gentility. Blue-collar people and college students lived in the buildings, and on Thursday evenings during the summer many of them walked together down to the free concert and dance in the park by the river. The yards were green and cool, sometimes bordered by tulip beds, and the people who lived in the apartments planted vegetable gardens between the alleyways and the back porches, which were usually enclosed with latticework. If a man chose to live in town, this was a fine neighborhood to raise a family in, Johnny thought.

When he woke Tuesday morning he was handcuffed to the railing of the bed and could not see out the window into the street, but even before the soft edges of his sleep had disappeared from his mind, he knew there was something different about this day. He could hear the sweep of rain on the window glass — not a shower, either, but a hard, driving rain that ran off the eaves and through the guttering and over the hospital lawn into storm drains. Johnny could hear the wet sound of automobile tires on the slickness of the streets, a deep roll of thunder resonating in the hills, the thick flapping of an American flag someone had forgotten to take down from the hospital pole, and he knew the summer drought was broken, that the fires that threatened his ranch up on the Jocko were turning into steam.

He pushed the button for the nurse who would come to the room and then tell the U.S. marshal on the door that Johnny needed to be unhooked so he could use the bathroom. The rain clicked on the glass, and he could hear a freight train blowing somewhere west of town, perhaps heading into Alberton Gorge. After the marshal unsnapped the cuff on his wrist, Johnny stood by his bed and gazed out the window at the dark green sogginess of the maples on the street, the cars driving with their lights on in the middle of the day, and the columns of smoke rising from extinguished fires on the mountainsides. All that separated him from the outside world was a pane of glass and a thirty-foot drop onto a spongy square of flooded lawn.

He used the toilet, then waited for the marshal to hook him up again.

"It looks like you're going to Fort Lewis tomorrow. Sorry to lose you, Johnny. You play a mean game of checkers," the marshal said.

He was a heavyset, prematurely balding man named Tim, who had a small Irish mouth and big hands, and was evidently addicted to the candy bars he carried in his pockets as a surrogate for the booze he was trying to get rid of at Twelve-Step meetings.

"Who told you that about Fort Lewis?" Johnny asked, lying back on the bed, the handcuff chain pulling tight on his wrist.

"Forget I mentioned it. That's true, you have the DSC from Operation Desert Storm?"

"Yeah, you want it?"

"Shouldn't kid like that," Tim said.

A floral delivery man tapped on the door and Tim let him in. The delivery man started to set a vase of cut flowers on the table by Johnny's bed. "Let me see that first," Tim said.

Tim peeled back the decorative foil wrapped around the vase, shifted the flower stems around in the water, and examined the greeting card inside the small envelope attached with a paper clip to the foil. Then he set the vase down on the table. "Looks like somebody sent you a nice bouquet. Can I ask you something?" he said.

"Sure," Johnny said.

"How'd you get messed up like this?"

"It was easy. I was me," Johnny said.

"You sound like you might be a Twelve-Step guy yourself."

"I'm not," Johnny replied.

As the marshal and the nurse left the room, Johnny glanced through the opened door and saw a group of painters pass by, carrying buckets, tarps, ladders, and brushes, all of them dressed in paint-flecked caps and coveralls. The last man in the group was an Indian from the res. His eyes, as unreadable as obsidian, swept across Johnny, then the door closed.

Johnny removed the card from the envelope on the flower vase and opened it. It read:

They still won't let me visit you, but look across the street at noon and you'll see your gal with the 8:30 blues. We're going to beat this, baby.
Love, A.

Johnny stared at the paper clip on the envelope, then looked at the glass in the window that separated him from the outside world. He looked at the glass a long time, then gave up whatever thoughts were on his mind and ate the breakfast an orderly brought in on a tray. At eleven-thirty, just before he was scheduled to be cuffed to a wheelchair and rolled down the corridor for X-rays, Johnny slipped the paper clip into his mouth between his gum and cheek.

The rain had turned to hail, and it bounced on the windowsill as brightly as mothballs against the grayness of the day. When Johnny closed his eyes and listened to the hail and the roll of thunder in the hills, he imagined a vast landscape where the mesas rose into steel-colored stormheads forked with lightning while down below the hooves of red ponies shook the earth. At this moment, for no reason that made logical sense, he knew his dreams were real and not fantasies and that all the gifts of creation still awaited him, were still his, as tangible as a woman's smile on the far side of a street on a rainy day.

That morning I left the office and went home, unable to work, concentrate, or think on any subject except the telephone threat that had been made against Temple and the child she was carrying. I had now talked to the sheriff's office, Fay Harback, and the FBI agent Francis Broussard and had gotten nowhere. Lucas had been set up on a bogus marijuana bust and suspended from the university, and Temple had almost drowned in the Blackfoot River after the brake-fluid line on our truck had been cut. No one was in custody for any of the damage done to my family, nor had anyone even been questioned. My own relationship with every law agency in the area had become that of gadfly and public nuisance.

Most television cop dramas make use of

433

the following storyline: A likable individual is raped or assaulted, or a hardworking family loses one of its members to a serial killer, or a blue-collar stiff with a juvenile felony on his record gets jammed on a bad beef and is about to be sent to the pen. What happens? A half-dozen uniforms and five detectives with shields hanging from their necks show up at the crime scene and invest the entirety of their lives in seeing justice done. Every law officer in the script, male and female, seems to have an IQ of 180 and the altruism of St. Francis of Assisi. They verbally joust with the rich and powerful, walk into corporate board meetings where they hook up CEOs, and are immune to the invective flung at them by an unappreciative citizenry.

The federal agents who wander into the script are even more impressive. They have tanned skin, little-boy haircuts, and the anatomies of California surfers. Their psychoanalytical knowledge of the criminal mind is stunning. Without hesitation, they conclude for the viewer that serial rapists possess violent tendencies toward women and people who plant bombs on airplanes are antisocial.

But my thoughts on the subject are cheap in design and substance. It's easy to be facile about law enforcement. The truth is the good guys are understaffed, overworked, underfunded, and outgunned. Most of the time the bad guys win, or if they do take a fall, it's because

434

a wrecking ball swings into their lives for reasons that have nothing to do with jurisprudence. If you have ever been a victim of violent crime, or if you have been threatened by deviates or sadists — and by the latter I mean wakened by anonymous phone calls in the middle of the night, surveilled by people you've never seen before, forced to take public transportation because you're afraid to start your car in the morning — then you know that what I'm about to say is an absolute fact: You're on your own.

Law enforcement agencies don't prevent crimes. With good luck, they solve a few of them. In the meantime, if violent and dangerous people intend to do you injury, your own thoughts become your worst enemies. The morning might start with sunshine and birdsong, but by noon it's usually filled with gargoyles.

I walked around the house aimlessly, trying to chase down each of my thoughts and hold it in a bright place in the center of my mind, face it down fair and square. But it was to no avail. Thunder ripped across the sky and rain pounded on the roof and swept in sheets across the hillside. Through the kitchen window I thought I saw L. Q. Navarro standing among the fir trees, wearing his pin-striped suit and ash-colored Stetson, his face lit briefly by a flicker of lightning.

Take this guy Mabus off at the neck. Smoke

*him and put a throw-down on the body and buy
your wife a trip to Hawaii,* he said.

I wish I could, L.Q.

*Don't think about it, just do it. Everybody
dies. You want this guy to kill your wife or unborn child or Lucas? Take care of your own and
screw the rest of it.*

That easy, huh?

*There's nothing wrong with this guy Mabus a
two-hundred-and-thirty-grain brass-jacketed hollow-
point wouldn't cure.*

But I did not listen to L.Q.'s words. Instead, I found Karsten Mabus's business
card, the one he had given me with his home
telephone number written on the back. I hesitated only a moment, then punched the
number into the phone, thereby beginning
the commission of the most cowardly act of
my life.

"Hello?" he said.

"It's Billy Bob Holland, Mr. Mabus."

"How you doin'?"

"I don't want my wife or boy or unborn
child hurt."

"I don't, either. But why are you telling me
this?"

"Call your guys off. I don't have the goods
from the Global Research boost."

"Mr. Holland, I couldn't care less about
that stuff. Look, can you and your wife come
out to dinner this evening? I realize it's late
notice, but —"

436

"Johnny American Horse dumped a metal box of some kind on my property. But I don't have it and neither does Johnny or his wife, Amber. Wyatt Dixon found it and has it in his possession."

My own words sounded strange and apart from me, separate from my life and the person I thought I was.

"Can you please tell me who in the Sam Hill Wyatt Dixon is?" Mabus asked.

"Leave Wyatt alone and he'll probably blow out his own doors. But whatever you do, just stay away from us," I said.

"At this point, gladly, sir. I guess I have a great personal flaw, Mr. Holland. I'm obviously a terrible judge of character," he said, and hung up.

CHAPTER 22

It was still raining when Johnny was wheeled in a chair down a corridor to the X-ray room by a nurse and the U.S. marshal, who ate a candy bar while he talked. Before leaving the room, Tim cuffed Johnny's right wrist to the arm of the wheelchair.

"You'll be back in your room before lunchtime. If you want, I can get you an extra dessert from the cafeteria," Tim said.

Johnny didn't answer. Out in the hallway the painters were erecting a scaffolding against the wall.

"Did you hear me?" Tim said.

"Sorry, I got a toothache," Johnny said, touching his jaw.

"If I don't cut down on my sugar, that's what I'm gonna have," Tim said.

"We need to take some pictures now. There's a waiting room to your left, just past the double doors," the X-ray technician said.

"Take good care of my man here," Tim said. He walked down the corridor and through the double doors, nodding to the painters as he passed.

"You have any pain in your left arm?" the technician said.

"None," Johnny replied.

"Did you feel a break in it?"

"No."

"I guess the government just likes to be careful. How's the wound progressing?" the technician said.

"Fine. You guys did a good job." Johnny pressed his fingers against his jaw and cleared his throat.

"Well, let's get you done here," the technician said.

"I hate to tell you this, but I got to use the toilet real bad," Johnny said.

"I wish you'd told the marshal that."

"Just wheel me over to the restroom. I'm not going anywhere," Johnny said, clinking the handcuff chain tight on the arm of the chair.

The technician took Johnny across the corridor and watched him fold up the wheelchair, work his way awkwardly into a stall, his right wrist still cuffed to the chair arm, then ease down on the toilet seat. "I'll come back in a few minutes," the technician said.

When Johnny heard the door click shut, he removed the paper clip from his mouth, straightened it, and inserted it into the lock on his handcuffs. It took him less than thirty seconds to spring the curved steel tongue that Tim had crimped into his wrist. Behind the door of the next stall he found a painter's cap and pair of coveralls hanging on a hook. He ripped off his hospital gown, pulled on the coveralls, and fitted the cap down on his head. He stepped out into the corridor just as the painters were passing by.

The last man in line was an Indian who was struggling with a rolled tarp that sagged heavily across his shoulder. Johnny picked up the end of the roll, dropped it on his shoulder, snugging the side of his face against the canvas, and walked out the front door of the hospital into the rain-swept breadth of the outside world.

But what Johnny saw was more than simply the outside world. The building and sidewalks and cars and telephone wires were gone. Under an ink-wash sky he saw hills that had turned the bright gold of haystacks in late summer, the fir trees and ponderosa pine like miniature forests in the saddles. He could see black-horn buffalo grazing in the grass along the river, and he could see lightning in the clouds beyond the hills where the four points of the wind and the Everywhere Spirit made their home. He saw muscular fish that were the dull tint of dried blood working their way up a stream, beating themselves to death on the rocks in order to lay their roe and hold their claim on the earth. He saw bears, mustangs, deer, elk, and winged creatures that lived under the great bowl of heaven the Everywhere Spirit had made with His hands and filled with both sun and rain in order to bring life to the corn and the grass, and in the midst of all this he saw thousands of wickiups whose lodge skins were painted with the signs of the moon and the passing of the seasons, and he knew these presences had long ago been ingested by the great vastness of the Everywhere Spirit and they now lived inside Him, as they lived inside Johnny's sleep, and hence they could not die.

And more important than all these things, he saw his wife, Amber American Horse, wearing the white buckskin dress of the Indian woman who had guided him through the Bob Marshall Wilderness, the purple glass beads that were shaped like teardrops on the fringe of her dress tinkling in the wind, her hand beckoning, as though both she and Johnny were about to embark on a journey from which neither of them would return.

Temple came home early that afternoon, unsure of where I had been all day. "Why didn't you answer the phone?" she said from the mud room, where she was hanging up her raincoat.

"I was in the barn," I replied, although I wasn't sure where I had been.

She walked into the kitchen. "Are you sick?"

"No, but I did something that I have a

hard time squaring with —"

"With what?"

"Honorable behavior is the term I'm probably looking for."

She waited for me to go on, her face sharpening.

"I called up Karsten Mabus and told him Wyatt had the goods from the Global Research break-in. It's between Mabus and Dixon now," I said. I felt my eyes shift off her face.

She was quiet a long time. Then she took a quart of milk out of the icebox and poured it into a glass, slowly, as though she couldn't concentrate on what she was doing. "Do you want something to eat?" she said.

"No."

"I didn't stop at the grocery because I thought we might go out."

"I'm not very hungry right now. We can go out, though, if you want."

"It's not important," she said, looking out the window now at the wetness of the trees and the mist floating on the hillside. She picked up her glass of milk and drank from it. "So Dixon has become shark meat?"

"He can take care of himself," I said.

"Right," she said. She poured her milk down the drain.

"What's wrong?" I said.

"Not much. It's our one-year anniversary. I have your present in the car. I'll go get it," she said.

A half hour later, I got a call from Francis Broussard at the FBI office. "Johnny American Horse walked out of St. Pat's Hospital today. You happen to know anything about it?" he said.

I couldn't assimilate his words. "He walked —"

"He used a paper clip to pick his handcuffs and went out the front door with some painters. We think one of his buddies from the res planted some workclothes in the restroom for him to change into. His wife was waiting for him across the street. The question is, how did he and his wife set it up and where did they go?"

"You think I had something to do with it?"

There was a pause. "No, but you're a personal friend and you know things about American Horse other people don't," he replied.

"Was Amber allowed to visit him?"

"No."

"How about his lawyer, Brendan Merwood?" I said.

"He was there twice."

"Anyone else?"

"No."

"You're sure?" I said.

Again the phone went silent, and I knew Broussard had already drawn conclusions that he didn't want to admit, at least to me.

"The escape couldn't have been set up

without Merwood's participation," I said.

"Yeah, that's a possibility, isn't it? But why would an oilcan like Merwood risk his career, plus serious prison time, on a pro bono case?"

"How about he's scared shitless?"

"I did some background on Mr. Merwood. He's represented a couple of Karsten Mabus's enterprises. Do you know where American Horse and his wife are hiding?"

"No, I don't," I said impatiently. "You're telling me Merwood is setting them up to get whacked?"

"You said it, I didn't."

"What about the painters?"

"We have an Indian from the res in custody. But he's D, D, and D, and I don't think that's going to change."

"He's what?" I said.

"It's the Indian concept of a dialogue with federal agents. 'Deaf, dumb, and don't know.' "

"Pick up Merwood and lose the paperwork. Move him to a federal facility and let him spend a couple of days in the bridal suite with a few swinging dicks who dig rap music."

"I can't imagine why the A.G.'s office was happy to see you make a career change. Call me if you hear from American Horse," he replied.

The Reverend Elton T. Sneed was not a man for whom the world was a complex place. He believed in Jesus, the flag, the devil, sin, camp meetings, Wednesday night services, helping his neighbor, tithing, jailhouse ministries, the restorative power of baptism, the gift of tongues, and the exorcism of demonic spirits, some of whom he called by name. The heroes and villains of the Old Testament moved in and out of his rhetoric as though they were contemporary figures who lived in the community. Unlike many of his peers', his sermons seldom touched on the subjects of sex or politics, primarily because he had no interest in them. For Elton T. Sneed, the critical issue for a preacher was the wrestling contest between Yahweh and Satan.

For Elton, a ministry meant the acquisition of power — the power to heal, to cast out unclean spirits, and to wash away original sin. Salvation didn't come with catechism lessons, attendance at church, or even the daily practice of good deeds. It came like the sun crashing out of the sky, crushing a person to the earth. "If you don't believe me, ask St. Paul what happened on the road to Damascus," Elton was fond of saying.

When Elton brought salvation to the willing, it was in the form of an exorcism that left them dripping with sweat and fear, or, if he baptized them, he pushed them under so many times they thought they were about to drown or had been mistaken for dirty laundry.

The problem for Elton was not his belief system but the consequences of it. If redemption and forgiveness of sin came with baptism, or if indeed the Holy Spirit descended through the top of the tent and entered the human breast, how could a Christian shun or turn away from a brother or sister whom Jesus had chosen to save?

Sometimes Elton's jailhouse converts seemed to be a bit shaky in their beliefs after they made parole. They showed up at the parsonage door, asking for money, perhaps smelling of marijuana, a couple of women in the car, their faces averted. In these instances Elton usually gave them money, provided he had any, then would be filled with depression, a sense of personal failure, and a question mark about the worth of his ministry.

But he consoled himself with the changes he had witnessed in Wyatt Dixon, even though some of Wyatt's friends were a challenge to Elton's attempts at unconditional charity. His church and his larder remained opened to the worst of the worst. Who was he to judge? If he'd been dealt the lot of these poor souls, he would have probably turned out as corrupt and profligate as they, he told himself.

Look at the two men who had just pulled their pickup truck into his yard. The evening light was weak, the western sun veiled by smoke from dead fires, but Elton could see the faces of the two men getting out of the truck, and he wondered if both of them had been in a terrible accident or malformed in the womb.

The shorter man had a gnarled forehead, like the corrugation in a washboard, a squashed nose, and missing teeth. His eyes were set too low in his face and his upper torso was too long for his short legs, so that he gave the impression of a walking tree stump.

His friend was tall, with the flaccid muscle tone of a gorged serpent, a disfigured mouth that looked as if it had been broken with a hard instrument, and a hairline-to-cheek burn scar that had tightened the skin on one eye into a tiny aperture, as though he were permanently squinting.

Elton stepped outside the door of the parsonage, which was actually a house trailer enclosed in a wood shell, and nodded at the two visitors walking up the incline toward him. The air was damp from the rain and smelled of smoke and river stone and wet trees, and he thought he heard geese honking high overhead.

"Hep you boys?" he said. There was grease on his hands from his dinner, and he wiped his hands on a paper towel.

"Looking for work. Man at the State Employment said you might get us on bucking bales here'bouts," the tall man said, his eyes going past Elton into the backyard.

"Haying is all done by machine today. Don't many buck bales no more," Elton said.

"We're not choicy," the tall man said. "Haven't ate for a day or so."

The two visitors stared at Elton, as though their problems had not only become his but somehow had originated with him. Elton put the paper towel in his pocket self-consciously. "I expect I could fix you something," he said. "But it looks like y'all need a job more than anything else." He tried to grin, and his face felt stiff and self-mocking.

"Nice of you to invite us in," the shorter man said, walking past Elton into his home. His friend followed him, passing inches from Elton's chest, the burned area on his face puckered like dried-out putty.

Elton stepped inside but did not close the door behind him. "I got peanut butter and jelly, if y'all don't mind something simple," he said.

But they seemed not to hear him. They looked at the meagerness of his possessions — the footworn carpet, the secondhand furniture, the imitation wood paneling on the walls — with the curiosity of people who might be visiting a zoo.

"Your wife here?" the truncated man asked.

"She died. Eight years back. In Arkansas. Say —"

"It's true y'all talk in tongues?" the tall man said.

This time Elton did not try to answer their questions because he knew they did not care about the answers he would give them. The truncated man sat down in a soft chair and clicked on the television, flipped the channels, his eyes like angry chunks of lead as he stared at several blurred images. He clicked the set off. "It's this Mideastern crap. That's all that's on there. Guys who wipe their ass with their hands shaking their fists at the camera," he said.

Elton remained silent, knowing in his heart of hearts that everything that was about to happen was part of a higher plan. *Just don't be afraid,* he told himself. *Think of the children of Israel in the fiery furnace. Think of Dan'el in the lion's den. Think of Paul and Silas locked in jail, the angel of the Lord flinging back their door in a burst of light.*

But he could not suppress the fear that was invading his body, stealing his courage and his faith, causing his face to twitch, his brow to break into a sweat, his buttocks to tremble. "It's Wyatt you're after, but he ain't here. He's trading some horses up at Flathead," he said.

"*You'll* do just fine, Preacher," the tall man said.

"Wyatt's friends are here. Three fellows y'all don't want to meet. They went up to the grocery for me," Elton said.

"They *were* here," the short man said. He

449

was still seated in the soft chair. His elongated forehead was tilted forward. He raised his eyebrows at Elton, as an ape in a cage might. "But they're not here now. That's because they're locked in the back of a van."

The room was silent again, so quiet Elton could hear his own breathing, an imperceptible creak under his foot when he shifted his weight. A drop of sweat ran into his eye, and he wiped it out of his eye socket with the heel of his hand.

The tall man took a carton of orange juice out of Elton's icebox, shook it, and drank directly from the carton. Then he glanced at his watch and exhaled his breath wearily. He wore a dark green shirt that was tucked into his khakis and dusty alpine boots, and his clothes gave off an odor like detergent that had been ironed into the fabric. He set the orange juice carton on the counter and looked at Elton evenly, his half-destroyed face seeming to study the forms of redress the world owed him.

"Wyatt took a lockbox that's not his and hid it someplace. We think it's on your property," he said. "My buddy here is gonna fill up the bathtub now and then the three of us is gonna clear up this whole problem about where that lockbox is located. You'll be doing a good deed. I'm here to give witness to that."

The eye that had been shrunken to the size

of a dime by the scar tissue on his face glistened brightly.

"You was raised in the church, I can tell. Why do you want to do this, boy?" Elton said.

"'Cause it makes me feel good," the tall man replied.

Outside, the evening light had gone from the sky, and through the open window Elton thought he could hear the dull clatter of stones under the river's surface and the sound of geese flying north, perhaps to a warm-water refuge that they would never have to leave.

I had not forgotten our anniversary, at least not entirely. I had bought Temple an Indian concho belt and a new western saddle, one made by a famous craftsman in Yoakum, Texas. I had iced down a bottle of non-alcoholic champagne and arranged for flowers to be delivered to the house. But after the telephone threat on her life, I had lost all consciousness of the date.

Then, rather than act on my anger and take it to Mabus with hot tongs, I had made a sacrificial offering in the form of Wyatt Dixon, and I knew in all probability I would never feel the same about myself again. I told Temple all these things, brought the saddle from the barn and splayed it across the gallery railing, popped the cork on the champagne, flopped two heavy trout wrapped in perforated tinfoil on the grill, and slipped the concho belt around Temple's waist. She stared at me, bemused, perhaps concluding, as she often did, that the man she lived with had long ago severed his ties with the rational world.

Temple went into the bedroom and put on a white lace dress and I put on a suit, then we both put on heavy coats and ate dinner on the side gallery. The rain had stopped, and for the first time in six weeks the moon rose into a clear black sky chained with stars. The meadow was pooled with water, and elk were drinking from the pools, their tails flicking, their racks as hard-looking as sculpted bone in the moonlight. Temple lifted her wineglass to her mouth and drank, her eyes on mine. I had never known a woman who had shadows inside her eyes, but Temple did.

"What's on your mind?" I said.

"It took courage for you to call Karsten Mabus. Back in the old days you and L.Q. would have done things differently. It's important for you to remember that, Billy Bob. Don't look back on what you did. You're a brave man."

"No, I'm not."

"I know you better than you know yourself. I always did. You fault yourself for your violence. But when you and L.Q. did those things down on the border, you did them to protect other people."

"L.Q. paid the price for it, Temple."

"He knew the risks going in. He was a brave man, just like you are. Don't treat him like a victim. Don't do that kind of disservice to either him or yourself."

The wind came up and made a rushing sound in the trees on the hillside, and a shower of wet pine needles sifted down the slopes of the roof. I got up from my chair and went around behind Temple and bit her softly on the neck. She reached behind her and clasped the back of my neck, pushing her fingers into my hair, tilting up her chin, her eyes closed.

We left the rest of our food uneaten and went into the bedroom. I slipped her dress over her head and lay her back on the bed, then lifted a strand of hair off her eye and kissed her mouth and the tops of her breasts and stroked her thighs. Then I undressed and lay down close against her, my body against hers, our feet, thighs, and stomachs touching, my face buried in her hair, my fingers tracing the stiffened points of her breasts.

When I was inside Temple Carrol, I could never understand how any moment of anger, fear, resentment, or suspicion could have come between us. Temple's skin glowed with love for the man she was with. Her arms, thighs, calves, mouth, her womb, the warmth of her breathing against my cheek, were the most encompassing, unrelenting expression of loyalty and affirmation I had ever experienced. She went about making love with a selfless abandon that was both humbling and beyond what any man expects. She was never stintful, never sought her own satisfaction, and was never dependent, self-conscious, or embarrassed. In fact, she radiated a kind of visceral purity, even in the way she perspired, that made me think of flowers opening, sunshowers, a salty wave full of kelp cresting inside a groundswell.

Later I placed my ear against her stomach and listened. Her skin was moist against the side of my face, and I could hear the whirrings of the life inside her. Then I kissed her stomach and her mouth and pulled the sheet over her breasts. "Don't catch cold. We've got the best baby in the history of babydom in there," I said.

She touched my cheek with her hand.

That's when the phone rang.

CHAPTER 23

It was Fay Harback, and she wasn't doing well with what she had to tell me. "We've got another homicide on the res. At the home of a minister named Elton Sneed. You know him?" she said.

"He's a Pentecostal of some kind. Wyatt Dixon belongs to his church," I said.

"He's dead, drowned in his own bathtub. I just got back from there. I don't know if I'm up to this damned job. Know that old joke about the definition of a liberal? A humanist who hasn't been mugged yet or something like that?"

"Start over, Fay."

"It looks like somebody held Sneed down in the bathtub, then tried to make it look like an accident. Water was all over the floor and the walls. He'd been stripped naked and dropped in the tub, but his shirt and undershirt were soaked with water and stuffed in the bottom of a clothes basket. The pants had water on the knees, and there were abrasions all over his arms and shoulders."

I was standing in the kitchen and had to sit down in a chair as she told me the details of Elton Sneed's death. There was a weak feeling in my chest, as though weevil worms had worked their way into my heart.

"You there?" she said.

"You have any suspects?" I asked.

"No, nobody saw anything. But that's life on the res. Nobody sees anything, nobody knows anything, but that doesn't stop them from complaining constantly about Whitey dumping on them and not enforcing the law. Look, Wyatt Dixon showed up while I was there and went apeshit. No, that doesn't quite describe it."

"I need to confess something to you —"

"Let me finish. Dixon cried. I didn't believe he was capable of feeling anything about anyone. But tears actually ran down his face. It took four cops to get him back outside. The coroner wanted to tranquilize him."

"Why didn't he?"

"We didn't want another homicide. What were you going to say?"

"Karsten Mabus knows Wyatt has the goods from the Global Research robbery. His people probably went after Reverend Sneed when they couldn't get to Wyatt."

"That billionaire or whatever out on Highway Twelve again?"

"Right."

"He's behind the attacks on Dixon?"

"Right. He owns Global Research. He plans to run for office here in Montana. Global Research is the outfit that sold

Saddam Hussein part of his chemical and biological weapons program in the eighties. I told you all this."

"Were you a fan of Marvel comics as a kid?"

"Don't make light of this, Fay. He's an evil man," I said.

"You said you were going to confess something to me? How does Karsten Mabus know Dixon has the stuff from the Global job?"

"I told him," I said.

"To get the heat off yourself?"

"Read it any way you want."

"I knew somehow you were involved in this. I just didn't know how. I have some crime scene photos. Maybe you should look at them."

"By assigning indirect responsibility to me, you're conceding that Mabus sent his men after the preacher."

"What I'm saying is —" But she had trapped herself and couldn't finish.

"Where's Wyatt now?" I asked.

"On the loose. You stop pulling strings on all these people. You stay out of a police investigation, too," she said, and hung up.

The kitchen lights were off, and I could hear the easy sweep of wind in the trees and the clatter of a pinecone on the roof. But the tranquillity of the night would not ease the pang in my heart. My call to Mabus had brought about the death of Elton Sneed, a gentle, decent man who had honestly served his vision of this world and the next. Also, for the first time, I had begun to seriously wonder about my assessment of Fay Harback.

The shooter who came onto Karsten Mabus's property that night would prove a mystery in many ways for both Mabus's security personnel and the investigators from the Missoula County Sheriff's Department. It was safe to say he did not enter the property from Highway 12, as the front gate was electronically locked at 9 p.m. and a sophisticated alarm system, including sensor lights, that ran the length of the fence line automatically activated at the same hour. Two boys who had been camping up on a mountainside behind the ranch said they had seen a lone horseman come off a ridge and follow a creekbed to the back of the property, then enter the woods and disappear. They said the rider wore a hat and had binoculars strung around his neck and perhaps was carrying a rifle in a saddle scabbard.

Whoever the shooter was, he wore western boots, because sheriff's deputies found their pointed, deep-heeled indentations in the soft bed of pine needles behind a flat-surfaced boulder that he used as his sniper's nest.

Just before midnight Karsten Mabus, dressed in an Oriental robe, fixed himself a sandwich and opened a bottle of carbonated grape juice, then relaxed on an elephant-hide couch and read *The New York Times.* Through the rear living room window, which rose all the way to the cathedral ceiling, he could see steam rising from his swimming pool, the underwater lights tunneling below the lime-green surface, the arc lamps above his horse barns glowing with humidity, canvas windscreens flapping gently against the red-clay background of his tennis courts.

It was a beautiful night, the stars cold and white in a black sky that occasionally flickered with heat lightning.

Karsten Mabus put away the newspaper, sat up on the couch, and bit into his sandwich. The shooter had worked his way into place now, on a hillside that provided him cover and also a panoramic overview of the grounds, perhaps one hundred yards out and one hundred feet higher in elevation than Karsten Mabus. The first round pocked a neat hole in the window glass and missed Mabus's head by inches, burrowing deeply into the cushions of a large chair against the far wall with hardly a sound.

Mabus removed the sandwich from his mouth and set it down on the plate, focusing his eyes on the hole in the glass, seemingly unsure of the event that had just occurred.

The second round caught part of the window framing, blowing wood and large shards of glass onto the carpet, the bullet ticking Mabus's cheek just above the jawbone, flicking a thread of blood across his skin.

He rose from the couch, touching his cheek, looking at the balls of his fingers, then began punching buttons on a keypad by the fireplace. In less than thirty seconds at least five armed men emerged from either the shadowy edges of the ranch or the servants' quarters over the garage. One security man, who had seen a muzzle flash, pointed toward the flat-surfaced boulder a hundred feet up on the hillside.

Two of the security personnel mounted an all-terrain vehicle and, with the other three security men behind them, roared up the hill toward the sniper's nest.

The shooter stood erect, firing from a lever-action rifle, and shot the driver of the ATV off the seat. The next shot caught one of the running men below the knee, knocking his leg out from under him as though the bone had been clipped in half with a cold chisel. The ATV caromed off a tree trunk and spun crazily down the side of a gulch.

The two wounded men and their three friends took cover behind rocks and trees, flattening themselves into the bed of pine needles, while the shooter fired four more rounds through the woods, the brass casings tinkling on top of the boulder he stood behind. Moments later the security men could hear the sound of a horse's shoes clopping on stone, then thudding on hard-packed earth through the timber.

Karsten Mabus watched it all from the terrace by his swimming pool, in full view of the hillside, his plate in one hand, his sandwich in the other. After he finished eating, he wiped his hands, combed his hair, and used his cell phone to request an ambulance for his two employees who had been shot.

But before he went back inside, he saw a horseman silhouetted on a ridgeline. The horseman seemed to stop, framed against the sky, the constellations bursting overhead, and look back at Karsten Mabus, perhaps through binoculars.

Mabus formed a pistol with his thumb and index finger, pointed it at the horseman, and winked.

At 1:15 p.m. Wednesday, I looked out the window of my office and saw two detectives from the sheriff's department escorting Wyatt Dixon in handcuffs through the rear door of the courthouse. But rather than accept the role of chained culprit and miscreant, Wyatt was the bucolic king in captivity. He was dressed in gray razor-creased western pants, a long-sleeved maroon cotton shirt, a wide silver necktie, and a soft-crowned hat tilted low on his forehead. His upper arms looked like hams inside his shirt, his sideburns etched against his jaws with a fresh haircut. He limped along without his canes, grinning at everyone he saw, his eyes manic, the manacles on his wrists like scrap metal he could snap in half if he chose. Jailhouse riffraff smoking cigarettes on the lawn cheered him as he walked by.

I crossed the street and entered the courthouse just as the elevator closed on Wyatt and the two plainclothes. I walked down the corridor to Fay Harback's office. She was talking to her receptionist, wearing a black suit, her small hands knotted in fists on her hips.

"What's the deal on Dixon?" I said.

"He's being interviewed."

"Not unless I'm present, he's not."

"You're Wyatt Dixon's attorney now?"

"Ask Wyatt."

"I don't have to. Now go fiddle with a divorce case," she said, turning her back to me.

"Why'd you bring him in?"

"We have two guys in Community Hospital with bullet holes in them. Our chief persons of interest are Dixon and Johnny American Horse."

"The gig out at Karsten Mabus's place last night?"

"Nobody's catching any flies on you," she said.

I rode the elevator upstairs. Wyatt was in

an interview room with the two detectives, the door partly open, his wrists uncuffed. The interview was not going as planned by the detectives, both of whom were standing while Wyatt sat. Their names were Boyle and Regan. Both of them had been investigators with Internal Affairs and were not well liked by their colleagues.

"It's real good of you fellows to bring me in and talk this thing out," Wyatt was saying. "I have invited Vice President Cheney to go duck hunting with me this fall, and I'll be telling him of the good work you boys are doing. I know he'd appreciate y'all's hep in chasing down them A-rabs what's been throwing camel shit through window fans all over the Mideast." Wyatt pushed a paper napkin across the table toward the detectives. "Write your names down so I can alert the Vice President to the kind of high-quality smarts that's on the job here in Missoula, Montana."

The larger of the detectives, Jimmie Boyle, slapped Wyatt's hat off his head. "You simple fuck, we're the last thing between you and a twenty-five-year jolt," he said. "Cop to it now, claim temporary insanity over the death of the preacher, and you might even skate. In the meantime, you pick the hair out of your teeth and show some respect for the only friends you got."

Wyatt reached down for his hat and set it

crown down on the table. Once again, I witnessed one of those mercurial transformations that seemed to take place in Wyatt, as though someone had clicked a switch in the back of his head. Between the time he stooped over for his hat and the time he looked back at the detectives, the clown's grin had gone from his face, replaced by the lifeless mask and glasslike eyes that made one think of the quiet that comes before a storm.

"I'm done here. Don't y'all be trying to use Reverend Sneed's death to jerk my chain, either," he said.

"You believe this asshole?" Boyle said.

"You heard him. You're done," I said, stepping into the room. "Charge him or cut him loose."

"How'd you get up here?" Boyle said. He had a large nose, the rim of one nostril threaded by a scar that looked like a piece of string.

I started to answer but didn't get the chance. Fay Harback came up behind us, her face tight with anger. "I want a word with you," she said, walking toward a coffee room.

When we were inside, she turned on me. "You don't listen, Billy Bob. You think you have the franchise on morality and can do and say whatever you want because you represent clients who have some kind of social handicap," she said. "The sniper at Karsten Mabus's ranch crippled one man and put a hole through the rib cage of the other. That said, my intuitions tell me Wyatt Dixon isn't the shooter. But he's told a number of people, including Darrel McComb, that Karsten Mabus may be the Antichrist. That means we have to clear him as a suspect, even though personally I think he's of diminished capacity and belongs in a mental institution.

"Regardless, I can't go forward in the investigation until he's excluded as a viable suspect. So while you're obstructing our investigation, you're also hurting your client . . . I seem to be losing your attention. Is this too complex for you to follow?"

"Darrel McComb told me you dimed him with I.A. I didn't believe him. But I've downgraded my opinion."

"Well, I'm not really interested in your —"

"You've been working against me from the jump, Fay. In one way or another, you've tried to thwart every initiative I've taken on Johnny American Horse's behalf. I think Johnny would be dead or in the joint if it wasn't for Darrel McComb. Some joke, huh? A right-wing redneck became the loose cannon in the script and screwed up the frame that somebody was trying to hang around Johnny's neck."

Her cheeks were glowing, her mouth a tight seam, her diminutive figure shrunken somehow inside her clothes, the skin below her mouth puckering. She clenched the top of her left arm, and for a second I seriously thought she might be having the beginnings of a heart attack.

She slapped me in the mouth, hard, her fingernails cutting my skin.

Then she walked to the door of the interview room, where the two detectives stared at us open-mouthed. "Kick him," she said.

I walked out the front door of the courthouse with Wyatt Dixon. The sun was out, the sky freckled with white clouds, the mountains green from the rain. Even though it was a business day, the streets were festive, filled with bicyclists and joggers, and a string band was playing under the trees on the courthouse lawn.

"Buy you a hot dog?" Wyatt said.

"Another time," I replied.

I could feel his eyes on the side of my face. "You just gonna let that woman pop you in the mouth like that?" he said.

"I'm used to it."

"No, something's crawling around in the woodpile. How you know it wasn't me dropped them men at Mabus's ranch?" he said.

"You would have used that fifty-caliber Sharps of yours. You probably wouldn't have missed Mabus, either."

"Maybe you give me too much credit."

466

I waited for the traffic light to change, then started across the street, hoping Wyatt would stay behind. He didn't. "You figure American Horse for it?" he asked.

"No," I replied, my eyes straight ahead.

"A man who'll use a knife on another man will do anything," he said.

"You have any more trouble with the D.A.'s office, you tell me about it. In the meantime, you make no statement to anybody from the D.A.'s office or the sheriff's department about anything," I said.

But Wyatt was not easily distracted from the subject at hand. "If it ain't me or American Horse, who's that leave, Brother Holland?"

"You got me. Have a good one," I replied.

He stopped at a hot dog cart where a man in an apron was selling dogs and ice cream under a striped umbrella. I walked on down the street toward my office, believing I was rid of Wyatt Dixon for a while.

Wrong.

"Your knowledge about all this don't add up to me," he said.

"The morning paper said the shooter fired several shots in quick succession," I replied. "That means he didn't use a Sharps. I also have the feeling the shooter picked up his brass or he wiped it clean before he loaded it into the magazine. Otherwise, the D.A.'s office would have latents that would have either implicated or cleared you. So what's that tell us? You're an innocent man."

But I could see his interest fading and a wan expression taking hold in his eyes. He took a bite of his hot dog, started to chew, then choked as though cardboard had caught in his throat. He spit his half-chewed food into a trash can and threw the rest of the dog in on top of it. His mouth was close to my face when he spoke again, his breath rife with the smell of meat and mustard. "Know why it wasn't me up on that hill? It's 'cause I wouldn't even try. Mabus cain't be killed with a gun. Cain't be killed by no normal means," he said.

"He's just a man, Wyatt."

"They held Elton Sneed underwater till his heart give out. His death's on me. I ain't never gonna get over this. I ain't never had no feelings like this before," he said.

He crossed against the light, swaying like a drunk man through cars that braked to a halt or swerved around him, their horns blowing.

A half hour later I drove to Community Hospital, located in the middle of the old federal reservation that was once Fort Missoula. In the 1870s Negro bicycle troops had been stationed there, ostensibly to help remove the Flathead Indians from the Bitterroot Valley and to control the Nez Percé, who, under Chief Joseph, almost de-

468

feated the United States Army. But today the old two-story, whitewashed stucco barracks, with their red-tile roofs, were administrative offices for the U.S. Forest Service, the parade grounds a golf course, and the Negro troopers who had ridden bikes with iron wheels rested under the maples inside a piked fence.

The names of the two shooting victims had been published in the morning paper. A receptionist gave me their room numbers.

"Can I talk with them?" I said.

"You have to ask the nurse," she replied.

Their rooms were next to each other on the second floor. I walked past the nurse's station as though I already knew where I was going and had permission to be there. The man who had taken a round in the rib cage was out of intensive care, sleeping in a flat position, an IV taped to his left arm. His hair was dark and curly, his jaws unshaved, his arms unmarked by tattoos. I didn't recognize him.

The second man, whose name was Jared Green, was another matter. He was sitting up in bed, watching the television set on the wall, a glass of fruit juice in his hand. His hair was blond, neatly combed, his head large, his facial skin like pig hide.

"You doing all right?" I said through the open door.

He clicked off the television set with a remote control. "Who are you?" he said.

I stepped inside the room. "You stopped my truck out on Rock Creek. You asked me to walk over to Karsten Mabus's limo. How you feeling?" I said.

"When the dope wears off, I'll tell you."

"You took a round through the leg?"

He flipped back the sheet to show me the knot of bandages around his knee. "Mr. Mabus send you?" he said.

"Not exactly."

"Nobody's been out to see me except the foreman. I got surgery scheduled for three o'clock this afternoon. The food here blows. Tell the nurse this catheter is like a snake hanging on my joint."

"Good luck," I said.

"Hey, come back here. Why you here?" he said at my back.

I drove back down a long street lined with maples flickering in the wind, past the golf course and several upscale retirement homes, then turned into the traffic that would take me back downtown. I clicked on the radio, the volume louder than normal, my hands tighter on the steering wheel than they should have been. I wanted to be around noise, stopped at the red light next to a car filled with high school kids or family people. I wanted to be in a crowded restaurant, at a rodeo, a state fair, a baseball game. I wanted to be anywhere except inside my head with my own thoughts.

Back at my office, I called Temple and gave her the names of the two shooting victims and asked her if she could run them.

"Sure. But what's the point?" she said.

"I just want to know who's working for Karsten Mabus."

She waited a beat before she spoke. "Where'd you go last night, Billy Bob?"

"For a carton of ice cream."

"I'll call you back later," she said.

It was almost quitting time when my phone buzzed. "It took me a while," she said. "These guys have lived all over the place, at least until they went to work for Mabus. That's the funny thing about them. They floated around the country, getting in trouble wherever they were, then they found a home with Karsten Mabus and changed their ways. Which guys like them don't do."

"Start with Jared Green," I said.

"He was a trainer at health clubs in Miami and Los Angeles. He was also a prostitute for an escort service in Naples, Florida. He was in a reformatory at Tracy, California, and spent eight months in the Broward County Stockade for breaking his girlfriend's jaw. He should have gone to Raiford, but the D.A. couldn't get her to testify. He's the one who got kneecapped?"

"He's the one."

"Same guy who stopped you on Rock Creek Road?"

"How'd you know?"

"Because you seem to have a personal interest in him."

"Can't you just give me the information, Temple?"

She paused, then ignored my irritability and went on. "His friend, Albert Burgette, has a bad-conduct discharge from the Navy and used to be a long-haul truck driver. He and some others guys also ran a home-repair scam. Each spring they'd roam around the West, knocking on the doors of elderly people, telling them their roofs had ice damage. Burgette was also charged with the hit-and-run death of an eleven-year-old girl, but it didn't stick. The cops in Fresno think his friends threatened a witness.

"In other words, both guys are genuine scum. Now do you want to tell me why you're so interested in these characters?"

"I guess you're right, they're not important."

"Where'd you go last night, Billy Bob?" she said.

At 5 p.m. I locked up the office and crossed the street to a workingmen's bar. I sat in back, near a brick wall with a painted-over window in it that gave onto an alleyway, and ordered a beer and a double shot. It was

472

a cool, dark place, with a lighted jukebox and neon ads for western beers on the wall. The people who drank at the bar were from the neighborhood and talked about sports and the opening of the streams that had been closed because of the forest fires, or they made jokes about their tabs and their jobs. I wanted to buy them a round, be among them, and have no cares other than the traffic I would have to negotiate before I was home, enjoying a fine supper.

But the images of two bullet-wounded men would not go out of my head.

I went back to the bar twice more for doubles, with a beer back. When I was on my fourth round, a huge shape stepped between my table and the glare of light through the front door.

"Didn't know you were a drinking man," Darrel McComb said.

"I'm just about to leave," I replied.

He sat down at the table anyway, with a longneck and an empty glass. His jaws were gritty with stubble, his clothes rumpled. "Tell American Horse he gave me the key," he said.

"The key?" I said.

"It'll make sense down the road." He poured beer into his glass and salted it. "One day I'm going to write the history of what happened down in Central America. Hitler said the victors write the history books. But

473

sometimes the victors leave big blanks in the story, know what I mean?"

"Yeah, I think so," I said, realizing he was either drunk or entering a new and perhaps terminal stage in his career. "Say that again about Johnny American Horse?"

"You bet, kemosabe," he said. He drank from his glass, then smelled himself and smiled bleary-eyed into my face. But he forgot whatever it was he intended to say.

I patted him on the shoulder as I left the bar, perhaps glad to have the problems I did and not someone else's.

I bought a hot dog and a Styrofoam cup of black coffee on the corner and ate the hot dog on a bench before I tried to drive home. After I pulled into the driveway I went straight into the bathroom, brushed my teeth, rinsed my mouth with Listerine, and showered the smell of booze and cigarette smoke off my skin and out of my hair. But I didn't fool Temple. Not about anything.

"Make a stop on the way home?" she said.

"I ran into Darrel McComb. He said something about Johnny American Horse providing a key for him. I couldn't figure out what he was talking about."

But Temple was not interested in the problems of Darrel McComb. "The thirty-thirty is gone from the rack," she said.

"Yeah, I took it to Sportsmen's Surplus. I

think the sight is bent," I replied.

I was sitting at the kitchen table. Through the side window I could see our horses drinking at the tank and shadows spreading across the valley floor. I felt her fingers stroking the back of my neck. "You're the best man I've ever known, Billy Bob," she said. "You're incapable of evil or meanness. If you've broken any laws, it was on behalf of the people you love."

I had to swallow at her words. I started to speak, but she didn't let me. She put her arms around me and hugged my head against her, her mouth pressed into my hair.

CHAPTER 24

Darrel left the bar and drove to his apartment on the river. He took a hit of white speed and washed it down with beer, then walked out on the balcony and looked out over the town. The rain had killed the fires and restored the glories of summer to western Montana. What a grand evening it was. He looked at the water coursing under the pilings on the Higgins Street Bridge, the glow of lights on the old Wilma Theater building, the red brilliance of the sunset among hills at the bottom of an azure sky, and he wondered how his life could have gone so wrong.

The answer was easy: He genuinely loved the place where he lived, but the place where he lived did not love him. And that's the way it had always been. He had loved causes that didn't love him. On all levels he had served people who had found him either odious or expendable, and the notion of being loved had long ago disappeared from his life.

Well, that was why hookers were invented, he thought bitterly, then felt both embarrassed and demeaned at the content of his own thoughts.

Get out of this funk, he told himself. He had never sought either pity or understanding for the life he had led. Years back, whenever he was asked why he kept re-upping in the Army, he had always replied, "It's three hots and a cot, Jack." You didn't share your feelings with people who don't pay dues. Let the fruits and tree huggers frolic in Golden Gate Park, he had always told himself. The men and women who protected them and would one day live in Valhalla required no recompense other than their own self-respect.

But for just a moment Darrel wondered what it would have been like if he'd had a wife or even a girlfriend like Amber Finley.

He went back inside, closed the glass door on his balcony, and forced himself to empty his mind of thoughts about Amber Finley. He opened another beer, bit down on another hit of white speed, and blew out his breath when he felt the rush take him. *That* was more like it.

He opened his computer file and began recording all the recent events concerning Karsten Mabus, Greta Lundstrum, Elton T. Sneed, and Johnny American Horse.

For a college guy, Holland didn't seem too smart, Darrel thought to himself. The key to taking down Karsten Mabus was getting inside his compound. But even though Darrel had made Greta his personal snitch, he had not figured a way to put her inside Mabus's place with a wire. Then American Horse had escaped from federal custody, which made him a likely candidate for the sniper shootings at Mabus's ranch.

The only other viable candidate was Wyatt Dixon. But Darrel didn't believe Dixon had the brains to get inside the property, shoot two men, and safely escape. It had to be American Horse. Or at least that was the case Darrel was going to make.

The shooting couldn't have happened at a more perfect time. Now Darrel had the leverage he had lacked earlier. It was just a matter of convincing Karsten Mabus that Greta and her boyfriend, one Darrel McComb, a disgraced police officer with no moral bottom, had information that could prevent another assassination attempt on Mabus's life.

He glanced at his breakfast table, where the tools of his trade rested like an ugly testimony to everything that he was: his Beretta, the sap he had beaten American Horse with, his cuffs, a switchblade knife, two miniaturized recorders with tiny microphones, a .25 hideaway and holster with a Velcro ankle strap, and a throw-down that had the serial numbers burned off.

Darrel finished recording the events of the last few days that were connected in any way to the homicides committed on the property of Johnny American Horse. He used the spell-check mechanism to correct any misspellings in the file, reviewed his prose for its accuracy and specificity, then decided to add another paragraph.

It read: "Please consider the following statement as my summation of my time on earth — *Hey, I never had to sell shoes at Thom McAn.*"

He exchanged the fourteen rounds out of the old magazine on his Beretta, inserting them into a new magazine with a taut spring, examined the surveillance equipment he had bought off an alcoholic P.I., and finished his beer out on the balcony. The sunset that had flamed at the bottom of the sky was almost gone, and a cool wind was blowing off the river. The evening shade had spread across the valley, the gold light on the eastern hills dying before his eyes, and he thought he smelled the autumnal odor of gas and dead leaves inside the wind. But surely fall had not already come, had it? Wasn't there another summer concert and dance on the river tomorrow night?

At 1:00 a.m. Thursday, someone reported a fire burning inside Brendan Merwood's downtown law office. Two fire trucks were dispatched, but when firemen and the security service searched the building, they found nothing out of the ordinary. By the time Brendan Merwood arrived at the scene, wearing his pajamas and bathrobe, the firemen were packing up to leave. Across the street, at the entrance to an alley, several homeless men had evidently started a fire in a trash barrel, and the firemen told Merwood the flames from the barrel had probably been reflected in the windows of the law office.

I've heard recovering drunks and addicts say they treat their own minds like dangerous neighborhoods they don't enter by themselves. All night I kept seeing the face of Elton T. Sneed and imagining the level of pain and fear he must have experienced before he died. How could I have been so foolish not to realize Mabus's people would target someone close to Wyatt rather than Wyatt himself, considering the fact he had already shot or torn several of them apart?

Wyatt had told me Sneed's death was on him. But it wasn't. It was on me.

Whether I liked it or not, my guilt had joined me at the hip with a man I had once considered the most repellent human being I had ever known.

I woke in the false dawn, and without waking Temple I took a croissant and a carton of chocolate milk from the icebox and drove up the Blackfoot to Wyatt's place.

It was cold in the canyon, the rocks up on the hillside pink inside the mist, a sliver of moon hanging above the fir trees. My boots

480

clanged on the steel swing bridge, while down below the river roared like rainwater flooding through a stone pipe. I could smell the odor of woodsmoke from Wyatt's kitchen and steak frying in a skillet, and I wondered briefly, considering the nature of my mission, if I would leave Wyatt's property alive.

He met me at his back door, shirtless, barefoot, a blue-and-white-freckled coffeepot in his hand. He stared at me blankly, his face marked from a lack of sleep. I waited for him to speak, but he didn't. "You wear a hat in your house?" I said.

"If it suits me," he replied.

"Can I come in?"

"I don't give a damn," he said, turning his back, flipping over the steak in his skillet.

"I told Karsten Mabus you had the goods from the Global job. I wasn't going to let my family take your fall, Wyatt," I said, standing no more than two feet behind him. I felt my mouth go dry, my hands open and close at my sides.

He forked the steak onto a plate and began browning three pieces of white bread in the skillet grease, his face bloodless, without expression, like a severed head upon a platter.

"Wyatt?"

"I heard you." He sat down at the table and started eating, cutting his meat with his right hand, forking it upside down into his mouth with his left.

481

"We can go after Mabus on environmental issues. Maybe he's violated federal laws in dealing with Saddam Hussein."

"I done give up on your thinking skills, counselor."

"I see."

"All them government people belong to the same club. Play golf together, let each other in on stock market deals, diddle the same women. Think you're gonna change that with some pissant civil suit?"

"I'm sorry about the reverend."

"You didn't have nothing to do with it. My farrier seen Mabus's people up on that ridge where I found the lockbox. They seen them unshoed hoofprints and put it together just like you and that FBI agent, what's-his-name, Broussard, done."

"Where's the lockbox?"

"Everything in it went FedEx last night for Dallas. It's going to some people got a newspaper down there, one I can trust."

"Which newspaper?"

He told me the name. I had to think a moment, then I remembered the publication. To call it right-wing was simplistic. At various times it had been an outlet for Birchers, members of the Paul Revere Society, and people who had used armed force to take over a county courthouse on the Mexican border. But that was not why I remembered the newspaper's name. To my knowledge, it had been the first news outlet in the country to publish the fact that a United States senator from Texas was involved in a huge swindle of the USDA and perhaps even the murder of a state agricultural official. This same senator would become President of the United States. But even though there might have been substance to the story, it was ignored by mainstream media because of the fanatical reputation of the publisher.

"I think you just gave away the ranch," I said.

He drank from his coffee cup and gazed out the window. "You was the shooter at Mabus's place, wasn't you?" he said.

"You never know."

"I talked with some folks on the res. They seen two guys looked just like the ones shanked me headed up the road to Reverend Sneed's house. I know where them yardbirds is at, Brother Holland. They're fixing to have a bad day."

"If I have knowledge you're about to commit a crime, I'm required to report it," I said.

He laughed to himself. "This from the man who capped them two security people on Mabus's ranch?"

"See you around, Wyatt."

"Hey?"

"What?" I said, looking back from the doorway.

"The trout start rising soon as the sun gets over the ridge. Sit down and have a cup," he said.

At 8:15 a.m. that same Thursday morning, Darrel pulled into a convenience store down in the Bitterroots, left Greta Lundstrum in the car, and called the office of Brendan Merwood on his cell phone. At first Merwood pretended not to recognize Darrel's name, but Darrel knew that to be Merwood's way of dealing with people whom he considered unimportant.

"I'm the sheriff's detective with the big ears and buzz cut you called a liar on the stand a couple of times," Darrel said. "I'm also the detective the department sacked as a drunk and general screwup."

"How good of you to call. What can I —"

"I found out where Johnny American Horse is holed up. I can put him out of commission myself or —"

"Stop right there, my friend. You've contacted the wrong party."

"American Horse used a thirty-thirty without a scope. Next time out, he'll have a better weapon and blow hair on your client's walls. You get on the phone and tell Karsten Mabus what I said. My number is on your caller ID. You have fifteen minutes."

Darrel clicked off his cell phone and got back in his Honda. Greta looked seasick, her makeup on too thick, a dirt ring around her throat.

"You going to stand up, Greta. Get all other options out of your head," he said.

"One day I'm going to fix you for this, Darrel."

"You already did."

"What do you mean?"

You betrayed me, he thought. But he let it go. "How's the recorder riding?" he asked.

"Like a tumor, if that answers your question," she said.

Five minutes later, his cell rang. "Where are you? We'll send a car to pick you up," Merwood said.

"Are you kidding?" Darrel said.

"You call it, then."

"Your office. Tell Mabus to bring his checkbook, too."

There was a pause. "When?"

"Twenty-five minutes," Darrel replied. He clicked off his cell phone and dropped it on the floor of the Honda. "Piece of cake."

"You really think Karsten Mabus is going to come downtown and write you a check?" she said.

"If he wants to stay alive. Wait here just a minute." He went inside the convenience store and returned with a large container of black coffee. "Nothing like it to get the day started," he said.

They drove into Missoula, passing the old

military fort that resembled Scofield Barracks in Hawaii, where Darrel had once been stationed. They crossed the new bridge over the Clark Fork, one that was lined with carriage lamps mounted on stanchions. Down below, Darrel could see the smooth rush of green water through the pilings, rafters bouncing through the current, and off to the left a sandlot baseball diamond couched between the bridge and the riverbank. This might be a hard place to let go of, he thought. He rolled down the window and let the coolness and smell of the morning blow into his face.

"You look mighty pleased with yourself," Greta said.

"When you add it all up and it comes out to zero, you got to take your kicks where you can," he said. "That make sense to you, Greta?"

"I don't know what I ever saw in you," she replied.

He waited until they were at the red light before he stared directly into her face. "Say that again?"

"We had fun for a while, didn't we? It wasn't all bad," she said. She let her eyes rove over his face. "Maybe there's still time."

The light changed. "You almost had me going," he said.

He pulled into the alley behind Brendan Merwood's law firm and parked between two nineteenth-century brick buildings. Then, with his large Styrofoam cup of coffee in his hand, he and Greta entered the back door.

Merwood had two law partners, but both of their offices were empty and the receptionist and secretary who usually worked behind a curved counter in front were gone as well. "Hello?" Darrel said.

Merwood stepped out of his office, porcine, solid, wearing a striped shirt with French cuffs, his brown skin shining as though it had been rubbed with tanning lotion. "Sit down. Please," he said. When he smiled his mouth had the dislocated stiffness of a patient in a dentist's chair.

The Venetian blinds were closed, the soft tones of the walls, carpet, and furniture even softer in the muted light, the interior of the office humming with the sound of the air-conditioning vents.

"Where's Mabus?" Darrel said.

Merwood didn't answer. Instead, three men wearing business suits came out of Merwood's conference room. Darrel remembered having seen one of them at his health club, a silent, lean-bodied man with silver hair who had smacked the heavy bag with murderous intensity.

"What's this?" Darrel said.

"We need to make sure everybody's operating in a pristine environment here," Merwood said.

"You know the routine," the man with

silver hair said. His accent was East Coast, from the streets, an over-the-hill wiseass who'd moved west after the collapse of the Mob, Darrel thought.

Darrel set down his coffee container on the counter, then placed his hands on each side of it. He spread his legs slightly, looking back over his shoulder. "I'm carrying, so don't get excited," he said.

He felt the man with silver hair pull the Beretta from the holster clipped onto Darrel's belt and slide the sap and switchblade out of his side pockets. The silver-haired man's hands groped Darrel in the scrotum, between the buttocks, between his thighs, and down both legs, retrieving the .25 hideaway and its Velcro-strap holster from Darrel's right ankle.

"This guy's a walking torture chamber," the man with silver hair said.

But Darrel was not paying attention to the man with silver hair. He was watching the other two security men as they searched Greta Lundstrum. They had told her to place her hands up against the wall and spread her feet, but they seemed to avoid touching her body in an invasive way, at least to any greater degree than was necessary. One man gingerly touched the inside of her thigh and stepped back.

"You want to deliver it up?" he said.

"Look the other way and I might," she said.

With her back to them, she lifted her skirt slightly, bent over, and untaped the recorder Darrel had put on her earlier.

"We were hoping to have reciprocal trust here, Mr. McComb, but that fact seems to have eluded you," Brendan Merwood said.

"That's a recorder, not a wire. It's just backup. This isn't a sting," Darrel said.

"And you want to sell Karsten Mabus the whereabouts of Johnny American Horse?"

"That pretty well sums it up. But right now I need to use the can," Darrel said, tapping the rim of his Styrofoam coffee with his fingernail.

"Do you believe this fucking guy?" one of the other security men said.

"Don't use that language in here," Merwood said. He blew out his breath. "Go with him." He gestured with his thumb toward the office restroom.

The silver-haired man and the one whom Merwood had corrected for his profanity went inside with Darrel. But Darrel did not go to the urinal. Instead, he began unbuckling his pants as he entered a stall.

"What do you think you're doing?" the man with silver hair said.

"I got to take a dump. I had clam linguine and a few brews last night. Want to hang around, be my guest," Darrel said. He squatted on the toilet and blew a gaseous explosion into the bowl.

When Darrel and the security men came out of the restroom, Brendan Merwood was talking on the phone. He said something into the receiver Darrel couldn't hear, then replaced the receiver on the carriage.

"How much do you want for your information?" he asked.

"I'll take that up with Mabus," Darrel replied.

"Are you serious?" Merwood said.

"I told you he was a hardhead," Greta said.

"These gentlemen here will take you to see Mr. Mabus," Merwood said. "Go out the back door, if you would."

"I want my twenty-five, my nine-Mike, my blade, and my sap back," Darrel said.

"We'll sack 'em up for you," the man with silver hair said. "Let me have your keys."

"What for?" Darrel said.

"There's a guy outside who'll drive your car. You come in ours," the man with silver hair said. He eased back the receiver on Darrel's .25-caliber automatic and looked at the round that was seated in the chamber. He laid his arm across Darrel's shoulders, tapping him good-naturedly with the pistol. "This is gonna work out, believe me."

Darrel thought he could smell the sweat and deodorant in the man's armpit. For a second Greta's eyes settled on his, gleaming with victory.

★ ★ ★

After I left Wyatt's place on the Blackfoot,
I went to the office and tried to work. But it
was no use. Why did I want to even pretend
I was an attorney? My deeds had proved over
and over again that I was little different from
Wyatt Dixon or Darrel McComb. There was
no psychological complexity waiting to be
discovered at the center of my life. The truth
was, I lusted to kill. It was cleaner, easier,
and simpler than the drawn-out processes of
the law. Jailhouses and prisons are filled with
people who are ugly and stupid and who
probably deserve to be there. But rich guys
don't stack mainline time, and men like
Karsten Mabus, no matter what they do,
never ride the needle. So why not kick it on
up to rock 'n' roll? I told myself.

I was almost convinced by my own rhetoric
when Hildy, my receptionist, buzzed my
phone. "I've got Amber American Horse on
the line. Want to take the call?" she said.

I hesitated, then said, "Put her on."

"Billy Bob?" Amber's voice said.

"Are you on a cell?" I said

"Yes."

"My phones are probably tapped. Get off
the cell and use a land line. Call me in fifteen minutes at a place where the bindle
stiffs smile at you from the walls. You
hearing me on this?"

She paused only a second. "Make it a half

491

hour. I have to drive. It's dangerous," she said.

"Hey, cowgirls never get the blues," I said.

"What?" she said.

But I hung up the phone before a trace could be made, then went out the back door of my office and down the alley to Higgins Street. I walked past a newsstand and the Oxford Bar and crossed the street to Charley B's. The walls inside were hung with the work of a West Montana legend, Lee Nye, who had been employed there as a part-time bartender in the 1960s and whose photographs of seamed, wind-burned faces were like a pictorial history of the American West and the landless blue-collar men who had built it.

The phone behind the bar rang five minutes after I arrived. The bartender picked it up, then handed it to me. "Hello?" I said.

"It's Amber," she said.

"How's Johnny?"

"His arm's better, thanks to Darrel."

"To Darrel McComb?"

"That's why I called. We're going to split for Canada. I wanted to thank Darrel for what he did. I've treated him unfairly."

"I'm just not reading you."

"You don't have to. You see my father?"

"No," I replied.

"If you do, tell him I said good-bye."

"Don't hang up."

"This is a great country, Billy Bob. But the bad guys are going to grind you up."

"I'm still your attorney, remember? How did McComb help Johnny?"

But she had broken the connection.

It was unwinding fast now, but I didn't know it, either because I was too close to my own problems or perhaps because I still did not appreciate the level of fear that Karsten Mabus could instill in others.

Just before noon, Romulus Finley came into the office. He looked stricken, as though he had just been informed an incurable disease had spread through all his organs. He stood in my doorway, his lips moving soundlessly, dried mucus at the corners.

"You want a glass of water, Senator?" I asked.

He stepped inside the room and closed the door behind him. He sat down in front of my desk, looking about uncertainly. "Have you heard from my daughter?" he said.

"Yes, I did. This morning," I replied.

"She called here?" he asked, his face lifting expectantly.

I didn't answer. At that moment I was convinced that not only did I have a tap on my line but Finley knew about it.

"Where did she call you? I've got to get word to her," he said.

"About what?"

"Everything. I think she's in harm's way," he said, gesturing vaguely. "She's mixed up. Her mother was an alcoholic. That's why all these problems started."

"I don't know where Amber is, sir."

I waited for him to speak, to make the admissions that would perhaps change his life and perhaps even save his daughter's. He looked hard at me, but his vision was focused inward on thoughts that only he was privy to. The moment passed.

"Well, I'll just find her, then," he said, rising from his chair. He glanced around the room like a man who was lost in the middle of a train station. "Her mother wouldn't stop drinking. I tried everything."

"Senator, is there someone I should call?"

"No," he said. "There's no one. No one at all."

CHAPTER 25

Darrel sat in the backseat of the Chrysler and gazed through the tinted windows as the city of Missoula slipped behind him. The man with silver hair sat on one side of him, a second security man on the other side, Greta up front in the passenger seat. The man with silver hair was named Sidney. He had taken off his coat and folded it neatly across his legs. There were bright stripes in his dress shirt, like thin bands of smoothed tinfoil, and a silver pin in his lavender tie.

"I know you from somewhere," Darrel said.

"The health club," Sidney said.

"No, before that. Maybe from Nicaragua or El Sal."

"Could be. Lot of guys were looking for a job back then. You?"

"A little bit. Nothing to write home about."

"Three hots and a cot, right?" Sidney said.

They went through Lolo and turned west on Highway 12, heading toward the Idaho line. Darrel was amazed at how green the hills had become after only one day's rain. Lolo Creek was boiling, the current filled with driftwood from the banks. Up ahead

Darrel could see the blueness of the sky above Lolo Pass and snow on the tip of St. Mary's Peak.

Then he looked through the back window for his Honda. It was gone.

"They stopped for something to eat. They're gonna join us. Don't worry about it," Sidney said.

"Yeah? That's my car. I want it back," Darrel said.

Sidney didn't answer. But Greta turned around in the front seat. "You're in good hands," she said.

When Darrel didn't reply, she said it again. But Darrel was now staring at the side of Sidney's face. "It was at El Mozote," he said. "On the Honduran border. December 1981. You were standing by the trench where all those peasants were buried."

"You got the wrong dude, Mac," Sidney said, staring indifferently out the side window.

The Chrysler's tires hummed around a slight bend in the road and Darrel saw the entrance to Karsten Mabus's ranch, the white-railed fences and breeding barns shining in the sun. But the Chrysler kept going, climbing a hill, rounding another curve that was layered with outcroppings of gray and yellow rock.

"Mabus is the guy I need to talk to," Darrel said.

"Sure," said the man on the other side of Darrel, and plunged a hypodermic needle into his neck.

For the next three hours Darrel McComb drifted in and out of a red haze that was like the sunrise down on the equator — hot, pervasive, blinding when you looked straight into it. Pain had become geographic, a conduit into past places and events, a tropical garden spiked with bougainvillea, lime trees, crowns of thorns, and rosebushes that bloomed in December. He saw the waxy faces of the dead, the firing-squad victims with their thumbs wired behind them, the sawed-off soldiers in salt-crusted uniforms and oversized steel pots, their M-16s leaking white smoke. And for the first time in more than twenty years he felt these images leaving him forever.

The pain his tormentors had inflicted upon him hadn't worked, and neither had the chemicals they had injected into his veins. At some point a cloth bag coated with insecticide had been fitted over his head, but that had not worked, either. In fact, it had even obstructed his interrogators' agenda.

"You think people are coming to help you?" Sidney said, bare-chested, squatting down eye-level with Darrel. "Take a look at who's having drinks by Mabus's pool."

Two of Darrel's tormentors lifted up the

chair he was strapped in and set it by a window in the log house high up on a mountain overlooking the back of Mabus's ranch. Sidney fitted a pair of binoculars on Darrel's eyes. "That's United States Senator Romulus Finley down there, pal. That's also your friend the district attorney, Fay Harback. They're on the pad, my man," he said.

But Darrel's eyes were too swollen to see.

"Light him up again," Sidney said.

Someone behind Darrel poured a bucket of water over his head, then an electrical surge struck his genitals and his nipples like a blow from a jackhammer. They hit him again. And again. And again. When he awoke, he was bleeding from the mouth.

Sidney had pulled up a straight-backed chair in front of him. He leaned forward, his lean stomach ridged, his chest patinaed with gray monkey fur. "Don't be a hardhead. I don't want to keep doing this to you," he said. "Just tell us where American Horse is. You'll get to live and make yourself a few spendolies at the same time."

The sun had gone behind the mountain, and in the shade the trees on the hillside looked cold and dark. But on a flat outcropping that jutted out over the canyon, Darrel thought he saw Rocky Harrigan gazing at the countryside, his heavy physique and the ledge he stood on bathed in sunlight. Rocky was wearing slacks, penny loafers, his aviator glasses, and his favorite goon shirt, a Hawaiian job printed with bluebirds and palm trees, the way he always dressed for an evening out. *Been waiting on you, old partner. Come on, we're going to have a fine time,* Rocky said.

Darrel saw him remove his shades and give the thumbs-up sign, then beckon Darrel to walk across the air and join him on the lip of a canyon that opened onto green valleys Darrel had never seen before.

Darrel's eyes closed, then opened briefly. "Got to tell you something, Sidney," he whispered hoarsely.

Sidney leaned down, his eyes close to Darrel's. "Go ahead, pal. You got the right attitude. Let's get this behind us," he said.

Darrel tried to muster the words but could not get them out. His teeth were red with his blood, his breath fetid, his eyes like slits in tea-colored eggs.

"Take your time. You can do it. You're almost home free," Sidney said.

Darrel lifted his lips an inch from Sidney's ear. "I was a good cop," he whispered, grinning self-effacingly at the effort it took him to speak.

One week later, a rock climber found Darrel's Honda and his body inside it at the bottom of a canyon just west of the Idaho line. The car's roof was crushed from the three-hundred-foot fall it had taken down the mountainside, and Darrel's body had been degraded by magpies and putrefaction, relegating the particular cause of Darrel's death to guesswork. But when the paramedics lifted the body into a vinyl bag, one of them felt a hard object behind Darrel's left calf muscle. The coroner scissored away the fabric, exposing a miniaturized recorder and microphone taped behind Darrel's knee.

The next three weeks passed for Johnny and Amber American Horse with little or no contact from the outside world. They stayed holed up in a cabin on the edge of the Bob Marshall Wilderness, a woodstove for heat, their water drawn by hand from a rock-dammed creek at the base of a canyon wall that stayed in shadow until late afternoon. The water from the pool was always cold and tasted like stone and fern and snowmelt, and at the bottom of the pool were schools of cutthroat trout pointed into the current, their bodies as sleek as silver and red ribbons. When Amber threw the canvas bucket heavily into the water, both her reflection and the schooled-up trout splintered into the rocks.

Years before, Johnny had built the cabin in a thickly timbered gulch that gave shade in the summer and protection from cold winds in winter and was hard to see from either the lowlands or the sky. The abandoned log road that led to the cabin had caved along the edges and was considered treacherous and unusable by both hunters and U.S. Forest Service personnel. On the first day of Johnny's escape from federal custody, he and Amber had parked Amber's vehicle behind the cabin, pulled a tarp over it, and covered the tarp with pine boughs. They used the woodstove only in the daylight hours and gathered only fuel that was dry and worm-eaten and would burn with maximum heat and little smoke.

The cabin was snug and watertight, stocked with canned beef and vegetables a cousin of Lester Antelope's had backpacked over the crest of the mountain. In wistful, self-deceptive moments Johnny and Amber almost believed their geographical removal from the outside world had somehow changed the legal machinery that was waiting to grind them up.

But if Johnny and Amber had forgotten the relentless nature of their enemies, Lester Antelope's cousin had not. He had left Johnny a Lee-Enfield carbine, a British officer's model with peep sights, a lightweight stock, and a bolt action that worked as smoothly as a Mauser's.

Then one night they heard sounds whose source they couldn't identify — a footfall in the woods, a tree branch snapping, shale sliding over rock surfaces on the hillside.

Johnny walked out in the trees and listened, the moonlight as bright as a flame on the pool where they drew their water. He came back to the cabin, poured a cup of cold coffee, and told Amber he had seen the freshly churned tracks of elk in the pine needles.

The next morning Amber saw Johnny oiling the carbine on the back step, pressing cartridges with his thumb down into the magazine, his skin netted with the sunlight that broke through the canopy overhead.

"We have plenty of meat. I wouldn't squeeze that off up here," she said, stepping into the doorway.

"A griz might try to get in at night. They can smell food a long way," he said.

"I'm not afraid of jail," she said. "Don't do what you're doing, Johnny."

His face was bladed, his cheeks slightly sunken. "You're not afraid of anything," he said.

"Losing you."

"If they nail us, it'll be for good. No second chances this time," he said.

"Don't say that. They don't have that kind of power."

"I let them take me without a fight. They asked me what I thought of the Atlanta Braves," he replied. He lowered his head and rubbed the oil rag along the carbine's barrel, his thoughts hidden.

She remained standing above him in the doorway, the wind blowing down from the crest of the mountain, through larch trees whose needles had turned yellow and were starting to fall. He locked down the bolt of the Lee-Enfield, a piece of cartilage pulsing on his jawbone.

"If they come for us, we go together," she said.

"That's no good. No good at all," he said.

She placed one hand on his shoulder for balance and sat down beside him. She picked his hand off the carbine and held it between hers. "If they come for us, we'll run. There're places in British Columbia they'd never find us," she said.

"That's right," he said, taking his hand from hers. "We don't have to worry about the griz, either. They're looking for food down low. They won't bother us."

He worked the bolt on the Lee-Enfield and jacked the cartridges from the magazine onto the ground. "See? All this was about nothing," he said.

But five minutes later, when she looked out the kitchen window, she saw him picking the cartridges for the Lee-Enfield out of the dirt and wiping them clean on his shirt before he stuck them in his pocket. That night, after she and Johnny went to bed, she thought she heard the engines of helicopters high above the trees.

She woke at false dawn. The cabin was cold, the woodstove unlit, and Johnny's side of the bed empty. She put on her jeans and Johnny's Army jacket and went out into the backyard. The privy door hung open, squeaking on its hinges. Her vehicle was still under its tarp and cover of pine boughs, the canvas stiff with frost. In the grayness of the woods she couldn't see the movement of a single warm-blooded creature — not an owl, a rabbit, a deer mouse, a hooded jay, or even robins, which only yesterday had filled the trees in flocks on their way south.

She went back inside the cabin and absently let the door slam behind her. The sound was like a rifle shot in her ears, and out in the woods she heard a large bird, perhaps an eagle, take flight, its wings flapping as loudly as leather in the dead air.

The carbine, she thought.

She went into the bedroom and pulled open the closet door, where Johnny had put the Lee-Enfield before he went to bed last night. But it was gone.

She dug her cell phone out of a drawer, then hesitated before clicking it on, trying to remember what she had heard once about law enforcement agencies tracking cell phones by satellite. Billy Bob had told her to get off the phone, that his own line was tapped. He had also told her to use a land line, she thought. She had done what he'd said, pulling the tarp and pine boughs off her vehicle and driving to a truck stop, taking a risk she didn't want to take again. No, satellite track or not, she would not leave the cabin again.

She activated the phone. As soon as she did, its message chime went off. She hit the retrieve button.

"It's Billy Bob. Call me at the office or home. Everything is okay," the recorded voice said. Then the transmission broke up.

There were three other messages with the same callback number on them, each of them impossible to understand. She rushed out the back of the cabin and climbed up the gulch until she was out of the timber, standing on a crag that overlooked a long, sloping mountainside covered with Douglas fir. She hit the dialback key on the cell and waited, her heart beating, her breath fogging in the cold.

The phone rang in my kitchen while Temple and I were eating breakfast.

"Amber?" I said.

"Tell it to me fast. My batteries are almost dead," she said.

"Where are you?"

"Tell it to me, Billy Bob. Hurry!"

"You and Johnny are free."

"Free?"

"Darrel McComb caught some of Karsten Mabus's thugs on tape. Johnny's clear on the homicides."

"Why didn't Darrel tell us?"

"Darrel is dead."

"Dead?"

"One thing at a time. How could Darrel know where you are?" I said.

"He brought antibiotics to Johnny's cabin. He'd followed me there once during his" — she hesitated — "during his voyeur stage. He figured that's where we were hiding. I can't think through this. How did Darrel die?"

"Mabus's men tortured him to death. Darrel had taped a recorder to his leg. He wouldn't give Johnny up."

"Oh, Billy Bob," she said.

"What?" I couldn't tell if she was expressing grief over Darrel McComb's death or at something she hadn't told me about yet.

"Johnny left before dawn with a gun. He believes the Feds have found us."

The cell phone made a crackling sound, then went dead.

In the predawn darkness Johnny had heard the thropping sounds of a helicopter and for a moment he did not know if they came from his dreams or somewhere above the gulch. He lay awake as the grayness of the dawn grew inside the trees, then sat straight up in bed when he heard, this time for sure, a motorized vehicle working its way up the log road.

He dressed and slipped the sling of the Lee-Enfield over his shoulder, put on a slouch hat, and without a coat walked out into the cold, up the hill into woods that were speckled with frost. He followed a deer trail to the top of the gulch, then entered a long, flat area where the trees were widely spaced and he could make out the log road that accessed his cabin.

He heard the helicopter again, but the wind was behind him and he couldn't be sure of the helicopter's location. Then he saw electric lights flashing below the rim of a mountain across the valley.

Could a logging crew be working there? The big companies were logging old-growth timber now, lifting out three-hundred-year-old trees by helicopter in the early morning and late evening hours so the companies' handiwork would not be seen in broad daylight.

But would they be logging when there was still fire danger in the woods, when a spark from an engine exhaust or even a chain-saw blade could set the undergrowth ablaze?

He dismissed the possibility of a logging crew. Someone else was out there. But so what? *Hokay hey,* he thought. They were dealing the play. Maybe they'd get a surprise about the hand they'd just dealt themselves.

The Everywhere Spirit and the grandfathers who lived with the four points of the wind would not fail him, he told himself. And with a renewed confidence in his vision of this world and the next, he rested behind a tree and watched the broken contours of the log road turn buff-colored and purple under the paling of the sky.

It did not take long for his worst fears to be confirmed. In the distance he saw government vehicles park on the log road and men file into the shadows of the trees, working their way up the slope in what would be a wide semicircle, sealing off any escape from his cabin.

Darrel McComb had turned out to be a rat after all, he thought.

He waited in the coolness of the trees, the Lee-Enfield's leather sling wrapped loosely around his left forearm, his left knee resting comfortably on a bed of pine needles. He watched the wind puff the mist out of the trees on the valley floor, then the sky became as light-colored and textured as weathered bone, stained at the bottom by the radiance of a red sun.

The men from the government vehicles were almost through the timber and about to enter an old clear-cut where they would be completely exposed. What fools, Johnny thought. He got to his feet and tightened the sling of his left arm, steadying the carbine against a pine trunk. He was breathing hard now, his heart tripping, a stench like soiled cat litter rising from his armpits. For just a moment he thought he heard the clatter of armored personnel carriers and tanks lurching over sand dunes, then he heard nothing at all, only wind and pinecones bouncing down the hillside

He wiped his eyes on his sleeve and opened his mouth to clear a popping sound in his ears. Up on the hill behind him he heard feet running and twigs breaking. When he turned, he saw a flash of clothing, like an olive field jacket, moving fast through the trees. Somehow they had flanked him and gotten around behind him.

But who cared? He'd waste them front and rear, blow brains and feathers all over the brush, and let the devil sort them out.

On the far side of the clear-cut he saw sunlight glint on brass, on a helmet, on steel, then the government men began to emerge out of the shadows. Johnny aimed through the peep sight on the point man's breast and felt his finger tighten inside the Lee-Enfield's trigger guard. In less than a second, a .303 round would be on its way downrange, per-haps starting to topple before it cored through its target.

Then he saw the green workclothes of the man he was about to kill and the red, white, and blue patch sewn above his shirt pocket. The man came on into the clear-cut, oblivious to the threat up on the hillside, a string of black and Indian Job Corps kids behind him, all of them carrying tools and surveyors' equipment.

"Johnny!" he heard Amber call behind him.

He stepped back from the tree and lowered the carbine, just as a helicopter lifted out of the next valley, its engine roaring, a huge log suspended by a cable from the airframe.

"Johnny, we're free! I talked to Billy Bob! We can go back!" Amber shouted, waving her arms.

The world seemed to tilt against the horizon. Johnny dropped the Lee-Enfield from his hands, the sling sliding off his bad arm, his eyes swimming. Then he picked the carbine up again, pulled the bolt free, and threw it down the hillside. He smashed the stock across the pine trunk again and again, the wood flying from the metal parts, as though he were vainly attempting to hew down an intransigent monument to his own rage.

"Did you hear me?" she said, skidding down the side of the hill, fighting to keep her balance, the Army field jacket she wore streaked with dew from the trees.

But he sat down on a rock, his head in his hands, and could not answer.

EPILOGUE

We had Indian summer that year. The nights were crisp, the days warm, the maples heavy with gold and red leaves all over Missoula. College kids climbed every day to the big white cement "M" overlooking the university, and hang gliders turned in lazy circles on the warm updrafts rising from Hellgate Canyon. The evening news at our health club showed brief clips of burned-out American Humvees in the streets of Baghdad but never images of the wounded or the dead. Nor did the camera visit civilian hospitals. The war was *there*, not here, and Indian summer came to us every morning like a balmy wind laced with the smell of distant rain.

I wished for a dramatic denouement to the events of the last few months, a clap of divine hands that would reassure us of an ontological order wherein evil is punished and good rewarded, not unlike the playwright's pen at work in the fifth act of an Elizabethan tragedy. But neither the death of Darrel McComb nor the revelations of the recorder he had hidden on his person could usurp the tranquillity of the system or dampen our desire to extend the beautiful days of fall into the coming of winter.

But Darrel's worst detractors had to take their hats off to him. He had created a preface on the tape, explaining how he had anonymously called in a fire alarm on Brendan Merwood's office, then had planted the recorder in the restroom when he entered the building with the firemen. The material on the tape caused the resignation of Fay Harback, who was discovered to have accepted large unsecured loans from a Mabus lending institution, and it brought about the arrest of Greta Lundstrum for the murder of Charles Ruggles. But Greta died in custody of coronary failure. And the security men who had tortured Darrel McComb to death and who had probably murdered Seth Masterson fled the area and to this date have not been found.

Romulus Finley and Brendan Merwood denied any knowledge of wrongdoing of any kind and were widely believed. If their careers were impaired in any fashion, I saw no sign of it. They played golf together on the links by old Fort Missoula, lifting the ball high above the fairways, their faces glowing with health and good fortune and the respect of their peers. Mortality and the judgment of the world seemed to hold no sway in their lives, but I sometimes wondered if Romulus Finley did not find his own room in hell when he had to look into his daughter's eyes.

If there was a dramatic turn in the story, it

was one that few people will ever know about. After the federal and state charges against Johnny American Horse fell apart, I saw Amber and Johnny coming out of the old city cemetery on the north end of town. The sky was an immaculate blue, the saddles in the mountains veined with snow, the maple leaves cascading like dry paper across the tombstones. I stopped my truck by the entrance and waved at Amber, who seemed lost in thought, a scarf tied tightly under her chin, a clutch of chrysanthemums in her hand.

"Oh, hi, Billy Bob," she said, as though awakening from sleep. "We couldn't find Darrel's grave."

"It's in back. I'll show y'all," I said.

We walked up a knoll, though trees, into shade that was cold and smelled of damp pine needles and fresh piled dirt. I could see rain falling on a green hill by the river, and the sun was shining inside the rain.

"You think the dead can hear our voices?" she asked.

"Maybe," I said.

"The sheriff told us Darrel was probably tortured for hours. At any point he could have given up our whereabouts," she said.

"They would have killed him anyway, Amber," I said.

Johnny took the flowers from Amber's hand and spread them on Darrel's grave. Then he

513

drew himself to attention and saluted.

"I think he'd appreciate that," I said.

When we came out of the cemetery, the sunshower on the hill by the river had turned itself into a rainbow. I saw Johnny's eyes crinkle at the corners, and I wondered if, in his mind, the Everywhere Spirit had just hung the archer's bow in the sky.

So maybe this story is actually about the presence of courage, self-sacrifice, and humility in people from whom we don't expect those qualities. Not a great deal was changed externally by the events I've described here. Wyatt Dixon's newspaper friends in Dallas published the story of Karsten Mabus's connections to the sale of chemical and biological agents to Saddam Hussein in the 1980s, but no one seemed to care. In fact, Karsten Mabus is currently underwriting legislation in the U.S. Congress that will open up wilderness areas in this country for oil and gas exploration while, at the same time, his companies are receiving contracts for the rebuilding of Iraq's infrastructure.

But as the old-time African-American hymn admonishes, I don't study war anymore. I made my separate peace regarding my own excursion into violence at Mabus's ranch, an event that left two men seriously wounded, consoling myself with the biblical account of Peter, who, after drawing blood with his sword in the Garden of Gethsemane, received only a mild rebuke from the Lord.

In fact, perhaps my greater sin was my presumption that violence, in this case the attempted assassination of Karsten Mabus, can change history for the better. As Wyatt Dixon suggested, Mabus cannot be gotten rid of by a bullet. Mabus is of our own manufacture, an extension of ourselves and the futile belief that the successful pursuit of wealth and power can transform avarice into virtue. His successors are legion and timeless. They need only to wait in the wings for their moment, then walk onstage to thunderous applause, their faces touched with an ethereal light.

I also knew that Mabus had a long memory and my story with him was probably not over.

But I refused to borrow tomorrow's trouble and make it today's concern. Our child would be born in spring, and each day Temple seemed happier and more lovely than the day before. During the fall she, Lucas, and I packed a straw hamper with supper and made a point of spending at least two afternoons a week fishing for German browns on the Blackfoot River, not far from the steel suspension bridge that led to Wyatt Dixon's house.

The river was low, the coppery color of tarnished pennies, the scales of hellgrammites wrapped like spiderweb on the great round boulders that jutted out of the current. Right at sunset the browns would take an elk-hair caddis or blond wolf with such hunger and force they would slap water up on the bank. But German browns begin spawning not long after Labor Day, so we kept none of the fish we caught and instead replaced them in the river, holding their fat bellies cupped in our palms, while they rested, bursting with roe, their gills pulsing, waiting to reenter the current and disappear beneath the reflections of sky, trees, and human faces that can appear and dissolve more quickly than the blink of an eye.

ABOUT THE AUTHOR

JAMES LEE BURKE, a rare winner of two Edgar Awards, is the author of twenty-three previous novels, including such *New York Times* bestsellers as *Bitterroot, Purple Cane Road, Cimarron Rose, Jolie Blon's Bounce,* and *Dixie City Jam.* He lives in Missoula, Montana, and New Iberia, Louisiana.

CARIOCA FLETCH

Also available in Large Print
by Gregory Mcdonald:

Fletch and the Widow Bradley

Gregory Mcdonald

CARIOCA FLETCH

G.K. HALL &CO.
Boston, Massachusetts
1986

Published in Large Print by arrangement
with William Morris Agency.

G. K. Hall Large Print Book Series.

Set in 16pt Plantin.

Library of Congress Cataloging in Publication Data

Mcdonald, Gregory, 1937–
   Carioca Fletch.

   (G. K. Hall large print book series)
   1. Large type books.   I. Title.
[PS3563.A278C37   1986]   813'.54   85–16378
ISBN 0–8161–3983–0 (lg. print)

Dedicated with affection and
admiration to Gloria and Alfredo Machado,
their family and friends

CARIOCA FLETCH

CHAPTER ONE

Naturally the samba drums were beating, rhythms beside rhythms on top of rhythms beneath rhythms. Especially just before Carnival did this modern city of nine million people on the South Atlantic reverberate with the ever-quickening rhythms of the drums. From all sides, every minute, day and night, came the beating of the drums.

'You cannot understand the future of the world without first understanding Brazil.' That was the way the trim, forty-year-old Brazilian novelist Marilia Diniz spoke. Informative. Instinctual. Indicative. The umbrella over the café table on Avenida Atlantica shaded her eyes, leaving her mouth in the afternoon sunlight. She shrugged her thin shoulders. 'Unfortunately, Brazil is beyond anyone's understanding.'

Marilia sat across from Fletch in a light dress with only straps over her pale shoulders. Marilia Diniz was the rare *carioca* who never went to the beach.

Laura Soares, more appropriately dressed in shorts, sandals, a halter, more

1

appropriately tanned golden brown, sat to Fletch's right. Laura would always go to the beach.

Fletch was dressed in the uniform he had learned to be innocent, egalitarian: shorts and sneakers.

In front of Marilia and Laura were glasses of beer, *chope*. Fletch had the drink he liked best in all the world: *guaraná*.

'Now that Fletch sees the *Praia de Copacabana* he will never go anywhere else,' Laura said. 'Maybe I will never even be able to get him to come back to Bahia.'

'I'll go back to Bahia anytime,' Fletch said. 'If your father lets me.'

'He'll embrace you. You know that.'

'I don't know.'

'The first truth about Brazil,' Marilia said, 'is its absolute tolerance.'

'Does Brazil tolerate intolerance?'

'I suppose so.' Marilia wrinkled her nose. 'You see, you cannot understand.'

Across the *avenida* stretched the huge, dazzling Copacabana Beach, from the Morror do Leme to his left, to the peninsula separating Copacabana from the beaches of Arpoador, Ipanema and Leblon to his right.

On the beach, among the brightly

2

colored umbrellas and blankets were thousands of golden brown bodies, all ages, sexes, their swimsuits so small on them only their skin, really, was visible, exercising, taking turns at the provided chin-up bars, reclining on sit-up boards, running. Within sight on the beach, Fletch counted fourteen soccer games in progress. Small children played at the water's edge, but most of the people in the water were doing disciplined swimming. Proportionately few on the beach were resting. The temperature was thirty-three degrees centigrade, about ninety degrees Fahrenheit; it was four o'clock in the afternoon, and the people's energy shimmered up from the sand more positively than reflected the strong sunlight.

At street corners to the right and left of where they sat drummed samba bands. Boys, men, from fourteen years of age to whenever, beat on drums of various sizes, various tones as if this were their last chance to do so, ever. The band to the right wore canary yellow shorts; to the left, cardinal red shorts. Immediately around each band, pedestrians stayed to give in totally to the samba awhile, dancing on the sidewalk, up and down the curb, among the cars parked pridefully anywhere. One or two drummers might stop a moment to wipe the sweat from their chests, bellies, forearms, drink a *chope* to make more sweat, but a samba band itself never stops, when it moves, when it stays in one place. A samba band's stopping is as fatal a thought as your own heart's stopping.

And the people passing on the sidewalk in front of the café, the pedestrians, going from corner to corner, band to band, businessmen dressed only in shorts and sandals, sometimes shirts, carrying briefcases, women in bikinis lugging bags of groceries, barefoot children running with a soccer ball, walked, lugged, ran, keeping the beat of the drums in their feet, their legs, their hips, their shoulders. This moving to the samba instead of just moving gives Brazilians the most beautiful legs in the world, having a true balance, an ideal proportion between muscular calves and slim thighs. The groups of gap-mouthed begging children, the cloth of their shorts worn so it almost did not exist, keep their bare feet moving to the rhythm of the drums, making the stillness, the steadiness of their huge dark eyes the more shocking, imploring. To provide a deception of class difference for the tourists, the café waiters wore black long trousers and white open shirts and real shoes, but even in their brushing crumbs from the tables, begging children away from someone they had implored too long, they somberly kept the samba beat.

'*Cidade maravilhosa!*' In his chair, Fletch stretched his arms over his head.

'Mysterious city,' said Marilia. 'Mysterious country.'

Fletch said: 'The guidebook says something like, "At first sight of Rio de Janeiro instantly you forgive God for what's visible of New Jersey."'

'I like New Jersey,' said Laura. 'Isn't that where Pennsylvania is? I thought so.'

'If you cannot understand the future of the world without first understanding Brazil,' Fletch said, 'I would like to understand more of Brazil's past. Granted, I came to Brazil rather quickly, without really expecting to, without being prepared, but once here I can find out very little of Brazil's history. Even Laura's father—'

Laura giggled and put her hand on his thigh. 'Brazil has no past. That's what

5

makes us so mysterious.'

Marilia shot a glance at Laura. 'You have not heard of *queima de arquivo*?'

A begging child came by and placed one peanut in front of each of them.

Laura laughed. 'A while ago a Brazilian airliner crashed on a runway. As anyone's airliner might. Within minutes a crew showed up to paint over the Brazilian how-do-you-call-them? insignias on the airplane. It is our way of preventing what has already happened.'

'It means "burn the record,"' Marilia said.

'It means "cover up,"' Laura said. 'It is the Brazilian way of life. That is why we are so free.'

'It has happened more than once,' Marilia said. 'A government takes power. In disapproval of all that has gone before, it burns the records of previous governments. Like confession, the idea has been to give us a fresh beginning.'

'So we are a nation of anarchists,' laughed Laura. 'We are all anarchists.'

'All histories are shame-filled,' Marilia said.

'Brazil's shames we have expunged by setting fire to them, sending them on the

6

wind.'

At a little distance from them, the pixie, a boy about six years old, watched them with disappointment. They were not eating their peanuts.

Marilia put her sunglasses on her nose and sat back in her chair. 'And you, Fletcher?'

Slowly, Fletch ate his peanut.

Instantly the small boy stepped forward and offered to sell Fletch a bag of peanuts.

Fletch took *cruzeiros* out of his sneaker and gave too many to the boy.

He opened the peanut bag and held it out to Marilia.

She shook her head. 'Do you practice *queima de arquivo*? Are you in Brazil to burn your record?'

'Many are.'

'It would make him Brazilian,' Laura said. 'Honorary Brazilian.'

'Is that why Laura's father does not like you?'

'My father likes him,' said Laura. 'Loves him. It's only that—'

'Her father,' Fletch said, 'is a scholar. A professor at the university. A poet.'

Now a dozen begging children were around his chair, whispering at him.

'Of course. Otavio Cavalcanti. I know him well. Laura is almost my niece. She should be staying with me, here in Rio.'

'He is intolerant of North Americans. I am a North American.'

Standing on the sidewalk near the curb, standing uncommonly still, was an old woman, a hag. A long, shapeless white dress hung from her neck. Dark pouches high in her cheekbones made it seem as if she had four dark eyes. All four eyes were staring at Fletch.

'That's not it, precisely,' Laura said. 'Fletcher can come here to Brazil, to sit in this café, drink *guaraná* and watch the women walk. My father is not permitted into the United States of the North anymore, to read his poetry at Columbia University. My father is intolerant of that.'

'I have read your father,' said Fletch. 'He speaks on behalf of the people.'

Across the sidewalk the woman in white was staring at Fletch as if he had dropped from the moon.

'And there is something else.' Laura shifted in her chair. 'You must admit it, Fletch.'

'What is it?' Marilia asked.

'My father feels Fletch does not see the

8

difference in the Brazilian people.'

'There is no equality like Brazilian equality,' Fletch said. 'I love that.'

'It is not the equality. . . .' Uncomfortably, Laura was looking at Marilia.

'Oh, yes,' Marilia said.

'My father says Fletch keeps trying to understand the Brazilian people through other people he has known. He cannot see the other side of us.'

'There is much I don't understand,' Fletch said.

'There is much you do not accept.'

Fletch grinned at his own joke: 'There is much I cannot see.'

'My father—'

'Your father is a member of a *Candomble*,' Fletch said. 'An intelligent man like that.'

Marilia twisted the cloth braided around her left wrist.

'But he loves Fletch. He says Fletch is surprisingly open, as a person,' Laura said.

'As a North American.'

'You cannot understand Brazil,' Marilia said from behind her sunglasses. 'Brazil accepts thieves. The United States of North America will not accept scholars and poets

9

who speak on behalf of the people.'

'Am I a thief?' Fletch asked. Clearly the hag staring at him from across the sidewalk thought he was something extraordinary.

'You said you came here rather quickly.'

'True.'

'You said you did not expect to come here. You were not prepared.'

'True.'

'You do business with Teo da Costa.'

'True.'

'Teodomiro da Costa is my good friend. In fact, I understand I will see you both at dinner at his house tonight.'

'Good.'

'Teodomiro da Costa makes a good business changing hard currencies, like dollars, into *cruzeiros*, into hard commodities, like emeralds, gold. He has become very rich doing so.'

At the word *cruzeiros*, the pixies around Fletch stepped even closer and raised the pitch of their imploring whispers.

Fletch said, 'I thought he drove a taxi.'

'Teodomiro da Costa does not drive a taxi.'

Fletch took more money from his sneaker and gave it to Laura to pay the waiter. When Laura paid, speaking

Brazilian Portuguese, the bill was sometimes as much as ninety percent less. He gave some *cruzeiros* to the smallest begging child.

'Marilia,' Laura said. 'In Brazil, a man's past is burned.'

'You may burn Fletcher's past,' Marilia said. 'That is all right. Laura, I do not want to see you burn your future.'

'There is no future, either,' said Laura. 'There is the piano.'

'The Brazilians wish for a future,' Marilia said.

'Past ... future,' Fletch muttered.

'I said something wrong,' Laura said.

'You are staying at The Yellow Parrot?' Marilia asked.

The Hotel Yellow Parrot was on Avenida Atlantica and known to be among the most expensive.

'Yellow Parrot,' said Fletch. 'You must admit some things in Brazil do not make sense.'

'Fletch is okay,' Laura said. Then she said something rapidly in Portuguese. 'My father loves him.'

Down the sidewalk to the right, stepping warily around the samba band sweating in canary yellow shorts, through the dancers,

11

came a North American woman, clearly from the United States, clearly newly arrived, in a light green silk dress moving on her body as she moved, green high-heeled shoes, wearing sunglasses and stupidly carrying her purse like a symbol of rank dangling from her forearm: the California empress.

Laura put her hand on Fletch's forearm. 'You okay, Fletch?'

'My God! I mean, why not?'

'Suddenly you turned white.'

'Let go of me.' Fletch flung off her hand.

He ducked beneath the table and began retying his sneakers.

Instantly there were the seven or eight heads of the pixies under the table with him, to see what he was doing.

Laura's head joined him under the table, too. 'Fletch! What's the matter?'

'*Estou com dor de estomago!*'

The pixies groaned in sympathy for him: 'Ooooooohh!'

'You are not sick from the stomach!' Laura said.

'*Estou com dor de cabeca!*'

'Ooooooohh!'

'You are not sick from the head!'

12

'*Febre . . . nausea . . . uma insolacao. . . .*'

'Oooooooohh!'

Seen relaxed in the shade under the table, Laura's legs were great to look at. Marilia's, although pale, were not so bad either. The sight made him feel better.

'Fletcher! What is the matter with you? Why are you so suddenly under the table?'

'That woman. That woman in green passing by. Don't look now.'

The heads of the pixies looked back and forth from Fletch to Laura intelligently, as if they understood.

'So? What about her?'

'She probably thinks I murdered her husband.'

CHAPTER TWO

'*Janio!*' With a frightening rush of long white dress through heavy green leaves, the old hag emerged from the bushes in front of them in the small forecourt of The Hotel Yellow Parrot. She was pointing her arm, her arthritically bent index finger at Fletch's face. '*Janio Barreto!*'

Fletch took a step back. His hand

13

gripped Laura's arm.

The hag took a step forward, her finger in Fletch's face. '*Janio Barreto!*'

He thought they had done quite well. They had left Marilia at the café, walked half a block to their right, through the samba band on that corner, ignoring the gestures to stay and dance for a while, turned right, right again on Avenida Copacabana, along that a few blocks, turning right again at the street just beyond The Hotel Yellow Parrot, carefully, looking first, hurried around the corner and the short way along the sidewalk and into the forecourt of the hotel. They were to use the beach entrance to the hotel, as Fletch was not wearing a shirt.

He had forgotten about the hag.

Now she was blocking their way into the hotel entrance.

'Janio Barreto!' she accused, wagging her bent finger in his face. 'Janio Barreto!'

Laura stepped forward. She put her hand on the old woman's sleeve and spoke in a soothing voice. Fletch recognized the Portuguese word for *mother* in what Laura said.

'Janio Barreto!' the hag insisted, pointing at him.

14

Laura spoke quietly to the woman some more.

The uniformed doorman appeared through the main door of the hotel and came through the forecourt to Fletch. 'Is there a problem, sir?'

'No. I don't think so. I don't know.'

The two women were talking quietly.

'Give her some money,' the doorman said. 'For charity.'

The hag was speaking rapidly now, to Laura.

The old woman kept glancing at Fletch. She was fairly tall and fairly slim, and clearly she could move fast to have gotten to the hotel before them, to have caught them. The leanness of her hands made her fingers seem all the more misshapen. Her brown eyes were huge, clear and intense; her face more wrinkled than drying, caked earth. Thin, iron-gray hair fell from her head like photographed lightning. Her high, cracked voice came through a few blackened teeth.

Now Fletch was hearing the Portuguese words for *wife, husband, father, sons, daughter, boat.*

Listening to the old woman, Laura began taking long, surmising looks at Fletch. Her looks seemed unsure—not of what the old

15

woman was saying, but somehow of Fletch. She was looking at him as if she had never seen him before, or seen him in quite this way.

His face politely averted, the doorman was listening too.

'What is she saying?' Fletch asked.

Laura waited until the old woman finished her sentence.

'She says you are Janio Barreto.'

'Who? What?'

'Janio Barreto.'

'Well, I'm not ... whatever. Whoever. Let's go.'

Laura's chin came forward a few centimeters. 'She says you are.'

The hag spoke some more, clearly repeating what she had said before, something about a boat.

Looking into Fletch's eyes, not smiling, Laura said, 'She says you are her husband.'

'Her husband. Ayuh.'

Laura repeated with firmness: 'She says you are Janio Barreto, her husband.'

Now Laura had the old woman's hands cupped in her own, gently, protectively.

'Of course,' said Fletch. 'Naturally. Certainly. She's not the first to say that, you know. Or the second. Tell me, does she have a settlement lawyer in California?' The doorman, having heard all, having understood all, turned his head and looked at Fletch. 'Tell her she'll have to get in line with her settlement lawyer.'

He smiled at the doorman.

The doorman was not smiling at him.

Laura said, 'You are her husband, Janio Barreto.'

'Hope she sues for settlement under that name. What is this? What's going on? Laura!'

Laura said, 'You died forty-seven years ago, when you were a young man, about as you are now. When you were this lady's young husband.'

'Good grief.'

'You are, how do I say it? Janio Barreto's aura. His other person. His same person.' Laura smiled. 'She is glad to see you.'

'I can tell.' Standing in the little forecourt of the hotel, surrounded by thick, deep green bushes, hearing the cars going by in the *avenida*, the voices of the children playing, hearing, of course, the beatings of the samba drums, Fletch felt coldness breaking over him, prickling his skin. 'Laura . . .'

Still gently holding the woman's hands,

17

Laura said, 'With this woman you have two sons and a daughter. Grown now, of course. They have children of their own. She wants you to meet them.'

'Laura, she wants money. I'm not taking on an extended Brazilian family.'

The doorman was still studying Fletch.

'You were a sailor,' Laura said. 'You earned your living from the sea.'

The old woman had turned, was facing Fletch, presenting herself to him.

Quietly, Laura said, 'She wants to embrace you.'

'Laura! My God...' Fletch could not help himself from moving somewhat backward, somewhat sideways. There were tears on the old woman's cheeks. Laura had let go of the old woman's hands. He felt a branch of one of the bushes against his bare back. 'Laura, what is this? What are you doing?'

'The important thing is...'

The old woman came to Fletch. She raised her arms, put them around his neck. Approaching him, her eyes were soft, loving.

'Laura!'

The doorman held up his hand as if to stop traffic. 'Wait, sir. There is more.'

18

The hag's cheek, wet with tears, was against Fletch's. She smelled terribly, of cooking oils, of fish, and of a million other things. Her body pressed against his.

He did not want to breathe. He wanted to gag. The branches from the bushes were stabbing into the skin of his back.

'The important thing is...' Laura's head was lowered. She spoke respectfully. 'Is that forty-seven years ago, when you were a young man, in another life, you were murdered.'

From the back of his throat, Fletch coughed over the old woman's shoulder.

Then Laura looked up at Fletch, her brown eyes moving rapidly from his left eye to his right to his left. 'Now you must tell your family who murdered you!'

Also with his eyes on Fletch's, the doorman nodded solemnly.

Her eyes settled in Fletch's, Laura said, 'Clearly you cannot rest until you do.'

CHAPTER THREE

'Of course,' Fletch said, coming out of the bathroom, a towel wrapped around his

19

waist, 'I really don't know how reasonable I want you to be.'

'I am very reasonable.'

Naked, long, lean, she lay across the rumpled white sheets of the bed reading *Newsweek*. Her wavy black hair fell over her face. The late afternoon sun through the shaded balcony window made consistent the gold in her skin.

'Laura Soares,' he said. 'From Sao Salvador da Bahia de Todos os Santos. Studied piano at the university in Bahia, then two years at the London Conservatory.'

'I did not like London Conservatory. There is little understanding of Brazilian music there. In a conservatory they conserve music, you know? They don't like to let it expand.'

'Sometimes gives concerts. Daughter of Otavio Cavalcanti, scholar and poet. And your mother cultivates orchids and takes photographs.'

'My mother grows flowers and takes pictures of them. She is trying to beat time.'

Fletch opened the shade more. Their room was at the back of the hotel, overlooking utility areas. Through tall

20

windows in the building across the area, Fletch watched a man painting a room. The man, in undershirt and shorts, had been painting the room during the day and well into the evening since they had arrived at The Yellow Parrot. It looked an ordinary, albeit big, room. The man was either a meticulous painter or had no other work waiting for him.

Fletch said nothing for a moment.

He had gone directly into the shower. The odor of the old woman had clung to him. His face was sticky from her tears, the back of his neck pasty from her caresses.

He had gotten himself thoroughly soaped when the shower curtain drew back and Laura stepped in. She helped him wash, even putting him on his knees in the bathtub, doubling him over, to scrub the back of his neck. She was kneeling before him in the bathtub, the shower water cascading off her head, shoulders, breasts. He began to clean her thighs with his tongue.

After they messed up the bed and each other to the sound of the samba drums coming through the windows, and lying quietly awhile until the sweat dried and made him feel cool, he went back into the shower.

Standing at the window he said, 'Questions . . .'

Reading from the magazine, the lean, naked Laura said, 'Half your diet should be carbohydrates.'

'You're reading about diets? You don't need to improve yourself.'

'My mother will be glad to hear about the carbohydrates. Am I saying "carbohydrates" right?'

'No. But I understand.'

'I don't think they talk about carbohydrates in London. I never heard the word. Pasta!'

'Don't you have any questions?' he asked.

'About pasta?' Still she did not look up from the magazine.

'About the woman in the green silk dress. I told you she probably thinks I killed her husband. She's come here to find me.'

'So?'

'You haven't asked me about that.'

'That has to do with your past. Anyone can make up a story and say it is the past.'

'You're not curious?'

'About the future. What time is it?'

22

He looked at his watch on the bureau. 'Nearly seven.'

'We cannot be too much on time at da Costa's for dinner. It is not polite to the servants. It gives them too much to do at once. Makes them nervous.'

'I have questions.'

'Probably. You are a North American.'

'Your father is Otavio Cavalcanti. You are Laura Soares.'

'That is the past, Fletcher old top.'

'I don't get it.'

'It has to do with who had the name in the past. Then you forget it. This article says you should eat much more chicken and fish than red meat. It says nothing of rice and beans. *Feijoada.*'

'Are you going to talk to me about that old woman?'

'Forget it, for now. She is not *Yemanjá.*'

'I am not Janio Barreto. Whoever.'

'She says you are. She recognized you. She says she studied you carefully while we were at the café. Did you notice her?'

'Yes.'

'She said you have the identical legs of her husband, the same stomach muscles from pulling the fish nets, the same proportion between your shoulders and

23

your hips. She said the slight slash of your navel is identical.'

'Laura . . .'

'Well, she should know.'

'I have never pulled fish nets.'

'You have the muscles from Janio Barreto.'

'Laura, not many Brazilians have my basic light coloring.'

'Some do. Janio Barreto did. Your heads are identical, she says, your eyes.'

'I had a similarity to the husband of the woman in the green dress, too.'

'Similarity has nothing to do with it. She says you are Janio Barreto, her husband.'

'Who was murdered forty-seven years ago.'

'Yes.'

'I'm a ghost? Is that what she's saying?'

'Partly that. No, you are yourself. You are Janio Barreto. You see, you came to Brazil. You see why, don't you?'

Fletch exhaled deeply. 'What is the old woman's name?'

'Idalina. Idalina Barreto.'

'What bothers me is that you listened to her. The doorman—'

'Why not?' Laura turned the page of the magazine. 'She was talking.'

24

'Laura, you seem to have no regard for the real past. Yet you listen to these impossibilities.'

She was studying some health chart in the magazine. 'What's real?'

'Which is more real to you?'

'Bananas are good for potassium,' she said. 'I think I knew that.'

'You won't let me explain. You won't explain to me.'

'Forget Idalina Barreto, as much as you can, for now.'

She flung the magazine aside and looked at him standing between the window and the bureau.

'How are we to know each other?' he asked.

She rolled more onto her back and held one leg, one arm in the air. 'By sharing your banana with me.'

He laughed.

'I need more potassium.'

'Potassium gluconate, I hope.'

'Come, come, Janio. I want some more of your potassium.'

'I'm not Janio.'

'Janio's potassium. Your potassium. Harvest your banana and feed me your potassium.'

25

'You're crazy.'

'Come, come, my Janio. It is ripe. I see that it is ripe. I will peel it with my teeth. Let me taste your banana.'

★   ★   ★

'Where's my shoe?' He regretted kneeling on the floor in his long white trousers to look under the bed for his shoe.

She came into the room and stopped. In the bathroom she had bathed and done her hair and also dressed in white slacks and an open white shirt.

'Why is this stone under our bed?'

Sitting back on his haunches, he showed her the small carved stone he found under the bed. 'It's a toad. It looks like a toad.'

'That,' she said.

'Why is there a stone under our bed?'

'The maid must have left it there.'

'The maid left a stone toad under our bed?'

'Put it back,' Laura said. 'It may be important to her.'

CHAPTER FOUR

'My father's here!' Laura dumped three teaspoonsful of sugar into her *cachaça*. 'I hear his voice.'

Courteously, Fletch took his glass of *cachaça* from the silver tray held out to him by a houseman. *Cachaça* is a brandy made of sugar-cane juice. In Brazil it is courteous to offer guests *cachaça*. It is courteous of guests to accept *cachaça*. Fletch had tried it with some added sugar, much added sugar, no added sugar. *Cachaça* was a taste he had not acquired.

With his glass of *cachaça* in hand, he followed Laura out onto the terrace.

Teodomiro da Costa's house was built somewhat upside down. Entering at street level, one went downstairs to the bedrooms and a small family sitting room, upstairs to the grand living room filled with splendid paintings and other *objets d'art*, upstairs again to a huge reception room complete with full bar. Off the reception room, high above Avenida Epitacio Passoa, overlooking the truly beautiful lagoon Rodrigo de Freitas, was a handsome terrace decorated with green, red, yellow flowering jungle plants.

Now in the reception room a long table had been set with crystal and silver for twelve.

Teodomiro da Costa did well exchanging currencies and commodities. Fletch had invested his money with him.

On the terrace Laura and Otavio were greeting each other with hugs and kisses and rapid talk in Brazilian Portuguese.

Wordlessly, Otavio then shook Fletch's hand.

'*Boa noite,*' Fletch said.

'Otavio has come here to meet with his publisher,' Laura said. 'He is staying nearby, with Alfredo and Gloria. Have you met them? Alfredo is a marvelous man, true Brazilian, so full of life, generous to a fault. Gloria is a marvelous woman, truly bright, so charming, with a large feminine soul.'

'Are they here?'

Laura looked around at the other people on the terrace. 'I don't see them.'

'They are preparing for the Canecao Ball tomorrow night,' Otavio said. 'I do not need to prepare. Poets are born in disguise.'

'And your mother?' Fletch asked Laura. 'She did not come from Bahia?'

'My mother,' said Laura. 'Orchids you can never leave.'

'They are worse than children,' agreed Otavio.

'Worse than I was, anyway,' Laura said.

Teodomiro da Costa came across the terrace to them. He was a tall man of sixty with the head of a bald eagle. 'Fletcher, it is good to have you back. Did you enjoy Bahia?'

'Of course.'

'Good. For dinner we are having *vatapa*, a typical dish from Bahia.'

Fletch smiled and took Laura's free hand. 'I made friends there.'

'But Cavalcanti is my friend.' Teo kissed Laura on the cheek. 'And Laura too.'

Otavio said, 'We are all friends.'

Teo took Fletch's *cachaça* and placed it on the tray of a passing houseman. He said something to the houseman. 'I have ordered you a screwdriver,' he said to Fletch.

'Is it called a screwdriver in Portuguese?'

Teo laughed. 'I called it orange juice, vodka, and ice.'

'I must figure out the words for it.'

'Not hard.'

'To say it rapidly. With firmness.'

29

'Come. I want you to meet da Silva.' Slowly Teo guided Fletch by the elbow across the terrace. 'Is Laura with you, or with her father?'

'With me.'

'Ah! You are so lucky.' Teo then introduced Fletch to another sixty-year-old businessman, Aloisio da Silva.

Immediately, da Silva said, 'You must come to my office. I have a new computer system. The very latest. Digital. From your country.'

'I would be very interested in it.'

'Yes. You must come tell me what you think.'

The houseman brought Fletch his screwdriver.

'Also, perhaps you have noticed my new building going up. How long have you been in Rio?'

'I was here for three weeks, then I was in Bahia for two weeks. I am back three days.'

'Then perhaps you have not noticed my building?'

'Rio is so vibrant.'

'Of course. It is in the Centro. Near Avenida Rio Branco.'

'I did notice a new building going up there. Very big.'

'Very big. You must come and see it with me. You'd be very interested.'

'I'd like that.'

'It is amazing what a difference computers make when it comes to building a building.'

Marilia Diniz appeared with her glass of *cachaça*. She kissed Aloisio and Fletch on their cheeks.

'Are you well, Aloisio?'

'Of course.'

'Rich?'

'Of course.'

Marilia forever remained a surprise to Fletch. She had to be the only person in Rio with no sun-color in her face. She saw people from a different perspective.

'Marilia,' Fletch said. 'Something happened to us after we left you.'

'Something always happens in Rio.' She sipped her *cachaça*. 'Listen. Teo has some new paintings. He has promised to show us them after dinner.'

★   ★   ★

'Otavio, perhaps you would help me to understand something.'

'Yes?'

Fletch and Otavio Cavalcanti stood alone at the edge of the terrace, looking at the moonlight on the lagoon. Otavio was drinking Scotch and water.

In Brazil, even distinguished scholars and poets are to be called by their first names.

'Does the name "Idalina Barreto" mean anything to you?'

'No.'

'She is not a famous eccentric?'

'Not that I know.'

Laura was across the terrace talking with the Vianas.

'I wonder if it is a scam.'

'A what?'

'A swindle. Some sort of confidence trick.'

'Ah, yes. Trick.'

'This afternoon Laura and I were accosted by an old woman, a *macumbeira* of some sort, maybe, dressed in a long white gown, an old woman. She said her name is Idalina Barreto.'

From the terrace the samba drums could be heard only faintly.

'Yes?'

'She said I was her husband.'

Otavio turned his head to look at Fletch.

32

'Her dead husband. Janio Barreto. A sailor. Father of her children.'

'Yes...'

'That Janio was murdered when he was young, at my age, forty-seven years ago.'

'Yes.'

'Are you hearing me?'

'Naturally.'

'She demands that I tell her who murdered me.'

Otavio was looking at Fletch as had Laura, as had the doorman at The Hotel Yellow Parrot. Then his eyes shifted in a circle around Fletch's head.

'Will you help me to understand this?'

Then Otavio took a drink. 'What's there to understand?'

★   ★   ★

At the long table at dinner they talked of the magic in much Brazilian food which provides so much energy, the masses of sugar usually placed in the coffee, in the *cachaça*, the sweetness of *cachaça* anyway, the *dende* oil in the *vatapa* they were having for dinner. The drink, *guaraná*, is without alcohol and also gives energy. It was said by the Indians that it cleared the blood

33

channels going to and coming from the heart. Fletch had discovered that it relieved tiredness.

Down the table, Laura said, 'Bananas are good for you, too. There is potassium in bananas.'

★   ★   ★

Then Marilia asked about the paintings Teo had bought.

'I'll show them to you after dinner. Perhaps, first, Laura will play for us.'

'Please,' said the Viana woman.

'Certainly.'

'Then I will show them to you,' Teo said.

Aloisio da Silva asked Fletch, 'Have you visited the Museu de Arte Moderna?'

'Yes.'

'I should think you'd be very interested in that building.'

'I am very interested in the building. It is a wonderful building. And I had a splendid lunch there.' The people at table became silent. 'There were few paintings in the museum when I was there.'

'Ah, yes,' Marilia said.

'I was thinking of the building,' Aloisio said.

'There was a fire . . .' Teo said.

'All the paintings were burned up,' the Viana woman said. 'Very sad.'

'Not all. A few were left,' Viana said.

Aloisio blinked at his plate. 'I was thinking the building would interest you.'

Fletch said, 'The paintings in the museum got burned. Is this another case of *queima de arquivo?*'

The silence at the table was complete.

From the head of the table, Teodomiro da Costa looked down at Fletch. A virus a few years before had given da Costa's left eye a permanent hooded effect, which became worse when he was tired, or wished to use it on someone. He was now using it on Fletch.

'It is a good thing, I think,' Fletch said into the silence, 'for the artists of each generation to destroy the past, to begin again. I think perhaps it is necessary for them.'

It was many moments, then, before conversation flowed smoothly again.

★　　　★　　　★

'You have Laura, I see. I am glad.' Viana sat next to Fletch on the divan in the living

35

room. They were waiting for Laura Soares to play the piano. 'You must be very careful of women in Rio.'

'You must be very careful of women everywhere.'

'That is true. But women in Rio.' He sipped his coffee. 'Even I. Late at night. Have found myself dancing with one of them. A man, you know. An operated-on man. It is more easy than you think to be tricked.'

'Not anything is as it seems in Brazil,' Fletch said.

'It is easy to be tricked.'

★   ★   ★

Laura played first some Villa Lobos, of course, then some of her own arrangements of the compositions of Milton Nascimento, somehow keeping in balance his romantic sweetness, his folkloric virility, his always progressing, complicated, mysterious melodic lines. At the side of the room, in a deep armchair, Otavio Cavalcanti dozed over his coffee cup. Then she played arrangements of other deeply folkloric Brazilian music Fletch did not recognize.

Laura Soares must have used piano

36

technique she learned at the London Conservatory, but she played none of the music she had learned there.

After everyone except Otavio, her father, had applauded, Laura said, 'Not so good.' She smiled at Fletch. 'I have practiced little the last two weeks.'

★   ★   ★

'We have come to see your new paintings, Teo!' So the young man first into the reception room announced. With his white open shirt and slacks he wore a forest green cape, a green buccaneer hat, green shoes. Immediately, his eyes found Fletch across the room.

'I've been waiting for you,' Teo said from the bar.

Just suddenly they were there, four young men dressed expensively, tailored perfectly, each in his own style, moving slowly, expectantly into the big reception room at the top of the house like a theatrical troupe taking over a stage. All but one had lithe bodies, the graceful ways of moving one would expect from fencers, acrobats, or gymnasts. The fourth was heavier, duller in the eye, maybe a little drunk, and moved

37

unevenly.

'Toninho!' the woman cried.

The Viana woman smothered him with kisses.

'Tito! Orlando!' No one seemed to greet the fourth young man immediately. Someone finally said, 'Norival! How do you find yourself?'

Tito was dressed entirely in black. His shirt and slacks had to have been fitted to him while they were wet. No seams showed in his clothes.

Orlando wore blue stripes down the sides of his white slacks, blue epaulettes on his shoulders.

And Norival was dressed as expensively, but somehow the earth-brown pockets in his light green slacks and shirt did not seem so amusing.

The people had surrounded the four young men, three of whom were uncommonly handsome, and were talking in Portuguese and laughing. Laura had gone to give each of them a hug and kisses.

Fletch ordered a *guaraná* from the barman.

Not only had the dinner been cleared from the long table in the reception room during Laura's recital, the long table itself had disappeared.

Their backs to the room, some paintings had been placed on the floor along one wall.

One easel had been set up in the best light of that room.

Now Toninho stood in that light, in front of the easel, making gestures with his arms which made his green cape ripple in that light. Whatever he was saying was making the people around him laugh. He seemed to be charming even his companions, Tito, Orlando, and Norival.

Laura's eyes were shining happily when she came back to Fletch.

'Who are they?' he asked.

'The Tap Dancers. They are called the Tap Dancers. Just friends of each other. It's just a name.'

'Do they dance?'

'You mean, professionally?'

'Yes.'

'No.'

'Sing?'

'No.'

'Do tricks?'

'They are just friends.'

'Fashionable, I think.'

'Aren't they sleek?'

Hand emerging from his cape, Toninho

39

came forward to shake hands with Fletch.

'Toninho,' Laura said happily. 'This is I. M. Fletcher.'

'Ah, yes.' Toninho's eyes were as brilliant as gems and as active as boiling water. 'Janio Barreto. I am Toninho Braga.'

'You know about that?' Fletch shook hands.

Toninho flung his arms up, sending his cape back over his shoulders. Clearly, in his eyes, he was enjoying his own act; possibly, confident in his virility, he was satirizing fashion, fashionable behavior. 'The whole world knows about that!'

Teo da Costa came into the group.

Laura said something to Toninho in Portuguese. Toninho answered, briefly, and she laughed.

'Fletcher,' Teo da Costa said quietly, 'within the next day or so, I would like to talk with you. Privately.'

'Of course.'

'Your father is not here. Not looking into your life . . .'

With great dignity, Teo's face was averted.

'Of course, Teo. I'd appreciate it.'

'Come, Teo!' Toninho exclaimed. 'The

paintings! We came to see your new paintings!'

         ★   ★   ★

One by one, Teo placed the paintings on the easel and let his guests study, enjoy them. They were by Marcier, Bianco, Portinari, Teruz, di Cavalcanti, Virgulino. For the most part they were clear, even bold, in the bright, solid earth colors. Especially did Fletch like one of a mother and child, another of a child with a cage. All the rhythms and colors and feelings and mysteries of Brazil were in the paintings, to Fletch.

         ★   ★   ★

Later, Fletch sat on the divan next to the sleepy Otavio Cavalcanti.

'You like the paintings?' Otavio asked.

'Very much.'

'Better than the museum building?' Otavio smiled. 'You are a North American. Everyone expects your passion to be for buildings and computers and other machines.'

'Yes.'

41

'Teo perhaps has the best collection, now that the museum is just a wonderful building again.'

'He must be careful of fire.'

To that, Otavio did not respond.

'Perhaps you can tell me this,' Fletch said to Otavio. 'Getting dressed tonight, looking for a shoe, I discovered a small carved stone under my bed.'

Otavio raised one eyebrow.

'A small stone. It was carved into a toad. A frog.'

Otavio sighed.

'Why would the maid put a stone toad under my bed?'

Slowly, heavily, Otavio Cavalcanti lifted himself off the divan. He went to the bar and got himself a Scotch and water.

★   ★   ★

'Come on.' Laura samba-walked across the room, holding her hands out to Fletch. He sat alone on the divan, thinking of *Ilha dos Caicaras*. He was thinking of himself as *Ilha dos Caicaras*, a small island in the lagoon. 'I worked enough. I played a little concert. Let's go with the Tap Dancers.'

'Where are they going?'

42

Otavio was drinking alone at the bar.

'Seven-oh-six. Toninho wants us to go with them. To hear the music. To dance.'

'Everyone?'

'Just you and me. And the Tap Dancers.'

Fletch got up from the divan. 'Why do I keep asking your father questions? Great scholar. I have never gotten an answer yet.'

Laura glanced at her father at the bar. 'Come on. If you have foolish questions, the Tap Dancers will have foolish answers for you. You'll get along fine together.'

CHAPTER FIVE

'Toninho must always make an entrance,' Laura said in the dark nightclub. 'I think he does so on purpose.'

'Do you really think so?' Fletch mocked.

Fletch and Laura had driven in his yellow two-seater MP convertible directly from the sidewalk in front of da Costa's house to the sidewalk in front of 706.

The Tap Dancers had disappeared in their own black four-door Galaxie.

At the door, Laura spoke to a young waiter, and instantly three tables for two were pushed together for them. Of course the band in the club was playing. The music would be nonstop. As soon as Laura and Fletch sat at the table, a waiter brought a bottle of whiskey with a marked strip of tape down its side, a pitcher of water, a bucket of ice and many glasses.

'What did you tell the waiter?' Fletch asked through the sound of the drums.

'That the Tap Dancers are coming.'

'They are that famous?'

'Everyone loves the Tap Dancers.'

'They're sleek.'

'Yes. They're sleek.'

In a moment, they appeared in the door. Each wore the mask of a cat over his face. There were four girls with them.

Even without making noise, they soon had everyone's attention. They began to sniff up and down the wall, along the tables, through a foreign lady's bouffant, curious about everything, until they found their own table.

Even the man who was singing at the moment laughed. The sound of his laughter through the amplifier in the middle of a song was delightful.

As the catlike Tap Dancers found their table and sat down, even those who were dancing applauded them.

One squeezed in beside Fletch and took off his mask. Toninho. Fletch expressed the appreciation of having been tricked that he had learned was appropriate in Brazil.

Fletch said, 'Laura suspects you make big entrances on purpose.'

Smiling, face flashing even in the near-dark, Toninho took off his buccaneer's hat. 'What's fun?'

Fletch said, 'What's fun?'

'Moving.' Toninho looked at his hand on the table, directing Fletch's attention to it. He raised and lowered his ring finger. 'That's fun,' he said. He raised his ring finger, little finger and thumb, and lowered them. 'That's more fun.' Then his hand on the table became terrifically animated, the fingers fluttering, doing their own crazy dance, the hand itself becoming some sort of a crazed rabbit trying to keep up its own wild beat. Watching it, Toninho laughed. 'That's most fun.'

'Have you ever had experience with paralysis?' Fletch asked. 'Have you ever been paralysed?'

Toninho's big brown eyes swelled. 'I have the wisdom to know that one day I will be.'

Introductions to the girls were made. Fletch got none of their names right, over the sound of the music. They clearly were glad and impressed to be there, to hear such good music, have access to the Scotch. Fletch calculated it had taken the Tap Dancers less than ten minutes to find these girls.

'Toninho,' Fletch said. 'Why would the hotel maid place a small carved stone toad under my bed?'

'A toad?'

'A frog.'

'Was there a frog under your bed?'

'Yes. There still is.'

'How do you know?'

'I found it while I was looking for my shoe.'

Toninho's eyes twinkled. 'What did you do with it?'

'I put it back.'

'That's good.' Toninho shed his cape then, and took a girl dancing to the dance floor.

For a while they all danced. The music was marvelous. Rather, Fletch danced. The Brazilians, including Laura, simply continued their being Brazilian, keeping the rhythm of the constant music anyway, their constant rhythmical movements anyway, onto the dance floor where they simply glided into full reaction to the music.

A young girl in leather jeans and a jersey which did not make it to the top of her jeans began to sing. She was extraordinarily good. They all sat at the table to listen to her.

The tape which ran down the side of the whiskey bottle was marked off in ounces. To calculate the bill, the waiter counted the ounces of whiskey missing from the bottle and charged them for that. The Tap Dancers' girls moved the whiskey level down the tape with happy alacrity.

The band did not stop when the girl put the microphone back on its stand. Everyone stood to cheer her and she danced into the dark at the back of the nightclub.

One of the Tap Dancers' girls, who had been staring at Laura, finally asked, in Portuguese, 'Are you Laura Soares, the pianist?'

'I play piano.'

Tito was sitting across from Fletch.

'How did you people know about Janio Barreto?' Fletch asked him.

'About your being Janio Barreto?' Tito

seemed to be correcting him.

'About that incident this afternoon.'

'Is it not something to know?' Tito's face was handsome and happy, too, but his eyes could not have Toninho's sparkle.

'How did you hear of it?'

Tito leaned forward across the table. 'We're all very eager to hear what you will have to say.'

'About what?'

'About how you came to die. Who murdered you.'

'Tito, Tito. Am I never to get sensible answers?'

'Tell me one thing, Janio.'

'Don't call me Janio.'

'Fletch. How do you think you came to be in Brazil?'

'I am a newspaperman from California. I had an airplane ticket.'

'How did you come to have the airplane ticket?'

'Sort of by accident.'

'You see?'

'No. I don't see.'

'Look around this room.' Without moving his head, Tito shot his eyes all the way to the left and moved slowly in a straight line all the way to the right. There

48

was something spooky in this controlled use of his eye muscles. 'Do you see others here like you?'

'What do you mean?' Mostly the room was full of young Brazilians, a few older Argentinians, the foreign lady with her large bouffant and small escort.

'Other newspapermen from California who "had an airplane ticket" and came here "sort of by accident"?'

'Tito...'

'No. You are here.'

'Why was I born?'

'Maybe that too.' Tito sat back. 'Now that you know what you must do, you will never rest until you do it.'

'What must I do?'

'Tell us who murdered you. Murder is the most serious crime.'

'Tito...'

A conspiracy of girls yanked Tito dancing.

Fletch finally poured himself a Scotch and water and sat back.

Then he and Laura danced awhile.

When it was very late in the night he found himself sitting at the end of the table with Norival, who was having difficulty keeping his eyes open and his tongue

49

straight, being told, even being asked, about various kinds of fish available in the South Atlantic.

Slowly it occurred to Fletch that Norival was talking to him as Janio Barreto, who had fished these waters fifty years ago.

Fletch decided it was time to leave.

As he stood up, he said to Norival, 'Much has changed in these waters in fifty years.'

He went to the dance floor and cut in on Orlando and asked Laura if they could leave.

★   ★   ★

Outside the nightclub, on the sidewalk, Toninho called after him.

Fletch turned around.

Again, Toninho said, 'Fletch,' but he did not approach. He stayed near the door of 706.

Laura sat in the MP.

Fletch went back to Toninho.

It would be dawn soon.

'Fletch.' Toninho cupped his hands around Fletch's left ear and put his lips in his cupped hands. 'A woman puts a frog under their bed to keep her lover from leaving her.'

Fletch stood back. 'It wasn't the maid?'

'Are you the maid's lover?' Toninho laughed. He slapped his thigh with his hand. 'Oh, Fletch!' He put his hand on Fletch's shoulder and shook him. 'Be glad.' Then he laughed again. 'Also because traditionally it is a live frog!'

CHAPTER SIX

'Restless.'

'Of course,' she said.

This was the third time he had gotten out of bed in a half hour.

The first time, he went to the bathroom and drank from the bottle of mineral water. Then he tried snuggling up next to Laura so that all of his front touched all of her back. She breathed deeply, asleep. The second time he put his head through the drapes and saw the daylight of another morning. No electric lights were on. In bed again, he tried lying straight on his back, his hands folded across his chest as if he were in a coffin, and breathing deeply. Even at that hour, from somewhere in the city he could hear the samba drums.

Now he put on his light running shorts.

Laura raised her head from the pillows and looked at him.

'I'm going for a run on the beach,' he said. 'Before the sand gets too hot.'

'Okay.'

'I can't get to sleep.'

'I know,' she said. 'Poor Fletch.'

She put her head back down on the pillows.

CHAPTER SEVEN

'Can you buy me a cup of coffee?'

Joan Collins Stanwyk.

She was waiting for him, smoking a cigarette, at a little table in the forecourt of The Hotel Yellow Parrot when he came back from his run. There were three crushed cigarette butts in the ashtray on the table.

Her eyes ran over the sweat gleaming on his shoulders, chest, stomach, even on his legs.

Having finished his run with a sprint, he was breathing heavily.

'That's the least I can do for you,' he said.

Two miles up the beach there had been a crew of men dressed in orange jackets fanned out like a search party cleaning the beach, and Fletch had run to them, and back. As he ran barefoot, he avoided several *macumba* fires smoldering from the night before. And he passed many dead wallets, purloined, stripped and dropped. Even at that hour, many other people were running on the beach. And a group of Brazilian men easily in their sixties were playing a full game of soccer barefooted in the sand.

Coming back across Avenida Atlantica, the roadway was almost unbearably hot on his bare feet, and it was not yet seven o'clock in the morning.

The bar, which was the middle door at the front of The Hotel Yellow Parrot, of course was closed. Fletch pressed the service bell beside the door.

'Let's see if that brings someone.' He sat across from Joan at the little table.

He folded his slippery arms across his slippery chest.

The forecourt, with thick green bushes headhigh on three sides, had brilliant streaks of morning sunlight in it.

This morning Joan Collins Stanwyk looked less the California empress. She was dressed in a light, tan slacks suit, white silk shirt, and sandals. Her hair was not in its usual impeccable order. Her face looked haggard; her eyes sleepless. She might still have been suffering jet lag; she might also have been suffering from her martinis and her cigarettes and, of course, from her recent widowhood.

'How are you?' he asked.

'I've been better.'

'Did you come here to find me? I mean, to Rio?'

'Of course.'

'How did you work it out? Where I went?'

'Did you forget Collins Aviation has its own security personnel? Mostly retired detectives who are very good at finding out things? Although, I admit, sometimes not fast enough.' There was no humor in the irony of her statement. 'And did you forget that I was born, bred, and educated to do a job? And that I'm rather good at it?'

She was the daughter of John Collins, who had built a mammoth airplane company out of his own garage in

California. Wife, now widow, of Alan Stanwyk, the late chief executive officer of that company. A famous socialite, executive hostess for both her father and her husband, famous blonde, long-legged, tennis-playing Californian beauty who had known her function in that world of fast cars and slow parties and had once, shortly before, surprised Fletch at how well she had performed, or tried to perform.

'I haven't forgotten.'

A waiter appeared.

Fletch ordered coffee for Joan and *guaraná* for himself.

She said, 'You're absolutely gorgeous, wet with sweat. You have the same build as Alan had, but there is so much more light in your skin.'

He tried to shave the sweat off his chest and stomach with the side of his index finger. 'I don't have a towel. I've been running. I—'

A slight jerk of her head stopped him. There was something smoky about her eyes. He was looking at a woman whose life, whose whole world, had been deeply violated by circumstances, probably for the first time in her life.

'If you came here for a full explanation—'

She stopped him. 'I need your help.' Her hand shook before she put her fingers against her cheek and stroked the area in front of her ear. 'Let's forget for now why I came here. Ironically enough, you're the only person I know in Rio, and I have to ask you to help me.' Her voice was very soft.

She collected herself while the waiter set coffee in front of her, the can of *guaraná* and a glass in front of Fletch.

'I knew you were here,' Fletch said. 'I saw you yesterday on the *avenida*. You were wearing a green silk dress. And carrying a handbag.'

'Oh, yes,' she said bitterly.

'I hid from you.' He poured his *guaraná*. 'I was just so surprised to see you. How did you find out where I was staying?'

'I just called all the best hotels, and asked for Mister Irwin Maurice Fletcher. I knew, of course, you could afford the very best accommodations.' Again, naturally, there was no humor in her irony. 'Just went down the list of first-class hotels. When I asked for you here, at The Yellow Parrot, they rang your room. No answer. So I knew where you were staying.'

'Why are you sitting in the forecourt

56

waiting for me at six-thirty in the morning?'

'I had no choice. It was the next thing to do, the only thing to do. After the most horrible night . . . I walked down from the hotel. While I was still up the block I saw you starting out for your run, going across the street. I wasn't about to run after you up the beach.'

'No.'

'I was robbed,' she said.

'Oh.'

'You say that with such aplomb. As if you knew it.'

'I guessed it.'

'How?'

'You don't know about Rio?'

'I guess not enough.'

'It's a marvelous place.'

'Terrific,' she said.

'You going to give me all the details?'

'You sound like you've already heard them.'

'I think I have.'

'Robbed twice.'

'Not a record.'

'Robbed of everything.' A tear appeared in the corner of her eye.

'Baptized,' he said.

'Last night, after I found out which hotel

you were in, I considered coming and camping out in the lobby until you showed up, but from what I've heard of Rio nightlife, that didn't make much sense.'

'No.'

'At least not for such a healthy, wealthy, attractive young man.'

At first Fletch thought he would let this irony pass over him. Then he said, 'I wasn't in.'

'So I went out myself. I went for a walk. Right along here.' She indicated the *avenida* beyond the hedge. 'Sat in a café, had a drink, watched the people, listened to the drums. Walked further, to another café, had a drink. Couldn't pay the bill. My purse was gone.'

'Yes.' In his saying just 'yes,' Fletch heard an echo of Otavio Cavalcanti. *Yes. Of course. What is there to understand?*

'My wallet was gone. All my cash. My credit cards.' Tears now were in both her eyes. 'My passport.'

'It happens to everyone I have heard of,' he said.

'My necklace was gone!' She seemed astounded. 'A diamond pin I was wearing on my dress!'

'Yes.'

58

'What bothers me most is that pictures of Alan in my wallet are gone. Of Alan and Julia.' Julia was her young daughter. 'No matter what you may think, I wanted those pictures of Alan. They're irreplaceable.'

Tears rolled down her cheeks.

Fletch said: 'Yes.'

She reached for a purse that wasn't there. 'Damn! I don't even have a handkerchief.'

Fletch shrugged his bare shoulders. 'I don't even have a sleeve.'

She sniffed.

'I explained to the waiter as best I could that I couldn't pay him. I'd been robbed. That I would come back and pay him today.' Joan Collins Stanwyk sniffed again. 'I swear, Fletch, all during my walk, nobody even touched me. No one bumped into me. How did they get my necklace? The pin off my dress? There wasn't even a tear in my dress. I felt nothing!'

'The future of Brazil,' said Fletch, 'is in surgery.'

'I went back to my hotel.'

'And your room had been burglarized.'

'How did you know?'

'You said you'd been robbed twice.'

'Everything!' she said. 'Everything except my clothes. My jewel case, my

59

traveler's checks.'

'Everything.'

'Everything. I haven't a thing. This morning I don't have a dollar, a *cruzeiro*, a credit card, a piece of jewelry.'

Fletch said: 'Yes.'

'I went downstairs to the hotel manager immediately. The assistant manager, that time of night. He came to the room with me, clucked and hissed and t'ched like a barnyard, figured the thieves must have come in over the balcony, scolded me for leaving the balcony door unlocked—Good heavens, I'm on the ninth floor. It was a warm night.'

'Took no responsibility.'

'I spent hours with him in his office. He said I should have left all my valuables in the hotel safe. Apparently they handed me a slip of paper when I checked in with that written on it. He took me back to my room and showed me the sign on the inside of the door advising me to lock the balcony doors, to put my valuables in the hotel safe. We went back to his office. I filled out lists of things that are missing. I kept asking him to call the police. For some reason, he never called the police.'

'No reason for disturbing them.'

'What do you mean?'

'They've heard the story, too.'

'Fletch, I was robbed. Of thousands and thousands of dollars' worth of things. Money, jewelry, my credit cards.'

Again Joan Collins Stanwyk sniffed.

'The police would know all that.'

'Will you help me?'

'Of course.'

She clutched her hands in her lap. 'I feel so violated.'

'Disoriented?'

'Yes.'

'Stripped naked?'

'Yes!'

'Totally lost without all your possessions?'

'Yes, yes!'

Fletch sat back in his chair. His sweat had dried in the air. 'I think that's part of the idea.'

'What are you talking about?'

'Who are you?'

'I am Joan Collins Stanwyk.'

'Can you prove it?'

Her eyes searched the stone floor of the forecourt. 'As a matter of fact, I can't. No credit cards. No checkbooks. No passport.'

'How does it feel?'

'How does what feel?'

'To be whatever you are right now.'

Her eyes narrowed. 'I did not come to you for psychological therapy, Mister I. M. Fletcher.'

'Thought I'd throw it in. No extra charge.'

'I need money.'

'Why?'

'I want to get out of that damned hotel. I want to pay my bill and get out of that damned hotel. I don't even have taxi fare.'

'Okay. But why don't you call home? To California? Your father?'

'He's on his yacht. The *Colette*. Trying to recuperate from Alan's—'

'And you came here, to look for me.'

She shrugged. 'Recuperation.'

'Doing your job. As you see it.'

'Yes.'

'Striving. Being Joan Collins Stanwyk, come hell or high water.'

'Are you going to help me? I want to go—'

'Tell me. Your family has offices stuffed with people looking out for you. Security personnel. Lawyers. Accountants. Why haven't you called them?'

Her head lowered. After a moment, she

62

said, softly, 'It's Saturday. In California, it's before dawn Saturday morning.'

He laughed. 'And you can't wait? You'd rather come to me, whom you pursued to Rio de Janeiro, than wait until your daddy's offices open?'

'I want to get out of that hotel. That man made me so angry.'

'It is essential to you, under the circumstances, that you talk to someone who knows who you are.'

She blinked at him. 'What?'

He put his forearms on the table. 'I was robbed. Wallet, cash, driver's license. Not my passport. My watch. My Timex watch.'

'Within the first twenty-four hours you were here?'

'Within the first six hours. People warn you, but you cannot believe it. You have to go through it yourself. It's a baptism.'

'What do you mean, *baptism*?'

'You learn to use the hotel safe, carry what money you need immediately in your shoe. And to not wear jewelry. Not even a watch.'

'Fletcher, I lost thousands of dollars, everything I have with me.'

'You lost your identity.'

'Yes. I did.'

'You lost your past.'

'Yes.' Joan Collins Stanwyk was frowning at the bushes.

'Do you feel more free?'

Now she was frowning at him. 'What?'

'Now you are equal, you see.'

'The people who stole my possessions aren't equal.'

'Oh, sure. That's widely dispersed. Come here a moment, will you?'

He got up from the table and stood in the opening of the hedge.

After a moment, she got up and came to him.

Together they looked across the city sidewalk where people were beginning to go about their daily business, across the wide city avenue filling up with taxis and commuters, to the beach, beginning to fill up with people of all ages walking, running, jumping, doing pull-ups, swimming.

Drums could be heard from down the road.

'There's not a pair of long trousers in sight, is there?' he asked.

'Very few shirts,' she said.

'No wallets. No identities. No class paraphernalia: no jewelry.' He looked at her tan slacks suit, silk blouse, high-heeled open-toed sandals. 'They have their bodies. Their eyes, their arms, their legs, their backs.'

'Their fingers, damn them.'

'I think we're being told something.'

'Have you gone Brazilian? In just a month?'

'Naw. I won't be *carioca* until I can walk across the *avenida* in bare feet at high noon.'

She turned to go back to the table. 'Sounds to me like you're giving some fantastic intellectual, political rationale for their out-and-out thievery.' She sat down at the table. 'But I guess you have every reason to.'

'To what?'

'To understand.'

'This lady I know...' Fletch too sat down at the table. 'She writes novels. I doubt I've got it straight, but she told me there is some ancient ritual here, a religious ritual, for which the food, in order to be acceptable by the ritual-masters, must be stolen.'

Joan Collins Stanwyk sighed. 'Enough of this. I've been robbed. I need help. If I weren't desperate, I wouldn't have come to you.'

'I guess so.'

'Will you please come to the police station with me?'

'If that's what you want.'

'I must report this.'

'It won't do any good.'

'Fletcher, I've been robbed, of thousands of dollars—'

'You have to pay a fee.'

'What?'

'To report a robbery to the police, you have to pay a fee.'

'You have to pay the police money to tell them you were robbed?'

'It's a lot of paperwork for them.'

She swallowed. 'Is that all it is? Paperwork?'

'Yes. I think so. In most cases.' He scraped his chairlegs on the stone pavement. 'You are warned, you see. Robbery here is not uncommon. No one can deny that. It is also common in New York, Mexico City, and Paris.'

She was beginning to have to squint into the sunlight to see him. A beam of sunlight was coming through a break in the hedge. 'But here, you say, they're doing you a favor to rob you.'

'You might as well think that.'

'They rob you with philosophy.'

'It's not considered such a bad thing to relieve you of your possessions, your identity, your past. What is yours is theirs is mine is ours...'

Her white face was stonelike. Her jaw was tight.

He said, 'I'm just trying to make you feel better.'

'Fletcher, are you going to let me have some money? Right away?' Her fingers gripped her temples. Her whole head shivered. 'At the moment, we won't go into the source of that money.'

'Of course. I'll bring some to your hotel. I have to get out of these wet shorts and shower and get them to open the hotel safe.'

'Very well.'

When she stood, she looked very pale and she seemed to sway on her feet. She closed her eyes a moment.

'You all right?'

'I'll be all right.'

'What hotel are you in?'

'The Jangada.'

'Very posh.'

'Bring lots of money.'

'We'll have breakfast together. At your hotel.'

'Yes,' she said. 'Come straight to my room with the money. Room nine-twelve.'

'Right.' He had been in a bedroom of hers before.

He walked with her to the break in the hedge.

'I'd send you back in a taxi,' he chuckled, 'but I'm not wearing shoes.'

Distantly, she said, 'I'd rather walk.'

CHAPTER EIGHT

There was no answer when he tapped at the door of Room 912.

He knocked louder.

Still the door did not open.

He knocked again and then placed his ear against the door. He could hear nothing.

As quietly as possible, in his own room at The Hotel Yellow Parrot, Fletch had showered and changed into fresh shorts, a shirt, sweat socks and sneakers. Laura was still sleeping. He left a note for her, *I have gone to the Hotel Jangada to have breakfast with someone I know.*

He had driven the short distance between the hotels in his MP.

68

After knocking on Joan Collins Stanwyk's door at The Hotel Jangada, he went back down to the lobby and called the room on the house phone.

No answer.

At the hotel desk, he asked the clerk, 'Please, what is the number of Joan Collins Stanwyk's room? Mrs Alan Stanwyk?'

The clerk consulted his plastic-tabbed file. 'Nine-twelve.'

'She hasn't checked out, has she?'

The clerk squinted at his file. 'No, sir.'

'*Obrigado.* Where is your breakfast room, please?'

Joan Collins Stanwyk was not in the breakfast room. She was not in the bar, which was open.

On the terrace of The Hotel Jangada were two swimming pools, one which was in the morning sun, the other which would be in the sun in the afternoon. Already a few were sunning themselves around one pool. Around the pool in the shade a few were having breakfast. Two fat white men had their heads together over Bloody Marys.

Joan Collins Stanwyk was not in the pools area.

On the ninth floor, Fletch knocked at her door again.

From the lobby he called her room again.

At the desk, he left her a note: *Came to have breakfast with you as arranged. Can't find you anywhere. You fell asleep? Please call me at Yellow Parrot. If I'm not there, leave message. Enclosed is taxi money.—Fletch.*

'Will you please leave this for Mrs Stanwyk? Room nine-twelve.'

'Certainly, sir.'

Fletch watched the desk clerk put the sealed envelope in the slot for Room 912.

★   ★   ★

'Teo? *Bom dia.*' Fletch phoned from The Jangada.

'*Bom dia*, Fletch. How are you?'

'Very pleased by your new paintings. Thinking of them has made me happy.'

'Me, too.'

'When do you want to see me?' Three North American oil-rig workers in heavy blue jeans got off the elevator, staggered across the lobby of The Hotel Jangada, and went straight into the bar.

'Any time. Now is fine.'

'Shall I come now?'

'We'll have coffee.'

70

CHAPTER NINE

'You do want coffee, don't you?'

'I guess I need it.'

A houseman had led Fletch downstairs in Teo da Costa's house to the small family sitting room. Dressed in pajamas, a light robe and slippers, Teo sat behind his glasses in a comfortable chair reading *O Globo*.

'Have a busy night?' Teo folded the newspaper.

'We went to Seven-oh-six. With the Tap Dancers.'

'It's a wonder you've had any sleep.'

'I've had no sleep.'

Standing, Teo nodded to the houseman, who withdrew.

'You look fresh enough. You look like you've been out jogging.'

'I have been.'

A look of concern flickered across Teo's haughty face.

Fletch said, 'I don't feel like sleeping.'

'Sit down,' Teo said. 'Is there anything bothering you?'

Sitting, Fletch said, 'Well, I arranged to have breakfast with this person I know, from California. When I went to the hotel, she wasn't there.'

'She went out on the beach, perhaps.'

'I had arranged to meet her less than an hour before I went to the hotel. She could have fallen asleep.'

'Yes, of course. In Rio, night and day get mixed up. Especially as Carnival approaches.'

The houseman brought two cups of coffee.

Teo sipped his standing up. 'People don't realize it, but Brazil's second-largest export is tea.'

After the houseman left, Fletch asked, 'You wanted to talk to me, Teo. Privately, you said.'

'About what you're doing.'

'What am I doing?'

'What are you going to do?'

'I don't understand you.'

'Brazil is not your home.'

'I feel very comfortable here.'

'What would you most like to do in this world?'

'Sit on Avenida Atlantica in Copacabana, eat *churrasco*, drink *guaraná*, and watch

Brazilian women of all ages walk. Listen to Laura play the piano. Go to Bahia, occasionally. Run, swim. Jump up and down to the drums. Love the people. I am learning a little Portuguese, a few words.'

'Do you mean to stay in Brazil?'

'I haven't thought.'

'How long have you been here now? Six weeks?'

'Something like that.'

'You've bought a car. You've met Laura.' Teo sipped his coffee. 'Don't you have any plans?'

'Not really.'

Teo put his cup and saucer on a table. 'A young man should have plans. You're a young man. From everything I can see, a very healthy young man. You are attractive. You have a brain. Because of the business we have done together, I know how much money you have. I do not know the source of that money, but I know you are not a criminal.'

'Thanks.'

'I am only speaking to you, Fletch, because I am sixty, and you are only in your twenties. Your father is not here . . .'

'I appreciate it.'

73

'It is not good for a young man to live without a plan.'

'Are you saying I should leave Brazil, Teo?'

'Brazil is a difficult place, even for Brazilians.' Teo scratched the back of his head and laughed. 'Especially for Brazilians.'

'Is this about Laura, Teo?' Fletch fixed Teo in the eye. 'Did Otavio Cavalcanti ask you to speak to me?'

Teo used his hooded eye on Fletch. 'Brazil is not that way. Not intolerant.'

'Otavio is.'

Teo laughed. 'Otavio Cavalcanti is one of the most liberal men we have. So liberal he cannot go to New York and read his poetry at a university.'

'About some things he is liberal. About his daughter . . .?'

'And what do you think of Otavio?'

'He is a great scholar and poet who does not answer my questions.'

'Brazil is difficult to understand.'

'Did Otavio speak to you last night, Teo?'

'Yes,' Teo admitted. 'He did. That is not what concerns me.'

'Laura put a frog under our bed.'

'Yes,' Teo said. 'So Otavio told me. You know what that means?'

'I do now.'

'You see, you do not know Brazil. Perhaps cannot know Brazil. There is so much here that came from the Nago and the Bantu, particularly the Yoruba. You can have no feeling for it.'

'Saravá Umbanda!'

'What did you do before you came here? You were a journalist?'

'I worked for a newspaper.'

'Then you must make a plan to work for a newspaper again. Buy your own small newspaper, somewhere you want to be. Understand the new technology of communications. Grow along the course you were on.'

Fletch sat silently a moment.

Then he finished his coffee.

'Teo, have you heard about this Janio Barreto ... situation? That I am someone who was murdered here forty-seven years ago—?'

'Yes. I was told about it last night. It worries me.'

'Why?'

'It worries me that you might not understand.'

75

'Of course I don't understand. Perhaps you could help me to understand.'

'I'm sure the woman—What's her name?'

'Idalina. Idalina Barreto.'

'I'm sure the woman is entirely sincere in what she believes. There is no scam, swindle. There is no trick involved, as you asked last night.'

Upstairs, a vacuum cleaner was being run.

'Teo, do you personally give any credence to such a thing?'

'Do I think you are a peri-spirit?' Teo smiled. 'No.'

Fletch said, 'Phew!'

'I worry that you won't know what to do about it.'

'What do I do about it?'

Teo hesitated a long moment. 'I don't know either. Brazil is one of the most modern nations on earth...' His voice dwindled off.

'I think I understand what you are saying, Teo.' Fletch stood up. 'I promise I will think.'

'It's just that your father is not here.'

'I will think of a plan.'

In shaking, Teo held Fletch's hand a long moment. 'The Tap Dancers,' he said,

'Your father would not want you to become a tap dancer on life.'

CHAPTER TEN

'Laura?'

The window drapes were open. The room had been made up. Fletch pushed the ajar door to the bathroom all the way open.

'Laura?'

There was a note for him on the bureau.

Fletch—

Otavio called. He is feeling too tired to stay for Carnival in Rio. He wants to be home in Bahia. He said this morning he feels too tired to travel alone, through all the Carnival crowds. So I am helping him travel to Bahia.

Surely I will be back Sunday. Enjoy the Canecão Ball tonight even without me. If you get too lonely without me, I have left you Jorge Amado's *Dona Flor and Her Two Husbands*—a great Brazilian classic. And I will bring you a present from Bahia— something I want for you.

Ciao,
Laura

Across the utility area, the man was still painting the room.

The phone rang.

'Janio?'

'Not here, at present.'

'Is Fletcher there?'

'Yes, he's here. I think.'

'Toninho Braga, Fletch.'

'How are you? Have you slept?'

'We thought you might like to spend the day with us. Drive up to a place we know in the mountains. Laura can go shopping.'

'Laura's gone to Bahia with her father.'

'That's well. Then will you come? A place we know, very amusing, very relaxing. It is important to get away during Carnival.'

'Toninho, I haven't slept. I went running.'

'This place is very relaxing. You can have a sleep there, after lunch.'

'Teo da Costa is expecting me for the Canecão Ball tonight.'

'Oh, we'll be back in plenty of time for that. We are going to the ball, too.'

'Who's we?'

'Just Tito, Norival, Orlando, and myself. Get away from the women a few hours.'

'I think I should try to sleep.'

'You don't understand.'

'I don't understand anything.'

'We are downstairs in the lobby, expecting you.'

'Toninho.'

'You will come?'

Fletch looked at the freshly made bed. '*É preciso terno?*'

Such was a tourist joke. In Brazil a suit was never necessary.

'You will need no clothes. Do you have money?'

Fletch felt the wad of *cruzeiros* in his pocket he had taken out of the hotel safe for Joan Collins Stanwyk. 'Yes.'

'Good. Bring your money. We will gamble. We will gamble and take your money away from you.'

'Okay.'

'You coming right down?'

'Yes.'

'You didn't say that.'

'I'll be right down.'

Before leaving the telephone, Fletch called The Hotel Jangada and asked for Room 912.

There was no answer.

He took a full liter of mineral water from the bathroom.

Before leaving the hotel room, Fletch checked under the bed.

The frog was still there.

CHAPTER ELEVEN

'*Bum, Bum,*' Toninho said.

The black four-door Galaxie was on the sidewalk close to the hedge in front of The Hotel Yellow Parrot. Around it, dressed only in shorts and sunglasses, were the Tap Dancers. Norival, the only one with his belly hanging over his belt, held a can of beer in his hand.

'*Bom dia*, Fletch,' Tito said.

'*Tem dinheiro?*'

Tito grinned. '*É para uso pessoal.*'

In front of the hotel, half in the road, half on the sidewalk, a samba band was beating its drums at full strength in the strong Saturday morning sunlight. At their center was an old pickup truck casually decorated with palm fronds, some of which had been dyed purple and red. Seated in the back of the pickup truck, facing backward, was a huge black *papier-mâché* monster. Its arms were out, to embrace; its eyes were big and shiny; its smile was friendly. A girl dressed only in a G-string and pasties sat on the monster's head, her legs dropping over its face. Of course she had gorgeous legs and a flat belly and full breasts. Her long black hair fell over her face. On the ground near the truck, a tall man in a long black evening gown and cherry-red face rouge danced wildly to the drums. A nine-year-old girl also danced in a black evening gown, while puffing a cigarette. A bare-legged middle-aged man danced while holding his briefcase. Perhaps there were fifty or sixty people dancing around the band.

'*Bum, bum, paticum bum,*' Toninho said.

Fletch tossed his plastic liter bottle of water onto the back-seat of the Galaxie.

'*Senhor Barreto,*' the doorman said quietly.

In one swift motion, Tito pulled Fletch's tennis shirt over his head and off him.

Orlando put his forefinger against Fletch's chest. 'Look! Skin!'

'He has skin?' Norival asked, looking.

Tito ground a couple of knuckles into Fletch's back. 'Muscle!'

81

'He is there?' Norival asked. 'Really there?'

'*Senhor Barreto*,' the doorman said, 'Mister Fletcher.'

'*Bum, bum*,' Toninho said.

Behind the doorman, tall, stately in her white gown, big-eyed Idalina Barreto came through the crowd. On each side of her she had a child by the hand. Three older children were in her wake. The children were clean enough, but the jerseys on the girls were too big or too small. Below his shorts, from above his knee, the ten-year-old boy had a wooden leg.

'*Janio Barreto!*' the hag shrieked over the sound of the samba band.

'Ah,' Toninho said solemnly. 'Your wife.'

The doorman stood back.

Tito handed Fletch his shirt rolled up into a ball. Fletch threw it into the car.

The old woman cackled rapidly. She was presenting the children to him.

'She says they are your great-grandchildren, Janio,' Tito said. 'Are you catching their names? The boy is called Janio.'

Fletch put his hand on the head of one of the small girls.

82

At first, Idalina Barreto smiled.

As Fletch ducked into the backseat of the black Galaxie, her voice became shrill. She pressed forward.

Toninho got into the driver's seat. 'Aren't you going to ask your wife if you may go gambling?'

Orlando got into the front passenger seat. Entering from the other side, Tito sat in the middle, beside Fletch. Norival sat near the left window of the backseat.

Fletch handed two of the children money through his back window.

Toninho started the car. '*Bum bum*,' he said.

As the car rolled forward, the hag's face continued to fill Fletch's window. Her shrieking voice filled the car.

'Ah, wives,' Tito said.

Soon the car bumped off the sidewalk and got into traffic on the *avenida*.

Through the rearview mirror, Toninho was staring at Fletch.

There were many cans of beer on the floor of the backseat of the car.

'*Bum, bum, paticula bum*,' Toninho said, driving through traffic.

'*Carnival*.' In the front seat, Orlando stretched. 'How nice.'

Toninho shook his head sadly. 'Think of driving off and leaving your wife and great-grandchildren that way! To go gambling! What is the younger generation coming to!'

'*Um chopinho?*' Norival held out a can of beer to Fletch.

'Not yet.'

Stuck in traffic, Norival handed the beer through the window to a child no more than twelve. Then he opened one for himself.

In the traffic near them was a big, modern bus. All that could be seen through the windows of the bus were bare, brown upper torsos, moving like fish in a net, the arms flailing the insides of the bus, the feet apparently stomping the floor with the rhythm, the faces raised in some song. The bus was being used as a drum, being played from the inside by more than one hundred fists, more than one hundred feet. The bus being used as a drum from the inside did not seem to impair its modern beauty or impede its rollicking progress through the traffic.

Finally the Galaxie turned into a side street and picked up speed for a short way until they came to another samba band almost clogging the street. A small seventy-year-old lady, all by herself, dressed in a

84

red dress and red shoes, a red plastic handbag hanging from one forearm, danced to that band, taking perfect small steps with perfect dignity.

Creeping the car past the samba band, Toninho shouted through the window at them, '*Bum, bum, paticum bum, prugurundum!*'

Some of the people who heard him waved.

'*Bum, bum, paticum, prugurundum,*' Fletch tried to say. 'What's that?'

'An old carnival song,' Tito said, picking a beer off the floor.

Norival was swallowing his third beer since getting into the car.

'What does it mean?'

'Nothing.'

★   ★   ★

After a while they were free of the city, and the car began climbing the narrow, twisting mountain roads. Behind walls and hedges were suburban homes. The higher they climbed, the more expensive were the houses.

Shortly Norival had to be let out to water some of the bushes. Then he started another beer.

Occasionally through the heavy green growth, the hedges, Fletch caught glimpses of Christ the Redeemer, thirty meters tall, over a thousand tons heavy, a half mile in the sky above Rio on Corcovado, arms stretched wide to welcome and embrace the whole world. Enough times, Fletch had heard the story of the Argentine fisherman who spent days outside *Baia de Guanabara* waiting for the statue to wave him in. Finally, he sailed his catch of fish home to Argentina.

At one point, Toninho said in English, 'You are not here long before you discover Brazilian music is not only the *bossa nova* of Vinicius de Moraes and Tom Jobim.'

'That is for export.' Norival licked the lid of his beer can.

'Perhaps Brazilian music is too complicated for others to understand,' Tito said.

'The melody, too, comes from the drums,' Fletch said. 'People are not used to listening to the drums for melody.'

For the most part, the Tap Dancers discussed which samba school would win the Carnival Parade. This matter is discussed in Brazil as fervently, as

86

passionately, as who will win the World Football Cup or the presidential election is discussed in other parts of the world.

Each of the big *favelas*, slums in Rio de Janeiro, presents a finished samba school for the Carnival Parade, complete with a newly written song and huge, ornate, intricate floats; hundreds of trained, practiced drummers; brilliant, matching costumes for thousands of people. The Carnival Parade is the total competition of sound, melody, lyrics, rhythm; sights, the stately floats, dazzling costumes, the physical beauty of the people dancing from that *favela*, the magical quickness of the kick-dancers; originality and vitality; minds and hearts of the people of each of the slums.

All the people in each *favela* work all the year on their *favela*'s presentation, being careful that their song for that year is well written, then spending many nights and every weekend practicing it, playing it, singing it, dancing it, promoting it in the streets; designing and making each of the costumes, for men and women, each more complicated than a wedding garment, by hand; designing and building their samba school float, usually as big as a mansion.

Every spare moment and every spare *cruzeiro* goes into making each *favela*'s presentation as beautiful, as stunning to the ear and the eye, the mind and the heart, as exciting as possible.

And the competition is most strictly judged, and therefore, of course, always the subject of much controversy.

As Fletch heard the Tap Dancers discuss these matters, which school had the best song for this year, possibly the best costumes and floats, as they knew of them, the best drummers and dancers, which did win and might have won last year, the year before, he heard the names and snatches of the songs that were now being heard everywhere, on the streets, from the radio and television. Months before Carnival, the new song of each samba school is offered the people like a campaign pledge and promoted like a political platform or an advertising slogan. The Tap Dancers discussed the various samba schools one by one, from the oldest, *Mangueira*, to one of the newest, *Imperio da Tijuca*; from one of the more traditional, *Salgueiro*, to the overpowering drum section of *Mocidade Independent de Padre Miguel*. Toninho seemed to think this year's winner would be

.

Portela, judging the song that school was offering and what he knew of the costumes. Orlando thought *Imperatriz Leopodinense* had the better song. Tito agreed with Toninho about *Portela*. Norival drank his beer, belched, and just said, '*Beija-Flor.*'

Fletch wiped the sweat off his skin with his rolled-up shirt.

Breaking into English, Toninho said, looking through the rearview mirror, 'Fletch, you should hope for Santos Lima to win.'

'Then I do.' Leaning forward, Norival gave Fletch a lop-sided look. 'But why should I?'

'You used to live there. That was your place. That is where Janio Barreto lived. And was murdered.'

For a moment, there was silence in the car.

Then Orlando began humming the song offered this year by *Imperio da Tijuca*.

★   ★   ★

'Orlando! Toninho!'

In the mountains, they had driven down a deeply shaded drive and pulled into the sunlight-filled parking area in front of an

89

old run-down plantation house.

Immediately there appeared on the front porch of the house an enormous woman, a good three hundred pounds, her arms out in either greeting or sufferance, in the identical posture of Christ the Redeemer.

'Good Lord,' Fletch said when he saw her through the car window.

Orlando and Toninho had gotten out of the front seat and opened the back doors.

The other side of the car, clearly Norival did not care whether he moved.

Fletch got out his side of the car. The mountain air was cooler on his skin; but, still, the sun was biting.

Around the corner of the house appeared a skinny young teenage girl dressed only in shorts. Her eyes seemed as sunken as in a skeleton's skull.

'Tito?' the woman shouted.

Tito got out of the car, grinning.

The other side of the car, Norival lumbered out, went quickly to the bushes not far away, and relieved himself.

Then behind the enormous woman imitating a statue there appeared a real statue, a *mulata*, a girl six foot four easily, perfectly proportioned, an amazing example of humanity. Her shoulders were

90

broad, her waist narrow, her legs long. Each of her breasts was as large and as full as an interior Brazilian mountain seen from the air. Each of her eyes was bigger than a fist and darker than a moonless night. Her black hair was long and flowing. Her skin was the color and texture of flowing copper. Dressed only in slit shorts and high-heeled shoes, she moved like a goddess in no great hurry to go out and sow the seeds of humanity upon a field. This amazing creature, this animate statue, smiled at them.

Fletch gulped.

'You brought me someone new!' the fat older woman yelled in English. 'Is he North American? He is so beautiful!'

'He has special problems, Dona Jurema,' Toninho laughed. 'He has special needs!'

'My God,' Fletch said. 'Where am I?'

Tito punched Fletch's bicep. 'At a different height in heaven.'

CHAPTER TWELVE

'Tricked,' Fletch said. 'A little place we know in the mountains. You guys have brought me to a brothel.'

Towels wrapped around their waists, he and Toninho were sitting in long chairs in the shade near the swimming pool. The back of the plantation house was even more dilapidated than the front. Paint was thin and chipped. The back door was lopsided on its hinges. The flower borders had gone years untended. Lilies grew in the swimming pool.

'Very relaxing,' Toninho said. 'I did say it was very relaxing.'

'So why do the well-loved Tap Dancers need a brothel?'

'Everyone needs a few uncomplicated relationships, no? To relax.'

They had entered the plantation house, each being fondled by the massive Dona Jurema as he passed her, her laugh volcanic, her fat layered like lava. The younger woman, Eva, smiling happily, stood aside, looking even more Amazonian inside the house. They had crossed the scarred foyer, gone through a large, vomit-smelling dark ballroom turned into a tavern, and out the back door.

Coming again into the sunlight, each of the Tap Dancers dropped his shorts and plunged into the swimming pool. With the encouragement of Dona Jurema and the smiles of Eva, Fletch had followed suit.

There were five white towels waiting for them when they came out of the pool. Their shorts had been piled neatly on a table near the back door.

The skinny young teenage girl brought them a tray with five glasses of *cachaça* and a sugar bowl.

Norival downed his *cachaça* in a gulp, asked for another, and collapsed on a long chair on the long side of the pool.

Tito was doing disciplined laps in the pool, stroking through the lily pads.

Orlando went into the house.

'What is that new North American verb?' Toninho asked. 'Interact. It is tiresome having always to interact, especially with women. The women here do not expect anything so profound as interaction.'

Dona Jurema came through the back door and let herself down the steps like a big bag of glass.

'So good of you to come, Toninho,' she said. 'Not many of the girls are up. Ah, it's a hot day. We had a busy night. We will have lunch for you in a while.'

'This man.' Toninho puts his hands on Fletch's forearm. 'This man has special needs.'

Jurema beamed at Fletch. 'It would be a sin if he is having difficulties.'

'He is not having difficulties, I think,' Toninho said. 'Are you, Fletch?'

'Only with the *cachaça*.' He put his glass down on the burned-out grass.

'A special need I'm sure you can satisfy, Jurema.'

Arms akimbo, the woman shrugged her shoulders. It was a seismic upheaval. 'We can satisfy any need. Why, an Air Force General we had here—'

'Toninho,' Fletch said. 'I have no special needs.'

'But you do,' Toninho said. 'A very special need. I am your friend. It is important to me that your special need be fulfilled.'

'I need sleep,' Fletch said, leaning back in his chair, closing his eyes.

'I know what you need.' Solemnly, Toninho said, 'My friend needs a corpse.'

Fletch's eyes popped open. His head snapped up. 'What?'

'I said you need a corpse. For the purpose of copulation.' To Jurema, he said, 'My friend has the great need to make love to a corpse.'

Jurema was not laughing. She was answering Toninho in rapid Portuguese. Her eyes, her face, her voice bespoke someone doing business.

'Because,' Toninho said, 'my friend is a corpse. Partly a corpse. Part of him has not had a woman in forty-seven years. Clearly, if we are to get the truth from him, his peri-spirit must be awakened.'

'Toninho!' Fletch said.

'It is true,' Toninho said to Jurema.

Behind Fletch's long chair. Jurema bent over. She put her hands on his breasts and put at least part of her weight on them. Pressing hard, she ran her hands all the way down his stomach, under his towel to his pelvis, then raised her hands.

She erupted in laughter. 'He seems alive. If the other part of him is as healthy . . .'

A cool breeze blew over Fletch. He resettled his towel.

'You see the problem,' Toninho said with dignity. 'Now. How can you help my friend?'

'Toninho. Stop it. You're gross.'

'A corpse for my friend? Someone young, dead, and pretty.'

'Toninho, this isn't funny.'

'Probably by Tuesday,' Jurema said.

'There are always such corpses available during Carnival.'

'Find a good one,' Toninho said.

Jurema waddled a short distance. Speaking to Toninho in Portuguese, incredibly enough she stooped over and picked a weed out of the burned grass. Her face flushed. She then lifted herself up the back stairs and into the house.

'Tuesday,' Toninho said. 'She'll have one for you Tuesday.'

'Toninho, I hope this is another of your jokes.'

Abruptly, in the same tone of voice, Toninho said, 'Your friend, Teodomiro da Costa, is to be respected.'

'I met with him this morning.' Fletch watched the sunlight flashing on Tito's shoulders as he swam. 'He had advice for me, which I respect. Especially at the moment.'

'In this country, seventy per cent of the business is run by the government, you see. To do well on your own, as Teo has, is to do very well indeed. Now tell me. In North America, there is a car which has what is called a slant-six engine. Can you describe it to me, please?'

Fletch told Toninho what he understood

of the slant-six engine, and that it had an especially long life. Sitting on Saturday morning in the mountains above Rio de Janeiro looking out into the sunlight, he felt his eyes crossing. He had not had that much of the *cachaça*. One moment Toninho was talking seriously of necrophilia and the next just as seriously about a slant-six car engine.

The young girl brought Norival his third *cachaça*.

'Ah,' Toninho said. 'Norival is an *arigó*. A simpleton, a boor, but a good fellow. If he were not from a rich, important family, he would be an *arigó*. His brother, Adroaldo Passarinho, is the same, exactly like him in every way. Look the same, act the same. His father has sent Adroaldo to school in Switzerland, in hopes there will be someone in the family this generation less than simple. *Arigó*.'

Tito climbed out of the pool and, not drying himself, dropped naked belly down on the grass.

In high seriousness and in great detail, Toninho then wanted to know about this new robot he had read about in *Time* magazine supposedly capable of understanding and obeying one hundred thousand different orders. Designed in Milan, manufactured in Phoenix with Japanese parts. What was the nature of the computer which ran it? How were the joints designed, and how many were there? What would the robot say when given conflicting orders? Would the robot know, better than a person, when it is breaking down?

In his towel, holding a fresh glass of *cachaça*, Orlando stood on the back steps of the plantation house. He sang. Of the four Tap Dancers, Orlando's muscles were the heaviest. His voice was deep, and he sang well.

> *O canto de minha gente*
> *Assediando meu coração*
> *Semente que a arte germinou*
> *E o tempo temperou*
> *Amor, o amor*
> *Como é gostoso amar.*

Norival raised his head from his long chair and hissed. Even from a distance, it could be seen Norival was not focusing. His head dropped back.

'Ah, the *arigó* never sobered from last night,' Toninho said.

'What's the song?' Fletch asked.

'An old Carnival song. Let's see.' Toninho closed his eyes to translate. Fletch had been slow to see how long Toninho's lashes were. They rested on his cheeks. '"My people's song makes my heart leap. The seed is sown by art and tempered by time. Love, love, how good it is to love."'

'That's a good song.'

'Oh, yes.'

With his glass of *cachaça*, Orlando wandered down to where they were sitting.

'Orlando,' Toninho said. 'Give Fletch a demonstration of *capoeira*, of kick-dancing. You and Tito. Make it good. Kill each other.'

Raising his head beside the pool, Tito said, 'You, Toninho.'

'Perform for the gods,' Toninho said.

Orlando looked into his glass. 'I've had a drink.'

'You won't hurt each other,' Toninho said.

'You and Orlando,' Tito said from the grass.

'It is important Janio sees *capoeira* from close up,' Toninho said. 'So he will remember.'

Glass still in hand, Orlando went to Tito and with his bare feet stood on Tito's ass.

99

Standing thus, he drained his glass, leaned over, and put it on the grass. Then he began to walk slowly up Tito's back.

'I can't breathe!' Tito said.

'And you can't talk?' Toninho asked.

'I can't talk, either.'

Then he wriggled free, spilling Orlando to the side, and jumped to his feet.

In a wide arc, he swung his right foot, aiming for Orlando's head.

Orlando ducked successfully, turned sideways and slammed his instep into Tito's side, against his rib cage. Orlando's towel dropped.

'Wake up,' Orlando said.

In a short moment, Tito and Orlando had the rhythm of it, had each other's rhythm. Gracefully, viciously, rhythmically, as if to the beating of drums, with fantastic speed they were aiming kicks at each other's heads, shoulders, stomachs, crotches, knees, each kick coming within a hair's breadth of connecting, narrowly ducking, sidestepping each other, turning and swirling, their legs straight and their legs bent, their muscles tight and their muscles loose, their fronts and their backs flashing in the sunlight, the hair on their heads seeming to have to hurry to keep up with this frantic movement. With this fast, graceful dance, easily they could have killed each other.

Eva had come onto the porch to watch. Her eyes flashed. A few faces of other women appeared in the upper windows of the plantation house. *Everyone loves the Tap Dancers . . . They're sleek.*

'Remember . . .' Toninho was saying. 'A skill developed by the young male slaves, in defense against their masters. They would practice at night, to drums, so if their masters came down from the big house, to look for a woman, they could pretend to be dancing. Thanks to—what is the word in English?—miscegenation, such skills ultimately were not needed . . .'

There was a loud *Thwack!* and Tito began to fall sideways. He had taken a hard blow to the head from the instep of Orlando's foot. The blow could have been much, much harder. Tito did not fall completely.

'I told you to wake up,' Orlando said regretfully.

Recovering, Tito charged Orlando like a bull, right into his midriff. Orlando fell backwards, Tito on top of him. Laughing, sweating, panting, they wrestled on the

101

grass. At one point their bodies, their arms and legs, were in such a tight ball perhaps even they could not tell which was whose.

Eva, moving like Time, went down to them.

Finally, Orlando was sitting on Tito and giving him pink-belly, pounding Tito's belly hard repeatedly with his fists. Tito was laughing so hard his stomach muscles were fully flexed and no harm was being done.

Standing over them, behind Orlando, Eva laced her fingers across Orlando's forehead and pulled him backward, and down.

Kneeling over Tito as he was, sitting on him, bent backward now so that his own back was on the ground, or on Tito's legs, Orlando looked up Eva's thighs. He rolled his eyes.

He jumped up and grabbed Eva by the hand.

Together Orlando and Eva ran down the grassy slope from the swimming pool and disappeared.

'You see?' Toninho said. 'Uncomplicated.'

After resting a moment on the ground, breathing hard, Tito rolled over and over and on into the pool of water.

'Your *Moby Dick*,' Toninho said abruptly. 'By Herman Melville?'

Fletch looked at Toninho, wondering what new surprise was coming. 'Yes,' Fletch said. 'I read it while waiting for a bus.'

'"Call me Ishmael,"' Toninho quoted.

'Not a bad beginning,' Fletch said. 'Simple.'

'Is it?' Toninho finished his *cachaça*. At the long side of the pool, Norival was finishing his fourth. 'Is that Ishmael meant to be some spirit of the United States? Some guardian?'

'Almost anything can be said,' Fletch said. 'And has been.'

'In a way, *Ismael* is the guiding spirit of Brazil.'

Fletch said nothing. Necrophilia, slant-six car engines, the nature of *arigó*, robotics, *capoeira*, now a discussion regarding American literature.

'I'm quite certain Melville stopped in Brazil on his voyages. Have you ever thought of that interpretation of *Moby Dick*?'

'Melville meant Brazil is the guiding spirit of the United States?'

103

'Maybe of the hemisphere.'

'Toninho . . .' Tito's forearms were flat on the edge of the swimming pool, holding his head up. Water streamed down his face from his hair. His right ear was red from Orlando's kick. 'I think we should do Norival a favor.'

Toninho looked over at Norival stretched out in the sunlight. Norival bubble-belched. 'Yes.'

Toninho stood up.

Together Toninho and Tito tipped the slow-reacting Norival out of the long chair.

Fletch went to watch what new trick they would play.

Each taking an arm, they dragged Norival, belly down, to the bushes. The towel dragged off him in the dirt. Then, methodically, standing behind him, Toninho and Tito each picked up one of Norival's feet. They raised him so that his shins were on their shoulders.

Not all that gently, somewhat from the sides, they kicked Norival's soft, upside-down belly with the insteps of their feet, once, twice, some more.

'*Arigó*,' Toninho said, kicking Norival's upside-down stomach.

'Empty out the sack,' Tito said. 'Very

practical.'

It didn't take too many kicks for Norival to begin vomiting his four *cachaças*, his numerous *chopinhos*, whatever was still in him from the night before.

Once he began vomiting, they dropped his legs on the ground.

Tito grinned at Fletch. 'Very efficient, yes?'

'It seems to be working.'

The other side of the swimming pool, Orlando and Eva were climbing back up the slope.

'Ah,' Toninho said, watching them. 'Five minutes is a long time in the life of such a *mulata*.'

Norival now was on his hands and knees, emptying himself into the bushes.

Bleary, drooling vomit, he looked up at them.

'*Obrigado*.' In Portuguese, he said to them, 'Thanks, guys.'

CHAPTER THIRTEEN

After lunch, it rained.

The five young men sat in their muddy

towels at a round table on the back porch of the old plantation house playing poker.

The humidity was complete, and even in the rain Fletch and Orlando and Tito had been in and out of the pool between hands. They would be either wet with sweat or wet with water, and the rain water, the pool water, seemed cooler. The only reason they sat under the roof to play was to keep the cards reasonably dry. Near them, their shorts were still piled on a small table, but the pile was messed up, as Norival had gone to his shorts and swallowed two pills from its pockets. They drank beer. There were many crushed cans near Norival's feet.

From under the porch roof, as he played, Fletch watched the rain fall on the pool and make mud puddles in the dead garden. He watched the flower-kissing birds sustain themselves with wings which beat so fast they were almost invisible, like auras on either side of their bodies, as they sucked sugar water from small vessels in the rafters.

Kick-dancing and flower-kissing birds.

After two or three hours of poker playing, it was clear who the winner was. Norival was careless, concerned more with his next *chope* than the cards. He seemed keyed-up anyway—for someone who had had so much to drink, even though properly evacuated before lunch. Fletch yawned. Tito, Orlando, and Toninho played cards in a way odd to Fletch. They did not seem to see the cards as they were, but as something else, something more. Always they believed in the next card too much. They believed in what the cards might be instead of what they were.

Fletch was collecting all the chips.

At one point, Toninho said, 'of course you cannot understand Brazil, Fletch. Three of us—all but Norival—have been to school in the United States. We cannot say we understand the United States, either. Everyone there is so anxious.'

'Very nervous,' Orlando said.

'Worried,' Tito said. 'Do I drink too much, smoke too much, make love too much, too little? Is my hair all right? Might someone see that my ankles are fat?'

'Does everyone *like* me?' Orlando guffawed.

'I'm so pretty!' Toninho said in falsetto. 'Don't touch me!'

Fletch strummed the table with his fingers. *'Bum, bum, paticum bum, prugurundum.'*

The noise of the rain pounding on the tin roof increased.

Eva came through the back door and stood, watching them.

She stood behind Norival and watched his last chips disappear in careless play.

She took his feverish head in her hands and turned it sideways, and leaned his cheek against her bare stomach. 'Ah, Norival,' she said in Portuguese. 'You are getting drunk again.'

'*Arigó*,' Toninho said, clearly hoping for a picture card and playing as if he had one.

Eva rotated Norival's head so that he was slipping off the chair. The front of his face was against her stomach. He breathed deeply a few times through his nose.

In a moment, Eva led Norival indoors.

Tito, Orlando, Fletch, and Toninho played silently.

Occasionally, concentrating, Toninho's lips would move as if he were talking, but no sound came out.

When Orlando won anything, no matter how much he had lost, his face would break into a marvelous grin. He would be ready to lose more.

At one point, when Fletch was raking in chips again, Tito murmured, 'Your peri-spirit is with you.'

'Is he telling you what cards we have?' Toninho asked.

'Doesn't need to,' Fletch said. 'I play with what I see I have against what I see you have.'

From inside there was a short scream.

Toninho chuckled. 'I guess Norival has a few surprises in him yet.'

'We know he cannot hurt Eva,' Tito said. 'He is only a stick in her fire.'

Then there was another, horrible, long drawn-out scream. It pierced the sound of the rain.

'They are playing,' Orlando said.

'Norival!' Toninho called in Portuguese. 'Mind your manners!'

Naked, Eva fell through the back door. 'Norival!'

Her hair was messed up. Her eyes were wild.

She sucked in breath and spoke in a rush.

Toninho said, 'She says Norival has stopped moving. That he has stopped breathing.'

Eva was shouting Portuguese over the sound of the rain.

'Has he passed out,' Tito said.

'No.' Alarmed, Toninho stood up. 'She

says he has stopped breathing!'

They all rushed inside.

More slowly, Fletch went with them, suspecting some new trick.

In the little room on the first floor, Norival lay on the rumpled, dirty sheets of an extra long bed. He was partly on his side, as if rolled into that position. He was naked and his stomach was slack. There was still a streak of mud on his leg.

Norival was grinning.

There was a happy, wicked gleam in his eye.

From the door, Fletch watched Norival's grin remain idiotic.

Norival's eyes did not blink.

Fletch joined the Tap Dancers at the side of the bed. With his fingertips he felt for a pulse in Norival's neck. There was none. Norival's pleased eyes did not blink.

As Fletch watched, slowly the grin disappeared from Norival's face. The lips became straight.

The happy gleam remained in his eyes.

A few inches in front of Norival's penis, the bed sheet was wet and stained.

'He is dead!' Orlando said in Portuguese.

Under his breath, Tito whistled.

Standing, his back straight, Toninho

said, 'Norival. You died *arigó*.'

'What do we do?' Orlando asked. 'Norival is dead!'

'How did he die?' Tito asked. 'Surely he has done this before. It hasn't been fatal.'

Orlando said, 'He can't be dead. Wake up, Norival! You'll miss Carnival!'

'He is dead,' Toninho said. 'Norival is dead!'

Eva filled the door of the small, dark room. Talking rapidly but more quietly now, she kept gasping, imitating a belch, grabbing her huge left breast with both hands.

'Died of a heart attack while copulating, I guess,' Fletch said.

Orlando said, *'Way to go, Norival!'*

'No wonder he was smiling!' Tito said.

'You saw him smiling?' Toninho asked.

'Definitely he was smiling,' Tito said.

Orlando nodded. 'When we came into the room, he was smiling!'

'He is not smiling now,' Tito said.

'But look at his eyes,' Toninho said.

'His eyes are still happy,' Tito said.

'And why not?' Orlando asked. 'Why not happy?'

At the door, Eva was beginning to look pleased with herself.

'But he's dead!' Tito said.

'But how he died!' Orlando said. He looked ready to shake Norival's hand. 'Well done, Norival!'

'A death in ten million,' Toninho said. '*Arigó!*'

CHAPTER FOURTEEN

The tall, slim, naked young man stood in the dead garden, the rain pouring down his body, his feet wide apart in the mud, his face up to the rain, his arms held high as if to catch the sky.

From the back porch, Fletch heard what Toninho said to the sky:

With God he lays down; with God he rises,
With the grace of God and the Holy Spirit.
May Thine eyes watch over him as he
    sleeps.
Dead, will You light his way
Into the mansions of eternity
With the tapers of Thy Trinity?

Fletch went down to Toninho in the garden.

'A prayer.' Toninho's face and arms lowered. His shoulders sagged.

Then Toninho looked over the hedges, out into mountain space in the rain. 'Not a worry.' Fletch could not make sure if there were tears mixed in with the rain on Toninho's cheeks. 'When you die copulating, you are certain to come back to life, soon.'

CHAPTER FIFTEEN

'Toninho! What do we do?' Tito asked in a hushed voice.

Toninho shook his head as if to clear it.

'Still, Norival is dead,' he muttered thickly.

While Fletch and the Tap Dancers were out of the room, Dona Jurema, the young teenaged girl, and one other woman from the house had washed Norival, put a fresher sheet under him, and laid him out straight.

Now in the small, dark room, Norival lay on his back, clean, naked. His eyes were closed. In his hands folded over his stomach were a few flowers which had seen

113

better hours. A candle flickered at the head of the bed; another candle at the foot of the bed.

Leaving a full bottle of whiskey in the room, Dona Jurema left the young men sitting around the bed in straight wooden chairs.

So they had sat for two or three hours. The thick candles had burned down only a few centimeters.

There was no measurement tape on that whiskey bottle. Their next drink from it would probably be their last. Fletch had had three or four good swallows from the bottle.

Even on the straight wooden chair across the bed, Orlando sat with his legs out straight before him, his chin on his chest, his thumbs hitched into the tops of his shorts.

'We must do something,' Tito said.

Toninho blinked.

'We cannot leave Norival here,' Tito said.

To Fletch, Toninho said, 'Norival comes from a rich, important family. His uncle is an admiral!'

'To die in a whorehouse,' Tito said. 'Full of booze . . .'

'And pills, I think,' Fletch said.

'His mother would be disappointed,' Tito concluded.

'But what a way to go!' Orlando muttered without opening his eyes or raising his chin from his chest.

'We must do something,' Tito said.

'We must move him.' Toninho drank from the bottle, saw that it was nearly the last of the whiskey, and handed the bottle to Tito.

'We must arrange some other death for Norival,' Tito said.

'Burn the record,' Fletch agreed. 'I see the point.'

'For the sake of his mother,' Tito said.

'He must not have died here,' Toninho said carefully. 'Not in the arms of Eva.'

'No,' said Tito. 'It would make her too famous.'

'Still.' Toninho winked. 'People will know.'

'Yes,' Tito said. He passed the bottle over Norival to Fletch. 'People will know how Norival died.'

'What a way to go!' Orlando muttered.

'But not his mother,' agreed Tito. 'Not his sisters.'

For a moment, while Fletch held the

bottle, they were silent.

The candles flickered and Norival did not breathe.

Through the open window came the sound of the rain on the tin roof.

'We must do something,' Tito said.

'The important thing is,' Toninho said, trying very hard to keep his tongue straight and to see things clearly, 'is to prevent an autopsy.'

'Yes!' Tito said forcefully at this great wisdom.

'Because Norival was full of booze and pills.'

'Despite our having emptied him out once,' Tito put in.

'And that would disappoint his mother,' said Toninho, losing his tongue in his mouth.

'Worth it,' Orlando muttered from his chest. 'A death in ten million. Good old Norival.'

'Wake up, Orlando,' Tito said. 'We must think.'

'No.'

Toninho kicked Orlando's legs and Orlando nearly fell off his chair.

Blinking, he looked at Norival laid out on the bed, holding the wilted flowers.

116

It was not yet dark, but the rain made the candles bright in the small room.

'Orlando, we must think of something.'

'*Queima de arquivo*,' Fletch said. 'I am learning Portuguese.'

'Truly,' Orlando said. 'We must do something. We must move him.'

'His boat,' Toninho said.

'Yes.' Orlando shook his head solemnly. 'His boat. Who now will want his boat?'

'Exactly,' Toninho said.

'Exactly what?' Tito asked.

Fletch took his drink from the bottle and handed it back across Norival to Orlando.

'Clearly.' Toninho spoke slowly, carefully. 'Norival died on his boat.'

'Clearly.' Tito looked at Norival as if for agreement. 'Norival would have liked that.'

Orlando said, 'I think Norival was satisfied enough with the way he died.'

'But we can say he died on his boat, Orlando,' Tito said.

'Off his boat,' Toninho corrected him. 'He died off his boat. He drowned. That should prevent an autopsy.'

'Yes,' Tito said. 'Poor Norival drowned. That should make his mother happy.'

'You're all crazy,' Fletch said.

'But Toninho,' Tito asked, 'how do we

117

get Norival to his boat? It is way down in the harbor. There is a gate to the docks. Guards. There are always guards at the gate.'

Again there was silence, as they considered the gate and guards leading to the dock where Norival's boat was.

Toninho took the bottle of whiskey from Orlando and finished it. 'We walk him.'

He placed the empty whiskey bottle on the bed, within Norival's reach.

Tito said something in Portuguese.

'We walk him right by the guards.'

Orlando said, 'This is a night the dead walk.'

'Broomsticks.' Toninho's eyes were now fully open. He was speaking perfectly clearly. 'Jurema must have brooms.'

Tito looked at the floor. 'I sincerely doubt that, Toninho.'

'Everyone has brooms. Tito, you get rope and rig a harness around Norival's chest. Under his arms. Orlando, you get brooms from Dona Jurema and saw them down to size. You know? So they will fit from the harness under his arms to his waist, so we can hold him up. We need some thick thread for his legs.' Orlando and Tito were studying Toninho carefully with

118

their eyes, putting all this together. Toninho jumped up. 'There is a book of tide tables in the glove compartment of the car. I shall figure out exactly where Norival must drown to come ashore and be found in the morning.'

'His wallet is in the car, too, Toninho,' Tito said. 'In the glove compartment. Norival must wear his wallet when he drowns, so when they find him in the morning, they will know who he is.'

'Otherwise they will not report the body,' Orlando said.

'They will report the body fast enough, if it's a Passarinho,' Tito said. 'Norival Passarinho.'

'You help too, Fletch. You get Norival's clothes, including his shirt.'

'You're all crazy,' Fletch said. 'What if we get caught with a corpse?'

Standing over Norival, Tito rubbed his own hands together. 'Not a worry, Norival,' he said. 'We'll see that you died decently.'

CHAPTER SIXTEEN

'Drive carefully, Toninho,' Tito said. 'We don't want an accident.'

Although he was not going fast, Toninho was not being all that successful at keeping the black four-door Galaxie to the right. They were swerving down the wet, twisting mountainside road. It was now fully dark. A Volkswagen, climbing the road, had just blared its horn at them.

'We don't want to be stopped by the police,' Orlando said.

'Drive as if you are driving a hearse,' Tito advised.

'I am driving a hearse,' Toninho said, swinging the wheel too much.

At Dona Jurema's, Orlando had sawed two broomsticks down to size. Tito bound Norival's chest with a rope harness. Toninho studied the tide tables and decided exactly where Norival was to drown in the South Atlantic Ocean. Together they fit the broomsticks into the harness and then dressed Norival.

While watching them carry Norival out of the old plantation house, Dona Jurema said to Fletch, 'Come Tuesday. I'll have a corpse for you.'

'Cancel the order,' Fletch said. 'We have a corpse.'

Toninho sniffed. 'Norival is not that sort of corpse.'

As they swerved down the mountainside, Norival sat propped up in the backseat between Tito and Orlando. The broomsticks were not visible beneath his shirt.

When they came to the first flat, wide road on the outskirts of Rio de Janeiro, Tito reminded Toninho again to drive slowly, to stay to the right. Toninho drove very slowly. Even two children on roller skates passed them.

Toninho looked through the rearview mirror. 'Norival never looked better. He holds his head up nicely.'

The car swerved a little.

'Careful, Toninho,' Tito clucked.

'The way he died, he should,' Orlando said. 'Not everybody—'

From behind them came the sound of a police siren.

'Oh, oh,' Toninho said.

'Go fast, Toninho!' Tito said. 'We have a corpse in the car!'

'No, no,' Orlando said. 'Stop.'

The result of following these conflicting orders was that the car shot forward a few meters and then bucked to a stop.

On the backseat, Norival rolled forward. His head struck against the back of the front seat.

'Oh, Norival!' Tito said in exasperation.

'It's all right,' Orlando said, pulling Norival back into a sitting position. 'He won't bleed.'

'Quick!' Toninho said. 'Open his eyes! He looks more real that way!'

Orlando reached over with his fingers and opened Norival's eyes.

The police car drew alongside.

Apparently staring straight ahead through the windshield, Norival's eyes gleamed with a wicked joy.

'What did I do wrong?' Toninho asked. 'These people have no respect for the dead!'

The conversation with the policeman of course was in Portuguese.

While it was going on, Fletch sat perfectly still in the front seat, trying not to look interested or concerned.

After they drove away from the policeman, Toninho, Orlando and Tito, choking with laughter, repeated the conversation in English for Fletch.

Policeman: Why are you driving so slowly?

Toninho: It's Carnival, sir. I don't want to hit any revelers.

Policeman: No one else is driving so slowly.

Toninho: Perhaps no one else is as good a citizen as I, sir.

Policeman: Back there, you swerved. You almost hit a parked car.

Toninho: I sneezed.

Policeman: God bless you, my son.

Toninho: Thank you, sir.

Policeman, shining his flashlight around the inside of the car, finally leaving it for a moment on Norival's joyfully beaming, unblinking face: Why does that guy look so happy?

Toninho: He always looks that way during Carnival, sir.

Policeman: Is he stoned?

Toninho, whispering: He's not all there, sir.

Policeman: Oh. Well, drive faster.

Toninho: Yes, sir.

★   ★   ★

'Tito, you stay with the car. Drive to where I showed you on the map. The beach. We'll be there in a few hours.'

Correct. They had driven by the gates to the dock where Norival's boat was. The gates were closed and locked. Not one but three guards stood at the gate chatting, two outside and one inside.

They drove up the street and parked the car against the curb.

It had stopped raining. The moon was threatening to come out.

They lifted Norival out of the backseat and stood him in the road between Toninho and Orlando.

'Here, Fletch.' Toninho handed Fletch a ball of heavy thread he had taken from Dona Jurema. 'Tie Norival's left ankle to Orlando's right, his right ankle to my left. See? It will work out. That way, Norival will appear to walk.'

Fletch tied Norival's left ankle to Orlando's right.

They lifted Norival a little off the ground on his broomsticks and Orlando walked in a circle around Toninho. Norival's movement was too slow.

'No, Fletch,' Toninho said, 'the line must be tighter. Norival must appear to be

124

taking the same size steps as Orlando.'

Kneeling on the wet road, Fletch retied the thread tighter, and then tied Norival's right ankle to Toninho's left.

Somewhere in the harbor, a ship's whistle blew.

Toninho and Orlando walked Norival up the road a little way. 'How do we look, Tito?'

'Lift your side higher, Toninho,' Tito said. 'His foot is dragging a little, your side.'

Toninho hitched Norival higher. 'That better?'

'Perfect,' Tito said. 'You'd never know he's dead.'

'Fine. Then we should go. See you at the beach in a few hours, Tito. Here, Fletch, you walk a little in front of us, in case things do not look exactly right.'

Slowly, in bare feet, Fletch walked down the rain-slicked road and up onto the sidewalk toward the gate to the boat dock. Each pocket of his shorts was bulging with a wad of *cruzeiros* he had won at poker.

He could not help looking around.

Eyes beaming in complete joy, arms stiff at his sides, although his shoulders propped up by broomsticks did look a little high,

125

Norival walked almost in step between Toninho and Orlando. Three close friends going down the street together. The harness kept Norival's head high.

Norival did trip going up the curb.

Down the road, Tito was driving the car away.

The three guards watched the four young men approach.

'*Boa noite*,' Fletch said to them.

'*Boa noite*,' they answered lowly, suspiciously.

Fletch stood aside.

'Ah, Doctor Passarinho!' One guard threw away his cigarette.

Again the conversation was in Portuguese.

Fletch kept looking up at the heavy, scudding clouds, hoping the moon would not take that moment to appear.

Guard: 'You are not going out on your boat tonight, are you?'

Toninho answered in his normal voice, not even trying to conceal the movement of his lips. 'Yes. Rio is so crowded. From Carnival. I need some peace and quiet.'

Orlando took a few steps in his circle so that the faces of Norival and Toninho were turned a bit away from the guards.

Guard: 'But there has been a heavy rain! It might rain again!'

Toninho/Norival: 'That will help keep the sea calm.'

Guard: 'They say the wind will come up.'

Toninho/Norival: 'Yes, well, I feel like a vigorous sail.'

Second guard: 'You look uncommonly happy, Doctor Passarinho.'

Toninho/Norival: 'I think I have met the love of my life.'

Guard: 'That will do it.'

Toninho/Norival: 'Yes. I doubt I will ever love anyone else.'

Third guard (inside gate): 'Ah, to be in love! To be young and in love! You look so happy, Doctor Passarinho!'

Guard: 'But if you go sailing now, you will be missing the parties! The grand balls! How can there be Carnival parties without the Tap Dancers?'

Orlando: 'No. Only Norival is going sailing. Because he is so stuck in love, you see. We came just to see him off. We will swim ashore. Off Copacabana.'

Second guard: 'I understand everything perfectly. He is in love... From the stiff way he walks, I should say he should not be with the young lady just now...'

Guard: 'Is that it? Ah! I see! So Doctor Passarinho, even though it is the middle of the night during Carnival, goes sailing!'

Third guard: 'What a man!'

Guard: 'What a gentleman!'

Toninho/Norival: 'Something like that.'

Guard: 'Norival Passarinho must do what is best, for himself and his young lady!' He signaled the guard inside to open the gate. 'What consideration!'

Orlando and Toninho marched Norival through the gate. True, Norival did walk as if he suffered one of the more virulent social diseases.

Fletch fell in behind them.

Toninho/Norival: *'Obrigado! Boa noite!'*

★　　★　　★

Aboard, Orlando removed the sail covers and had the mainsail up in almost no time at all.

Toninho released the bow line and gathered it in.

As soon as the mainsail caught the wind, Fletch, at the tiller, released the stern line and, letting it trail in the water, took in the main sheet.

Facing aft in the cockpit, Norival

beamed delightedly at his friends taking him sailing.

While Orlando was running up the jib, Toninho came aft and took the tiller. 'I know the harbor,' he said. 'We do not want to run into someone's boat in the dark while one of us is dead.'

Fletch gathered in the stern line. 'Not in the S.S. *Coitus Interruptus*.'

The moon came out.

In the moonlight, Norival's whole face beamed. But when the boat heeled, he fell over sideways.

'Can't have him rolling around,' Toninho said. 'He might go overboard before we mean him to.'

Fletch relieved Norival of his rope harness and the broomsticks and sat him up in the leeward corner of the cockpit. He tied a light line around his shoulders to a stanchion behind him.

'The things we do for our friends,' Toninho muttered, coming about.

Now Norival was sitting to windward, leaning unnaturally forward as if being seasick. But he was still beaming.

Orlando joined them in the cockpit.

Laughing, then, they translated the conversation with the guards for Fletch.

'*What a gentleman!*' Orlando kept repeating.

Then Orlando said, 'Norival loved this little boat.'

At the tiller, Toninho said, 'Who'd think Norival would be one to go down with his ship?'

Orlando laughed. '*What a gentleman!*'

★ ★ ★

'We're just about there,' Toninho said.

Ashore, as they came around a point, a car's headlights went on and off three times.

'Yes!' Toninho said. 'There's Tito. He must see us.'

At first, sailing south in Baia de Guanabara, Fletch had tried to sleep. He lay on the deck, a cushion under his head. He regretted leaving the rest of his mineral water in the car. Despite the drinks he had had, sleep was impossible.

The sky was clear now. The breeze was from the northeast and steady. The little sloop moved nicely through the water.

To starboard, *Cidade Maravilhosa*, Rio de Janeiro, passed slowly, laid out under the moonlight. There were a few fires on

130

the beach. The street lights, the lights in the tall apartment buildings and hotels along the shore dimmed the stars above. From offshore, the samba drums were heard from all parts of the city in a soft jumble. Like no other city Fletch had seen from such a perspective, Rio has peculiar black holes in its middle, the sides of its cliffs, *Morros da Babilonia, de São João, des Cabritos, Pedra dos dois Irmãos*, its surprising, irrepressible jungle growth within the city. Above all in the moonlight, arms out in forgiveness, stood the statue of Christ the Redeemer.

At some point, sitting in the cockpit opposite Norival, Orlando had said, 'We will have to go to Canecão Ball.'

'Yes,' Toninho said. 'However late.'

'We will have to find the Passarinhos,' Orlando said, 'and say that Norival went sailing.'

'Janio, you must stay with us so we will be believed.'

'I should return to The Yellow Parrot.'

'No, no. There will not be time. You come to my apartment. You can wear my costume from last year. We are the same size.'

'I seem to be the same size as everybody,'

131

Fletch said. 'Alan Stanwyk, Janio Barreto, Toninho Braga...'

'Tito will drive fast and we will dress and go in a hurry.'

'The tickets Teo gave me for the ball are at The Yellow Parrot.'

'You can use Norival's. He won't be needing it.'

They sailed another few kilometers. Ashore, again Tito flashed his headlights three times.

'All right.' Toninho punched Fletch's leg. 'Take the tiller, Senhor Barreto. It is no surprise to us you know how to run a boat. Orlando, assist Norival. Make sure he has his wallet in his pocket.'

'He has his wallet.'

'His death would never be reported, unless they know who he is. Whoever finds a Passarinho body will expect money for reporting it.'

Fletch sat, tiller in hand, keeping the course along the shore.

Toninho went below.

Soon from the small cabin came a heavy pounding. Then a splintering sound. Then gurgling.

The boat veered to port. Instantly, it became unmanageable. The sails luffed.

Fletch released the tiller.

Toninho came up the companionway and tossed a hammer overboard.

'We are near enough the rock for people to believe he hit it,' Toninho said. 'And now for Norival.'

Together, Toninho and Orlando lifted Norival, his eyes still beaming happily in the moonlight, brought him to the gunwale. Gently, they dropped him overboard.

For a moment, the two young men stood on the deck, staring down into the water. Toninho's lips moved. Orlando crossed himself.

'He'll be on the beach by dawn,' Toninho said.

The little boat first had come about, put its nose up into the wind, both sails luffing. Then the bow began to sink. As it did so, it fell off the wind, the sails filled again, and, twisting, it began to capsize.

'Come, Janio!' Toninho shouted. 'You don't want to keep dying at your age!'

Orlando dove overboard.

Only after Fletch dove did Toninho scramble off the sinking boat.

The water was exactly body temperature, as was the air. In irrepressible, sensuous delight, Fletch stroked through the buoyant water toward *Cidade Maravilhosa*.

The wads of money in the pockets of his shorts came to feel like stones in the water.

After a hundred meters, he stopped swimming. He looked around to see if anything of the boat was still visible. He could not be sure. There was something white on the water, possibly the side of the hull, possibly the sails.

Then, from near the boat came a loud yell. '*Aaaaaaaaarrrrrgh!*' Water was thrashed.

'Toninho!' Fletch called. 'What's the matter?'

Silence.

'Toninho! What happened?'

Fletch was just starting to swim back when Toninho's steady voice came calmly across the water surface: 'I swam into Norival. . . .'

CHAPTER SEVENTEEN

'We must be very casual,' said Tito, now a movie Indian.

They were entering the Canecão Night

Club.

'What is the number of the Passarinho box?' Orlando asked.

'They're always in box three,' Toninho answered.

'Da Costa is in box nine,' Fletch answered.

Relieved of the corpse, Tito drove the black four-door Galaxie back to Copacabana fast enough to satisfy any police.

In the car, Fletch gulped down the rest of his liter of water.

At Toninho's apartment on rua Figueiredo Magalhaes, Toninho, Tito, Orlando, and Fletch shaved and showered in assembly-line fashion.

The Tap Dancers were to dress as movie Indians in breech-clouts, soft thigh-high boots, and war paint. Norival's breech-clout did not fit Fletch, unless he wanted to spend the rest of the night holding it up with his hand.

Toninho dug his last year's costume out of a closet and tossed it to Fletch: a one-piece shiny satin movie cowboy suit, complete with mask, frayed leggings, and spangles. Fletch wriggled into it.

'Toninho. This is a scuba suit?'

'It fits you perfectly. Here are the boots, the hat, the mask.'

'It fits like a scuba suit.'

Toninho, Tito, and Orlando then sat in a circle decorating each other's faces, chests, backs with movie war paint, with great speed. Finished, they looked as if they had already sweated through a war.

While they were doing that, Fletch decorated Toninho's apartment by draping wet *cruzeiros* every conceivable place, to dry.

'Remember,' Tito said. 'Very casual.'

At Canecão Night Club, Orlando opened the door to the Passarinho box.

'Orlando!' people exclaimed. 'Tito! Toninho!'

The people in the box just stared at the masked movie cowboy.

Below them, the huge floor of the Canecão Night Club was jammed with people in bright costumes at little tables, on the dance floor, wandering around. Across the hall on the large stage was an enormous band, mostly of samba drums, but of horns and electric guitars as well.

Everyone in the Passarinho box made much of the Tap Dancers' costumes. As there wasn't much to the costumes, in fact

136

they were making much of the Tap Dancers.

In turn, Toninho, Orlando, Tito exercised the courtesy of not knowing who people were and expressing great surprise when, for example, Harlequin revealed himself to be Admiral Passarinho.

'You're very late!'

'Oh,' Toninho equivocated. 'We just found the box.'

'Who's this?' a woman asked.

'Janio Barreto,' Toninho muttered.

'I. M. Fletcher.'

Senhor Passarinho was dressed as *Papai Noel*. 'Where's Norival?'

'He went sailing,' Tito said.

'Sailing? It is storming out!'

'The storm is over,' Orlando said.

'Sailing? On the night of the Canecão Ball?'

'We saw him off,' Toninho said. 'Fletch did too.'

'Sailing? Why would he go sailing the night of the Canecão Ball?'

With apparent concern, Toninho said, 'Norival has been acting very serious lately.'

'He has been talking of taking up a career,' Orlando said.

'That would be nice,' said *Papai Noel*.

'It is a question of what he does best,' Tito said.

'Norival has his talents,' Orlando said.

Toninho said, 'Perhaps he wanted to think.'

'Norival becoming serious?' asked Harlequin. 'Then it is time for me to retire!'

'No, no,' Toninho said. 'You don't know Norival as we do. When Norival sets his mind to something, he is apt to die trying.'

'Norival can be very sincere,' Orlando said. 'About some things.'

'Yes.' Accented by war paint, Toninho's eyes crossed. 'Norival is one to die trying.'

'Norival is not coming to the ball at all?' Harlequin asked.

'He went sailing,' Toninho said lamely. 'To come to some conclusion . . .'

'Ah, what a son!' *Papai Noel* said. 'Probably drunk somewhere! These tickets cost three hundred North American dollars each! Norival, Adroaldo . . . Why does a man have sons? As soon as they grow as big as he is, they ignore him! They take, but do not give!'

Fletch was introduced to Senhora Passarinho, who sat aside, watching the

138

dancers on the floor. A lady with mild, vague eyes, she was dressed as a circus clown.

'Ah!' she said. 'Norival went sailing! Of course, he never was one for parties! A quiet, sensitive boy, always. He wrote poetry, you know, when he was younger. I remember one poem of his, where the cockatoo bird was meant to represent his school principal...'

'You see,' Tito said aside to Fletch. 'We could not disappoint that lady with the truth.'

'Clearly.'

'It would kill her.'

'Have a drink!' ordered Harlequin. '*Cachaça?*'

Toninho grinned broadly. The worst was over. '*Nao, Senhor.* We must go find girls.'

'Of course you must!' boomed *Papai Noel*. 'The night is as young as you!'

'Just make sure they're not men disguised surgically!' Harlequin warned.

'If I find someone special, I shall bring her to you,' Toninho said, 'to check out.'

Harlequin roared in laughter.

Outside the box, Fletch said, 'Toninho, are you going back to the beach in the morning to make sure Norival came ashore?'

'Oh, no.' Toninho adjusted the top of his boot against the bare calf of his leg. 'Today is Sunday. We must go to Mass.'

★　　★　　★

Teodomiro da Costa was standing at the little bar at the back of his box.

'Who is this?' he exclaimed. 'I don't recognize you!'

Fletch stared at him the appropriate time through his mask.

Everyone else in the box was facing forward, listening intently to the singer of the moment.

What was left of the Tap Dancers had gone looking for girls.

'You scare me, Senhor Gunslinger! What do you want?'

'It's me, Teo.'

'Who?' Teo leaned forward, staring through the eyeholes of Fletch's mask.

'Fletch!'

'Ah!' Teo feigned a look of great relief. 'Then come have a drink.'

The barman Teo had brought from his house began to make Fletch a screwdriver.

'It's so late,' Teo said. 'It is nearly three

140

o'clock in the morning. Did you fall asleep?'

'No.'

'I thought not.'

'Without Laura, I went for a tour of the suburbs. Got back late.'

'In a bus?'

'Something like that. A big car.'

The singer stopped singing.

'Oh, Fletch! Beautiful costume!' the Viana woman said. 'Where did you get it?'

'I mugged someone on my television set.'

'It fits you . . .' She looked below his waist. '. . . handsomely.'

'Frankly, I feel like I'm walking behind myself.'

'You are, darling. You are.'

Teo introduced Fletch to his other guests. Besides the Vianas and the da Silvas, there was a famous Brazilian soccer player who could not stop dancing around the box by himself; his wife, who was taller than he, and probably heavier; a broker and his wife from London, who put on their Wegman—Man Ray masks for Fletch; Adrian Fawcett, who wrote about music for *The New York Times*; an Italian racing driver and his girl friend, who was very young indeed; and the young French film star Jetta.

Everyone marveled at Fletch's costume, and he at everyone's. Teo was dressed somewhat as a tiger, with a short tail. His tiger head rested on the bar table. Staring unblinkingly through glass eyes, the tiger head reminded Fletch somewhat of Norival in his last moment. But Norival's eyes were much happier.

Jetta was dressed in a nurse's cap and costume, white shoes. Her nurse's skirt was not even as long as the Tap Dancers' breechclouts.

In films, he had seen more of Jetta.

Fletch took off his mask and movie cowboy hat and stood at the rail and watched the swirl of color and flesh below him.

A few of the drummers were going off the stage; others were coming on. The music would never stop.

At three places on the huge floor, between the dancing area and the tables, were tall, raised, gilded cages. Inside, three or four magnificent women dressed only in G-strings and tall headgear writhed to the music. Outside, crawling around the cages, trying to attain sufficient footholds in their high-heeled shoes to writhe to the music, nine or ten women dressed in G-strings and tall headgear crawled around like big cats on their hind legs. Each of the gilded cages was a locus of writhing brown bare asses and huge, shaking brown bare breasts.

Beside him, Teo said, 'The floors of the cages are elevators; they go up and down so the women can get in and out without being accosted by the crowd.'

'They must be seven feet tall,' Fletch said.

'They are all over six feet.'

'What about the women outside the cages?'

'They were not women.' Teo sipped his drink.

'They are.'

Teo said, 'They are exhibiting the superb work of their Brazilian surgeons.'

From a distance, Fletch could see no difference between the women inside the cages and the women outside the cages.

Once before, in New York, he had been fooled.

'No one hardly ever accosts them,' Teo said. 'Very sad, for them.'

The music picked up, and all the people, those dancing, those at the tables, those in the boxes, began singing/chanting the song presented by *Imperio Serrano* that Carnival. Fletch stumbled over the lyrics. He could never make his Portuguese sibilant enough.

All the tanned people, the brown people, the black people were moving to the rhythm and singing the lyrics of the song presented by a single samba school together, something about how indebted Brazilian people are to the coffee bean, and how they should respect the coffee bean like an uncle.

Adrian Fawcett, drink in hand, stood at the rail to Fletch's left. 'Brazil is what the United States would like to think it is.'

'I used to work for a newspaper,' Fletch said. 'A reporter.'

'What do you do now?'

'Do? Why must I do? I am.'

Jetta stood the other side of Fletch. After Eva, after watching the women in the gilded cages, Jetta-off-the-screen seemed small.

'Really what do you do?' Adrian asked.

Fletch said, 'I don't know.'

Jetta said, 'Teo said there would be someone young for me to dance with.'

'I feel one hundred years old at the moment.'

'I have heard that story,' she said. 'You

are someone who died, years ago, murdered, and has come back to life to reveal your murderer.'

'Did you ever hear anything so crazy?'

'Yes,' she said. 'Will you dance?'

Fletch wanted to crawl into a corner of the box, to sleep. He was sure he could do so, despite the drums, the horns, the guitars, the singing. 'Of course.'

Excusing themselves from the box, they went to the dance floor.

The people swirling around them were dressed as rabbits and rodents, harlequins and harlots, grande dames and playschool children, villains and viscounts, convicts and cooks, pirates and priests.

Surprising to Fletch, Jetta seemed a wooden dancer. She clung to Fletch as she might to a log in the middle of the sea. He suspected she resisted such music.

A few meters away, Orlando, breechclout flapping, was dancing wildly with a woman in a blond wig. The concentration in his eyes as he danced put him in another world. The woman's dress exposed only one breast totally.

At the edge of the dance floor, a dozen men stood absolutely still, staring up, their mouths agape. Above them was a woman

145

sitting on the rail of a box, her bare buttocks hanging over the rail. The woman herself was not visible: just her bare buttocks hanging over the rail.

Jetta followed Fletch's gaze. 'Brazilians are so relaxed about their bodies,' said the young French film star. 'So practical.'

Feeling almost intoxicated with sleeplessness, Fletch envisioned Tito and Toninho turning Norival upside down in the bushes, kicking the vomit out of his stomach; Tito and Orlando, naked, kick-dancing, then wrestling, laughing, on the burned-out grass; the magnificent Eva standing in the door of the small, dark room where Norival lay dead, clutching her left breast with both hands, looking mildly pleased with herself; harness and broomsticks and calculating where a corpse dropped into the tide would be by dawn . . .

Jetta ran her hands up the smooth sleeves of Fletch's shirt to his shoulders and said, 'You were so late in coming.'

Even though dancing, sleep passed through Fletch's brain like a curtain dragging across a stage. 'I had to sit up a sick friend.'

146

CHAPTER EIGHTEEN

Alone in his room at The Hotel Yellow Parrot, Fletch first dialed The Hotel Jangada and asked for Room 912.

There was no answer in Room 912.

Not even taking off his movie cowboy suit, he fell on his bed. He thought he would sleep immediately. It was nearly seven o'clock in the morning. He was not used to going to sleep at seven o'clock in the morning.

Getting up, he dropped his clothes on the floor. Then he crawled beneath the sheet.

Even at that hour of the bright morning, the sound of a samba combo could be heard from somewhere in the street. He rolled onto his side and pulled the pillow over his ear. Eyes closed, flesh wavered everywhere in his mind: big, soft, pliant breasts with huge nipples swinging to the beat; long, smooth backs danced away from him; brown buttocks dimpled as they moved; gorgeous long legs bent and straightened as feet pressed gently against the earth, the dance floor in the rhythm of the melodic samba drums.

Fletch got out of bed and called Room Service for breakfast.

While he waited, he took a long, hot shower.

Alone, a towel around his waist, he ate breakfast sitting in a corner of his room. For once, the man across the utility area was not painting the room.

He called The Hotel Jangada again, again asked for Mrs Joan Stanwyk in Room 912.

Again there was no answer.

He closed the drapes against the bright morning and got into bed.

He tried lying like a statue on a crypt, like Norival dead on the bed at the old plantation house, flat on his back, his hands crossed on his stomach. He tried counting the members of a woman's pole-vaulting team leaping over the barrier. At the nineteenth redhead taking her turn with the brunettes and blondes going over the barrier, he knew sleep was unattainable.

He called The Hotel Jangada again.

Heavily slogging around the room, he opened the window drapes.

He pulled on clean shorts, a clean tennis shirt, socks, and sneakers.

Outside the hotel, in the brilliant sunlight, the small boy, Idalina's great-grandson Janio Barreto, was waiting for him.

The boy grabbed Fletch's arm. He hobbled along with Fletch, speaking rapidly, softly, insistently.

Fletch shook the boy off and got into his MP.

On his wooden leg, the ten-year-old Janio Barreto ran after Fletch's car, calling to him.

CHAPTER NINETEEN

'*Bom dia*,' Fletch said to the formally dressed desk clerk at The Hotel Jangada. 'There is a problem.'

Instantly, the man was solicitous. He put his forearms on the reception counter and folded his hands. 'Are you a guest of this hotel?'

'I am staying at The Hotel Yellow Parrot.'

The desk clerk was only a little less solicitous. The Hotel Yellow Parrot was a good hotel, too, more traditional, not so flashy. All the good hotels in Rio de Janeiro exactly doubled their rates during Carnival.

Fletch had already telephoned Room 912 on the house phone, gone to the door, checked out the breakfast and pool areas. No sign of Joan Collins Stanwyk. The note he had left for her was still in the Room 912 box behind the reception desk.

He spoke slowly and distinctly: 'Someone who is staying at your hotel, a North American woman named Mrs Joan Stanwyk, talked to me yesterday morning at about this time, at my hotel. We arranged to meet almost immediately here, for breakfast. She was to walk from there to here. All I had to do was to get something from the safe of The Hotel Yellow Parrot, shower, change clothes (I had been jogging), and follow her in my car. I left The Hotel Yellow Parrot about a half hour after her, and drove straight here. She did not answer the house phone. She did not answer when I knocked on her door. She was not in the breakfast room, the terraces, the swimming pool areas, the bar. She still doesn't answer. I'm afraid something must have happened to her.'

The desk clerk smiled faintly at this story of a jilted lover. 'There is nothing we can do, Senhor. We must respect the privacy of our guests. If the lady does not wish to see you, or hear from you...' Raising his hands from the counter, he shrugged.

'But, you see, she needs something from me. Money. She had been robbed of everything.'

Again the man shrugged.

'I left her a note.' Fletch pointed to the note still in its slot behind the man. 'The note is still there.'

'People change their plans rapidly in Rio during Carnival.' The man smiled. 'Sometimes they change their whole characters.'

'Will you let me into her room, please?' Fletch had already tried to jimmy the lock to Room 912. It was an advanced lock, designed for only the most advanced burglars. 'I worry that something must have happened to her. She may need help.'

'No, sir. We cannot do that.'

'Will you go yourself?'

'No, sir. I cannot do that.'

'Will you send a maid in?'

'It's Carnival.' The desk clerk looked at the lobby clock. 'It is early. People sleep odd hours. They do not want disturbance.'

'She's been missing twenty-four hours,' Fletch said. 'It is now a police matter.'

The man shrugged.

Fletch said, '*Onde é a delegacia?*'

★　　★　　★

'Is there a police officer who speaks English?'

'Spik Onglish,' the police officer behind the tall desk said. 'Quack, quack.'

Fletch turned his head so a younger police officer down the counter could hear him. 'Anyone here who can speak English?'

Down the counter, the younger officer picked up a phone, dialed a short number, and spoke into it.

After he hung up, he held the palm of his hand up to Fletch, either ordering him to stop or suggesting he wait.

Fletch waited.

The lobby of the police station was filled with regretful revelers. On the floor and along the bench sat and lay men and women of all shapes, sizes, colors, in nearly every state of dress and undress, sleeping, trying to sleep, blinking slowly, holding their heads. Some of the revelers were in Carnival costumes, now in tatters: a queen; a mouse; ironically, a magistrate. One hairy man, asleep with his mouth open, was dressed only in bra, panties, and garter

152

belt. A fat woman, eating cookies from a bag, was dressed as the Queen of Sheba. Five or six of the men had cuts and bruises on their heads; one had a nasty long cut down the calf of his leg. Even with no glass in the windows, the room smelled putrid.

While Fletch waited, a man dressed only in tank trunks entered. A long-handled knife stuck into the area between his chest and his shoulder. He walked perfectly well. With dignity, he said to the police officer at the high counter, *'Perdi minha máquina fotográfica.'*

From the bottom of a flight of stone stairs, a heavy police officer beckoned Fletch to come to him.

'My name is Fletcher.'

The man shook hands with him. 'Barbosa,' the man said, 'Sergeant Paulo Barbosa. Are you North American?'

'Yes, sir.'

The sergeant heavily led Fletch up the stairs. 'I have been to the United States. To New Bedford, Massachusetts.' He led Fletch into a little room with a desk and two chairs. The sergeant sat in the chair behind the desk. 'I have cousins there, in New Bedford, Massachusetts.' He lit a cigarette. 'Have you been to New Bedford,

Massachusetts?'

'No.' Fletch sat down.

'It is very nice in New Bedford, Massachusetts. Very sealike. It is on the sea. Everyone there fishes. Everyone's wife runs a gift shop. My cousin's wife runs a gift shop. My cousin fishes.' The sergeant brushed cigarette ashes from his shirt when there were no cigarette ashes on his shirt. 'I truly believe the Portuguese bread is better in New Bedford, Massachusetts than the Portuguese bread in Rio de Janeiro. Some of it. Ah, yes. New Bedford, Massachusetts. I was there almost a year. I helped my cousin fish. Too cold there. I could not stand the cold.'

The man sat sideways to the desk, not looking at Fletch. 'Are you enjoying Carnival?'

'Very much.'

'Ah, to be young, handsome, healthy in Rio during Carnival! Can you come closer to heaven? I remember.' Then he brushed cigarette ashes off his shirt which were truly there. 'And rich, too, I suppose.'

In a corner of the room behind the desk was a gray steel filing cabinet, with three drawers.

'It must be a busy time for the police.'

'It is,' the sergeant agreed. 'We get to enjoy Carnival very little. Everything goes topsy-turvy, you see.' He smiled at Fletch, slyly proud of this idiom. 'Topsy-turvy. Men become women; women become men; grown-ups become children; children become grown-ups; rich people pretend they're poor; poor people, rich; sober people become drunkards; thieves become generous. Very topsy-turvy.'

Fletch's eyes examined the typewriter on the desk. It was a Remington, perhaps seventy-five years old.

'You were robbed . . .' the sergeant guessed.

'No,' Fletch said.

'You were not robbed?'

'Of course I was robbed,' Fletch said. 'When I first came here.' The sergeant seemed to be relieved. 'But I am not bothering you with such a small, personal matter.'

The man smiled happily, in increased respect for Fletch. He turned and faced Fletch, now ready to listen.

Again, slowly, carefully, Fletch told Sergeant Paulo Barbosa the facts of his meeting Joan Collins Stanwyk at The Hotel Yellow Parrot, arranging to bring money to

The Hotel Jangada, as of course she had been robbed, to have breakfast with her ... her not being at the hotel yesterday or today ... not picking up the note he had left for her ...

Another cigarette was dropping ashes on the sergeant's shirt. He was quick to brush them away.

'Ah,' he said, 'Carnival! It explains everything.'

'This is not a crazy lady,' Fletch said. 'She is a woman of many responsibilities. She is a healthy, attractive blonde woman in her early thirties, expensively dressed—'

'Topsy-turvy,' the sergeant said. 'If you say she is not a crazy lady, then during Carnival, she becomes a crazy lady! I know! I have been on this police force twenty-seven years. Twenty-seven Carnivals!'

'She has been missing for over twenty-four hours.'

'Some people go missing all their lives! They come to Brazil because they go missing from some place else. Don't you know that?'

'Not this lady. She has a magnificent home in California, a daughter. She is a wealthy woman.'

'Ah, people during Carnival!' The

sergeant puffed on his cigarette philosophically. 'They are apt to do anything!'

'She could be kidnapped, mugged, hurt, run over by a taxi.'

'That is true,' the sergeant said. 'She could be.'

'It is very important that we find her.'

'Find her?' The sergeant seemed truly surprised at the suggestion. 'Find her? This is a huge country! A city of nine million people! Tall buildings, short buildings, mountains, tunnels, parks, jungles! Are we supposed to look on top of every tall building and under every short building?' He sat forward in his chair. 'At this time of year, everyone becomes someone else. Everyone wears a mask! There are people dressed as goats out there! As porpoises! Tell me, are we to look for a goat, or a porpoise?'

'For a blonde, trim North American woman in her early thirties . . .'

'Topsy-turvy!' the sergeant exclaimed. 'Be reasonable! What can we do?'

'I am reporting the disappearance of a female North American visitor to Brazil—'

'You've reported it! If she walks into the police station, I'll tell her you're looking for her!'

'I don't see you taking notes,' Fletch said firmly. 'I don't see you making up a report.'

The sergeant's eyes grew round in amazement. 'You want me to type up a report?'

'I would expect that, yes.'

'I should type up a report because some North American woman changed her plans?'

'A report should be filed,' Fletch insisted. 'Any police force in the world—'

'All right!' The sergeant opened his desk drawer. 'I'll type up a report! Just as you say!' He took a key from his desk. 'You want me to type up a report, I'll type up a report!' Standing, he went to the filing cabinet and inserted the key into its lock. First he looked in the top drawer, then the middle drawer. 'Anything to keep the tourists happy!'

From the bottom drawer, he took out a typewriter ribbon. It appeared to be just about as old as the typewriter.

The sergeant blew dust off the typewriter ribbon.

'Never mind.' Fletch stood up. 'I get the point.'

From a telephone kiosk on the sidewalk outside the police station, Fletch called Teodomiro da Costa.

Teo answered the phone himself.

'Teo? Fletch. I knew if you were asleep, your houseman would tell me.'

'I have to wait for some Telexes from Japan. I am preparing to sell some yen.'

'Teo, that woman I mentioned to you yesterday morning, the North American, is still missing. The note I left for her at The Hotel Jangada has not been picked up. She has no money, no identification. I have been to the police. They tell me there is nothing they can do. The people at The Hotel Jangada will not let me into her room. She may be very sick, Teo, or—'

'Of course. I understand. I think the first thing is to inspect her room. She was a healthy woman, you say?'

'Very healthy. Very sensible.'

'Where are you now?'

'Outside the police station.'

'I'll meet you at The Hotel Jangada.'

'Teo, you've been awake all night.'

'That's all right. This could be a very

159

serious matter, Fletch. Just let these Telexes arrive, and I will be right there.'

'Thanks, Teo. I'll wait in the bar.'

CHAPTER TWENTY

'What is the woman's name?'

'Joan Collins Stanwyk,' Fletch answered. 'Room nine-twelve.'

Fletch was on his second *guaraná* when Teo appeared in the door of the bar of The Hotel Jangada. Even in shorts and a tennis shirt, the dignity of Teodomiro da Costa was absolute.

At the reception counter, Teo spoke with the same clerk with whom Fletch had spoken.

Fletch stood aside and listened.

Clearly, in Portuguese, Teodomiro da Costa introduced himself, explained the situation as he knew it and stated his request: that they be permitted to inspect Room 912.

Again, with all apparent courtesy, the desk clerk refused.

The conversation became more rapid. Teo said something; the desk clerk said

160

something; Teo said something, smiling politely; the desk clerk said something.

Finally, drawing himself up, giving the desk clerk his hooded eye, Teodomiro da Costa asked the rhetorical question which is magic in Brazil, which opens all doors, closes all doors, causes things to happen— or not happen, according to the speaker's wish—which puts people in their places: '*Sabe com quem está falando?*: Do you realize to whom you are speaking?'

The desk clerk withered.

He got the desk key to Room 912 and led the way to the elevator.

★   ★   ★

'Do you see anything amiss?' Teo asked.

While the desk clerk stood at the door of Suite 912, jangling the key in his hand, Teo and Fletch had searched through the living room, bedroom, bathroom, terrace as well as they could.

'Not a damned thing,' Fletch answered. 'Except that Joan Collins Stanwyk isn't here.'

The rooms were freshly made up, the bathroom undisturbed, the bed not slept in. Going through the drawers, closets, even going through the medicine chest and suitcases, and other immediately conceivable hiding places, Fletch had found no money, no jewelry.

'One thing is significant, Teo,' Fletch said. 'Yesterday morning, Joan was wearing a tan slacks suit and a silk shirt. I cannot find the slacks suit and the shirt here in the suite.'

'She could have sent them to the hotel cleaners. You don't know what other clothes she had.'

'Not likely. She wanted to move out of this hotel as soon as I brought money.'

'Then it is likely she disappeared somewhere between The Hotel Yellow Parrot and here.'

'Yes.'

Standing back on his heels at the door, the desk clerk rattled the key against its chain.

'What do we do now?' Teo asked. 'You're the investigative reporter, newly retired.'

'Check the hospitals, I guess.'

Teo thought a short moment. 'There is really only one hospital where they would have brought anyone sick or injured between The Yellow Parrot and here. We can check that one out.'

Fletch said, 'Let's do so.'

★　　★　　★

'What do we do now?' Teo asked again.

They stood in the hospital lobby.

Teo had explained to the hospital administrator the disappearance of a blonde North American woman, in good health, more than twenty-four hours before, who had already been robbed of her money and identification.

The administrator clucked about Carnival, was most understanding although not alarmed, and permitted Teo and Fletch to walk through the seven floors of the hospital, checking the beds of every reasonable unit.

The administrator had said there were many people without identification in the hospital during Carnival. She would be grateful to have any of them identified.

'I don't know.' Fletch's eyes wanted to close in sleep, in discouragement, perhaps to think.

'I don't see what else we can do,' Teo said.

'Neither do I.'

'Once in a while you have to let time pass...' Teo said.

'I guess so.'

'Let things right themselves.'

'She could be anywhere,' Fletch said. 'Anything could have happened to her. Should I check all the hospitals in Rio?'

'That would be impossible! Then check all the hotels and hospitals and jails in Brazil, one by one? You can't live so old!'

'I guess not.'

'Let time pass, Fletch.'

'Thank you, Teo. Sorry to keep you up.'

'You have done your best, for now.'

'Yes...' Fletch said, uncertainly. 'I guess so.'

CHAPTER TWENTY-ONE

Before again pulling the drapes closed in his room at The Hotel Yellow Parrot, Fletch noticed that across the utility area the man was back painting the room. 'If he doesn't finish soon,' Fletch said to himself, 'I'll go across and help him.'

In bed again, hearing the samba drums from two or three combos in the street,

Fletch tried his best to sleep. He breathed deeply, evenly, a long time, to convince his body he was asleep.

His body was not fooled. He was awake.

His mind was crowded with wriggling flesh, with people dressed as rabbits and rodents, harlequins and harlots, grandes dames and playschool children, villains and viscounts, convicts and crooks, pirates and priests. *Clearly, you cannot sleep*, Laura had said. *Did you fall asleep?* Teo had asked. *I thought not.* With a fat Queen of Sheba eating cookies from a bag. With the sight of a man walking well with a long knife sticking out of his chest, reporting to police that he had lost his camera.

Idalina Barreto had been on the sidewalk in front of The Hotel Yellow Parrot when he returned. The wooden-legged great-grandson was with her. She had some sort of rag doll in her hand.

As he hurried into the hotel, she yelled and shook the rag doll at him.

Again he put the pillow over his head. Again he insisted he go to sleep. He thought how tired his legs were, from dancing with Jetta, from . . .

It was no good.

'*Bum, bum, paticum bum.*'

Heavily, he got out of bed. He opened the drapes again.

He looked up the number of Marilia Diniz in the telephone book.

'*Prugurundum.*'

He dialed her number. It rang five times.

'Marilia? Good morning. This is Fletcher.'

'Good morning, Fletcher. Are you enjoying Carnival?'

'Marilia, I know it is Sunday morning, during Carnival; it is wrong of me to call; but I need to talk to you. I have not slept since Thursday.'

'You must be enjoying Carnival.'

'It is not exactly that. Are you too busy? Can we meet somewhere?'

'Right now?'

'If I don't get sleep soon ... I don't know what will happen.'

'Where's Laura?'

'She went to Bahia with her father. She'll be back later today.'

'You need to see me, before you can sleep?'

'I think so. I need to understand something, do something. I need advice.'

'You are disturbed?'

'I lack in understanding.'

'Come over. Do you know how to get to Leblon?'

'Yes. I have your address from the telephone book. Are you sure it's all right if I come now?'

'I ignore Carnival. I am here.'

★   ★   ★

'Trouble between you and Laura?' Marilia asked.

In her little house in Leblon, behind a high wooden fence, Marilia Diniz led Fletch into a small study.

'I saw you in a car with the Tap Dancers yesterday.'

Fletch did not dare ask her what time of day, or night, she saw them; whether all the Tap Dancers were blinking. 'I relieved them of some money, playing poker.'

At the side of the study, Marilia was adjusting a disk in a word processor. 'The Brazilian male,' she said, 'is known for his energy.'

'There's magic, high energy in the food.'

'The Brazilian male is slow to give up his ... what? ... his immaturity.' She started the word processor and watched it operate a moment. 'At seventy, eighty, the Brazilian male is still a boy.'

The word processor was whizzing away, typing manuscript. 'Forgive me,' Marilia said. 'This is my routine for Sunday mornings, making manuscript of my week's work. She sat in a comfortable chair near her desk and indicated Fletch should sit on a two-person sofa. 'I used to have a typist, but now? Another job lost. Teodomiro arranged this word processor for me.'

Fletch sat.

'You look healthy enough,' pale Marilia said. 'Glowing.'

'I have already been to the police station this morning. A woman I know, from California, showed up at my hotel yesterday morning, early. She had been robbed. I told her I would bring her money, immediately. Walking between my hotel and hers, she disappeared.'

'Ah, Carnival . . .'

'Really disappeared, Marilia. With Teo's help, I checked her suite at The Jangada. Her clothes are still there. She has no money, no passport, no credit cards, identification.'

'You are right to be concerned,' Marilia said. 'Anything can happen during

Carnival. And does. Is there any way I can help you?'

'I don't think so. We went through the hospital for that district. Teo says I just must wait.'

'Waiting is hard.'

'That's not why I came to see you. As I said on the phone, I have not slept since Thursday.'

'No one sleeps during Carnival.' Then Marilia said, 'So I guess you don't want any coffee.'

'No, thanks. Do you know about this old woman who says I am her murdered husband come-back-to-life?'

'Someone mentioned something about it, the other night at Teo's.' Marilia glanced at her word processor. 'You tell me about it.'

'Okay.' On the divan, Fletch put his hands under his thighs. 'When you, Laura, and I were having that drink at the café on Avenida Atlantica, Friday afternoon, an old woman in a long white dress came along the sidewalk and apparently saw me. She stopped near the curb. She stared at me until we left. Did you happen to notice her?'

'I'm ashamed to say I didn't.'

'She was behind you.'

'Is the old woman the reason you disappeared under the table?'

'No. That was because of this other woman, from California, who walked down the street just then. I was surprised to see her.'

'The woman who has since disappeared?'

'Yes.'

Marilia got up and checked her word processor, scanned the processed manuscript.

'When Laura and I entered the forecourt of The Yellow Parrot, this old hag jumped out of the bushes at us. She was screaming and pointing her finger at me. Laura talked to her calmly.' Marilia sat down again and listened to Fletch expressionlessly. 'The old woman said that she recognized me. In an earlier life, I had been her husband, Janio Barreto. That forty-seven years ago, at about my present age, I had been murdered. And now I must tell her who it was who had murdered me.'

Marilia said nothing.

Fletch said, 'Laura said, "Clearly you will not rest until you do."'

'And you have not rested.'

'I have not slept.'

'You think the old woman has put a curse

170

on you?'

'Marilia, she hangs around outside my hotel, accosts me every time I go in or go out. She brought her great-grandchildren to the hotel to meet me. This morning she was there on the sidewalk, yelling at me and shaking some kind of a voodoo doll at me.'

'A *calunga* doll.'

'Whatever.'

The word processor finished its work and turned itself off.

Marilia said, 'An interesting story.'

'No one will help me to understand,' Fletch said. 'Otavio Cavalcanti will answer none of my questions, about anything. He just nods and says Yes. Teo says he doesn't understand, doesn't know what to do. I can't understand whether Toninho Braga is making a joke out of it or whether there is some part of him that is serious. Worst of all, I can't understand Laura at all. She's an intelligent woman, a concert pianist. She seems to have no curiosity about my background, but she seems to give this Janio Barreto matter some credence.'

Marilia sighed. 'Ah, Brazil.'

'I can't tell if everyone here is playing some kind of an elaborate joke, a trick on me.'

171

'What do you think?'

'I don't know. Laura says I won't rest until I reveal this murderer, and I haven't. Teo seems to say he is not surprised I am not sleeping. The Tap Dancers just don't expect me to sleep. How can I figure out what happened in Rio de Janeiro a generation before I was born? Am I to die of sleeplessness?'

'Did the old woman say you wouldn't sleep until you answered her?'

'I don't know. Laura talked to her. In Portuguese that was way above my head. I believe the old woman did say so. Why else would Laura have said so?'

'And you believe all this?'

'Of course not. But I'm nearly going crazy with sleeplessness.'

Marilia's eyes traveled around the stacks of books in her study. 'What's the question?'

'First, could this all be an immense practical joke Laura and the Tap Dancers are playing on me? The Tap Dancers seemed to know all about it before they ever met me.'

'Could be,' Marilia said.

'They're all friends. I'm the foreigner. Surely it is easy enough to hire an old

172

woman, some children, a ten-year-old boy on a wooden leg?'

Marilia frowned. 'A small boy on a wooden leg?'

'Yes. Supposedly the great-grandson. Named Janio Barreto, of course.'

Marilia said, softly: 'Or it could be that you are Janio Barreto, and you were murdered decades ago, and you have come back to Rio to reveal who murdered you.'

Fletch stared at her. 'Are you in on this, too?'

'Fletcher, my new friend from North America, you must understand that most of the people in this world believe in reincarnation, in one form or another.' Marilia stood up and went to her word processor.

She began to tear and stack the pages of her manuscript.

'Marilia, may I point out to you that while you and I have been sitting in this room talking about ghosts and curses and *calunga* dolls, a magnificent, modern piece of technology quietly has been typing your manuscript in the corner?'

'This will not be read in your country.' She placed the stack of new pages under a manuscript on her desk. 'I am not

173

translated and published in the United States of the North. The publishers, the people there have a different idea of reality, of what's important, what affects people, what happens, of life and death.' She sat in her soft chair. 'Have you at least had breakfast?'

'Yes.'

'Then what shall we do?'

'Tell me straight out if I should take this matter seriously.'

'It is serious, if you're not sleeping. You can become quite ill from not sleeping. You can drive your car into a lamp post.'

'Marilia, nothing in my background prepares me for this. I was employed as an investigative reporter for a newspaper, dealing with real issues, police corruption—'

'This is not real?'

'Can it be real that I was murdered forty-seven years ago? That I have come back from the grave?'

Marilia chuckled. 'It's real that you've come back to Rio de Janeiro. It's real that some old woman thinks so. It's real that you're not sleeping. Ah, Carnival!' Marilia said. 'People go crazy during Carnival!'

'I don't intend to be one of them.'

'Reconciling differing realities,' Marilia apparently quoted from somewhere. 'What does your education and training, as an investigative journalist, tell you to do in a situation which perplexes you?'

Fletch thought a short moment. 'Find out the story.'

'My training says that, too. So let's go find out the story. Where do the Barreto family live?'

'Someone mentioned ... Toninho mentioned ... Santos Lima. Toninho said I had lived in the *favela* Santos Lima.'

'Let's go there, then.' Marilia stood up and took the bunch of keys from her desk. 'Let's go find out the story.'

CHAPTER TWENTY-TWO

'Have you ever been in a *favela* before?' Marilia asked.

'I have been in slums before. In Los Angeles, New York, Chicago.'

They had driven slowly past The Hotel Yellow Parrot. None of the Barreto family was at that time waiting in front of the hotel.

Fletch had parked the MP where Marilia told him to, on a city street a few blocks from the base of the *favela*.

'Last week, our industrial city of São Paulo produced ten thousand Volkswagen cars,' Marilia said. 'And twelve thousand, eight hundred and fifty babies. That is the reality of Brazil.'

The *favela* of Santos Lima rose straight up a mountainside not all that far from the center of Rio de Janeiro. For the most part it was made of hovels stuck together by various materials, bits of lumber from here and there, packing crates, tar paper. A single roof might be made of over a hundred pieces of wood, tin, aluminum. A favorite patch was a flattened tin can nailed over a hole. A few were old, solid houses, all very small, and most of these had been painted at one time or another, purple, green, chartreuse. Some of the little stores, which mostly sold rice and beans and *chope*, looked somewhat permanent. As with most residential districts, the houses looked more solid, slightly more prosperous, the higher they were in the *favela*. The sewage from the higher houses flowed down muddy streets to settle under the lower houses.

As they entered the *favela* and began to climb, radios blared music from every direction. In a nearby shack, a packing crate really, a samba drum was being tuned. At a distance a large *bateria* of drums could be heard practicing.

Marilia Diniz and Fletch attracted much attention. Almost instantly they were surrounded by thirty, forty, fifty small children barefoot in the mud and sewage. The teeth of a few of the older children had rotted to stumps. Only a few of the very young had the distended bellies and skinny legs of malnutrition. Generally the bodies of the children old enough to fend and rummage for themselves, those over the age of six, although skinny, were well formed, as quick as darting fish. Their fingers tugged lightly at Marilia and Fletch; their imploring voices were low. For the most part, their eyes were bright.

'Well over half the population of Brazil is under nineteen years old,' Marilia said. 'And half of them are pregnant.'

Marilia then asked the children for directions to the home of Idalina Barreto. In response, they fought for her hand to guide her there.

Fletch followed along with his own

gaggle of children. Perhaps a dozen times he felt their hands slip into and out of the empty pockets of his shorts.

The women looked at him through their doorless doors and glassless windows with blank expressions on their worn faces, neither friendly nor unfriendly, not particularly curious. Their expressions indicated more that they were thinking about him, the life that they had glimpsed here and there; the big, clean buildings he had lived in, the airplanes he had flown in, the restaurants he had dined in, the accoutrements of his life, cars, telephones, air conditioners. There was little resentment in their look, as there was little resentment in their not being familiar with snow. His was a different life, vastly different, as different as if he had lived on Venus or Mars: too different to generate emotion.

A man called to Fletch in Portuguese from a bar counter under a tin roof. 'Come! I'll buy you a little beer!'

'Thanks,' Fletch answered in Portuguese. 'Maybe later!'

And of course Fletch wondered about their lives as he walked through their world. To do without everything he knew, even a little money, privacy, machinery, in most cases, work. To do without everything but each other. He wondered if he could adapt to such a life, but only as he wondered if he could adapt to life on Jupiter or Saturn.

As they passed a small home, a toothless, bald old woman in a rocking chair in the shade looked at Fletch through rheumy eyes. *'Janio!'* she shrieked. *'Janio Barreto!'*

She tried to get out of her chair, but fell back.

Fletch just kept moving.

As they turned the corner around a sizable pink building, Fletch spotted young Janio Barreto down the dirt track. The boy hurried away on his wooden leg— doubtless, to broadcast the news that Fletch was coming.

The Barreto home was not very high in the *favela*.

Idalina Barreto stood tall in the door to her home, hands on her hips. Janio and other small children were in front of the house. Her eyes narrowed as Marilia and Fletch approached.

'Bom dia,' Marilia said. She introduced herself. She explained that they had come to hear all about Janio Barreto and what

179

had happened to him forty-seven years before.

The hag pointed to Fletch and, in her crackly voice, asked some question about Fletch.

Marilia said, 'She wants to know if you will tell her what happened. Why you were murdered, and who murdered you.'

There was no humor, no irony, in Marilia's face.

Sleepless, slightly dizzy in the bright sunlight, surrounded by a swarm of whispering children, Fletch shook his head. 'I don't know.'

★   ★   ★

As Idalina Barreto led Marilia and Fletch into her home, she dispatched children to find various relatives and bring them here.

The inside of the house was a space protected from some of the elements by walls of many boards of different shapes and sizes, nailed together at different angles under a patched tin roof.

The interior was impeccable. The dirt floor was reasonably dry and freshly swept. Plates, pans, cups, and glasses near the basin sparkled. A round table in the center of the room was polished. On it was a pretty embroidered cloth, and on the cloth was a bowl of fresh flowers. The *calunga* doll was also on the table. Chairs of various styles and sizes were around the walls of the room.

On the wall, either side of a battery radio, were magazine pictures of Jesus and the Pope.

A vast crowd was collecting outside the house.

Marilia said, 'Idalina would like to know if you'd like coffee.'

'Yes. Thank her.'

Idalina flicked her wrist, and more children darted out.

Then she sat in a tall-backed wooden chair with wide arms. She gathered the hems of her long white dress around her ankles.

She indicated with a sweep of her hand that Marilia and Fletch should be seated in chairs of their choosing.

Fletch took a humble seat in a kitchen-styled chair.

As they waited silently, children brought them cups of very strong, very sweet coffee.

A few adults came into the room, four women, two men. They were introduced to

Fletch as Idalina's children and grandchildren. Fletch stood to greet each of them and didn't really get their names.

Each stared at him, round-eyed. They didn't seem willing or able to breathe normally. They backed into chairs along the walls.

Finally, the one for whom everyone apparently had been waiting arrived: a man in his fifties, shirtless, in proper black shorts and sandals. His hair was neatly combed.

'I speak English,' he said, shaking Fletch's hand. 'I am Janio Barreto Filho. I have worked many years as a waiter, in Copacabana.' He stared into Fletch's eyes a long, breathless moment. Then, old enough to be Fletch's father, he said, 'I am your son.' In one movement, he hugged Fletch to him and embraced him hard. There was a choked sob in Fletch's ear. 'We are so glad you have come back.'

CHAPTER TWENTY-THREE

'I will speak English so good as I can,' the middle-aged Janio Barreto Filho said.

'Mother says to me you want me to bring to life for you the facts of what happened.'

'Yes,' Fletch said. 'Please.'

'If this will help you tell us who murdered you . . .'

Barreto Filho sat in a cushioned chair along the back wall of the house. Stately as a duchess, Idalina Barreto sat in her tall chair along the side wall. Fletch and Marilia sat along the other side wall.

Adult relatives sat in the other chairs. Four stood near the door. Children sat on the dirty floor. The windows were filled with people listening.

The area in front of the house was crowded with people.

From somewhere in the neighborhood the distinct sound of a television ceased.

But, of course, practicing drums could still be heard.

As Janio Barreto Filho spoke, he was interrupted, questioned, reminded, and corrected by his mother and other adults inside and outside the house. Marilia helped to translate the difficult parts.

Listening intently, as the room under the tin roof in the sun became hotter, the air thicker, Fletch put together a continuous narrative to take away with him, to dissect and analyse later.

This may be a story, Janio Barreto Filho said, of a father who may have been right.

After all these years, my mother would like to know.

My father, Janio Barreto, was a handsome man, fair of hair and skin, well built, very lively, believed to be the best dancer in all the *favela*, maybe all of Rio de Janeiro. At least people say they enjoyed watching him the most. Sometimes, serving young people from North America, one or two from Chile or Argentina, in the hotels of Copacabana, I have thought of him, as this was always as he was described to me, light in color and as unconcerned with the sad little things in life as a rich person.

It is said he came from near São Paulo, perhaps the descendant of one of the North Americans from the South of the United States who came to that area at the end of your Civil War, to try to continue their plantation, slave-owning lives there. Many such came, and, of course, such is the beauty and seductiveness of our women, it was not long before they too became a part of the Brazilian population, their children having black and Indian blood and therefore unable to keep their brothers and sisters in bondage.

But you were truly fair, and came to the *favela* Santos Lima like a welcome thunder-storm in midwinter heat, casting your bolts of lightning everywhere. Why you came here, perhaps you could tell us now.

You were fourteen or fifteen when you arrived, full of your juices, full of laughs and smiles, being here, there, everywhere at once. As soon as you came to the *favela*, everyone could not have enough news of you: *Where is Janio? What has Janio done now? Did you hear what Janio did last night?* When the pantaloons of the corrupt policeman were pasted on the statue of Saint Francis, when the new bicycle of the storekeeper was found in a bedroom of the brothel, when the shit-dam suddenly appeared around the big house a few of the faithful had built for the strict North American missionary, everyone knew you did it, and laughed with you, and stroked your fair hair.

The prestige of any girl you lay with rose in the *favela*. I suppose some of the girls lied about this, as it seems impossible to me—a man who enjoys life as much as any other—that one boy could have granted such prestige to so very many girls. In my own youth, being your acknowledged son, too much was expected of me. Going down the street I had to protect myself, not only from girls, but from their mothers as well. It is true that the *favela* Santos Lima is known to have many more fair people than any other *favela* in Rio de Janeiro.

Of course you took on friends, a gang of three or four boys, two of whom were Idalina's brothers. Together you spent the days on the beaches, wrestling, swimming, playing soccer, the nights drinking and dancing and gambling, increasing the prestige of girls individually and raising mischief.

Now, Idalina's father was a man of great dignity. Although he worked as a conductor on a trolley car, he spent his life studying to be a bookkeeper. He never succeeded in finding work as a bookkeeper, but he prepared himself. It was his fervent wish at least to hand on to his sons the idea of being a bookkeeper.

He did not share in the *favela*'s general idolatry of Janio Barreto. He felt you were leading his sons astray, giving them a liveliness that was not natural to them or in keeping with the idea of keeping books.

Through people he knew at the samba school, finally he succeeded in getting his sons jobs on a fishing boat. But the old men who owned the fishing boat made the condition highly irksome to old Fernando that they would only hire his sons to work on the fishing boat if they could hire Janio Barreto as well. Whether the idea was that they believed my uncles needed your leadership and brains, even though at first you knew nothing about the sea, being from the interior of Brazil, or whether it was the idea of the elders to get you to sea and therefore away from the *favela* some hours of the week and therefore cut down on the mischief and population growth, or whether they wanted, by being your employers, to be the first to know and tell of your pranks is unknown to me. To get his sons employed, Fernando had no choice but to agree.

187

So you went on the fishing boat with the Gomes brothers, and soon there were stories of a dead cold fish five feet long being put in the bed of the most precise bachelor in the *favela* while he slept (it was sad he never slept in his bed or ate fish again), of a fishing-boat race which caused an older captain, whom you had taunted unmercifully, to become so determined to win at any cost that he rammed his own dock under full sail at such high speed he smashed his boat to slivers.

Fernando put up with all this with resignation. At least his sons had jobs, and there was hope that after a while working hard at sea, they would come to the idea of bookkeeping.

But when you began to call upon his daughter Idalina, coo to her through the window, spread flowers you stole from the cemetery all over the roof of the house, Fernando went into a rage.

Nor did he consider it funny when, on the night of his Saint's Day and perhaps he had had a bit too much to drink and lay in a stupor, you came along and shaved off only half of his mustache.

Then, at the age of eighteen, when

most young men consider it wise and appropriate to be humble, apparently goaded by Fernando's open disapproval of you, you announced to the whole *favela* your intention of making Idalina your wife.

The *favela* was delighted. They knew marriage would do you no harm, not slow you down or make you less entertaining.

Idalina was delighted. It did not disturb her to be marrying the liveliest boy in the *favela*, or that her bond to you in marriage would have to be made of elastic.

Fernando fell into a mood so black for weeks he could not think of bookkeeping. He spent his time keeping his eye on Idalina. He argued with the air.

'Am I the only sane man in the world to see that Janio Barreto is a bad boy and no match for my Idalina? He has done enough to me, in keeping my sons from thinking in assets and debits! Why does he want a wife when he has every girl in the *favela* spitting at each other over him? He will never stop! Does he want to marry my daughter and continue his wild life just to torment me? It is as natural for him to be a husband as it is for a tomcat to pull a wagon!

'Idalina, he is no good! At the first difficulties of life, he will wander away! Already he has wandered from his home once! I want to know why! Once a man has wandered from his home, he is never to be trusted! He will wander again!

'Believe me, he will end up beaten in a gutter! That will not be a husband to be proud of!

'Probably dead! Some day someone will put a knife to him, and that will be the end of your husband, Janio Barreto, and of your marriage!'

The weight of the *favela* was on the side of the young lovers, of course, as people who are not directly involved in a situation always prefer romance to reason, and while Fernando stewed in his deep gloom, you and Idalina were married.

Now, as you must remember, not only were you known to be able to dance better and for a longer time than anyone, with more admiring eyes upon you, also you brought to the *favela* many new things about kick-dancing, *capoeira*, it

190

being a skill which really developed in the interior. You taught the young men in Santos Lima more about *capoeira* than people knew in all the other *favelas* in Rio.

At that time, the Carnival Parade was beginning to become more organized from just a street competition among the *favelas* to the more formal presentation and attraction it is today.

Immediately, the samba school of Santos Lima became most famous for its troupe of *capoeiristas* you had trained. Santos Lima still has the reputation as having the best *capoeira* group in Rio de Janeiro.

But the first prophecy of Fernando came true.

You did not return immediately from Carnival that year. For days afterwards you were missing.

Finally you returned to Santos Lima from somewhere in the city. It was clear you had been physically beaten, and very badly. Your body was black with bruises. There were knife cuts on your upper arms and shoulders. Your face was as lumpy and welted as the bed of a couple married fifty years. You dragged yourself home like a beaten dog. Obviously, you had ended up beaten in a gutter.

People remarked, in hushed voices, the change in you. Silently you sat in your little house, licking your wounds. You never said what happened. You spoke to no one. Your laughter was not heard anywhere in the *favela*. You never went out and embarrassed Idalina by being with other women, to such an extent Idalina was beginning to lose her pride in you.

This is as I have the story from my mother and my uncles. Is your life beginning to come alive for you?

Then the second prophecy of Fernando came true.

After sitting quietly at home, not working, not playing, for almost all of Lent, you rose up and, carrying nothing, taking nothing with you except the working shorts you wore roped around your waist, you walked down the *favela* without a salutation to anyone, and disappeared. You wandered away.

Everyone was sure you were gone for good. Fun had gone from the *favela*.

Everyone commiserated with Fernando for having an abandoned

daughter and two small grandchildren living out of his pocket, and congratulated him on the accuracy of his prophecies.

But the next winter, nine months later, you came back. You sailed into Guanabara Bay in a fishing boat you said was your own, a big boat ten meters long. You said you won it playing cards in Uruguay. The name painted on her side was in Spanish, *La Muñeca*. Surely you had sailed a long way. You were as thin as a street dog and very badly sunburned across your nose and shoulders. Some people said you went to Uruguay and stole the boat. Did you?

So now you had your own fishing boat.

In the inactivity caused by your absence, one of the Gomes brothers had become too fat to fish, the other too drunken. They both said they wanted to stay ashore now and think about bookkeeping.

You took on another young man, younger than you, named Tobias Novaes, to help you fish.

You worked hard. Shortly, you had a house near the top of the *favela*, higher even than Fernando's house. And for every married year, you had a child from your wife, Idalina. And every one of those children had children to play with their own ages who were also partly fair and looked as much like them as cousins.

At about your present age, it happened that a girl younger than you, who was as fair of hair and skin as yourself, came to the *favela*. Immediately, the *favela* said, 'Oh, poor Idalina! This one will be serious! If they love themselves, how can they not love each other?'

And it was noticed that you became more serious then, worked longer hours, seldom looked up from your work. It was as if you were trying to ignore the inevitable: Ana Tavares, her name was.

But the inevitable is the inevitable, and as if your seed were transmitted by the wind, it was soon seen that Ana Tavares was glowing in her pregnancy.

This was especially noted as Ana Tavares was only waiting out the year to be old enough to join the convent of The Sacred Heart of Jesus. People marveled that a girl who spent so many hours of the day and the night kneeling before the statue of the Blessed Virgin could become pregnant. They attributed it to the wind.

Spending just as much time in prayer as always, Ana did not explain or complain.

Her father, however, whose life had not been as saintly as is recommended, was outraged. It had been his fondest wish to have a daughter a nun to pray for his soul before and after it departed.

You, having no father or brothers to attack, and being too young and strong, too expert a *capoeirista*, to attack, laughed for days after old Tavares attacked your father-in-law, Fernando, for his trouble-making son-in-law. Your father-in-law did not defend you. He too carried such rage at you that he yelled back at Tavares, and the two fathers of women became so enraged thinking about you that soon they were beating each other with their fists, then rolling on the ground, apparently fighting about which had the greater rage against you.

In truth, the son of Ana Tavares was entirely fair. She became the wife of a carpenter, and the boy—most likely another of your sons—became a *Puxador de Samba*, a singer of great repute in the samba school.

Yes, Oswaldinho there, in the window, is a son of that son of yours. You see how fair he is? Clearly, he has your blood, as have I.

Then the third prophecy of old Fernando came true—really came true.

One night you did not come home. You did not come home most nights. You were still young and perhaps by now considered it your obligation to entertain the *favela* with your tricks and to continue increasing your ever-growing audience by copulation.

But after this night in particular, after a heavy sea storm, you were found on the beach, face down, with your throat slit ear to ear. Your blood had drained from your neck into the sand. Your shorts and hair and skin were caked with salt water, as if you had swum a long way to shore.

People say that in that particular spot on the beach, it has been impossible to light a fire or even light a match, ever since.

Your boat, *La Muñeca*, was missing, and never seen again.

Never seen again also was the boy who had helped you on the boat, Tobias Novaes.

For many years it was believed you had been murdered by young Tobias, although that surprised people, as it was generally believed he was a good boy. People thought he had slit your throat and stolen your boat.

But years later, his father got a letter from him, saying he had become a monk in Recife. Instantly, they had a letter written to him, asking if he had murdered you and stolen your boat.

The answer came back, eventually, that he hadn't known you were dead and that he felt himself greatly indebted to you as it was your example, and the example of your life, which had made the unworldly, serene, contemplative life of a monk seem so ideal to him.

For all these years your murder has been a mystery. There were so many people who could have killed you. Someone in the *favela* who did not like a trick you played on him? Did Tobias murder you for the boat? Did Uruguayans come and murder you and take back their boat? Or had the boat wrecked in the storm? How about old Tavares? He believed your preventing his daughter, Ana, from becoming a nun, surely condemned him to hell. . . ?

My grandfather Fernando made three predictions about you. That you would end up beaten in the gutter. You were beaten up, but you survived it, became your old self again. That, sooner or later, you would wander away. You did, but you came back. That some day, someone would take a knife to you and kill you. That happened.

My mother, Idalina, who is very old now, as you see, wants to know the truth of these things. Who murdered you, and why?

How is it that her father was so right about you?

CHAPTER TWENTY-FOUR

'What Laura says is true,' Fletch said to Marilia Diniz across the lunch table. 'Anyone can tell you any story, and say it is the past.'

Leaving *favela* Santos Lima totally unsatisfied, Fletch and Marilia led a parade of plucking pixies and curious adults down the hill and along the city street to his car.

He had made his courtesies, thanked Janio Barreto Filho for the story, shaken hands with all the adults, thanked Idalina for her coffee and hospitality, generally wished the *favela* well in the parade of the samba schools that night, but left the airless little house as soon as he could. The heat in the room had become almost unbearable. But the eyes of everyone told him how unsatisfied they were. They had expected the story of Janio Barreto to bring his memories alive so he could tell them before leaving who had been his murderer.

Solemnly, Fletch promised he would think over the whole story.

He and Marilia drove to Colombo, a sparkling clean tearoom noted for its great pastry.

Marilia asked, 'Do you still think it is a joke being played on you by Laura and the Tap Dancers?'

'I don't see how it can be. All those people in the door and windows, all those people in the street had heard the story before, knew parts of it well enough to correct Janio, add elements to it—and all with high seriousness. If it is a trick, it's the most elaborate trick conceivable.'

Their waffles were warm and tender.

199

'You have heard the story now,' Marilia said. 'What is the answer?'

'How would I know?'

Marilia's eyes flickered at him. 'All right. But use what you do know, use your training. You were trained as an investigative reporter . . .'

'Yeah: investigating how come the city's water pipes run an extra five kilometers to avoid the property owned by the water commissioner. Big deal. This is not quite the same sort of situation.'

'Nevertheless . . .'

'Investigative reporters do not make guesses just to satisfy people with a conclusion to a story.'

'But investigative reporters do think, don't they?'

'Think about documented facts. How can I think about something that happened on a beach in Rio de Janeiro forty-seven years ago? However long I am in Brazil, I will never be that prescient. Or postscient.'

'What will you tell them?'

Fletch made sure there was syrup on each part of his waffle. 'I suppose I'll tell them the kindest thing I can think of: Uruguayans came and slit his throat and took their boat back. It would be kinder than blaming someone in the *favela* dead or alive.'

'Janio said he won the boat playing cards.' Marilia chewed thoughtfully. 'There is some evidence he did.'

'What evidence?'

'If you stole the boat, even from a different country, wouldn't you change its name?'

'Of course. I suppose so.'

'The name of the boat was in Spanish. *La Muñeca*. He never changed its name. They said after Janio was found dead, *La Muñeca* was missing. Never seen again.'

Fletch sighed.

Marilia said, 'And if Uruguayans killed Janio Barreto, why didn't they kill Tobias Novaes as well? He would have been on the boat with Janio.'

'Perhaps the Uruguayans appeared after they docked.'

'Could be,' Marilia said.

'After Tobias wandered off to become a monk. Marilia, that's too big a coincidence in timing. How could Tobias wander off to become a monk without telling anyone what he was doing, just before Janio got his throat slit?'

'There had been a storm at sea. I have

heard of people becoming very religious, very suddenly, during storms at sea. They make deals. Spare my life, oh Lord, and I will devote the rest of my life to singing Thy praises.'

'Maybe.'

'I think the boat sank. And both Janio and Tobias swam ashore. Tobias to join a monastery; Janio to get his throat slit.'

'That's fine. It's great to guess. But how can we know?'

Again, Marilia's eyes flickered.

Fletch said, 'Tobias himself is a good bet as the murderer. Surely he wouldn't be the first to commit a heinous crime and then, after a while, so weighted with guilt, he hies off to a monastery to spend the rest of his life atoning.'

'True. Tobias could have killed Janio. He could have stolen the boat. But after years of being a monk, could he have lied about it?'

Somewhat in imitation of Tito Granja, Fletch crossed his eyes.

'After years of atonement,' Marilia said, 'Tobias would know he would be risking his soul to lie.'

'"Risking his soul,"' Fletch repeated. 'That brings up the father of the girl who

202

was going to be a nun. What was his name? Tavares. Apparently he thought he was going to end up in hell anyway. Why wouldn't he have killed Janio?'

'He might have. Still, murder is the greatest crime. And there is always the possibility of personal salvation.'

Fletch looked at Marilia's bracelet. It was made of rotting braided cloth. He had seen many such bracelets in Brazil. He had difficulty understanding the significance of them.

'Fernando,' Fletch said. 'Idalina's father. Certainly he hated Janio. Over a long period of time. He got into a fistfight over him.'

'Kill his son-in-law? Leave his daughter a widow, his grandchildren fatherless?' Slowly, Marilia said, 'I suppose so. Fernando apparently thought Janio not a very good husband or father.'

'And he had reasons to be envious of him. Fernando could never find work as a bookkeeper. Then Janio shows up with his own boat. Becomes a prosperous man. Even gets to live in a house higher up in the *favela* than Fernando.'

Marilia, a slim, trim woman, surprised Fletch by ordering one of the bigger, more sugary pastries.

Fletch said, 'You know, once you make prophecies about someone, there is the instinct to help them become fulfilled.'

'Fernando said someone would take a knife to Janio and kill him, and it wasn't happening fast enough to satisfy Fernando, so he did the job himself?'

'I suppose prophets have to work at their reputations, as much as anyone else.'

'Mmmmm. So what will you do, Fletcher? What will you tell these people?'

'I don't know. I'm not about to point the finger at a monk. Or at the grandfather of the family. Or at the memory of some other deceased citizen whose daughter was deflowered by the victim. Any one of hundreds of people could have done in Janio.'

'Now that you've heard the story, will you be able to sleep?'

'Will I?'

They finished their pastries in silence.

Fletch said, 'Marilia, tell me about that bracelet you're wearing.'

Self-consciously she touched it with the fingers of her other hand. 'Oh, that.'

'I see many people, men and women, wearing these cloth, braided bracelets.'

'Just a superstition, I guess.' Her face flushed. 'You make a wish, you know, for something you hope will come true. As you make the wish, you put on this braided bracelet. You wear it until what you wish for comes true.'

'Supposing what you wish for doesn't come true?'

Slightly red-faced she laughed. 'Then you wear it until it falls off.'

'You believe in such a thing?'

'No,' she said quickly.

'But you're wearing such a bracelet.'

'Why not?' she asked, resettling it on her wrist. 'It does no harm to act as if you believe in such a thing, just in case it is true.'

*   *   *

Outside the restaurant they stopped at a kiosk. Marilia bought *Jornal do Brasil* and Fletch bought *Brazil Herald* and the *Latin America Daily Post*.

A healthy-seeming curly-haired man of about thirty was leaning against Fletch's MP. It appeared he was waiting for them.

He spoke rapidly, happily to Fletch.

Then, seeing he wasn't being understood, he spoke to Marilia.

She answered him, happily enough. While talking with him, she opened the small purse tied to her wrist, took out some money, and gave it to him.

The man stuffed the money into his shoe.

Then he leaned against the next car, a Volkswagen bug.

In the car, Fletch asked, 'What did he want?'

'Ohhhh. He said he had been taking care of the car for us while we were away. It is for him to take care of the cars along this section of curb, he said.'

'Is it?'

'He says so.'

'Who gave him charge of this section of curb?'

'No one. It is just something he says.'

Fletch started the car. 'If it is just something he says, then why did you give him the money? Why didn't you just tell him to get lost?'

Flustered, Marilia was looking into her handbag, perhaps rearranging the interior. 'I suppose I owe it to him because I just had such a nice lunch.'

CHAPTER TWENTY-FIVE

'Fletch?'

'Yes?'

'Toninho Braga, Fletch. Look what time it is.'

'Shortly after noon.'

'That's right. And so far no one has reported finding Norival's body.'

Over the phone, Toninho's voice sounded more hushed than alarmed.

Fletch had driven Marilia Diniz to her home in Leblon, thanked her for accompanying him to the *favela*, repeated he still had no way of solving a forty-seven-year-old murder mystery, but he would return to the hotel to try to sleep.

His room at The Hotel Yellow Parrot had been cleaned. The unslept-in bed had been freshly made up.

He telephoned The Hotel Jangada and asked for Joan Collins Stanwyk in room 912.

No answer.

Across the utility area, the man was still painting the room.

He was about to strip, to shower, to

darken the room, to get into bed again, to try to sleep, when the phone rang.

'Toninho,' he said. 'It's Sunday. A big day of Carnival. Communication is slow.'

'That's exactly it, Fletch. There would have been hundreds, thousands of people on that beach, shortly after dawn.'

'Finding a body—'

'Norival is not just a body. He is a Passarinho. That would be news.'

'First the police have to be summoned—'

'Yes, the police would be summoned. But we left plenty of identification on Norival's body. The people who found the body would be quick to tell the Passarinho family, the radio stations. The police would be even quicker. They would compete for the attention of the Passarinho family.'

'I don't see what you're saying. You put Norival's body in the water. He was dead. He has to come ashore somewhere, sometime, if you were right about the tides.'

'I was right about the tides. Where's Norival?'

'How would I know?'

Fletch looked down at the soft, smooth countenance of the bed.

'Fletch, we must go make sure someone finds the body of Norival.'

'Toninho, I'm not sure I can take many more disappearances today, of persons dead and alive.'

'You must come help us look, Fletch. That will make four of us. We can comb the beach.'

'You want to go beachcombing for a corpse?'

'What else can we do? We put Norival's body there to be found, not to be lost. What if he were lost forever? There would be no Funeral Mass. He would not be properly buried. His family might think he ran away.'

'His boat would be missing.'

'Sailed away. To Argentina! Think of his poor mother!'

'His poor mother.'

'Such a thing would kill her. Not to know what happened to her son.'

'Toninho . . . I still have not slept.'

'That's all right.'

'"All right"?'

'You must help us. Four searching is better than three searching. It is a long beach.'

'Toninho . . .'

'We'll pick you up in ten minutes.'
The phone line died.

CHAPTER TWENTY-SIX

'Perhaps we should check with Eva,' Tito said. 'Norival might have gone back to her.'

'Norival was happy with Eva,' Orlando said.

Of the four young men walking along the beach, only Fletch wore sandals. He knew himself not sufficiently *carioca* to walk along a beach in the midday sun in bare feet.

Toninho, Tito, and Orlando had picked Fletch up in the black four-door Galaxie.

On the sidewalk in front of the hotel, the youngest Janio Barreto on a wooden leg silently watched Fletch get into the car and be driven away.

The drive to the beach where Norival was scheduled to appear had been as fast as possible through the Carnival crowds.

At one place on Avenida Atlantica perhaps as many as a thousand people in tattery costumes jumped up and down around a big samba band moving forward only a few meters an hour on the back of a flatbed truck. Never had he seen so much human energy spent in so little forward motion.

On the way to the beach they listened silently to the loud car radio.

The discovery of Norival Passarinho's body was not yet news.

The beach was filled with bright umbrellas, mats. Families and other groups picnicked and played.

Orlando said to Fletch: 'It is said if a person dies copulating, he is guaranteed to return to life soon.'

'For Norival, the process might have been very quick,' said Tito.

Spread apart only somewhat, they walked along the water's edge, looking for Norival perhaps washed up dead but thought asleep, some crowd of gossips with news of something unusual having happened, the corpse of the Passarinho boy being found, police barriers, markers, something, anything.

'Do people say the same thing in the United States of North America?' Orlando asked.

'I don't think so,' Fletch said. 'I never heard it.'

'People in the United States of North

America don't die while copulating,' Toninho said. 'They die while talking about it.'

'They die while talking to their psychiatrists about it,' Orlando laughed.

'Yes, yes,' said Toninho. 'They die worrying about copulating.'

'People of the United States of North America,' Tito scoffed. 'This is how they walk.'

Tito began to move hurriedly over the sand, his head and shoulders forward of his body, legs straight, not pivoting his hips at all, his hands dangling loosely beside him like a couple of cow udders, his eyes staring straight ahead, an expectant grin on his face, each foot landing flat on the sand. The impression was of a body being pushed at the shoulders, falling forward, each foot coming out and landing at the last second to keep the body from falling flat on its face.

Fletch stopped walking and laughed.

For a while, then, he walked slightly behind his friends.

'Yes,' Tito said. 'Norival may have revived.'

Fletch asked, 'Is it true everyone goes slightly crazy during Carnival?'

Toninho said, 'Slightly.'

212

'If the way to life eternal,' Fletch asked, 'is to die copulating, then why don't people just copulate constantly?'

Orlando sniffed. 'I do my best.'

A man carrying two metal cylinders containing iced maté passed them. Each container easily weighed one hundred pounds. He would sell the maté in little cups to people on the beach. The man was in his sixties and he was walking rapidly enough to pass the four young men. His legs looked like the roots of trees hardened by time.

'This is crazy,' Fletch said. Perhaps lying in the sun on the beach would make him drowsy enough to sleep.

Dead wallets, stolen and emptied, were on the beach like birds shot from the sky.

Toninho scanned the surface of the ocean. 'There is not even a sign of his boat. That, too, should have come ashore.'

'The boat sank,' Tito said.

'Maybe Norival sank,' Orlando said.

'Maybe Norival is alive and we are dead,' Fletch said.

Orlando looked at him as if he had just offered a possibility worth consideration.

They were coming to the end of the beach.

Nearby was a group of very young teenage girls in bikinis. Five of the eight were pregnant.

Toninho said, 'Absolutely, Norival was to come ashore somewhere along here.'

'Let's ask,' Fletch said. 'Let's ask the people on the beach if they've noticed a Passarinho floating by without a boat.'

'It leaves only one thing to do,' Toninho said.

'Go home to bed,' Fletch said.

'Swim along the beach,' Toninho said.

'Oh, no,' Fletch said.

Toninho was looking into the water. 'It is possible Norival is lurking somewhere just below the surface.'

'That would be just like Norival,' Orlando said. 'Playing some trick.'

'*Arigó*,' Toninho said.

'I need sleep,' Fletch said. 'Not a swim.'

'Yes,' Tito said, 'Norival was apt to be a bit slow, sometimes, to show up.'

'Last night, when I swam into Norival,' Toninho said, 'he was more under the surface than I would have expected.'

'Right,' said Tito. 'We shall swim along the shore and see if we bump into Norival.'

'Oh, no,' said Fletch.

'Leave your sandals here,' said Orlando.

'Not even a North American can swim well wearing sandals.'

★ ★ ★

On the way back in the car they listened to a long news broadcast. Mostly, it was about Carnival Parade that night, and certain controversies which had arisen concerning it. One samba school was insisting the theme they had chosen to present had been usurped a little bit by another samba school. At least, the themes of the two schools were believed by one school to be dangerously similar.

In all that long broadcast, the discovery of the corpse of Norival Passarinho was not reported.

CHAPTER TWENTY-SEVEN

'You're not becoming a Brazilian,' Laura Soares said over the dinner table. 'You're becoming a Carnival Brazilian.'

When Fletch dragged himself back to his room at The Hotel Yellow Parrot, sunburned, caked with salt, the bottoms of

215

his feet fried from just the walk up the beach from the ocean to the car, Laura was waiting for him, curled up in a chair studying sheet music, full of questions about where they would dine, full of enthusiasm for spending the night watching the Carnival Parade from Teodomiro da Costa's box.

Tiredly, he greeted her. She helped him shower. On the bed he wanted to sleep. She teased him into giving her a warmer greeting than he thought possible in his sleepless condition. They showered again.

She was dressing when he came out of the bathroom.

On the white trousers and white shirt he had laid out to wear that night, she had placed a wide, bright red sash.

'Is this for me?' he asked.

'From Bahia.'

'Am I to wear it?'

'To the Carnival Parade. You will look very Brazilian.'

'I am to wear a red sash without a coat?'

'Why would anyone wear a coat over such a beautiful red sash?'

'Wow.' After he dressed, she helped him adjust it. 'I feel like a Christmas present.'

'You are a Christmas present. A jolly

Christmas present wrapped in a red ribbon for Laura.'

They decided to dine in the dining room which was on the second floor of The Hotel Yellow Parrot.

Through the floor-to-ceiling open windows they could see the *macumba* fires on *Praia de Copacabana*. Believers spend the night on the beach tending a fire, having written a wish, or the name of their illness, on a piece of paper which they launch in the first moments of the outgoing tide. On the first night of the year especially there are thousands of fires on the beach.

The hotel restaurant was said to be one of the best in the world. It was rare in that the restaurant's kitchen was exactly twice as big as the seating area.

They ordered *moqueca*, another Bahian speciality.

'You did not even read Amado's *Dona Flor and Her Two Husbands* while I was gone.'

'Tell me about it.'

'You said you could not sleep, of course, but you did not even read.'

'Somehow I kept busy.'

'Gambling with the Tap Dancers?'

'I relieved them of some of their

217

inheritances.'

'I dare not even ask you about this country inn they took you to.'

'It had a swimming pool.'

'Riding around all day. So late to the Canecão Ball. Cristina said you were dressed as a movie cowboy.'

'An outfit I borrowed from Toninho.'

'I saw it in the closet.'

'I looked real sleek.'

'That you danced hours with that French film star, Jetta.'

'There was no one else to dance with her.'

'I'm sure.' Laura mixed her *pirao* with her *farofa com dendê*. 'Brazilians are not like this all the time. Only during Carnival. Brazilians are a very serious people.'

'I'm sure.'

'Look at our big buildings. Our factories. Our biggest-in-the-world hydroelectric plant. Everything here runs by computer now. At the airport, all the public announcements, in each language, are done by computer voices. And you can understand what they are saying perfectly.'

Through the window Fletch started to count the *macumba* fires on the beach.

'Marilia Diniz and I went this morning to

the *favela* Santos Lima to see the Barreto family, to hear the story of Janio Barreto's life and death.'

Laura did not seem interested in that. 'You should read the novels of Nelida Piñon. Then you would know something of Brazilian life. Not just Carnival foolishness. Things are very different here in Brazil.'

'I know,' he said. 'The water goes down the drain counter-clockwise.'

'Anyway...' She removed a bone from her fish. 'Last night, in Bahia, I agreed finally to do this concert tour.'

'Concert tour? You're going on a concert tour?'

'Pianists who stop playing the piano stop being pianists,' she said.

'Where are you going? When?'

'In about a month. Bahia first, then São Paulo, Rio de Janeiro, Recife. Friends of my father have been urging me to do this, setting it up for some time.'

'I guess they want you to get serious.'

'I am an educated pianist. I've had good reviews. I like the idea of bringing so much Brazilian music to the piano.'

'You will have to work very hard to go on such a tour.'

'Very hard.'

'Practice a lot.'

'A very lot.'

'Do you want dessert?'

'Of course.'

They ordered cherry tarts.

'Fletcher,' she asked, 'what are you serious about?'

'Sleeping.'

'Serious.'

'I'm serious about sleeping.'

'Sleeping is necessary, I guess.'

'I am seriously worried. You remember that woman I was to have breakfast with yesterday morning at The Hotel Jangada?'

'Who is she?'

'The woman in the green dress we saw on the *avenida*.'

'You didn't want to see her.'

'I do now. Her name is Joan Collins Stanwyk. She's from California.'

'That was clear, from looking at her. Her eyes looked as if she were watching a movie.'

'She's disappeared.'

'People disappear in Brazil, Fletch.' Laura didn't seem to want to hear about that, either. 'What time are we to arrive at Carnival Parade?'

'Teo suggested about ten o'clock. I doubt

he'll be there much earlier than that.'

'I've never watched Carnival Parade from a box before.'

'I think he suspects this is the only year I'll be here for it.'

Laura said nothing.

For a moment, Fletch watched her finish her cherry tart.

Then Fletch gazed through the window at the *macumba* fires on the moonless beach. A cheer was sent up from a samba crowd on the *avenida*.

He said, 'Carnival . . .'

'The point of it is to remember that things are not always as they appear.'

CHAPTER TWENTY-EIGHT

'Welcome to the Samba School Parade!' Teodomiro da Costa said in the tone of a ring-master. He stood just inside the door of his box overlooking the parade route. He wore jeans and a T-shirt. On front of the T-shirt were printed a black bow tie and ruffles. In a more personal tone, he asked, 'Have you eaten?'

'At the hotel.'

He looked into Fletch's eyes and spoke just loudly enough for Fletch to hear him over the fantastic noise. 'You have not slept.'

'Not yet.'

'Have a drink.'

'*Guaraná*, please.'

Teo repeated the order to the barman.

'Laura!' Teo hugged her to his chest. 'Did Otavio get home all right?'

'Of course. He just pretended to need help.'

'I think that's what you do with daughters. You pretend to need their help when, actually, you do.'

The box was bigger than Fletch had expected, big enough for twenty people to move around in comfortably, to see, even dance, plus room for the sandwiches and drinks table, the barman.

Adrian Fawcett, the writer for *The Times*, was there, the Vianas, the da Silvas, the London broker and his wife, the Italian racing car driver and his girl friend. Jetta looked at Fletch with the resentment of someone who had been danced with but not loved. She did not look at Laura at all.

Everyone marveled at everyone else's costumes, of course. Laura was dressed as

222

an eighteenth-century musician, in breeches and knee socks, ruffled shirt front, gray wig. The Viana woman asked Laura if she had brought her piano to accompany her costume.

As Fletch moved forward in the box, glass of *guaraná* in hand, he had the sensation that Rio's volume knob was being turned up. Thousands of drums were being played in the area. Hundreds of thousands of people were singing and chattering and cheering.

Across the parade route, the stands were a sea of faces inclined toward the sky. Above the bright lights aimed on the route, thick, hot, smoky air visibly rolled up the stands and formed a thin gray cloud overhead.

'Rio de Janeiro's Carnival Parade Class One-A is the biggest, most amazing human spectacle in the world,' Teodomiro da Costa had said, inviting Fletch. 'Except war.'

The parade starts at six o'clock Sunday afternoon and continues until past noon Monday. About twelve samba schools, of more than three thousand costumed people each, compete in the parade.

'I'm not sure I can stand three more days

of Carnival.' Even speaking over the noise, Adrian Fawcett's voice was a deep rumbling chuckle. 'Days of elation or depression have the same effect on people, you know. I'm drained already.'

'It's a mark of character to be able to survive Carnival intact,' Laura answered. 'It's a matter of having the right attitudes.'

She beamed at Fletch.

Fletch said: 'It's all beyond belief.'

'Next is *Escola Guarnieri*.' Teo peered over the rail at the *bateria* in the bull pen. 'Yes, that's Guarnieri.' Then he said to Fletch, 'After that comes *Escola Santos Lima*.'

The parade route, on Avenida Marques de Sapucai, is only a mile long.

To the left along the parade route are the stands, built as high as most buildings, crammed with tens of thousands of people. They arrive in the stands, take and protect their seats, bake in the sun, eat their sandwiches, hold their bladders, chatter and sing beginning at noon, a full six hours before the parade starts. Almost all stay in their seats for the full twenty-four hours.

To the right along the parade route are the boxes, vastly expensive vantage points, some done up in bunting. In the boxes are government dignitaries, Brazilian and foreign celebrities, and people who are simply rich.

The parade route between its two sides is as wide as a three-lane road.

It is as wide as the line between shade and sun, sickness and health, tin and gold.

Also along the right-hand side of the route, ten meters high in the air, are the watchtowers where sit the various parade judges, one for costumes, one for floats, one for music, one for dancing, etc. They sit immobile, expressionless, alone, many behind dark sunglasses so that not even a flicker of an eye may be a subject of comment and controversy. Their names are not released to the public until the day of the parade. And so complicated and controversial is their task that the results of their judging are not announced until four days later, on Thursday.

Diagonally across the parade route from da Costa's box, to the left, is the bull pen filled with hundreds of costumed *ritmistas*, the *bateria* of drummers of *Escola Guarnieri*. Their drums are of all sizes and tones. It takes the drummers up to an hour to put themselves into their proper places in regard to each other, to get their rhythms up, their sound up. Now their rhythm and their sound are full, and fill everyone at the parade, fill their ears, their brains, their entire nervous systems, control the beatings of their hearts, make their eyes flush with blood, their hands and feet move involuntarily, their bones to vibrate. This is total sound, amplified only by human will, as primitive a sound as Man ever made, the sound of drums, calling from every human, direct, immediate response, equalizing them in their numbness before the sound.

Everyone in da Costa's box is standing at the rail. Laura has taken off her wig and opened the collar of her eighteenth-century-styled shirt. The faces of everyone at the rail shine with sweat. Their eyes, their lips protrude slightly, as if the sound of the drums reverberating within them were seeking a way to burst out of them. The veins at their temples throb visibly to the beat of the drums. Being host, Teo stands back behind the people at the rail. Being tall, he can still see everything.

Down the parade route from the left, passing the *bateria* in the bull pen like the top of a T comes the *Abre-Alas*, the opening wing of Guarnieri's presentation. This group of *sambistas*, moving of course to the sound of the drums, wear bright, ornate, slightly exaggerated costumes presenting a hint of the time and place of the samba school's theme, in this case nineteenth-century Amazon plantation ball gowns, their hoop skirts a little too wide, the bodices a little too grand, the bouffants a little too high; for the men, spats a little too long, frock coats a little too wide in the shoulders, top hats a little too high. This is the slave's view of plantation life. The exaggeration is a making fun. The exaggeration also expresses victory over such a life.

Immediately behind the *Abre-Alas* comes a huge float stating the literary theme of Guarnieri's presentation. On the slowly moving truck invisible beneath the float is a mammoth book open for all to see the letters G.R.E.S. GUARNIERI (*Gremio Recreativo Escola de Samba Guarnieri*). It is desired that the spectator know that it is of history that the school portrays, a kind of written, authoritative history, which may be a kind of joke, too, or an exaggeration, as there is very little authoritative, written history.

Then comes the *Comissão de Frente*, a line of formally dressed men doing a strolling samba. It is desired that the spectators accept these aging *sambistas*, honored for their contributions to past Carnival Parades, chosen for their grace and dignity, as the samba school's board of directors. Few, if any, actually are directors. The real directors are working hard in the school's parade, all sides of it at once. The presentation—dancers, drummers, floats on trucks and flatbeds, floats that are pushed by hand—must move at exactly one mile an hour, without gaps or holes, keeping the balances of colors and movements perfect.

Behind this line of dignitaries comes the first and most distinguished dancing couple, the *Porta Bandeira* and the *Mestre Sala*, the Flag bearer and the Room, or Dancing Master. These are mature people, in their prime, dressed in lavish eighteenth-century costumes regardless of the theme, those decided by everyone in the *favela* to be absolutely the best dancers, those dancers everyone else most enjoys watching. Their dance step is incredibly complicated, to most people an incomprehensible wonder, with patterns within patterns, movements within movements. They too must move forward in their dancing at exactly one mile per hour. And while she dances, the lady of the couple must carry a flag, the samba school's emblem on one side, the symbol of that year's theme on the other side, waving it so that both sides are visible to everyone.

It is obligatory that every person in the parade, every dancer, dignitary, drummer, director working or parading must constantly be singing the *samba enredo*, the song presented by that school that year, as loudly and as well, as continuously, as he or she can.

As the *Alas* come by, the theme of the school's presentation becomes more and more clear, however broad the theme may be. An *ala* is a group of hundreds of vigorously dancing people identically dressed depicting some aspect of the theme. Here one *ala* is costumed as Indians from the Amazon Basin, dancing steps suggestive of that cultural area. Another *ala* is again of plantation life, the costumes modified, of course, so that the beauty of the people of that *favela*, their flesh and movement, the joy of the dancers' bodies may be revealed and enjoyed by all.

In among the *alas* come the *Figuras de Destaque*, the prominent figures which

229

relate to the theme, in this case mythically huge figures of Amazonian plumed birds and monkeys.

All these groups cross in front of the *bateria* of drummers filling the air with sound in the bull pen.

In da Costa's box, Jetta in particular wilts. Her greatly abbreviated costume of a Foreign Legionnaire looks hot and heavy over her breasts and hips. Her back leans against a stanchion. Her chin is on her chest. Her eyes are open, watching, but glazed.

The most important obligatory *Ala* of any presentation is that which honors the earliest history of the samba parade in Rio de Janeiro. After the drought of 1877, women who had emigrated from Bahia danced slowly down the main street of Rio in their long white gowns on the Sunday before Lent, inviting the men to join them, as they had done in Salvador. So here comes the *Ala das Baianas*, scores of older women, usually the blackest in the *favela*, dressed, dancing in the flowing white robes of Bahia.

The *passistas* cause the greatest excitement and appreciation. Young people from the *favela*, the youngest fully formed, girls and boys, the most beautiful and most handsome, clearly the most athletic, as near naked as possible without being cumbersomely nude, dance down the parade route together acrobatically, tumbling, doing cartwheels, climbing each other, leaping off, being caught by others a centimeter before disaster, all the while singing, of course, doing all this in a choreography so intricate, so closely timed it has taken them the full year to study it, learn it, practice it. Some of the young men may have developed a *capoeira* routine which is so graceful while so vicious, so rife with genuine danger, that the sight of it might stop the spectator's heart if the drums weren't controlling the heart, keeping it going.

Adrian Fawcett says something to Fletch.

Fletch yells, 'What?' but cannot hear even his own voice.

Adrian cups his hands over Fletch's ear and yells with his full voice, virtually taking a full breath to blow out each word: 'Think if all this energy, planning, work, skill the year 'round went into revolution instead!'

Fletch nods that he heard him.

Interspersed among the *alas*, a few

231

alegorias have passed, huge floats depicting scenes from the Amazon, one a section of jungle bejeweled by women in G-strings suggesting plumed birds in their tall, bright, feathered headpieces; slim boys–men with the heads of snakes slithering over the rocks; children with the heads of monkeys dancing in the trees. Another *alegoria* depicts an Indian village, live fire centering thatched huts, costumed Indians dancing with mythical fish-headed and monster-headed figures.

In the middle of the presentation comes a small float, a disguised pickup truck, really a sound truck with amplifiers aiming every direction. On the back of the truck-float, dressed formally like a nightclub singer, stands the *Puxador de Samba*, microphone close to mouth, singing over and over at fullest personal volume, belting out the lyrics of the samba school's song for that year:

> Like the Amazon flows our history,
> Deep, mysterious and wide,
> Of many brooks and streams,
> Magically providing us with life.

After a few more *alas* does the *bateria*

begin to pull out of the bull pen and join the parade. An entire army of drummers, perhaps a thousand or more powerful men from the ages of fifteen to whenever, uniformly dressed in dazzling costume, all beating their drums in patterns practiced all year, all singing, all dancing despite the size of their drums, pass by. The sound is overpowering. It is perhaps the maximum sound the earth and sky can accept without cracking, without breaking into fragments to move with it before dissipating into dust.

Near the end of the parade comes the samba school's principal *alegoria*. In this case, for *Escola Guarnieri* that year, a nineteenth-century riverboat slowly comes down the parade route, if not full-sized at least impressively huge—as white, as delicate, as ornate as a wedding cake. Its prow moves majestically down the street high above the heads of the *bateria*. The bridge is proud in its height. Steam comes from its funnels. The cap of its whistle funnel rises and lowers, and doubtlessly the sound of a steamboat whistle comes out, but so high is the level of sound generally that even a steamboat whistle cannot be heard fifteen meters away. The white, gleaming hull moves by slowly. The mere sight of the upper decks and into the interior cabins and ballroom of the ship instantly creates the feeling of a grander day, grander people, a grander way to travel, to move, to be. Sedately move the side wheels of this riverboat, exactly as if they were thrusting water behind them. And as the riverboat passes, its stern turned up to be high above the final dancing *ala* behind it, the last to disappear down the stream of swirling costumed dancers and drummers, instant yearning for it fills the heart, the instant and full desire to experience again the passing of this ghost, this *alegoria* of the past.

★ ★ ★

'I think you're going to have to tell me that there is life after Carnival,' Fletch said.

At the bar table at the back of the box, Teo laughed and handed him a sandwich.

Other people were coming to the back of the box for drinks and sandwiches.

'Does everything become real again?' Fletch asked.

Adrian Fawcett said, 'Reality has hunkered down somewhere in my gut, assumed the fetal position, and promises only in whispers to return.'

The sound level had lowered to the merely very loud. Across the parade route, the *bateria* of *Escola Santos Lima* was organizing itself in the bull pen.

Jetta put her hand on Fletch's shoulder. 'Are you supposed to be some kind of a present?'

She looked thoroughly sound-struck, sight-struck, mind-blown, and jaded.

He smoothed his bright red sash.

'I'm a present,' Fletch said. 'Maybe I'm a past. Maybe I'm a future.'

'And did you come *par avion*?'

Chewing, Teo said, 'Did you and Laura come by subway?'

'Yes, Teo,' Fletch said honestly. 'Never have I seen an underground transportation system so modern, so quiet, so clean.'

Dressed like a Christmas package and as an eighteenth-century musician, Fletch and Laura had ridden Rio's subway to Carnival Parade at Teo's suggestion. Everyone had told them they could not get a car or a taxi within kilometers of Avenida Marques de Sapucai.

The ten-year-old Janio Barreto had followed Fletch and Laura from The Hotel Yellow Parrot to Avenida Marques de

Sapucai.

In the subway station he ducked under the turnstile onto the platform. Fletch thought the underground official saw him, but the man took no notice. Who would keep a wooden-legged boy off public transportation because he had no money? On the train, Janio stood away from them, not looking at them, not speaking to them.

Fletch pointed him out to Laura, briefly told her about him.

She seemed particularly disturbed by being followed by a small boy on a wooden leg.

Janio hobbled after them through the dark back streets to the Carnival Parade. At the entrance to the boxes he was stopped. Security was very heavy there, very official. Even with tickets, Fletch and Laura physically had to force, squeeze themselves through the bodies of the guards. They would not let anyone, even or especially a ten-year-old boy on a wooden leg, through the entrance to the boxes without a ticket.

'Yes.' Fletch was aware Teo was watching his face. 'A magnificent subway.'

The Italian racing-car driver came to the bar table. 'There are some Indians out there calling for you.'

'Me?' Fletch asked.

The racing-car driver jerked his thumb over his shoulder, indicating the area beyond the box rail.

Laura was dancing in the center of the box with Aloisio da Silva. The heat had caused her leggings to drop over her patent leather shoes.

On the packed earth between the box and the pavement of the parade route stood Toninho Braga, Orlando Velho, and Tito Granja. Again they were dressed as movie Indians. In that light, their shoulders and stomach ridges shone with sweat.

'Jump down!' Toninho shouted.

Fletch put perplexity on his face.

Cupping his hand over his mouth, Orlando shouted, 'We need to talk to you!'

'Later!' yelled Fletch.

'About Norival!' shouted Toninho.

Tito waved his arm to encourage Fletch to jump down to them.

Fletch turned around.

Dancing with Aloisio, Laura's eyes were on Fletch's face.

Her own face was so expressionless it was unfathomable.

From behind him, Fletch heard the name *Janio* shouted.

He jumped the three meters from the box down to the Tap Dancers.

CHAPTER TWENTY-NINE

Toninho clapped Fletch on the shoulder. 'You look Brazilian with that red sash. Probably just the way you did fifty years ago.'

'Laura brought it to me from Bahia.'

The four young men walked along the area between the boxes and the parade route.

Fletch said, 'I was in a *favela* this morning. I don't see how the people in a *favela* can afford to put on such a presentation, all these drums and costumes and floats.'

'It takes every *cruzeiro*, and then some,' Toninho said. 'By the way, I have lots of your money, your poker winnings, at my apartment. It's safe there. And dry.'

'Thousands of beautiful costumes,' Fletch mused. 'Each must be individually made.'

Tito said, 'Everyone in a *favela* pays dues to the samba school every week. Also, the samba school gets some subsidy from the government for Carnival Parade. It's good for tourism.'

'The *jogo do bicho*,' Orlando said. 'The *jogo do bicho* pays a lot.'

'The illegal numbers game,' Toninho said. 'The people who run the illegal numbers games give a lot of money to the samba schools for Carnival Parade. It's their way of giving some of the money back, paying taxes—'

'Because they've been stealing from the people all year,' Tito said. 'Stealing their false hopes.'

'It's good public relations for *jogo do bicho*,' Tito said. 'A business expense.'

They had passed two or three of the judges' viewing towers.

Tito turned around and walked backwards. 'Here comes *Escola Santos Lima*, Janio. Some of your descendants are parading.'

'*Escola Santos Lima* has the best *capoeiristas* in all Rio de Janeiro,' Orlando said. 'Maybe all Brazil. A huge what-would-you-say squadron of them.'

Toninho held Fletch's elbow. 'Listen. Norival has not appeared.'

'You miscalculated, Toninho. Miscalculated the currents. His body must have

239

been carried out to sea.'

'Not possible. Remember last night when I was swimming ashore? I swam into Norival. That proves that already he was floating toward the beach.'

Against the noise of Carnival Parade the four young men held their heads close together as they walked.

'It would be terrible if Norival were eaten by a shark,' Tito said.

'You don't see Norival as fish food?' Fletch asked.

'If it looks like he has just disappeared,' Orlando asked practically, 'how do we tell his family he is dead?'

'His poor mother,' said Tito.

'His father will be awfully angry,' said Toninho. 'And Admiral Passarinho . . .'

'They will never forgive us for burying Norival at sea without them,' Tito said.

'How would they ever believe us?' asked Toninho.

'You have a problem,' Fletch admitted.

'The tide has been in and out and soon comes in again.' Toninho looked sick. He looked as if the tide, with all its wiggly life, were passing through his own stomach and head.

'What do we do?' Orlando asked.

Fletch said, 'Got me.'

'What does that mean?'

'I haven't any idea.'

'You are our friend, Fletch.' Toninho still walked with Fletch's elbow in hand. 'You helped us with Norival.'

'Now you must help us think,' said Tito.

'I don't think I can,' said Fletch. 'Someone I know who is alive has disappeared. Other people tell me I died forty-seven years ago and must name my murderer. I haven't slept. I am drunk with the sound of the drums. Norival has died and disappeared. Everything is becoming less real. How can I answer if I don't understand?'

They had walked half the length of the parade route.

Fletch stopped. 'I must go back.'

'Yes,' said Tito. 'He must see Santos Lima parade.'

'You will tell us if you think of anything?' Toninho asked.

'Sure.'

'Now we cannot fish the whole ocean hoping to catch the corpse of Norival,' Orlando said.

'We'll telephone you,' Toninho said.

'Tomorrow, after the parade is over.'

★　　　★　　　★

If it were not for his wounds, Fletch would have been willing to believe that finally he fell asleep and dreamed the most horrible dream.

As it was, later he was unsure of when he had been conscious and when he had been unconscious.

Dizzy with sleeplessness, having somewhat the sensation of intoxication from the constant sound of Carnival drums, perhaps staggering a little, alone he began to walk back along the parade route to Teodomiro da Costa's box. His eyelids were heavy, his vision diminished in that glaring light. The *Abra-Alas* of *Escola Santos Lima* passed by, the first *alegoria* reminding the spectators to expect a literary theme. The walk back to da Costa's box seemed as big a chore as crossing all Brazil on foot. He was aware of the passing of the *Commisão de Frente*. He stopped, swaying, trying to focus in the glare on the dancing of the *Porta Bandeira* and the *Mestre Sala*. Their dance steps were too quick, too intricate for him to follow with his eyes. At the first *ala*,

242

he staggered forward again, only dimly aware of the passing of the thousands of dancing, singing people, the swirling costumes and flesh to his right.

Once back in Teo's box he would curl into a corner and sleep. For only an hour. People might be amazed or insulted at his sleeping during Carnival Parade, but he could not help it. He would arrange with Laura to wake him after an hour so people would not be too insulted. Even in that noise, he could, he had to sleep.

Just as he was comforting himself with this decision, using it to strengthen him to make it all the way back to Teo's box, strong hands pushed suddenly and hard against his left shoulder.

Instead of looking at who had pushed him, Fletch tried to save himself from falling. The edge of the parade route's pavement shot out from under him.

Someone pushed him again.

He fell to his right, into the parade.

A foot came up from the pavement and kicked him in the face.

Staggering from the blow, arms raised to protect his head, he looked around him. He was just inside the edge of perhaps a hundred young men doing their

243

murderous, practiced kick-dancing. A foot landed flat against his stomach. Immediately, the air was gone from Fletch's lungs. Gasping, he tried to duck sideways, back to the edge of the parade.

Again he was pushed, hard.

Spinning, he fell more deeply into the group of *capoeiristas*. He was surrounded by fast-moving, swinging legs striking at crotch height, stomach height, shoulder height, head height. A blow landed against the back of his right knee. He fell against someone. All around him flashed intense eyes. *Aw, shit*, was in Fletch's head, *I'm messing up their presentation. A damned North American, a tourist*. He was being kicked from all sides. The eyes of the *capoeiristas* were seeing him, popping in amazement at his being there, but usually only after they had pirouetted, when it was too late for them to stop their momentum, avoid kicking him.

I don't belong here.

Someone had pushed him into the *capoeira* troupe, not just once but three times. Whoever pushed him doubtlessly was still between him and the edge of the parade. Arms over his head, Fletch ducked. Keeping as low as possible, he began to scurry across the parade route to the far side, toward the stands.

A hard kick in the stomach lifted him off his feet. He came down hard on his left foot. He kept moving forward, through the muscular bare backs shining with sweat, the wildly flailing legs, balancing arms. Without air or the ability to breathe, he felt he was drowning in an ocean of churning arms and legs. The sound of the drums, the sound of the men singing in short, practiced phrases, rushed in his ears. He was being kicked and kicked. Even the gray pavement of the parade route was heaving beneath his feet.

He didn't see the foot that came up from the pavement and kicked him in his face. A cracking noise blasted his ears as his head snapped up and back.

A firm hand against his waist ejected him from the parade.

There was hard-packed earth beneath his feet. The *capoeiristas* were now a meter behind him.

Blood was on his hands. From his nose and ears and mouth blood was pouring down inside and outside his white shirt. It disappeared into his red sash.

He turned, half-conscious, to see if he

could spot whoever had pushed him into the *capeira* troupe.

The *Ala das Baianas* was passing by. A few of the tall black women in long white robes saw him, grimaced at his bloody appearance as they sambaed to the edge of the pavement and turned back.

His eyes wanted to close. He knew he had to go to ground somewhere.

Clutching his ribs, he turned toward the stands. A few people were pointing to him. Most were moving their heads, their shoulders to look beyond him, at the parade.

He staggered, fell toward the stands.

People he approached on the bottom tiers of seats stood up in horror at his appearance, to get away from him. Maybe one or two women were screaming. A few men were shouting at him, angrily, pointing at him. He could not hear the women screaming or the men shouting. He could only see their mouths move.

He knelt down and put his head and shoulders between the second and third tiers of seats. Whoever had pushed him into the *capoeiristas* had intended murder. Perhaps he had succeeded. Chances were good he would follow his quarry until he was sure he had killed him. His head under the seats, Fletch reached out, grabbed a couple of metal uprights and pulled himself through.

Fletch crawled beneath the stands.

He lay on his back on the dirt, the bottoms of the seats, the bottoms of the spectators just above him. He had been kicked in the stomach so many times he could not breathe.

Vomiting turned him over, got him up on his knees, got him gagging, breathing again. Blood from his nose and lips joined the more forceful stream of vomit.

On his knees, he backed away from his mess.

Stomach muscles quivering from the blows, arms and legs shaking, he remained on hands and knees coughing, trying to clear his throat of vomit and blood.

A meter ahead of him, the people who had risen from their seats, allowing him to crawl under the stands, were sitting in their seats again, pounding their feet like pistons again in rhythm to the drums, cheering on the biggest and most amazing human spectacle in the world except war. Fletch knew they could not hear him retching and choking. He could not hear himself. He was sure his appearance to them was as unreal as the rest of the spectacle they were watching.

After a while he crawled backward farther to give himself more headroom, more air.

Sitting cross-legged then, he put his head back to try to stop the bleeding from his nose. He remembered the crack he had heard when he got that final kick in the face. He did not think his neck was broken, nor his back, nor his head.

Above him rose, as far as he could see, the undersides of the stands. Pieces of skirts, the undersides of thighs, a few dangling feet. A sandwich wrapper floated down and landed near him in the dirt.

The light under the stands was weird. It was midnight. There was no illumination under the stands. The powerful light from the parade route filtered under the stands through the densely packed bodies above. Nodes of light, apparently sourceless, quivered in midair.

Streams of light wavered at odd angles to each other.

His crotch hurt, his stomach hurt, his ribs. His head had been hit from every direction.

Fighting the temptation, his body's demand to stretch out, to go to sleep, become unconscious, he lifted himself to his feet. It took him three tries to become upright.

He fell forward, and caught himself. A *chope* can fell from the stands and landed near his foot. He put one foot forward and fell on it. Maintaining upright balance seemed important to him. One hand rubbed an ear; the other tightly held his ribs. He gasped.

Later, he supposed he had moments of unconsciousness as he stood there.

He saw a man walking along under the stands. About to wave to him, making some gesture he needed help, Fletch noticed how oddly the man walked. Fletch looked more closely. The man's steps were short, high, fast. He landed first on his toes and then his feet rolled forward to his heels.

The man's feet were backward. His toes were behind his legs.

The hands pressing against his ribs Fletch lowered to press against his stomach.

He blinked blood from his eyes.

A headless mule cantered out of the dark under the stands, slowly turned, and cantered away.

Fletch fell forward on his feet several steps. Now truly he was the walking North American, falling forward. Each step, his feet barely prevented his falling on his face.

Out of the dark at Fletch's left appeared another man, walking, bouncing slowly. He was to cross in front of Fletch.

As he passed Fletch, the man's head, backward on his shoulders, turned and smiled. His eyes and teeth shone even in that light.

In an impossible angle from his head, one of his arms raised. He pointed to Fletch's right.

Standing very close to Fletch was an old man in an oversized coat. The man's hair was thin and gray. His eyes were sad.

He raised his arms toward Fletch.

Fletch backed away.

Only hair came out of the old man's sleeves, not hands or wrists.

Again, Fletch's head snapped.

Someone kicked him hard, on the muscle of the upper left side of his back.

Brushing away the old man with hair for hands, Fletch spun slowly on the hard-packed earth.

He saw the second blow coming at his

chest. He did not know how to avoid such a blow from the foot. He could not duck it. Moving sideways, slowly, stupidly, he still caught the full force of the blow.

His feet caught him as he fell backward.

A man, a wiry old man, was kick-dancing in front of him. Groggy, Fletch admired the perfectly executed pirouette.

And as the man's face turned to him, a beam of light through the stands shone fully on the face of a goat. Through the mask's eye-holes gleamed steady brown eyes.

The man's instep hit Fletch hard on the side of the head.

Fletch's head felt it was traveling through space by itself.

Reeling. Fletch saw the small boy standing not too far away on his wooden leg.

'Janio!' Fletch yelled. Blood bubbled from his throat to his lips.

In all that noise, he could not even hear his own voice.

His shoulders pumping unnaturally, the small boy ran away.

The *capoeirista* was real. He was in front of Fletch, behind him, all around him. The blows from his feet were real.

251

The man behind the goat mask was kicking Fletch to death.

Fletch tried to keep his legs together, yet not fall over. He tried to keep his back to the man, which was impossible. Hunkered down, he tried to keep his hands over his head, his elbows protecting his ribs. Falling this way, that, he tried to get away. The *capoeirista* was on all sides of him at once. Each blow from his feet opened Fletch's body for another blow.

Fletch received a hard kick in his throat, perhaps a killing kick.

Then one more kick in the back of his head.

He was face down in the dirt.

Consciousness was coming and going like an old song on a high wind. Blood was pouring from his face, particularly his nose again, but he could not get a hand to it.

His legs would not get him up. They would not obey orders, they were well beyond the necessary impulse to get up and run.

The man in the goat's mask grabbed Fletch's hair and twisted his head sideways and up. Fletch's whole body rolled sideways. He was lying on one hip.

A knee either side of him, the man knelt

over Fletch.

For a second the man's hand was flattened on the ground in front of Fletch's nose. In one of the odd flashes of light, Fletch glimpsed a ring on the man's finger. A ring with a black center. Intertwined snakes rose from that center.

Farther along the ground, Fletch saw a piece of wood sticking into the ground again and again as it came closer. Paired with the stick of wood was a boy's leg.

Pulling Fletch's hair, the man in the goat mask twisted Fletch's head forward and back.

With his other hand, the man was doing something under Fletch's chin.

Fletch felt a nice warmth on the side of his neck.

The nice warmth of blood.

The man was slitting Fletch's throat.

Then, as if hit by a great wind, the man was blown sideways. He sprawled into the dirt beside Fletch.

Above them were many legs, strong men's legs.

In one incredibly smooth, lithe movement the man was up, on his feet, on one foot. The other foot on a straight leg was whirling through the air. From the ground, Fletch saw all the other legs, the legs of his rescuers, back away.

The toes of the man in the goat mask then dug into the ground with the grip of a sprinter. They were gone in a blur.

Heavily, the other feet went after him.

The wooden leg still stuck in the ground nearby, next to the boy's bare leg.

'Janio, I need help.' On the ground, Fletch managed to get a hand to his throat. He stuck his finger in the knife hole. *'Janio! Socorro!'*

Fletch knew he was not being heard. He could not even hear himself.

It was not sleep then, into which Fletch fell.

CHAPTER THIRTY

He was conscious when the phone began ringing, but it rang five or six times before he could get rolled over, stretch his arm out to it, and pick up the receiver from the bedside table.

'Bom dia,' Fletch said into the phone, not believing a word of it.

'Fletch! Are you better?'

By now, Fletch knew Toninho's voice over the telephone.

'Better than what?'

'Better than you were when we found you.'

Fletch's memory was far from perfect. His brain had begun to clear only shortly before noon. He still tasted blood.

Lying on the ground under the stands at Carnival Parade, he remembered seeing from close-up the creases of Toninho's or Tito's belly.

He remembered being carried, it seemed for kilometers, under the stands. The sky was full of human feet and legs pounding in rhythm. The noise was no longer of singing, pounding samba drums. It was all just roar.

Then they were out from under the stands, and still he was carried a long, long way. The sounds abated. The air became clearer. The sky was high and dark.

'We're getting good at lifting bodies around,' Tito said. Why was he speaking English?

'Bury me at sea,' Fletch instructed them. 'The fish will appreciate dessert.'

As they carefully fitted him into the back seat of the four-door black Galaxie, Fletch saw the ten-year-old boy standing next to the car. His eyes were round.

'Hey, Janio,' Fletch said. '*Obrigado.*'

During the ride in the car, he lost consciousness again. He remembered none of it.

He remembered being walked into the lobby of The Hotel Yellow Parrot. Orlando was holding him up.

The doorman and the desk clerk hurried around, each questioning Toninho and Tito in Portuguese. Toninho and Tito were placating.

The ride in the elevator took forever.

Finally, Fletch was on his own bed. Being on his bed was so unexpected, so wonderful, he sucked in great gobs of breath. And passed out again.

He remembered Toninho working up and down his naked body, squeezing, testing, looking for breaks in Fletch's bones.

'My neck,' Fletch said. 'Is my head on straight?'

Orlando came in from the bathroom with wet towels. He and Toninho washed Fletch down, even turning him over, gently, to do so.

As the towels passed in and out of

Fletch's sight, they became pink, and then red.

The formally dressed desk clerk arrived with bandages and bottles of antiseptic.

He took away the wet, bloody towels and Fletch's blood-soaked clothes.

'Not my sash,' Fletch complained. 'Not my beautiful red sash.'

'Your bloody red sash,' Toninho said.

'Laura gave me that bloody red sash,' Fletch said. 'She brought it from Bahia.'

'He says he'll burn your clothes,' Tito said. 'A sacrifice to the gods. They get only a little of your blood. You live.'

'Ow.'

Toninho was applying antiseptic to a hundred places over Fletch's body. He stuck the antiseptic-soaked face cloth into the small slit in Fletch's throat.

Consciousness was lost again.

They rolled Fletch this way and that, to put a fresh, dry sheet under him. The desk clerk was back in the room. He was trying to fold a wet, bloody sheet while not letting it touch his clothes.

With his fingers, Fletch discovered plaster stuck to various parts of his body: his shins, ribs, face, neck. He did not remember their being put on.

257

'Should I stay with him?' Tito asked.

'He'll be all right,' Toninho said. 'He needs a few hours of meditation. There's nothing really wrong with him.'

'Except that someone tried to kill him,' Orlando said.

'Yes,' Toninho said. 'It looks that way.'

'He did not succeed,' Fletch announced from the bed.

'No,' Toninho said. 'He did not succeed.'

Softly, Tito said, 'He almost succeeded.'

The room was black. Fletch did not remember their leaving.

Through the dark night he listened to the samba drums. The sound was not coming from the street. It was coming from various televisions throughout the hotel, around the neighborhood. An announcer's voice came and went over the sound of the drumming and singing. Rio de Janeiro's Samba School Parade was continuing.

He did not sleep. Some unconsciousness other than sleep came and went like a presence in the dark room. It came closer and went away.

He did not move. No part of his body wanted to move. Every muscle in his body had been kicked at least once. The skin and tissue against his bones throbbed. For a while, the thighs of his legs would hurt; he would think about them, then his shoulders; and he would think about them, his back, the area high in his stomach just below his ribs. Even his fingers and toes hurt. Anything was better than thinking how his head hurt. His head felt as if the inside had been kicked loose from the outside and rattled.

Laura would return. Sometime during the morning. Or perhaps within an hour after the parade was over, by two or three in the afternoon. How could she know, at the parade, he had been kicked almost to death? All she knew was that he had left the box to take a walk with the Tap Dancers. She would return.

Daylight came through the balcony drapes. Then direct sunlight entered the room. The television coverage of Carnival Parade continued. The room grew hot.

In his bed he experimented moving an arm. Then the other. One leg. He dug his fingers into his left leg to cause it to move. Slowly, he rolled his head back and forth on the pillow.

His head was clearing. He had not been unconscious for a long time now.

It was nearly noon when he could resist no longer.

Slowly he rolled himself to the edge of the bed. Heavily he lifted himself up. The semi-dark room went out of focus for a minute. He took a step forward. There was no part of his body which did not hurt.

After using the toilet, he turned on the bathroom light and looked at himself in the mirror. To his regret, his head was on frontwards and stared back at him. Swollen eyes, bruised cheek-bones, jaws. One ear was inflamed. There was still blood in his hair. A shower would cause his bandages to fall off. Backing up, he saw the blue bruises on his upper arms, his chest. The top of his stomach was purple.

Brushing his teeth gingerly, he spat blood into the basin.

Then he returned to bed and waited.

Laura would come and they would have food. He would tell her what had happened to him. Would she listen? What had happened to him? Would she be interested, or would this be a level of reality which didn't interest her much? While he talked, would she be hearing something else? As he was leaving the box to join the Tap Dancers, her face had been inscrutable.

What did the fact of the wooden-legged boy following them through the subway mean to her it did not mean to him?

Laura had not returned by the time Toninho called.

'You must be better,' Toninho said. 'You've had almost twelve hours to meditate.'

'I need twelve years.'

'Who tried to kill you?'

'I'm thinking about that.'

'Ah, Carnival,' Toninho said.

'He was wearing a goat mask,' Fletch said. 'A man in his sixties, I'd say. He tried to kick me to death.'

'He must have slipped into the personality of the goat. Carnival does that.'

'No goat has such training in *capoeira*.' Fletch wanted to switch the phone to his other ear. Then he remembered his other ear had slipped into the personality of a tomato.

'The news is that Norival has showed up.'

'Great! In one piece?'

'Yes. He came ashore way down the coast, a hundred kilometers south of where we thought.'

'I always thought that boy would go a

long way.'

'Apparently he got caught in a current, which took him south, then ashore. He was on the beach this morning. A jogger found him. They are bringing his body up now.'

'Good. Great. All your worries are over.'

'The report so far is that he drowned. His boat broke up and he drowned.'

'That's good. So Norival did die at sea. His mother will be so glad. Admiral Passarinho will be ecstatic.'

'So we'll see you at the funeral home in about half an hour.'

'What? No way. Toninho, I can't move.'

'Of course you can move.'

'Why should I go to the funeral home?'

'To help us distract the officials.' Toninho's voice fell to the conspiratorial. 'To distract them from any idea of an autopsy. We need to stand around in a circle and say, yes, he drowned. We saw him go sailing and indeed he certainly did drown. They're more apt to believe you, you see. They don't know you as well as they know us.'

'I don't think I can move.'

'You must move. If you don't make yourself move now, you'll stiffen up, like Norival, and not be able to move for days.'

Fletch hesitated. He remembered past injuries. 'You're probably right.'

Still, he had had no real sleep.

'Of course I'm right. The funeral home of Job Pereira. On rua Jardim Botanico. The business part of the road.'

'I'll find it.'

'I'll bring all your gambling winnings to you.'

'You needn't bribe me.' Fletch tried sitting up in bed. 'On the other hand, maybe you do.'

CHAPTER THIRTY-ONE

At the funeral home of Job Pereira, Fletch tried to find a door-bell to ring, a door on which to knock. There was neither.

It was a large stucco and stone house sitting in the deep shade of its own trees.

'Hello?' he called. 'Anyone?'

The quiet from inside the building was tomb-like.

He stepped into the coolness of the foyer. There was no reception desk, still no bell to ring. There were short, dark potted palms in each corner.

'Hello?' Fletch called.

The only response was a faint echo of his own voice.

It had taken him longer than the promised half hour to get from The Hotel Yellow Parrot to the funeral home of Job Pereira.

Sitting on the edge of his bed, he had ordered food from Room Service.

While still at the telephone, he called The Hotel Jangada and asked for Room 912.

No answer.

No, Mrs Joan Collins Stanwyk had not yet picked up the envelope Mr Fletcher had left in her box.

Every step, every movement, however small, caused him pain. He opened the drapes to the balcony. Across the utility area, the man was painting the room. Perhaps the man's permanent job in life was to paint that room. Fletch opened the door to the balcony. The air was warm and dry and felt good. The televisions were still blaring the news of Carnival Parade.

Life goes on.

Shaving was like walking barefoot through a field of glass. Finished, he had to affix one more bandage to his face.

Alone, with stinging lips and sore jaws, he ate breakfast.

Every minute, he thought Laura might return.

Finally dressed in a pair of clean shorts and a T-shirt, sneakers and socks, he went down in the elevator. The desk clerk and the few other people in the lobby glanced at him and immediately looked away. Despite the glue stuck to various parts of his face and body, he gathered he no longer looked like a Christmas package.

The *avenida* in front of the hotel was emptier than he had ever seen it. Citizens either were still watching Carnival Parade or were worn out by it and sleeping.

Finally a taxi picked him up. All the streets were empty. All the way to the funeral home, the taxi radio kept up an excited description of the last *escola* to parade.

'Hello? Anyone here?'

The funeral home was lifeless. There was not even the sound of a radio or television reporting the parade.

Fletch limped into a big room to the left of the foyer. Heavy, waisted velvet drapes on the windows cut down the light in the room.

Several open coffins were on display in the room. Each was on its own fancy trestle. He looked in one. It was empty. A coffin sales room. He moved from coffin to coffin, looking in each. The coffins ranged from polished pine to brass-studded mahogany.

He heard a sound behind him.

A seemingly tired, lazy voice said, 'Hello?'

Fletch turned around.

In the door to the room, white as sea foam, the brighter light from the foyer behind him softening his outline, clearly stood Norival.

Norival Passarinho.

Dressed in white shoes, white slacks, white shirt. His belly hung over his belt. Damp hair fell onto his forehead. His face was puffy.

Norival Passarinho!

Fletch blinked.

Norival blinked.

Fletch sucked in cool air from the coffin display room.

'Ah, Janio Barreto.' Norival shambled toward Fletch. Norival even put out his arm to take Fletch's hand. 'At last I get to meet you properly!'

The room rose.
Fletch fell.

CHAPTER THIRTY-TWO

Fletch knew he was in a small, dark place.

Becoming conscious, he could hear no natural sounds except the sound of his own breathing. The air was stale.

He was lying on his back. His head was on some kind of pillow.

Only when he moved his right hand and immediately came to the edge of the space, a soft wall, did he realize how small the space was. The same was true when he moved his left hand.

The space he was in clearly was no wider than a long, narrow bed. He ran his hands up the satiny walls. The ceiling of the space was immediately on top of him, only a few centimeters above his chest, his chin, his nose.

A very small space indeed.

His fingers brushed against something else. Paper, fairly stiff paper. Both hands felt over the object lying beside him in the small space. His fingers told him it was a paper bag, with papers in it.

Fletch tried to think where he had last been, what had happened to him, at what he had been looking when . . . Coffins!

'Aaaaaaaaarrrgh!' Fletch's roar surpised and deafened himself. 'I'm not dead?'

In that terrible enclosure, he tried to get his hands up, to prise up, raise the lid of the coffin. His heart was pounding in a lively manner. His face poured sweat.

'Hey, out there!'

Horrified, he realized he might be trying to yell through six feet of sod.

'Hey, up there! I'm not dead yet! I swear to it!'

He could not get his arms, hands at the right angle to lift. The coffin lid was heavy. His beaten muscles quivered and ached but accomplished little.

'Aaaaaaaaarrrgh! Somebody! Anybody! Listen! I'm not dead yet!' The air in the coffin had become exceedingly warm. '*Socorro*! damnit!'

By itself, it seemed, the coffin lid rose.

Instantly, the air became fresh and sweet.

He blinked stupidly at the light of day.

Laura's head was over the coffin, looking in. 'Ah, there you are,' she said.

Lying flat, sucking in the good air, Fletch said nothing.

'What are you doing in a coffin?'

Fletch panted.

'You do look like you belong in a coffin.'

'I saw Norival,' he said. 'Norival Passarinho.'

'Norival's dead,' she said.

'I know!'

'Apparently he went sailing alone at night. His boat hit a rock or something. He drowned.'

'I know!'

'His body washed up this morning. Very sad. Poor Norival.'

'I know all that, Laura. But, listen! I came here to the funeral home. Toninho asked me to. I was alone, in this room.' Fletch peered over the edge of his coffin and established that he was still in the coffin display room. 'And I turned around, and there, in the door, stood Norival! Norival Passarinho! Blinking!'

'Norival?'

'He spoke to me! He said, "Janio Barreto." He came forward. He walked across the room at me. He tried to shake my hand!'

Laura wrinkled up her nose. 'Norival

269

Passarinho?'

'Yes! Definitely!'

'After he was dead?'

'Yes! I know he was dead!'

'It couldn't have been Norival Passarinho.'

'It was Norival Passarinho. Dressed in white. All in white.'

'You saw Norival Passarinho walking around after he was dead?'

'He said, Norival said, "Ah, Janio Barreto,"' Fletch lowered his voice to the sepulchral. '"At last I get to meet you properly."'

'You saw Adroaldo Passarinho.'

'What? Who?'

'Adroaldo. Norival's brother. They're just alike.'

Fletch thought a moment. 'Adroaldo?'

'Yes. Adroaldo was very surprised when he put out his arm to shake hands with you, and you fainted.'

'I fainted?'

'Well, you fell on the floor without apparent what-do-you-call-it? premeditation.'

'Adroaldo Passarinho?'

'You didn't know Norival had a brother?'

'Yes. Of course. But he was so white!'

'He's been in school in Switzerland all winter.'

'Laura...'

'Fletch, I think you're not surviving Carnival. It's beginning to affect your mind.'

'What am I doing in a coffin?'

Laura shrugged 'I suspect the Tap Dancers put you in there. After you fainted.'

'Why?'

'One of their little tricks.' She giggled.

'Very funny!' Stiffly, he began to pull himself up, to sit up in his coffin. 'God! I thought...'

'It is funny.'

He picked up the paper bag and looked into it.

'What's that?' she asked. 'Your lunch? Enough to tide you over to the other world?'

'My poker winnings.'

'Ah, they buried you with all your worldly wealth. All your illgotten gains. So you can tip Charon after he rows you across the River Styx.'

His time in the coffin had stiffened his muscles again. 'How come you're here?'

'Toninho called me at the hotel. Said you had fainted. I should come in the car and pick you up. Adroaldo and the others had to go with Norival in his coffin to the Passarinho home.'

Fletch's heart had slowed, but he was still sweating. 'What if you hadn't come? I could have run out of air—'

'Why wouldn't I have come?'

'Supposing the car had broken down, or—'

'You could have gotten yourself out of there.'

'I could have died of cardiac arrest.'

'Were you that frightened?'

'Waking up in a closed coffin is not something one expects to do—under any circumstances.'

She was studying his face. 'You're a mess.'

'I got nearly kicked to death.'

'They told me. Your whole body like that?'

'At the moment, I am not very sleek.'

'Was there any reason for it you know of? I mean, getting attacked?'

'I think so, yes. Help me out of this damned coffin, if you don't mind.'

'Also, there was another message for you

at the hotel.' She balanced him by holding onto his hand. 'A Sergeant Paulo Barbosa of Rio de Janeiro police would like you to call him.'

'What did he say?'

'Just left a message. How much trouble are you in?'

'Oh, my God.' A body wounded in every part is painful to lift out of a raised coffin and set on two feet on the floor.

'You really are a mess,' Laura said. 'The car is just outside.'

'You'd better drive.'

'Seeing the last vehicle you tried to drive is a coffin . . .'

'Not by choice, thank you.'

'We'll go back to the hotel. The Parade is over. It was really wonderful. You missed most of it.'

'I'm sorry about that.'

'Fletch, you always seem to be someplace you're not supposed to be, doing something you're not supposed to be doing.'

'Got any other news for me?'

'Yes.' They were crossing the wide, cool foyer of the funeral home of Job Pereira, heading for the dazzling sunlight beyond the front door. 'Paul Bocuse is the chef at Le Saint Honoré. I've made reservations for tonight, in your name. Have you forgotten the ball at Regine's? That's tonight. Tomorrow, I thought we'd drive up and have a quiet lunch at *Floresta*.'

'You mean Carnival still isn't over?'

'Tomorrow night it's over. I'm not at all sure you'll make it. I'll have to start preparing for my concert tour soon enough. Not a worry. We'll go back to the hotel and rest now.'

'No.'

'No? You want to go play soccer now?'

'I want to go to *favela* Santos Lima now.' Over the top of the small yellow convertible, she gave him a long look. 'I'll never rest until I do. You said so yourself.'

'I don't think I know the way.'

'I do.' He lowered himself gently onto the hot passenger seat. 'Just follow my directions.'

CHAPTER THIRTY-THREE

Sore with wounds, dazed with sleeplessness, Fletch walked into *favela* Santos Lima like a *Figura de Destaque*. The sun was searingly, blindingly hot.

274

Laura traipsed along a few steps behind him.

The children of the *favela* followed him too, of course, but they walked at a distance from him, quietly. As they climbed the hill, adults from the little houses and the little shops followed them.

By the time they were in front of Idalina Barreto's house, they were a large crowd.

The tall old woman recognized Laura immediately. Hands on her hips in the doorway of her little house, she began talking to Laura even before Laura got to the front of the house. The old woman asked, repeated some question of Laura.

The crowd outside the house was quiet. They wanted to hear Fletch's answer.

Laura said, 'She wants to know if you've come to identify your murderer.'

Fletch said, 'I think so. Tell her I think so.'

Laura frowned. 'Are you serious?'

'Is anything serious?'

'How do you mean to do that?'

'I mean to walk slowly through the *favela*, look into everyone's eyes. I shall identify my murderer.'

'Just like that?'

'Just like that.'

275

'I don't believe...' She looked around at all the people quietly awaiting Fletch's response.

'What don't you believe?' he asked. 'What do you believe?'

Fletch waited a long time for her to answer. He asked, 'Would you like to believe I'm about to perform magic? That I'm about to do a trick?'

Still Laura did not answer.

'Would you like to believe, as some of these people do, that I am Janio Barreto returned from the dead after forty-seven years to point out my murderer?'

'I believe...' In the heat of the sunlight, Laura took a deep breath. 'I don't believe you should play with these people.'

'Am I playing?'

'At least some of these people believe this story. Because the old lady wants them to believe. The others are just curious. They love any story.'

'Anybody can make up a story and say it is the past. Right?'

'Identifying someone as your murderer, as the murderer of Janio Barreto, would be a very serious thing for these people.'

'I hope so.'

'You have no idea what they might do to

such a person.'

'I can guess.'

'Fletch, you must tell me what you know.'

'You want a fact?'

'I want something.'

'Okay, Laura, here's a fact: The person who murdered Janio Barreto forty-seven years ago truly believes I am Janio Barreto returned.'

'How do you know that?'

'Look at me.'

'I don't think you should play with the, what's-the-word? credibility of people.'

'I am taking advantage of the credulity of only one of these people.'

'Someone believes—'

'Someone either believes I am Janio Barreto returned. Or he has decided to act as if he believes I am Janio Barreto returned, just in case it is true.'

In the sunlight, Laura sighed.

Now there were even more people standing around outside Idalina Barreto's house awaiting his answer.

The child Janio Barreto had appeared. Of all the people in the *favela*, he stood closest to Fletch.

'Please tell the old woman I am here to

identify my murderer.'

Laura started to speak to Idalina, but then stopped.

Instead, she said to Fletch: 'You're putting it to me too, aren't you?'

'Hell, Laura, we haven't even gotten to know each other.'

'All this will be on your head,' she said.

'Fine. My head is so sore now, it doesn't matter.'

Speaking loudly, as if making an announcement, Laura answered the old woman.

The crowd cheered. Many gave the thumbs-up sign.

The old woman asked another question.

Laura said, 'Do you really mean to just walk through the *favela*, up and down the streets, until you point someone out?'

'I want to see, to look into the eyes of everyone in the *favela*. Tell her, if the murderer is here, I will find him.'

Laura translated, in a less robust voice.

Idalina Barreto came out of the shade of her doorway.

In the sunlight, she took Fletch's arm.

Together, Laura walking behind them, the people from the *favela* all around them, Fletch and Idalina Barreto began to walk

278

through *favela* Santos Lima.

★   ★   ★

'I know your trick,' Laura finally said to Fletch in a low voice. They had been walking a long time. Her hair had collapsed with perspiration. 'You're going to walk through the whole *favela* and point no one out.'

'Maybe,' Fletch answered. 'Would that permit me to sleep?'

Favela Santos Lima was far more extensive than he thought. It was a senseless warren of streets and alleys and footpaths. The banged-together, stuck-together hovels seemed placed by the whimsy of the moment, or some invisible convenience. On some of the paths only he and Idalina could walk abreast. The stream of their followers flowed a kilometer behind them in some places.

'We're having our own Carnival Parade,' Fletch said to Laura.

'Not bloody likely.'

Sweating, the middle-aged Janio Barreto Filho appeared and asked what was happening. His mother told him *Janio Barreto* wished to look into the eyes of everyone in the *favela*. He would identify his murderer.

Janio Barreto Filho organized boys and men to walk ahead of Fletch and Idalina and get all the people out of their homes so Fletch could look into their eyes as he passed.

It was the afternoon after the Samba School Parade, and most of the people in the *favela* were sleeping. Barreto's squad called through the windows of their homes, entered, awakened people, and politely asked them to come outside. *No, no, it is not the police. It is an important matter. To solve an ancient matter having to do with the* favela. *We are about to find out who murdered Janio Barreto, a long time ago*. Shy of most clothes, faces puffy with tiredness, the people stood at their doors rubbing their eyes in the sunlight.

Perhaps they understood a feat of legerdemain was about to happen: a voice from beyond the grave was about to speak. Perhaps they understood nothing but that someone had asked them to wake up and stand outside a moment. Something interesting was passing by. Sleepy or curious, they cooperated.

Fletch asked Laura, 'Are you deciding

what you believe now?'

'All these people.' Laura looked back at the river of people following them. 'Many of them are laughing at you.'

'I would hope so,' he said.

'Turning this into a joke. Is that what you're doing?'

'Isn't it a joke?'

'You're going to lead them around in a circle and then say there is no such person as your murderer here.'

'Perhaps.'

As he walked, Fletch was becoming less stiff. He was thirsty. The sun was stinging his various wounds on his face and arms. His head throbbed like a samba combo. A few times, the bright sunlight dimmed on his unnaturally. He stumbled. Idalina Barreto's grip on his arm was strong.

Of course he did not know if he was going up and down every path in Santos Lima. He had to leave that to his guides. It certainly felt as though he was going up and down every path, looking into the eyes of every person in Santos Lima.

'I'm going back,' Laura said. 'Here are the car keys. I'll take a taxi.'

'No,' said Fletch. 'Stay with me.'

'I don't care to see out the end of this act

of yours.'

'It's not an act.'

Fletch was seeing the people of *favela* Santos Lima. He was seeing males and females, the old, the young, the tall, the short, the beautiful, the ugly, the misshapen, the healthy, the insane, the doddering, the dignified, the ashamed ...

Ahead of him on a narrow path, he saw a lean, gray-haired man dressed only in shorts leave a house. He crossed the path and entered another house.

Walking more quickly, Fletch approached that house.

In excitement, Idalina Barreto gripped his arm even tighter. She kept up with him.

Young Janio Barreto looked up into Fletch's eyes. Then, calling others he ran ahead and into the house.

Fletch entered the house. It was empty. There was a doorless back door.

From behind the house came the sound of young Janio Barreto calling loudly.

As Fletch went through the house, the mob following gathered speed. They went through the house and round the house.

Now they had the idea they were pursuing someone.

'What are you doing?' Laura said.

'Madman!'

Fletch looked back. A wall of the little house they had just gone through fell flat in the dust. The other three walls fell forward but did not collapse. The twisted tin roof kept three of the walls up.

'You're out of your mind!' Laura said. 'There is no understanding this!'

Above the little house he came to a wider path. To his left down the path, young Janio Barreto held onto the black shorts of the gray-haired man he knew Fletch was pursuing. Other boys, men, surrounded the man.

More slowly now, Fletch walked toward the group in the middle of the path.

As he approached, one of the young men said to the grayhaired man, 'Just let him look into your eyes, Gabriel.'

'*Gabriel Campos!*' Idalina Barreto shrieked in her highest crone's voice. '*Gabriel Campos!*'

Clearly the man wanted to bolt. He was surrounded now by twenty strong young men, by more than thirty children. He was being approached by more than one hundred fellow citizens of his *favela*.

With dignity, he stood his ground. His body was mostly light, sinewy muscle. The top of his stomach was pumping hard. The man had not moved that far, not moved that fast, to be so out of breath. Not for a man in his condition. A disingenuous smile played on his lips.

'*Gabriel Campos!*' Idalina shrieked. Then she shouted something about Janio Barreto.

Standing close to him, Fletch looked into the eyes of Gabriel Campos. He had seen those eyes before.

Gabriel Campos' eyes flickered. He looked at the crowd and back at Fletch.

His smile came and went like a flashing light.

Slowly, Fletch raised his hand.

He pointed his index finger at Gabriel Campos' nose.

Fletch already had checked the ring the man was wearing. It had a black center. Intertwined snakes rose from that center.

Instantly, Gabriel Campos ducked. Throwing back his elbows, he darted backward through the circle of young men, children, knocking over a child.

Idalina Barreto shrieked.

Others began to yell, move forward.

Two of the young men grabbed for Gabriel Campos.

Campos kicked one in the stomach; the

284

other in the face.

It seemed everyone was trying to lay a hand on Campos. With tremendous skill, ducking and dancing, he kicked free of the crowd.

He turned and ran up the path.

Shouting, young men ran after him. Tripping over each other, almost all the men and children who had been following Fletch joined the pursuit. Yelling, some lifting their skirts up, many of the women pursued Gabriel Campos as well.

Shrieking *Gabriel Campos! Gabriel Campos!* tall old Idalina Barreto went after him in her rapid, sturdy pace, losing ground in the midst of this marathon.

Fletch sat on a nearby rock.

Dor de estomago ... de cabeca ... febre ... nausea.

★　　★　　★

A few meters away, Laura Soares was in a group of women from the *favela*. They were all talking at once. Most of them were pregnant and therefore could not join in the pursuit of Gabriel Campos.

Laura was asking questions. She kept looking across at Fletch.

Higher up in the *favela*, the chase was still going on. On a road along a ridge, Fletch saw Gabriel Campos running between the houses. Easily one hundred people were streaming after him. He had a good lead on them.

Idalina Barreto's high, shrill shriek dominated all other sounds. '*Gabriel Campos! Gabriel Campos!*'

* * *

From somewhere down in the depths of the *favela* came the sound of a samba drum.

After a while, Laura came over to Fletch. She stood over him a moment without speaking.

Fletch said, 'I'm awfully tired. And I still have to call Sergeant Barbosa of the Rio police.'

Laura said, 'His name is Gabriel Campos.'

'I heard.' He looked up to where Idalina Barreto was. The old lady had climbed far fast. 'I hear.'

'The women say he was your friend when you were boys. He, one other boy, and the Gomes brothers. Who are the Gomes brothers?'

286

'Idalina's brothers.'

'See?' she said. 'You do know.'

'I was told, Laura. Yesterday. I was told.'

'You taught them all the skill of *capoeira*. Of everyone, Gabriel learned the best. After you were killed, he was master of the *capoeira* school of *Escola* Santos Lima. For years, he was famous for it. One year, he was even *Mestre Sala*.'

'I see. He wanted Janio—his teacher—out of the way.'

'He was placed on the board of directors of the samba school.'

'He would never have had such honors if Janio were alive.'

Laura made some sign in the dust with the tip of her sandal.

'I must get sleep.' High in the *favela*, the pursuit, the shouting continued. Fletch said, 'I wonder what they will do with him.'

'I don't want to know. How, why did you pick out Gabriel Campos? You must tell me.'

'You mean, did Gabriel Campos murder Janio Barreto forty-seven years ago?'

'Did he?'

'I don't know.' Beyond exhaustion, Fletch stood up from the rock. 'But I do know that, disguised as a goat, last night he tried to slit my throat.'

CHAPTER THIRTY-FOUR

'I forget if you said if you have ever been to New Bedford, Massachusetts,' Sergeant Paulo Barbosa asked.

'No,' Fletch said into the phone. He sat heavily on his bed in The Hotel Yellow Parrot. 'I have never been to New Bedford, Massachusetts.'

Laura had gotten Sergeant Barbosa on the line. Placing the call had seemed too complicated to Fletch in his sleepless condition.

'It is very nice in New Bedford, Massachusetts,' Sergeant Barbosa told him again. 'Much too cold, of course, for me. When you go back to your country, you must visit New Bedford, Massachusetts.' Fletch noticed the presumption that sooner or later everyone does go back to his country. It was the same presumption Idalina's father made of Janio Barreto. 'You must visit my cousin's gift shop in New Bedford, Massachusetts. She has everything in her gift shop that every other gift shop has.'

'All right.' Fletch's head was nodding. 'I promise.'

'That would be very nice. Now, about that North American woman you lost . . .'

Fletch's eyes popped open. 'Yes?'

'I don't think we have found her.'

'Oh.'

'What we have is a telephone call from the mayor of a very small town on the coast, south of here three hundred kilometers. The town of Botelho. It is very nice there. Very sealike. It is on the ocean. You should visit there anyway.'

'Yes,' Fletch said drowsily. 'I'll visit there, too. I promise I will.'

Laura was pulling the drapes closed against the sunlight. She had already stripped for bed.

'The mayor of Botelho said that on the weekend, Saturday, I think it was, a North American woman showed up there in Botelho.'

'Perhaps somebody told her she should visit.'

'Very likely. It is a nice place. I have taken my wife and children there.'

'Did you have a nice time?'

'A very nice time.'

'Good.'

'The mayor said this woman just wandered around for the afternoon by herself, on the beach and so forth, you know?'

'An American tourist—'

'After dark, she went into the very excellent seafood restaurant they have there. I brought my wife and children to eat there.'

Kneeling before him, Laura was taking off Fletch's sneakers and socks.

'Was it good?'

'Excellent. This woman ate her dinner.'

'A North American woman tourist went to a small resort town—'

'Botelho.'

'Botelho, yes. Spent the afternoon on the beach and then had dinner in a seafood restaurant.'

'Yes, that's right. After dinner, she said nothing. Instead of paying she went straight into the kitchen and began washing dishes.'

Laura pushed Fletch onto his back and began taking off his shorts.

'That's not Joan Collins Stanwyk.'

'She's been there ever since. Two days.

Washing dishes. Eating. The man who owns the restaurant has given her a little bed to use.'

'Joan Collins Stanwyk never washed a dish in her life. She wouldn't know how.'

'She is a blonde North American or English lady. She speaks no Portuguese.'

'How old is she?'

Kneeling over him on the bed, Laura was taking off his shirt. The telephone wire went through the sleeve.

'Quite young, the mayor says. Slim. In her twenties. Maybe her mid-twenties.'

'Sounds to me like some female derelict from the Florida Keys washed up on a Brazilian beach.'

'Botelho. The beach is very nice there.'

'I'm sure.' Laura was sliding Fletch's legs under the sheet. 'Why did the mayor of Botelho call the Rio police about this lady?'

'Saturdays a tour bus from Copacabana hotels stops in Botelho. The mayor thought she might have gotten off the bus. So he called this police station. He asked if we were looking for a murderess of her description.'

'A murderess?'

'Truth, he doesn't know where she came from. Or why. Botelho is a small town. He is a small mayor.'

Finally in his bed, to sleep, Fletch thought a moment. Then he said, 'I don't think so, Sergeant. Joan Collins Stanwyk didn't have any cash on her, but she is a wealthy, responsible lady, a lady of great dignity. She has many options open to her. All the options in the world. I can't see her ever going to a resort and getting a job washing dishes in a fish-and-chips joint.'

'Fish-and-chips? Ah, you are speaking London English.'

'Anyway, Joan Collins Stanwyk is in her thirties.'

'I didn't think this would be the lady.'

'I'm sure it's not.'

'Topsy-turvy. Do you remember what I said about topsy-turvy?'

'In fact, I do.'

'This is a very topsy-turvy world. Twenty-seven years I have served with the Rio police. Believe me, I have seen topsy-turvy.'

'I'm sure you have. Thanks for being in touch with me, Sergeant.'

*   *   *

Laura was in the bed beside Fletch.

292

'So,' she said, 'they have not found the woman you are looking for.'

'No. Just some English-speaking woman has showed up washing dishes in some fish restaurant down the coast.'

Into the dark, Laura said, 'The police just want you to think they are doing something about the disappeared lady.'

'Probably.' He turned on the bedside light.

'What are you doing?'

'Just calling The Hotel Jangada,' Fletch said. 'See if she has returned.'

'Want me to help you?'

'This one I can do myself,' he said. 'I've been practicing.'

At the Hotel Jangada, Room 912 did not answer.

The desk clerk said Mrs Joan Collins Stanwyk had not checked out.

Nor had she picked up the note Fletch had left for her.

CHAPTER THIRTY-FIVE

Fletch—

I could not wake you up.

293

I tried and tried. A few times I thought you were awake, because you were talking. What you said made no sense. Did you know you talk in your sleep?

You said you were on a big white riverboat, and the sky was full of buttocks.

You said you had your goat, or someone was trying to get your goat. You seemed afraid of a kicking goat. Then, remarkably, you babbled on about an ancient Brazilian mythical figure, the dancing nanny goat.

How do you know about such things? Sometimes, when you were talking in your sleep, your eyes were open, which is why I thought I was succeeding in waking you. You said something about a man with his feet turned backward, another mythical figure, and when I asked, 'Fletch, do you mean the *capoeira*?' you just stared off like some sort of a *almapenada*, a soul in torment. You also mentioned other Brazilian hobgoblins, the man with his head on backward, the headless mule, and the goblin with-hair-for-hands. You talked about being pursued by a one-legged boy, and when I asked, 'Fletch, do you mean the *saci-perêrê*?' you stared a long time before saying, 'Janio Barreto . . . Janio Barreto . . .'

Amazing thing is, you didn't know the

names of any of these Brazilian scary figures. You seem to be seeing them in some sort of a nightmare. You were sweating profusely. Do you think you had a fever? I am amazed you have such bad dreams of such hobgoblins, like a Brazilian child, when you have never heard of them or read of them, as far as I know.

Later, when I tried again to wake you, you said, 'Leave the dead alone!'

Maybe you frightened me. A little.

I canceled our reservation for dinner at Le Saint Honoré. I gave our tickets to the ball at Regine's to Marilia, who gave them to some people she knows from Porto Alegre.

Your body is a real mess.

I decided what you need is rest.

I have gone back to Bahia. Carnival is almost over, for this year. I must start organizing my music for the concert tour.

Perhaps you would come to Bahia and advise me of what music you think should be included in the programme.

Now maybe my father will be interested in talking to you—now that he knows you have studied up on such things as the *boi-tatá* and the *tutu-marambá*!

Ciao,
Laura

Fletch had awakened into bright sunlight. He was very hungry. He was very stiff. His body was sticky with sweat.

For a long moment, he thought it was still Monday afternoon and the sun had not yet set.

'Laura?' The hotel room was totally quiet. There was no noise from the bathroom. 'Laura?'

From the bed, he noticed that her cosmetics, all those bottles which issued smells if not beauty, were gone from the bureau. None of her clothes were around the room. Her suitcase was gone from the rack.

His watch was on the bedside table. It read five minutes past eleven. Even in a topsy-turvy world, the sun did not shine brightly at five minutes past eleven on Monday nights.

Slowly it dawned on him it must be five minutes past eleven Tuesday morning.

He had slept seventeen hours.

Having to ask individually each part of his body to move, he got up from his bed and walked across the room.

Instead of Laura's cosmetics on the

296

bureau was Laura's letter.

He read it twice.

Had he really talked so much in his sleep, said all those things to Laura? What's a *boitatá* and a *tutu-marambá*? Indeed, he must have frightened her.

Vaguely, he remembered having bad dreams. The boy, Janio Barreto, was following them down that crowded, dark slum street to Carnival Parade. In bright floodlights, Fletch was hunkered down in a swirling mass of bodies, brown eyes popping in surprise at seeing him there, being kicked from every direction. Again he was under the stands at Carnival, where he did not belong, looking through his own blood at a man walking by slowly, his head on backward, turning to smile at him . . .

In the bathroom, he tore the bandages off himself. Scabs had formed nicely. Red marks had turned purple, and purple marks had turned black.

Hadn't Laura seen the big white riverboat floating sedately down the stream of swirling costumes? Hadn't that been real?

Gingerly, adding no more cuts to his face, Fletch shaved.

Janio Barreto following them through the subway to Carnival Parade had meant something to Laura it had not meant to him. What had her letter said? *Saci-perêrê*. What's a *saci-perêrê*?

The warm water of the shower felt good on his body. The soap did not feel so good on some of his wounds.

In fact, Laura had not really asked him what happened to him under the stands at Carnival Parade. She thought anyone can tell a story and say it is the past. Even after his pointing out Gabriel Campos at Santos Lima, she did not really ask. She only asked how, why he pointed out Gabriel Campos.

He did not dry himself after the shower. Instead, he just wrapped the towel around his waist. The air felt too good on his wet body.

His mind a jumble, he went out onto the balcony. A small samba combo was playing, probably outside a nearby café. Across the utility area, the man was still painting the room.

Laura thought it was funny the Tap Dancers had left him in a closed coffin with his bag of money. He had seen Norival Passarinho walk after he was dead. On broom sticks, his ankles tied to the ankles of Toninho and Orlando. Then Fletch had seen Norival Passarinho really walk after he was dead, really talk. Adroaldo Passarinho. Well it *was* funny.

Fletch was dead. He had died forty-seven years ago. At Dona Jurema's mountain resort the Tap Dancers had tried, maybe as a joke, to arrange a corpse for him. People believed he could answer a question older than himself. Who had murdered Janio Barreto? And he had answered it. Apparently, Fletch had seen mythological figures which were not a part of his own culture. Of course, they must have been just costumed revelers under the stands. Were they? He had helped the dead Norival Passarinho walk, in a crazy, drunken scheme. Then he had believed he saw Norival Passarinho walk, heard him talk. Fletch had come back to life. He was in a closed coffin.

For Fletch, the line between life and death had become narrower. It was so narrow, it really could be funny.

Across the utility area, the man painting the room looked at Fletch.

Fletch had not realized he was staring at the man.

Fletch waved.

Grinning, the man waved back at him. He waved his paintbrush.

Fletch blinked. *He has damned little paint on that paintbrush, if he does not hesitate to wave it at someone, in a room he has been painting for days!*

Fletch laughed.

The man waved his paintbrush again.

Across the utility area the two men laughed together.

Fletch gave the man the thumbs-up sign, then went back into his room.

★   ★   ★

He telephoned The Hotel Jangada.

Room 912 did not answer.

Mrs Joan Collins Stanwyk had not checked out.

Yes, there was a message awaiting her in her mail slot.

Drinking mineral water from a plastic liter bottle, Fletch read Laura's note a third time.

Then he called Teodomiro da Costa and arranged to meet with him that night. He would be late, Fletch said, as he intended to drive to the village of Botelho and back.

Teo recommended the seafood restaurant there.

Reluctantly, Fletch knelt. His cuts and bruises protesting, he leaned over until his head was only a few centimeters from the floor.

He peered under the bed.

The small, carved stone frog was gone.

CHAPTER THIRTY-SIX

'What are you doing here?'

Joan Collins Stanwyk, dressed in shorts which were too big and a T-shirt which had some slogan on it in Portuguese, stood across the rough restaurant table from Fletch.

'Eating.'

'But how do you come to be here?'

'I was hungry.' He continued eating.

'Really,' she said. 'How did you find me?'

Her eyes were round in amazement.

'Brazilian police apparently are not always as casual as they like to appear.'

The restaurant was a patio with a roof

over it on the beach.

'Can you join me?' Fletch asked. 'Or aren't the help allowed to sit with the customers.'

'I can buy you a cup of coffee,' she said.

In sandals, she went across the restaurant to the serving tables.

He had enjoyed the drive through Rio's suburbs, through the Brazilian countryside down the coast. He enjoyed sucking in good air and seeing the real things of the countryside, real rocks and trees, real cows and goats. Good roads had been laid out against the day Brazil's past would catch up with her future. As he drove farther, most of the traffic he passed was on foot.

It had not taken him long to tour the village of Botelho. A short dock poked into a long ocean. The fish warehouse was no more than a shed. In the tiny church was a powerful, crude crucifixion. Less than a dozen fisherfolk bungalows facing the sea dozed in the shade of their own groves.

At the entrance to the open-air seafood restaurant he spotted Joan. Standing with her back to him in the kitchen area, Joan Collins Stanwyk, Mrs Alan Stanwyk, was placing plates and glasses in a vat of steaming water. He watched her dry her

302

hands and begin shelving clean plates.

It was early for dinner. The only other customers in the restaurant were five fishermen at one table chatting over *chopinhos*. A young waiter gave Fletch a menu and understood as Fletch pointed to a soup and a fish entrée.

Brown paper sack on the bench beside him, Fletch gazed out over the beach to the ocean. Sooner or later, Joan Collins Stanwyk would turn, look through the serving apparatus, see him. He left her the option of ignoring his presence. He would go away again without speaking, if that was what she wanted.

The fish chowder was the best he'd ever had.

He was halfway through his fish entrée when Joan crossed the restaurant and spoke to him.

Now she sat across from him at the long, rough table. She had placed a cup of coffee before each of them.

'I'm glad you're all right,' he said, still eating.

'Have an accident?'

'No, thanks. Just had one.'

They both laughed nervously.

'You look like someone really beat on

you.' Especially did her eyes fasten on the small scar on his throat.

'I ran into an enraged nanny goat.' Her face put on patience. 'That is the story I have decided to tell, to say is the past.'

Joan's face looked better than when he saw her Saturday morning. There was good color in her skin and her eyes were clear. So far, she had not lit a cigarette, which was unusual for her. She was wearing no makeup at all. It was also obvious her hair had received little attention in the previous four days.

'It really was good of you to seek me out,' Joan said. 'Have I been much trouble?'

'I was worried about you. I've been stood up for dinner before, often, but seldom for breakfast.'

'Not very nice of me.'

'It's okay. I had breakfast anyway.'

'Well.' She looked into her coffee cup.

'The food here is very good.'

'Isn't it? I love it.'

'Very good indeed. You wash dishes in this establishment?'

'Yes.'

'Didn't think you knew how.'

'It's not one of the more artful skills.' She showed him her hands. 'Aren't they beautiful?' They were red and wrinkled.

'They look honest.'

She fluttered her hands and put them in her lap. 'I feel like a schoolgirl who's been caught playing hookey.'

'It's just nice to know you're alive.'

'Any questions I might have had about you and Alan's death...' She looked into Fletch's face, then at the scar on his neck, then into her own lap. '...I don't have now. The money—'

'I'm willing to do my best to try to explain.'

In truth, Fletch wondered if Joan, in her extreme competence, was making some sort of a bargain with him.

'Not necessary,' she said. 'I know as much as I want to know. I pursued you to Brazil out of some sense of duty.'

Numbly, she repeated, 'Some sense of duty.'

He pushed his empty plate away. He realized Joan Collins Stanwyk was expected to wash it.

He sat silently, gazing out to sea. He waited until she understood that he was not questioning her.

She was sitting on her bench, her back straight, leaning on nothing. 'I walked away from you that morning, Saturday morning, away from your hotel, to walk to my own hotel. You had said some things I had never heard before. I became angry in a way I had never been angry before.

'Suddenly I realized that here I was, a grown woman, stumbling along in the morning sunlight in tears because someone had stolen my little pins. My pinky rings! Little plastic cards with my name on them!'

Fletch said, 'Also irreplaceable photographs of your husband, Alan, and your daughter, Julie.'

'Yes. That profoundly bothers me. But I realized what a spoiled brat I was. I am. Skinny little beggar children were dancing all around me as I walked along, their hands out, whispering at me. I waved my arm at them, and through tight jaws shouted, *Oh, go away*! Couldn't they understand that I had lost a few of my diamonds, my credit cards, to me a negligible amount of cash? How dare they bother me at seven o'clock in the morning for money for food?

'I became truly angry at myself. What a superficial, supercilious bitch. What a hollow person. I had spent the night whining at the poor assistant manager at the hotel. I rushed to you at first light, to whine to you. And here I was virtually swinging at hungry kids.'

She said, 'Joanie Collins had lost a few pins.'

Fletch sipped his coffee.

'Then I had a second thought, based on what you had said.' Her index finger was feeling along a short crack in the table. 'In a most peculiar way, I was free. I had been relieved of my identity. My credit cards had been stolen, my passport. It almost meant nothing that I was Joan Collins Stanwyk. At least, I couldn't prove it immediately to anybody. I couldn't go up to anybody, in a store or something, and say, "I'm Joan Collins Stanwyk," and make it mean anything. As you said, I was just arms and legs: one more person walking naked in the world.

'I liked that thought. Suddenly I liked the idea of being without all that baggage.'

From behind the serving apparatus, a tall, slim man was peering out at them. He was looking from Joan to Fletch to Joan again with apparent concern.

Fletch said, 'You're still Joan Collins Stanwyk.'

'Oh, I know. But, for the first time in my

life, it didn't seem to mean much. I saw that it didn't have to mean much.'

Again Fletch permitted his question to remain tacit.

'When I got to The Hotel Jangada, a tour bus was waiting. I didn't know where it was going. I joined the people, the women in their short silk dresses, the men in their plaid shorts, and got on it. No one asked me for a ticket, or money. Obviously I belonged to a group from The Hotel Jangada. I belonged with these people. I stole a bus ride here.'

Fletch smiled. 'Thievery is infectious.'

'The bus stopped here for lunch. I didn't have lunch. I couldn't pay for it. What a new fact! What a new feeling! I wandered around the beach. I let the bus leave without me.

'I wondered who I was. Really was. Really am. I wondered if I could survive a full day without cash, without credit cards, without my identity. I wondered what life would be like, for just a few moments, if I couldn't pull something out of my purse and say, "Here I am, now do as I ask, please; give me..."' She smiled at herself. 'It was getting dark. So I came here and had dinner. I sat over there.' She indicated a

308

bench near the door. 'I felt as guilty as hell.' She put her elbows on the table in a most unrefined way, her chin on her hands. 'Then I went and washed dishes for them.'

'Is it fun for you?'

'It's harder than tennis. I daydream about having a proper massage. God, last night I wanted a martini so badly.' She shrugged. 'I can't understand a word of the language. It's so soft, so sibilant.'

The tall man, wiping his hands on an apron, finally was approaching them.

Joan's face was happy. She said, 'This noon, a well-dressed couple arrived for lunch. German, I think. In a Mercedes, behind a uniformed driver. I found myself looking at her over my pile of dirty dishes. Somehow it made me angry that she only picked at her lunch. Of course I understood. She has to keep her figure...'

The man stood behind Joan, looking at Fletch. He put his hand on her shoulder.

She put her hand on his.

'Fletch, this is Claudio.'

'Bom dia, Claudio.'

Fletch half rose, and they shook hands.

'Claudio owns this place, I think,' Joan said. 'At least he acts as if he owns the place. He acts as if he owns the world. It may just be Brazilian masculinity.'

Assured she was all right, and apparently without conversation in English, Claudio left the back of his hand against Joan's cheek for a moment, then went back to the kitchen.

'Are you here forever?' Fletch asked. 'Have you decided upon dish-washing as a career?'

'Oh, no. Of course not. I love Julie. I love my father. I must get back. I have responsibilities. To Collins Aviation. I'm the best fund-raiser Symphony has.'

Fletch put the brown paper sack on the table.

'Just leave me here for a while,' Joan said quietly. 'Let me play truant from life for a short while, from being mother, daughter, from being Joan Collins Stanwyk. Leave me be.'

'Sure.' He pushed the paper bag across the table at her.

'What's that?' she asked.

'The money I was bringing you Saturday—enhanced by poker earnings. For when you decide to get back.' She looked into the bag. 'Surely enough to get you back to Rio, pay a hotel bill for a few nights, pay for Telexes.'

'How very nice.'

'Poverty is easier to slip into,' Fletch said, 'than to climb out of.'

She reached across the table and took his hand. 'How do you know so much?'

'Just the wisdom of the masses. Also,' he said, 'you must still have the key to your suite at The Hotel Jangada.'

'I must have. It must be in a pocket of that pants suit I was wearing.'

'Get it for me. I'll check you out of the hotel. I'll leave your luggage with the concierge, for when you want it.'

'I will want it,' she said. 'I'm sure I will.'

While Fletcher paid the waiter, Joan told him about bathing in the warm ocean, how hot the sun was at midday, how much she liked the smell of fish, it was so real, the sounds of something she thought might be tree-frogs at night.

'You sound like you're at summer camp,' he said.

'No. At summer camp someone else washed the dishes. And,' she smiled, 'there were only girls.'

Fletch waited by his car while she got the key to her suite at The Hotel Jangada. It was still daylight. Customers were beginning to arrive for dinner.

As Joan crossed the small parking lot to him, some of the customers stared after her, perplexed.

'Do me one other favor, will you?' she asked.

'Sure.' Fletch had known there would be a second part to the bargain. There are always two parts to a bargain.

'When you go back to the States, to California, back to your own reality, don't ever tell anyone that this crazy thing happened to me, that I did this crazy thing. That you found me washing dishes in a fish joint in some nameless little town in Southern Brazil.'

'The town has a name.'

She laughed. 'You know, I don't know what it is?'

'Botelho.'

'Will you promise me that?'

'Sure.'

'I mean, everyone needs a vacation from life. Don't you agree?'

'A vacation from reality.'

She handed him the key. 'I'm paying for a suite at The Hotel Jangada, and sleeping more or less on the beach in Botelho.'

Fletch said: 'Topsy-turvy.'

CHAPTER THIRTY-SEVEN

'Did you enjoy your dinner in Botelho?' Teodomiro da Costa asked.

'It was excellent,' Fletch answered.

'Yes, that's a good restaurant. I'm not sure it's worth the ride . . .'

It was late when Fletch got back to Rio, by the time he arrived at Teo da Costa's home on Avenida Epitacio Passoa.

When the houseman had shown Fletch into the downstairs family sitting room, Teo was looking sleepy in a dressing gown in a comfortable chair. He was reading the book *1887—The Year Slavery in Brazil Ended*. From under the reading light, Teo's eyes traveled over Fletch's various visible wounds, but he did not comment on them.

'Want a nightcap?'

'No, thanks. I won't be here that long.'

Stiff from Carnival, from his wounds, from the long ride, Fletch sank comfortably into the two-seater divan.

In the little sitting room was a handsome big new painting by Misabel Pedrosa.

'And did Laura enjoy Botelho?'

'Laura has gone back to Bahia.

Yesterday, I finally fell asleep. She couldn't wake me up. She had to go back to begin preparing for her concert tour.'

'Yes,' Teo said slowly, 'I gathered you might have cleaned up that mystery of who murdered Janio Barreto forty-seven years ago. There was a most peculiar report in *O Globo* this morning. A small item, saying Gabriel Campos, past *capoeira* master of *Escola* Santos Lima, was found on the beach, his throat slit. A woman from the *favela*, Idalina Barreto, is helping the police in its inquiries.'

'I pity the police.'

'Apparently she was found on the beach lighting matches, trying to set fire to the corpse of Gabriel Campos.'

'Did she succeed?'

'That's what's peculiar about *O Globo*'s report. It says that legend has it that no one has ever succeeded in lighting a fire in that exact spot on the beach in almost fifty years.'

'Teo, I'd like some of the money you've invested for me to be available for the education of the current young generation of the descendants of Janio Barreto.'

'Easily done.'

'Especially young Janio. He has a

wooden leg. It will be harder for him to make a living without an education.'

'Yes.'

Fletch fingered the scar on his throat. 'I believe he saved my life.' Then he chuckled. 'He might even think of becoming a bookkeeper.'

Teo placed his history book on the table beside his chair. 'And did you find your lady friend from California? What's her name, Stanwyk?'

'Yes. She's all right.'

'What happened to her?'

'She fell out of her cradle. She's enjoying a few moments crawling around the floor.'

Obviously tired, Teo cast his hooded eye across the darkened room at Fletch.

'Brazil is the future,' Fletch said. 'Who can see the future?'

'And you,' Teo asked, shifting comfortably in his chair. 'Did you enjoy Carnival?'

'I learned some things.'

'I'd love to know what.'

'Oh, that the past asserts itself. That the dead can walk.' Fletch thought of the small carved stone frog that had been under his bed. 'That the absence of symbols can mean as much as their presence.'

As if digesting all this, Teo blinked his hooded eye. He did not ask questions.

'Teo, driving so far today by myself, through the incredible Brazilian countryside, I think I settled on a plan.'

'No need to tell me what it is,' Teo said. 'Any more than there is to tell your father what it is. As long as you have a plan.'

'I've decided to try writing a biography of the North American western artist Edgar Arthur Tharp, Junior. It seems an opportunity to get some things said about the North American's view of the artist, the intellectual, of the North American spirit.'

Teo repeated, 'As long as you have a plan.'

'It is the spirit of things which is important, isn't it?'

Teo said, 'Norival Passarinho's funeral is tomorrow. Will you attend?'

Fletch hesitated. 'Yes.' He stood up. 'Why not?'

Teo stood up as well. 'And will you visit Bahia before you leave?'

At the door, Fletch said: 'To say good-bye.'

*　　*　　*

For a moment, Fletch sat quietly in the dark in the small yellow convertible outside Teodomiro da Costa's home.

A few doors from Teo's, a last Carnival party was in progress. It was Shrove Tuesday night.

A couple dressed as the King of Hearts and the Queen of Diamonds scurried across the sidewalk from a taxi into the house.

There was the sound of laughter coming from the house. Singing. Above all, the sound of a samba combo. Of samba drums *beating, rhythms beside rhythms on top of rhythms beneath rhythms. From all sides, every minute, day and night, came the beating of the drums.*

'*Bum, bum, paticum bum.*' Fletch started the car. '*Prugurundum.*'

Most people in the world Fletch had known had stopped hearing the melodies from the drums.